THE RULER OF THE GALAXY

Moses Solomon

The Ruler of the Galaxy

Part 1: Hidden Point

ISBN: 978-0-9894902-7-6
eISBN: 978-0-9894902-8-3
ISBN-10: 0989490270
Library of Congress Catalog Card Number: xx-xxxxx

Printed in the United States of America

To my wife,
with all my love,
for now and forever.

My sincere thanks go to Lisa Gilliam, my editor; Dana Henderson, for his inspiring artwork; Rodney Hatfield, for his marketing expertise, Mason McCann Smith, for his guidance on "Timegazer;" and my wife, for all her love and support and her great ideas.

Additional thanks go to Suzy Vitello, Lesann Berry, the Rev. Sara Fischer, and Maureen Kay; the late Steve Malick, Michael Stack, and Steven Wallace; C.S. Cole, Andrea Letourneau, the late Mary Rosenblum, and Ron Root; Margo Ander, Allan Anderson, Kyle Fahrbach, Sandra Grace, Andy Jones, Satnam Kaur Khalsa, Karin Ott Kristensen, Gregg Macklin, and Amie Waller; and Blake Swensen and Terry Light for all the helpful comments on the journey to publication.

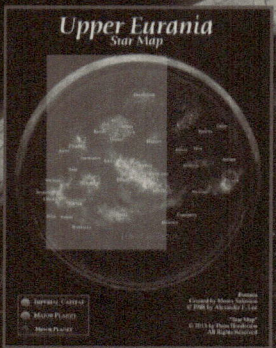

Upper Eurania
Star Map

G-7

G-6

BROZA

KEARO

G-5

GASSIL

HERON

PHARRY

ARCHARION

CHERINO

BREAME

ALTILANO

BEXEL

KELOVA

ALSCRAS

ONGLUS

SESTIA

TOUTLE

Lower Eurania

THE RULER OF THE GALAXY

OF THE

HIDDEN POINT

Prologue: In the Beginning

As told in *The Songs of the Euranians*, the first human, Euae, was created on the tropical planet of Amahl, while a rival being, a reptiloid named the Troggle, was created on the neighboring volcanic world of Sigorum. Over time, the human and reptiloid races flourished into vast civilizations. With advancements in science and technology, both developed spaceflight, leading to their eventual meeting and the inevitable outbreak of war:

"...and a titanic conflict raged between the reptiloids of Sigorum and the humans of Amahl. After many years of devastating battles, the humans gained an advantage over their enemies and sought to end the long war with an all-out invasion. When the great Adelph led the human military forces on a final landing against the reptiloid cities, large grotesque beings—covered in writhing tentacles, with incisor-lined beaks, multifaceted eyes, and oversized wings—emerged with great wrath from the depths of Sigorum and attacked. The human armies fought with great fortitude, but their laser cannons and sonic grenades peppered the monstrous beings without effect.

"As the battle turned in favor of the reptiloids, bolts of pink and green light, swathed in swirling gray clouds, heralded the approach of a being of pure energy. A vortex whirled amidst the smoke and smog that blanketed the skies, the howl of the entity echoing with gale-like force. The humans fled in terror, and the reptiloids bowed down in reverence to their creator. A rainbow of deadly energy showered down on the humans, slaughtering them by the thousands. Within minutes, the surface of Sigorum was littered with the burnt remains of Adelph's retreating army.

"At this darkest, most dire moment of human existence, a shattering roar erupted, and a whalelike silhouette darkened the skies. Swarms of blue light descended from the underside of the bulbous shadow, impacting the surface with mile-high explosive bursts. Arches cracked, towers fell, reptiloids were slaughtered by the thousands, and black clouds plunged Sigorum into darkness.

"Two shafts of green light pierced the clouds, enveloping the vortex in a bright green halo. The vortex's howl changed into a terrifying scream. The swirling colors flared, and the bolts grew into a tumultuous cascade. The remaining humans watched in awe as the vortex paled and faded away, the demonic scream echoing into the gale of the night sky.

"The green shafts of light then receded. The silhouette ascended through the stratosphere and disappeared into the recesses of space. The enemy had been defeated. The war was over."

Sigorum had been rendered uninhabitable by the devastating power of the *Gramm*, the weapon of the gods. Adelph and his battle-weary forces released a multitude of prisoners, captured over the many years of war, then withdrew, leaving the few reptiloids still alive on Sigorum to die with their planet. Though the humans had been saved from extinction, Amahl had also been devastated by the long war. And so, the survivors embarked on a long migration to the distant star cluster of Eurania, where they reestablished human civilization.

Over the course of the next seven millennia, their descendants expanded throughout the star systems to build a vast interstellar empire. Exploration ships launched from the empire, and distant settlements were established in the Upper Euranian region, on frontier planets such as Sestia, Onglus, and Bexel, and on long-forgotten worlds in Lower Eurania. The Imperial capital, Etolis, became the shining beacon of human existence.

Then an unforeseen interstellar cataclysm—the sudden eruption of the Great Nebula—destroyed the core worlds of the empire, isolating the settlements in Upper and Lower Eurania and leaving them to develop on their own.

Part 1

Timegazer

1. The Shaman

In the Year 1540 of the Sestian Calendar

Morgan reached over the steering controls, pulled a small lever, and activated the little Buggy craft's hyperdrive. Beyond the front window, the fabric of space sheared open like a gaping maw, revealing a gray void with pinpoint lights that whisked across the side windows. On the rearview monitor, mounted on top of the dashboard, the streaking lights of the void disappeared into a tiny patch of stars in the distance. He reached down to the center console, switched on the autopilot, and released the yoke. Glancing sideways at Rayna, Morgan said, "Alone at last."

Rayna unfastened her straps and wrapped her arms around Morgan's neck. He closed his eyes when he felt the warmth of her soft skin. She ran her fingers through his hair, which he kept barely short enough to avoid violating the military dress code. Her cheek snuggled against his, and her dark, wavy, shoulder-length hair settled over his shoulders. She hummed a soft melody as she brushed a tuft of his dark hair from his forehead.

He opened his eyes and gazed at her. "Six months was too long."

Six months apart while Rayna's cruiser, *Pouton*, escorted Alscrasian merchants through pirate-infested routes along the perimeter of the Great Nebula. Six months of passing messages through the intermittent relays of the comm-exchanges while his cruiser, *Ocelot*, patrolled the Alscrasian border.

That Morgan served under Rayna's father made things "interesting."

Captain Choff had never warmed to Morgan in the two years since he and Rayna had graduated from the academy. When they began their assignments, Rayna had asked Morgan to be understanding of her father. At first, he tried, accepting any and every assignment given. But after the captain ordered Morgan down to the hot, cramped engine room to inventory spare parts—tedium appropriate for an enlisted recruit, but not for an officer—and then reprimanded him for reporting back without changing into a clean uniform, all effort at understanding jettisoned out the disposal tube.

"Captain Chump" reminded Morgan of a mercurial foreman he had once apprenticed under who had favored some while coming down hard on others. Though he worked hard and had risen to become second officer in a short time, Morgan felt certain the tension existed because the captain didn't care for his only child's relationship with a guy from the working-class streets of Alscras.

Now, with both of their ships tied up at the same space fortress for maintenance work, Morgan and Rayna finally had an opportunity to go on leave together. The trip to Toutle, a nearby resort world of the far-flung Onglan League, would take a full day. Except for a close passage to Volon, a sparsely populated planet the wormhole curved around, the trip should be uneventful.

Rayna whispered in his ear, "Where did we leave off six months ago?"

She gave his ear a gentle nibble, and Morgan's desire swept over him. He flashed a hungry smile, undid his straps, tossed them aside—and with them, his shirt—and pressed her close. Her top fluttered to the floor, landing on top of his. Their lips met and they pulled themselves out of the pilot's seat and down to the floor.

A violent jolt rocked the spacecraft, interrupting Morgan and Rayna's climactic moment.

"*Dox!*" Morgan cursed as an alarm blared. Nothing could be more annoying than to be stopped by a blown engine relay. But alone out here in space, anything more than that would be a real problem.

Another alarm sounded as a mass of multicolored particles streaked past the front window. A tremor shook the little ship, forcing Rayna to brace herself against the back of her seat. Outside the window, the layered folds of hyperspace collapsed around them, and a starfield settled into place.

Morgan's mind raced. What kind of particle beam could break out of normal space? Checking the monitor, he saw the blue-green world of Volon come into view just as another beam —one that covered the entire width of the front window—fired from the planet. "Hang on, Rayna!" The strike sent rough shivers through the craft.

"Who's shooting at us?" Rayna checked the telemetry data from the shot.

This was one mystery Morgan wanted no part of. The Buggy broadcast no military signals, and to his knowledge, Volon was not advanced enough to build a weapon like this. He

switched off the autopilot, took hold of the steering yoke, and
fired the boosters to pull the craft away from Volon. "Get the
life-suits."

Rayna reached up and released the overhead compartment, allowing two bright orange emergency jumpsuits to roll
out. She tossed Morgan's bundle onto the helmet hook next to
him, and she quickly donned her suit, fastening the quick-action
seals and hanging the helmet on the hook next to her side of the
console.

"Can this Buggy take all this?" Rayna strapped herself
into her seat and took the controls.

"Don't know." Morgan quickly zipped into his jumpsuit
and strapped himself back into his seat. "*Tatiki!*" he cursed,
struggling with the steering. "The handling stinks."

"I *told* you to take the Comet," Rayna scolded, "instead
of this piece of—"

A wide, twisting band of light, streaming all the colors of
the rainbow, lanced out from Volon and smothered the front and
side windows, completely enveloping the Buggy. A hot-pink bolt
of energy leaped out from a vent, arced across the instrument
panel, and struck the bank of data monitors, shorting out two of
the gauges in a shower of sparks. Morgan's hands jerked loose
from the yoke as the bolt flashed through the steering column.

He pivoted his head at the sound of Rayna's scream.
Struck by the bolt in a blinding flash of light, she lurched into
convulsions.

"Rayna!"

Rayna slumped in her seat, unconscious.

A red alarm annunciator flashed on the dashboard. In the
center of the instrument panel, the gyro-stabilizer erupted in a
cloud of black smoke. A second later, the main engine blew out

with a booming concussion that blasted the back wall, propelling a shower of smoking shrapnel through the cockpit.

"*Shat'oq!*" Morgan cursed as he watched the planet spiral toward them.

They fell toward the equator like a meteor. With one hand clamped like a vise on the steering gear, Morgan reached over with his other hand to yank Rayna's crash restraints over her, snapping the full-body harnesses over her regular seat straps. He hit the emergency signal to broadcast an automated distress code in all Imperial dialects, then secured his own emergency restraints.

"Stay with me, Rayna." Coaxing the last vestiges of power from the crippled engine, Morgan tried to steady the ship's descent with short thruster bursts and a steely hand on the yoke. "Come on!" he urged the Buggy.

Miraculously, the craft righted itself just before entering the upper atmosphere. Morgan fought to keep the craft stable as it glided down. Sweat broke out under his jumpsuit. On the front window, the fiery friction of the craft streaking through the atmosphere obscured his view of the descent. The automatic temperature alarm sounded an alert each time the cabin temp increased an additional five degrees. Soon, the air started to feel suffocating.

Morgan glanced over at Rayna. She lay limp under her restraints, her eyes still closed, her breathing remaining slow though steady. With some systems on the blink and others totally dark, he could barely maintain his precarious hold over the craft's descent.

The Buggy emerged through the clouds, and when the heat broke, the temp alerts ceased. Bright sunlight gave Morgan a clear view of the landscape. A snow-peaked mountain range passed by below them. Beyond lay a vast forest. Keeping his eyes glued to the flight path ahead, Morgan reached overhead and switched on the automatic landing sequence. No data appeared on the ground-tracking monitor; not even a beep sounded. He tried the switch again. Again, no response. He looked up and saw black scorch-marks along the edge of the panel.

"*Dox!*"

The forest rushed toward them, and he drew in a deep breath to steel his nerves against the inevitable crash landing. Morgan gave Rayna one more glance. Her helmet was hanging out of his reach. He pulled his own helmet off its hook and slapped it over her head, the magnetic seals fastening.

Now close enough to see individual trees whisk by, he tried to steady his breathing. His heartbeat raced as he guided them down the last few feet.

The craft mowed down a line of treetops, the rough bumps jarring the ride down. Without warning, the trees gave way, revealing a formation of jagged boulders marking a break in the forest. Everything jumped with a loud concussion as the base of the craft hit the tallest boulder. The craft toppled at an awkward angle. The force of the impact jerked and twisted Morgan against his emergency straps. The steering yoke yanked out of his grasp, nearly ripping his hands from his wrists. The Buggy hit the ground and bounced several times, part of the dashboard erupting into another cloud of foul black smoke. The overhead landing control panel burst out in an explosive flash of energy and tumbled down on Morgan.

Amidst the chaos, he reached out for her. "Rayna—"

As the tumbling panel struck his head, an old proverb flashed in his mind: *At the end of life, the souls that follow Almighty Euranus will find Eurania.* Then he blacked out.

~ ~ ~

Morgan had met Rayna during their first year at the military academy. The previous week, Otho Ennuk, a burly country boy in canvas cutoffs, had bested him in both weightlifting and running. So Morgan challenged "Oggy"—Morgan's new nickname for Otho—to a Zahrin-style unarmed bout at the gym. Before he knew it, Otho bopped a good one to Morgan's head, sending him sprawling to the mat.

His first upside-down glance at Rayna blade-bouting along the far wall triggered a pure, physical attraction in him. The other females at the gym looked to him like bulked-up male athletes with female features. But Rayna, in a ponytail and purple leotard, wielded the long Zahrin rypniblade with graceful body gyrations and rolls that excited his young male instincts. The rhythm of her footwork reminded him of a dancer's. Her blocks and swings against her sparring partner, though, were as powerful as anyone else's in the gym. He rolled over and watched as she grabbed both ends of her weapon and thrust the flat edge into her opponent's face, knocking him into the rear wall.

She both inspired and distracted Morgan. He refocused and quickly floored the larger Otho with a surprise reverse throw to the mat, finally triumphant.

She smiled at him, and he felt sure she had noticed him staring at her earlier from across the gym. He smiled back and, feigning nonchalance, challenged an available big body—a tall, square-jawed blonde with bulging muscles—to a bout. Unfortunately, his mind wandered again, and in less than ten seconds, an open hand thrust into his face and stunned him backward to an awkward thud on the mat.

"Sorry about that," the big body said with a smile.

Otho shook his head at Morgan. "That was awesome."

Morgan looked up, sighed, and took Otho's hand to pull himself up. To his surprise, Rayna also ran over to him.

"Are you all right?" She stifled a laugh. "You really should keep your eyes on your opponent."

Morgan didn't know whether to feel embarrassed or try a line. "Hi, I'm Morgan. Are you available for dinner?"

"What?" Rayna's mouth gaped.

"This one moves fast." Otho winked at Rayna. "Better watch out."

Rayna threw her head back and laughed. "I don't believe this."

Morgan smiled at her. "Yes?"

Of course, she accepted. And with her help, Morgan and Otho, and later their mutual friend Lon Prowzi, became much better Zahrin combatants.

A few weeks later, after having discovered a poorly maintained orchard less than a mile from the campus, he whispered to Rayna to sneak away from Otho and Lon and abandon an uninspiring technical writing lecture.

Morgan enjoyed amusing Rayna with moments of mischief. The daughter of a straitlaced military man, she seemed to delight in taking an occasional chance to push her boundaries, and this seemed a perfect opportunity.

This time, however, they had barely stepped out among the overgrown groves when a trio of oversized workers, covered from head to foot in juice stains and reeking with the stench of alcohol, apparently intoxicated with the fermentations of the overripe fruit, jumped them.

Morgan, reverting to his brawling instincts, bulled his way through all three until two of the men grabbed hold of him. His shirt tore open as they swung him about. The third hammered a fist to his face. Stunned, he crashed backward into a tangle of tree trunks.

"Let go!" Rayna yelled.

Morgan struggled to right himself, his vision slowly clearing. He saw the three attackers surrounding Rayna, two of them grabbing hold of her arms. To his amazement, Rayna gritted her teeth and leveraged their hold on her, launching herself into the third, belting both boot heels into his chest with a loud, vicious crack and upending him over a mass of thorny bushes.

Otho and Lon ran into the orchard, seemingly from out of nowhere. Otho grabbed a broken branch and pummeled one of the men to the ground, while the smaller Lon helped Rayna dispose of the other with a barrage of punches and well-placed kicks. Poor Morgan sat, recovering from the blow to his head, until Rayna ran over to him.

"Oh no," Rayna said, placing both hands around his face.

"It feels like a black eye coming," Morgan muttered.

"At least it'll be an impressive one," Otho said, offering Morgan a hand up.

Morgan grimaced, struggling to his feet. "I guess I'm glad you guys followed us here."

"Thanks, guys," Rayna said, brushing off a few twigs.

"Next time," Lon said with his light Sestian accent, "maybe you won't skip class."

Morgan sighed, disgusted, and turned to Rayna. "How did you manage that move?"

"Zahrin combat isn't just for exercise," she replied, giving his eye a light kiss. "Are you all right?"

Morgan stared at her, stunned by her display. He felt dumbfounded, but he wasn't sure if it was from his poor showing or her brilliance in the fight. At that moment, the only thing he knew for sure were his feelings for Rayna.

~ ~ ~

"Rayna?"

Morgan's voice was barely audible. His head throbbed with pain. A stinging sensation radiated from his shoulders down his arms, and a dull ache racked his chest from the tug of the restraints. A blur of red and yellow lights blinked on the dashboard, indicating a complete failure. Unsure of how long he had been unconscious, Morgan took a long, slow breath and waited for his vision to clear.

Two sections of the dashboard still smoldered. As the pain began to subside, he turned on the vent to blow some of the thick smoke out of the craft. The astro-nav computer read: *Memory reset.* He rubbed his head with his hand and found it smeared with blood. The distress signal that he had activated as they went down had stopped, the comm unit dead. This was not how their leave was supposed to be.

"Rayna?" He turned his head.

Her seat was empty, the unfastened straps dangling down the sides. Her helmet lay on the floor.

He gasped, his heart racing. What had happened while he was out? He ripped his buckles open, threw his straps aside, staggered to his feet, and scanned the cockpit wreckage. The overhead panel lay on the floor behind his seat, dented and scarred with black scorches from the blowout, with a tiny smear of blood from Morgan's head.

"Rayna!"

Morgan looked at the tousled pile of clothes on the floor, his hands trembling, his heart pounding like a cannon, a nauseous panic rising up.

Then he saw it—the airlock was ajar, opened wide

enough for a person to fit through. The doorframe itself was cracked, apparently broken during the crash. *There!*

He opened the locker, grabbed the belt with his gun and the charcoal-gray vest that held a pair of short silver skiloblades, and fastened them on. Then he put on his lightweight jacket over the vest and the weapons. The jacket's dark umber color would conceal his bright orange top and help him blend into the surrounding forest, in case he encountered hostile Volonians or animals. Now ready, he climbed through the broken airlock and stepped out.

Morgan plunged into the forest, his eyes scanning the thick layers of dark green foliage, broken branches, and splintered tree trunks, looking for a sign of Rayna. He knew nothing about the people of Volon or why modern development had seemed to skip over this planet. Volon wasn't unique. There were plenty of lush worlds throughout the Euranian star cluster. However, those that remained undeveloped lay along the perimeter of the Outer Territories, not situated within an organized region like the Onglan League. Obviously, Volon wasn't as primitive as the reports indicated. He struggled with conflicting thoughts of what to do should he encounter a Volonian.

Movement in a nearby clearing caught Morgan's eye. He sneaked close enough to make out three humans standing together. Two men in skullcaps—a muscular one with red lightning bolts tattooed on both arms and a bulky firearm hanging from his belt, and another in a short brown robe covered by a metallic jacket sporting a spider print—had their backs to Morgan. A woman in an off-white cape with a similar spider image and a hood was speaking to them in low tones, in an unfamiliar language.

Native Volonian tongue, Morgan guessed. Since Volon sat

within the borders of the Onglan League, Morgan decided to try the lower-Onglan dialect that he had learned during his academy years. He knew he would speak with a peculiar accent, but it didn't matter. He cleared his throat and approached them.

One of the Volonian men stepped away, giving Morgan a clear view of the Volonian woman as she knelt down to the grass, next to the body of a woman lying on the ground in an orange jumpsuit.

Rayna!

The woman bent down and put her hands over his beloved's face. As Morgan broke into a sprint toward them, a faint golden glow began to emanate from the woman's hands, bathing Rayna's head in a warm field of light. Without warning, a web of blinding sparks filled the halo, covering Rayna's face with static.

Morgan yelled in Onglan, "What are you doing to her?" He instinctively reached under his jacket and whipped out his charge-lock gun, his fingers flipping the switch to arm the weapon's charge-pak loader. "Get away!"

The tattooed Volonian drew his firearm and pointed it at Morgan.

The woman stood and held up her hands. "Thakian, no." The glow in her hands faded away.

For an instant, Morgan thought he saw a red light in her brown eyes. He glanced down at Rayna, her face no longer enveloped in the woman's field of light. Rayna's eyes were closed, and she lay unconscious, as she had been in the Buggy.

The armored man stepped forward, shouldering Thakian aside to speak to Morgan. "The woman is hurt." He spoke in a lightly accented Onglan. "We brought her from the wreckage so that Jairesse can help her."

Morgan hesitated, unsure. Could he believe them? He had heard stories of races outside the empire exhibiting unusual abilities—some that healed, some that killed. He knelt next to Rayna, took her hand, and felt for her pulse. Slow, faint, but what alarmed him was the coolness of her skin. Anything was possible, and he struggled to think objectively.

Kneeling next to Morgan, Jairesse spoke in a soft, even tone. "She will not awaken without my help." She removed her hood and straightened her long, wavy blonde hair. "If I do not help her now, she will soon die."

Morgan's gaze swung from Volonian to Volonian. His fingers itched on the trigger, but he took a deep breath to steady himself. "What's her condition? What can you do for her?"

He heard a long, deep gasp; his eyes returned to Rayna, his free hand still holding hers. Had she stopped breathing? Seconds passed, and then Rayna gasped again. He squeezed her hand, his fingers rubbing hers. Again, she seemed to stop breathing. Then she gasped again.

If Jairesse was telling the truth, and he prevented her from helping, and Rayna died, he could never live with himself. His eyes moistening, he lowered his hands and nodded. "If any harm comes to her…" He paused, aware of the rapid beat of his heart, the throbbing pain of his headache, and the tremble in his hands. "Sorry." His sweaty palms tightened on his gun. "She is… very special to me."

"I understand." Jairesse removed her cape, revealing a golden robe. "What is her name?"

"Rayna." Clearing his throat, Morgan said, "Her name is Rayna Choff."

The armored man stepped forward and held out his hands. "I am Adonair."

Morgan eyed Adonair, then Jairesse, and finally Thakian, still holding his firearm, still suspicious. "Morgan Teggo." So far, the Volonians seemed friendly enough, a touch old-fashioned with their natural-fiber clothing and their small electronic items either attached to their waists or hanging from their necks. It was all consistent with what he thought Volonians might be like. Could he trust them? "Please, help her."

Jairesse knelt at Rayna's side with one hand hovering over Rayna's forehead and the other over Rayna's chest. She closed her eyes for a few seconds, then stood back up and said to Adonair and Thakian, "Please gather seven *quellates*."

The two men immediately ran into the forest.

Jairesse told Morgan, "Place her hands across her chest."

Staying on guard, Morgan put his gun down, took Rayna's hands, and crossed them over her heart. Then he took up his gun again, and they waited in silence, Morgan holding out hope for a sudden revival without any further intervention.

Adonair and Thakian soon returned with plant specimens, which they handed to Jairesse.

She turned to Morgan and held out the seven plant specimens to him. "Place this large purple vine across her collar, this small golden flower over her forehead, this red stem in the grasp of her right hand…"

Morgan hesitated, unsure of what Jairesse had in mind. The flowers appeared plain and ordinary, like decorative pieces. These were the *quellates*?

He re-holstered his gun under his vest and accepted the plant samples. He laid the purple vine across Rayna's collar and placed the golden flower on her forehead. He gently opened the fingers of her right hand and wrapped them around the red stem. As he continued, he kept his eyes on Rayna's face. Her gasps for breath seemed to be less frequent, the ominous stretches of utter stillness longer.

Morgan didn't see how a handful of flowers could help, and he struggled with the foreboding feeling that he might lose Rayna, but he couldn't deny the brief display of power Jairesse had exhibited—whatever that had been. He wished he understood what was going on and how, exactly, Jairesse's primitive setup would save Rayna. When he finished placing all seven specimens, he stepped back and waited with bated breath.

Jairesse knelt, held her hands close to either side of Rayna's head, and took several deep breaths. A faint glow emerged in the palms of her hands. Jairesse tilted her head back and raised her arms skyward, her sleeves falling aside to reveal glowing silver bracelets with etchings of unfamiliar symbols. She began uttering a soft melodic chant that flowed as smoothly as gentle waves of water.

"Ooooo, kha'tha, duolu, Oscanos, kha'tha, duolu, Gheriah, pan'dithy."

Morgan had no clue what Jairesse was doing. The chant felt almost musical. Rayna loved to sing. Was this Jairesse's way of reaching Rayna's brain activity? Would the glowing hands warm Rayna? He squeezed his fists to steady himself and calm his nerves.

"Ooooo, kha'tha, duolu, kaandathi, maandathi, pan'dithy."

Jairesse brought her arms down, her glowing hands together, lowered her head so that her face disappeared behind a cascade of her golden hair, and dropped her voice to a whisper that felt primitive, almost pre-human.

"Hicith, cislema, jaka-jaka…"

The chant no longer felt soothing to Morgan. Instead, it

now sounded like rodent murmurings, animalistic.

Rayna's face remained unchanged, unmoving, as if resting in peace.

Jairesse placed one hand on the top of Rayna's head, the other on her waist, and her singing changed to a soft atonal wordless melody.

Morgan crossed his arms to steady their tremble. His heart pounded, and he felt a drop of perspiration slither down his side. He recognized two words from Jairesse's chant. Oscanos and Gheriah were the names of two deities of the mythological pantheon that many Euranians—both those who resided within the Central Empire and those outside—still worshipped. As far back as he could remember, he had never believed the ancient stories. But even aboard *Ocelot*, many did.

Morgan shook his head at the sight of Jairesse kneeling beside Rayna, the glow from her hands spreading over Rayna's body to form a halo. This was not the sort of modern medical treatment Rayna needed. If he could only get her back to the space fortress, she would be in better hands. This was religion, nothing more, and Rayna's life lay in the hands of a shaman.

Hours passed. Adonair and Thakian silently sat with their backs against nearby trees. Jairesse and Rayna remained unchanged, the chanting continuing in a low whisper. The sun, having passed overhead, began to set, the shadows of the forest lengthening, the air beginning to cool.

Morgan's muscles had stiffened from the tension, and his head felt bruised from the bump. He was exhausted. Feelings of hope and helplessness jumbled his thoughts. He could only keep watch over Rayna. How long could he wait for Jairesse and her mystic ritual? But he had no choice. They were stranded; he had to take the chance that Jairesse might be right.

He was tired. He couldn't decide what was best for Rayna. He had to stay strong, for himself and for her.

At twilight, Jairesse opened her eyes, and the glow faded away. She took three deep breaths and rose to her feet. Rayna still lay next to Morgan, unchanged. With a sweep of her hand, Jairesse brushed the plant specimens to the grass.

Morgan jumped to his feet, startled by the sudden move. "Is she...all right?"

"Her injuries were severe," Jairesse said, donning her cape. "She is still healing within, but she should recover with time, adequate rest, and no further stress." She gently placed her hand—now without any trace of the glowing light—on Morgan's arm. "You can relax. Your beloved will live."

Morgan desperately wanted to believe Jairesse, but he did not see anything that looked different about Rayna.

"When will she awaken?"

"She may be able to hear you." Jairesse stepped away. "Perhaps you can awaken her."

"Rayna?" He could only hope. He knelt at her side, took her hand, and spoke to her in Alscrasian. "Rayna? It's Morgan. I'm right here. Hey, you're going to be fine." He brought her hand to his face. It felt reasonably warm. He felt her pulse. Slow and steady. "Can you hear me in your dreams?" He let out a nervous chuckle. "*Dox*, your father's going to have my head, for sure. What should we tell him?"

He watched her chest rise and fall. Her breathing now seemed steady and normal. If he didn't know the truth of the situation, he would have guessed that she was simply in deep sleep, without any ill effects. But she still wasn't responding. He could still lose her, and the thought terrified him. "Come back to me, please." His voice cracked.

He held her hands in his, closed his eyes, and lowered his head. If there was any truth to the Euranian Ancestors, now would be a good time for them to show themselves and save her.

"Come back to me, please..."

A distant voice in the darkness. From where? Come back —to where? The voice was familiar, a voice that had remained with Rayna for years.

"Morgan?"

Was it just a thought, or had she spoken?

"Rayna!" The voice was strong now.

She felt a firm squeeze in her hands. Her heart came alive, strong beats pounding inside her chest. Deep breaths, almost uncontrollable, sucked cool air in. Then, a gentle kiss on her lips. Soft. Warm.

Her eyes opened, and she saw his face.

It was Morgan. The happiness he radiated—the wide smile beaming from his face—energized her. He always made her happy. But then she paused to take in the mass of trees and boulders surrounding them. "Where are we?" For a moment, she felt confused, before the memories rushed back. "The particle beam..."

"How do you feel?" he asked.

With Morgan, it was always first things first.

She took in a deep breath. Her muscles felt deflated. "Tired." Still on the ground, she wiggled her arms and torso. "Stiff, sore, but not painful." She quickly put her hand on his chest. "Is this Volon?"

"It is," Morgan said as he helped Rayna stand.

He motioned toward a nearby woman with golden hair. Switching to Onglan, he introduced, "Your healer, Jairesse." He eyed the unfamiliar woman. "I don't know how I can thank you."

Jairesse crossed her arms. "You may consider relaxing your guard. You are among friends."

Morgan lowered his eyes and nodded.

"Thank you," Rayna said to Jairesse. She didn't know what for, but it didn't hurt to be polite. She bowed and, to her surprise, came back up dizzy enough to fall backward.

"Whoa!" Morgan quickly caught Rayna in his arms.

"Sorry." Rayna gave an embarrassed smile as she steadied herself. The loss of balance was something she hadn't expected.

"Please take care," Jairesse cautioned. "You are still recovering."

Something had happened to her—something she couldn't wait to find out about.

As a full moon rose over the nearby mountain range, Morgan introduced Adonair and Thakian to Rayna, who immediately began peppering the Volonians with questions about what had happened to her.

Jairesse stepped forward, her hand up, interrupting Rayna's questions. "Your *suromila* was blocked," she said.

Morgan didn't recognize the word. Was it more of Jairesse's mysticism? He glanced at Rayna, who looked lost.

"My what?" she asked.

"The center of your being," Jairesse explained as she sat down on the ground. Adonair and Thakian followed suit, sitting on either side of her. "It is what makes human beings different from all other animal life. Another day, and your life force would have deteriorated to the point of death." She paused and spread her arms out. "We who are humans are connected to the *Pankoulda.*"

Hearing yet more unfamiliar Volonian babble, Morgan waved Rayna over.

"What is it?" Rayna asked him.

"You're not going to get anything useful from her," Morgan said, nodding his head toward Jairesse. "Just a lot of obscure Volonian religion."

Rayna stared at Jairesse. "I want to hear it." She walked back, sat down with the others, and waited for Jairesse to continue.

After thinking it over, Morgan also sat to listen.

"Deep in the center of our being," Jairesse began, "the *Pankoulda* reach across space and time to regenerate our life force with their thoughts. When you are alone and very quiet, you can sense their presence. Not just our animate life energy but our intelligence springs from the *Pankoulda.* Our thoughts, our feelings, all of our emotional bonds with one another."

Morgan looked away. It was all mystical talk, matters he never gave much credence to. As a platoon officer, Rayna was used to encountering native life and their unfamiliar ways, so he wasn't surprised that she wanted to listen. But Rayna was always too headstrong, and he didn't see how Jairesse's religious exposition connected to what had happened to Rayna.

"With your *suromila* blocked, you were no longer connected to the *Pankoulda,* the source of higher life." Jairesse paused. "Do you understand? Your mind and soul cannot live without the sustaining presence of the *Pankoulda.* Even though your bodily functions could be mechanically maintained, you— Rayna Choff—would have ceased to exist."

Rayna ran her hand over the grass, her gaze following the movement of the blades. "So, I was fortunate to have been found by someone like you who understood all this."

Jairesse nodded. "You are restored now. You only need to regain your strength."

Morgan eyed Jairesse, Rayna having voiced exactly what he was thinking. He would be forever grateful that she had saved Rayna, but Jairesse's choice of words in describing the possibility of Rayna's death was too foreign for him to accept. If Rayna hadn't been physically injured, would she have died of an empty mind? This Volonian woman was still a mystery—perhaps too mysterious for comfort. "Forgive my ignorance, Jairesse, but... who are you?"

Jairesse only smiled at Morgan.

Adonair said, "She is the priestess of our temple. What she explained to you is privileged knowledge that's been passed down from the ancient days." He crossed his arms. "Who are you, and where are you from?"

Morgan said, "Obviously, not from Volon." Adonair's question was fair enough, a crash landing in their forest probably not a common occurrence. "We were shot down by a powerful particle beam. You must have seen it?"

"Are you referring to the *Hruvrah*?" Thakian asked. "It sent shock waves throughout the valley."

"*Hruvrah*?" Morgan asked, raising an eyebrow.

Thakian made an arc-shaped motion with his arm. "The rainbow of the gods."

"Rainbow..." Morgan remembered the particle beam exhibiting rainbowlike colors. "The beam that hit us was a straight shot from the ground into space." He caught Adonair glancing toward a distinctive twin peak in the mountains. Did the Volonians know something? "What's the *Hruvrah*?"

After a brief but awkward pause among the Volonians, Jairesse spoke. "It is a prophecy. Its appearance marks the beginning of a period of turmoil and conflict unseen since the ancient days." Her face turned ominous as she spoke. "As the priestess of our temple, it is my duty to seek out the Timegazer and learn what is to come upon us."

Morgan shook his head and looked at the ground. He didn't believe in any religious prophecies, local or interstellar. But the so-called *Hruvrah* was the particle beam that had nearly killed him and Rayna. He had to find out who was behind it and why it had fired at a passing Buggy that posed no threat. An advanced weapon among these simple people just didn't make sense.

"A subject strictly for the temple," Adonair quickly interjected. "You need not be concerned about it."

Morgan paused. Adonair's curt response was disturbing, especially after all of Jairesse's lifesaving help and friendliness. Was Adonair harboring a secret? Morgan glanced at Rayna to see if she'd picked up on anything they'd said. Switching to Alscrasian, he said, "I need to think a little bit. Are you feeling well enough to stand?"

Rayna nodded with a reassuring smile.

Switching back to Onglan, Morgan said to her, "We should go work on the comm unit." He turned to the Volonians. "We need to call for a rescue, the sooner the better."

After rising to his feet, he helped Rayna up and they walked slowly and deliberately back to the wreckage of the Buggy. Taking deep breaths and swinging his arms, Morgan pondered the Volonians with each step. Especially Adonair.

After stepping back inside the ruined craft, Morgan went straight to the pilot's seat and opened up the receiver, while Rayna retrieved her weapons from the locker. Within minutes, Morgan had panels open, circuits and feeders removed and carefully laid in a row on the floor among the scattering of debris, and the main array component extended from its bay as far as the bent tracks would allow it. He inspected the unit and discovered that a relay set, while intact, had one of its connections jarred loose during the landing. After reconnecting the relay, the receiver began beeping and the monitor displayed a message header on its screen. Relieved that the fix was so simple, Morgan silenced the beeper and opened the full message.

"BG-832, this is Space Fortress C, acknowledging reception of your distress signal.

"We are analyzing the craft telemetry attached to your signal. Preliminary indications are that you sustained a time distortion from a particle shower which interfered with the operation of the craft's systems.

"Please send us your current status. Space Fortress out."

Morgan closed the message and sat back in his seat to consider their situation. He looked out the window, past the lush forest, and studied the mountain peaks in the moonlight. The valley lay quiet, with only an occasional animal call in the distance. A flock of small birds with glowing amber eyes flew past a nearby mountain peak. A large flying reptile, also with glowing eyes, glided over the treetops.

He still puzzled over why no one had ever developed this world. Given its location within the territory of the Onglan League and an abundance of natural resources, it would have made sense for the Onglans to establish a presence here, if no one from the Central Empire did. And yet the mysterious particle beam attested to the fact that someone with advanced knowledge was here.

Rayna sat down in her seat and put two cups of water on the dashboard. She pointed at his forehead. "You should bandage that up."

Morgan nodded but kept working on the comm unit. He had enough of a hunch about the Volonians and the particle beam to consider following them. But given Rayna's weakened condition, he felt uncertain about placing her in a potentially dangerous situation.

Rayna took a sip. "You didn't believe a word of what Jairesse said, did you?"

Morgan emptied his cup in one mouthful. "Where is your *suromila*? In your heart?" He held both hands over his chest. "Your brain?" He made a bowl with his hands and placed it over his head. "Your liver?" He thumped his right side. "You know the liver is the energy generator of your body."

She laughed. "I assume *Pankoulda* is just a local name for the Euranian Ancestors. Lam'ba believes in them," Rayna said, referring to Lon by his nickname.

"He has no choice," Morgan remarked. "He was raised by monks."

"And didn't someone say Mr. Lendus was ordained?" Rayna asked, referring to the *Ocelot* executive officer.

"That's just a rumor." He winked and closed up the panel. "Well, the good news is that the comm's working now. The bad news is that nothing else is." He paused. "I have a hunch I want to follow. The rainbow—"

Rayna held up her hand. "I know what you're thinking— that we need to track down the particle beam. But wouldn't it be better to send for a squad from the space fortress?"

Morgan shook his head. "We don't have enough hard information to request a mission." He looked Rayna over.

"I'm fine, if that's what you're wondering," Rayna said, sounding a bit insistent. "The dizziness is gone. I have no broken bones, and I don't see any of my blood anywhere—unlike someone else we know. If I weren't up to the task, I'd let you know."

Morgan wasn't totally convinced, but Rayna seemed to be regaining her strength. Would she really be up for what amounted to a self-directed investigation? "Well, if we could join these Volonians while they're here with us, they might lead us right to the source of the particle beam." After pausing for one final minute of consideration, he decided to take Rayna at her word. He reached for the transmitter set, adding, "If my hunch is right, that is."

Rayna nodded, then went silent. She looked down at the floor and asked, "What really happened to me during the crash?"

Morgan saw from Rayna's furrowed eyebrows that she was now serious. "I don't think we'll know for sure until we get back to the fortress."

"Morgan, don't stall, please." Rayna said. "What did you see?"

There was no point in avoiding the subject. "I was knocked out, too," he began, "but they left me alone. When I woke up, you were missing, so I searched until I found you, lying unconscious in the clearing with the three of them gathered around you."

Morgan stopped to choose his next words with care. He looked away from Rayna and cleared his throat.

"I honestly didn't know what to do. She said that if she didn't help immediately, you would die. Your hands were cold, and your breathing was slow and labored. You were gasping, and there were long pauses in between, as if you'd stopped breathing."

The memory still gave Morgan chills. He couldn't believe he could talk so calmly about it to her.

"Jairesse sang some kind of mystical chant. She used no medical instruments, no drugs or medicine. She didn't even touch you. She had me place little flowers all over your body, and then"—he held out his hands— "her hands glowed as she put them near your body. And she stayed that way for the whole day. When she was done, she declared that you were going to be all right."

He took a deep breath, his eyes returning to meet hers. "Whatever it was, it worked. But I don't understand what she did to revive you."

"Morgan," she said, "it scares me to think that Jairesse might have been right."

He took her hands and held them steady. "Rayna, you're okay, and that's what matters."

"Morgan," Rayna said in a semi-scolding tone. She stared at him in silence.

"Rayna, what is it? Tell me."

She looked down and sighed. "Maybe I'm just... Did I ever tell you about when my mother died?"

"You said you were really small."

"Did I ever tell you I was alone with her?" She looked at Morgan, who shook his head. She rarely showed any hint of vulnerability, to him or anyone else. But now, her eyes seemed a silent request for reassurance. "I don't know how long we were together. I just remember watching her breathing slow, just like what you said, as if she were tiring and it was hard for her to breathe. Her hands cooled first, and when her forehead also became cold, I knew she would soon be gone. I've never forgotten how still she lay, and how lonely I felt."

As she described her mother, Morgan remembered Rayna's condition, his feelings of helplessness, and the fear of losing her.

"Was I like that?" she asked.

Morgan embraced her. "You're going to be okay, Rayna." A thought occurred to him. "You know, we've only Jairesse's word to go on. There's no real data to support her interpretation. When we get back to the space fortress, Dr. Creatoun will check you over. Then we'll know what really happened, and that will be that."

When he released her, she smiled and nodded. "Okay."

"So, on this other matter..." He changed the subject and reached again for the transmitter set.

"Just don't report what happened to me," Rayna said. "I don't want my father to get all agitated while we're still here."

"Uh-huh." Brushing aside her concern, Morgan switched on the transmitter. "Space Fortress C, this is *BG-832*, on the surface of Volon, Lieutenant Teggo speaking. Our craft is not flyable, after crash-landing. We await a rescue craft." He glanced over at Rayna, who was mouthing a "no-no-no" gesture at him. "Ensign Choff was briefly knocked unconscious during the crash but is recovered now." This was for her own good, Morgan decided. "She will require a full examination upon our return."

Rayna threw her hands up in disapproval.

"In the meantime, we have met three Volonians who gave us assistance." He glanced at Rayna. She looked steamed. For Morgan, there was no need to report his hunch about following the Volonians just yet. "Teggo out."

He switched off the transmitter and faced Rayna's glare.

He'd seen that look before. "Just planning ahead, that's all."

"I hope Dad slaps you down!"

"Rayna..." His brain scrambled to salvage the conversation. The last thing he wanted was another confrontation with Captain Choff and another sentence to the supply room. "I was just thinking of your health. Because I care."

She seemed taken aback. "If you cared, you'd consider my feelings on matters like these."

Morgan stopped—it was true. He tended to forget that, in many ways, she was his equal. In some things, she was his superior. After all, she was a platoon officer, trained to establish landings in unfamiliar settings, learn about the locals, and deal with hostile encounters.

"You know you're not cleared for duty, don't you?" He softened his voice. "There's no medical officer here."

Rayna frowned. "I told you I'm fine."

Morgan sighed. "You may be a squad leader—"

"*Platoon* leader," Rayna corrected him. "I command *three* squads."

"—but I still outrank you."

"Not by much."

Morgan didn't want to give in, even though she was just as headstrong as he was. "You're determined, aren't you?" He thought it over. "All right, I'm listening."

"Morgan, I have to come along with you." Her facial muscles were clenched, stern.

Morgan's shoulders slumped.

"I can't just sit here, all alone. I'll go crazy." Now, her voice softened. "I need something like this job to take my mind off of all this."

Morgan sighed; he knew her next line by heart.

She took his hands. "You always make me feel better." She looked into his eyes. "Maybe that's why I love you."

It was no use. Again. "And I love you, too." He gave in, smiling at her. "If Jairesse says you're okay, then I'll be okay with you going."

She jumped out of her seat, threw her arms around him, and gave him a passionate kiss. They pulled themselves out of his seat and down to the floor, picking up where they had been interrupted by the crash.

Morgan and Rayna emerged from their craft, both armed and jacketed. With handheld lights to guide their way through the darkness, they rejoined the three Volonians.

Morgan immediately addressed Jairesse. "It will be about a Volonian day before a rescue craft arrives."

Jairesse turned to face Rayna. "I should examine you before we depart." She peered into Rayna's eyes, placed her hands over Rayna's temples, and waited until a soft golden glow from her hands enveloped Rayna's head.

Morgan held his breath, tense from the sight of Jairesse's red eyes.

"You are whole, but weak," Jairesse pronounced. "Take care to avoid danger, so that nothing disrupts your *suromila*."

"I understand," Rayna said, her voice sounding slightly muffled from within the halo.

Jairesse bowed her head and withdrew her hands. The golden glow faded away, and her eyes returned to normal.

Morgan took Rayna's hand. "Are you sure you feel all right?"

"For the two-hundredth time, I'm fine." There was a hint of annoyance in her voice.

"We should go," Adonair urged Jairesse. "The rest of our party awaits our return with the holy commandments of the Timegazer."

"Yes." Thakian led everyone a short distance through the trees to a smaller clearing, where a big-wheeled, box-shaped transport rover sat.

"Volon is modernized?" Morgan asked, surprised.

"Enough to be practical," Adonair said, opening a panel next to the door. "We receive the interstellar widecasts from the empire. But we're not like you, with advanced spaceships. We live simpler here."

"Wait." Motioning with his hand toward his gun, Morgan said, "We should accompany you into the mountains."

"There's no need." Thakian's face was cold, the muscles of his jaw tensed.

Jairesse smiled, her hand raised to calm Thakian. "Thakian is a Master of the *Illito*, our people's warriors. He will protect me during the journey. And Adonair is also accompany-ing me." She spread her arms out. "Thank you for your offer. Morgan and Rayna, may the *Pankoulda* bestow their blessings onto you." She bowed to them.

Morgan was about to insist on following when a sharp howl pierced the cool night air. A flame-red flying reptile, its eyes a bright yellow and its fang-lined jaws gaping, leaped out of a nearby tree and plunged toward them.

"Everyone down!" Morgan yelled. He and Rayna ran to opposing sides of the clearing, their charge-lock guns in hand.

Jairesse screamed as she and Adonair dove for cover un-der the rover chassis. Thakian pivoted to face the predator, his firearm drawn, but had to dive to the ground as the beast swiped at him with its massive talons.

"Fire!" Morgan ordered.

He and Rayna pummeled the flying reptile from both sides, catching it in a crossfire of high-energy shots until it crashed to the ground in a bloody, smoking heap, its final, dying cries echoing through the forest.

Morgan approached the animal, his gun still pointed at it. "Thakian? Are you okay?"

Thakian only huffed with disgust as he got to his feet, ignoring Morgan, while Rayna helped Jairesse and Adonair out from under the rover.

"It's dead." Morgan gave the smoldering reptile a firm nudge with his foot. The stench of burning flesh drifted through the air. He eyed Thakian, then turned to face Jairesse. "Are you sure you don't want us to accompany you?"

2. The Fountain of Eternal Passage

The gentleman sat in meditation, surrounded by a circle of five squat green candles that illuminated him from his feet up to his waist. He closed his eyes, took five long deep breaths, and relaxed his muscles. A faint aroma, a hint of pomira tree bark mixed with sulfur, entered the nostrils of his pointed nose. He took five more slow breaths and let the out-of-body-inducing vapors seep in. His mind loosened its focus as puddles of pink and gray colors flowed in. A quiet voice whispered to him.

A vision of oversized foliage took shape in his mind. Leaves of an assortment of trees covered the terrain. A rough path knifed through the dense forest. Patches of undergrowth pushed through the dirt, between the pebbles that littered the lane. Tiny reptiles slithered or crawled across the path. Flying insects darted back and forth between the small bushes at the base of the trees. A single mollusk ate a collection of small eggs.

"Visitors," a voice whispered.

With his mind's eye, the gentleman spied fresh tread tracks in the bare path. He then saw a transport rover rolling over the rough terrain. Another inhale, and the vision faded before he could identify the travelers inside.

Morgan peered over Thakian's shoulder at the front window of the transport rover. Outside, the forest was thinning, revealing the foothills of an abrupt mountain range. The ride became bumpy as the terrain grew jagged, littered with bare rock. Steep, craggy formations shot two thousand feet skyward, where low-lying charcoal-gray clouds drifted past pointed peaks that occasionally blocked the moonlight.

Thakian gave Morgan a hard stare, cold enough to make Morgan back off. Morgan knew that he and Rayna needed to tread lightly. Jairesse had overruled both Thakian and Adonair on bringing Morgan and Rayna along, and while both Volonian men were obedient, they were obviously resentful.

"How do you do this?" Morgan turned and asked Jairesse, his hands held up, emulating her. "Are there others who have the same power as you?"

Jairesse shook her head. "Only one other, and she is very young. Very undisciplined and childlike, but she is learning well for her age. Someday, she will succeed me. It is her calling."

Soon, the rover drove up the rocky incline and onto a mountain pass. One side rose straight up, a sheer wall; the other side fell into a steep chasm. Morgan peered out the window and saw the surging rapids of a dark green river far below. A giant brown sea snake flailed in the foam. They reached the end of the drivable pass, a cul-de-sac flanked by drops on both sides. A vertical wall towered before them. After pointing the rover's headlights at a small cave-like opening recessed ten feet up in the wall, they disembarked from the vehicle.

"I don't like this." Thakian scanned about in all directions with his handlight, grunted at Adonair, and drew his firearm. "Wait here."

Morgan put his hand on Thakian's shoulder. "You're not

going alone, are you?"

Thakian shrugged Morgan's hand away. "I am a Master of the *Illito*."

"Let us go with you," Rayna said.

"It is my purpose," Thakian said with a stern face. "It is my honor."

Morgan was stuck. Whatever rank Thakian held, they had outclassed him earlier, and Morgan didn't want to heap more insult on a tradition-bound mindset. "This may be more than a one-person job."

Thakian shook his head.

Morgan looked at Adonair and Jairesse, both stoic, and gave in. "All right, we don't want to be disrespectful."

Thakian grunted, turned away, and climbed the giant rocks with an athletic agility that impressed Morgan. Within seconds, Thakian reached the opening. After peering inside with his handlight, Thakian proceeded into the cave.

A being in black waited behind a grouping of jagged boulders, crouched in the darkness of the cave, eyes unblinking, its wings folded, its foreclaws curved and tensed, its keen ears discerning every sound.

It froze as a shaft of light sliced through the darkness. A tall human took one measured step at a time, shining a handlight from side to side, until he stood directly below the black, shadowy being.

The human looked about, examining the ancient ruins littering the interior of the cave: statues of humans, semi-humans, and beasts, chair-like pieces of varying shapes and sizes, and the remains of once-functional machinery, fallen, cracked, and corroded. The being widened its eyes and saw the image of a red lightning bolt on the man's muscular upper arm.

It was a warrior.

The man suddenly swung his light up. The being ducked its head, whipped its wings about, and camouflaged itself as a large rock until the light passed over it. When it heard the man step away, it reopened its wings and stealthily followed.

Soon, the man reached a bend, and as he paused to shine the light into the darkness that enveloped the depths ahead, the being extended its foreclaws, its wings held taut, its eyes squeezed into a squint, its lips pulled back to expose its incisors.

The warrior took two steps around the corner, then stumbled over an unseen depression in the ground. The large shadow-like being sprang down and smothered him, its wings wrapping around his face, choking off his cry.

Outside, all heads pivoted at the desperate cry from within the cave.

"Thakian!" Jairesse yelled.

Morgan and Rayna drew their guns, bounded up the boulders, charged into the cave, and paused a moment for their eyes to adjust to the utter darkness. They pulled handlights out of their jacket pockets and flipped them on, Rayna's pointed ahead into the darkness, Morgan's swinging from side to side at an assortment of animal-head statues and other ruins lining the walls.

As they rounded the corner, Rayna pointed at a shadowy figure running away into the distance.

"Wait," Morgan said, nearly tripping over a body. He stooped down and shone his light on the face. "*Krok!* It's Thakian!"

He and Rayna sprang into defensive positions over Thakian's body, their lights scanning about them, their guns at the ready.

Adonair and Jairesse ran in and knelt beside Thakian. Jairesse cradled his head. Morgan glanced down and saw Thakian's eyes settle into narrow slits, his head limp in Jairesse's hands.

"Jairesse..." Thakian murmured, barely audible. He suddenly coughed up a mouthful of blood, his body convulsing as he began choking. "The Xaturi..."

"Thakian!" She looked to Adonair, her eyes pleading for help.

Adonair picked up Thakian's light and shone it on Thakian's now-pale face. Thakian calmed, and Jairesse felt for a pulse along his neck, but after a few seconds, she could only shake her head.

"Thakian..." Her voice trembled. "Don't leave us."

A warm, gentle breeze blew into the cave. It grazed over them, light as feathers, before disappearing into the depths. As it passed, Thakian expired.

"No..." Jairesse's face contorted with sadness, and she lowered Thakian's head. She placed her hand on Thakian's forehead and broke down. With tears streaming down her face, she put the *Illito* warrior's firearm into his right hand, took both of his arms, and crossed them over his chest.

Morgan instinctively put his hand on Jairesse's shoulder and helped her steady herself. He glanced at Rayna and was struck at how she stared at Thakian's face, seemingly lost in thought. If he knew it would be this deadly, he wouldn't have let her come on this trip, not so soon after her brush with death.

He took a step over to Rayna, but when she looked at him and said, "We should move them outside, for safety," he felt reassured that her mind was still on her job.

Jairesse regained her composure with a deep breath. She placed her hand on Thakian's chest, lowered her head, and began chanting.

"Memono G'pathi amenno, Oscanos.

"Thakian potho li dactus, Gheriah.

"Abethi demni…"

Morgan and Rayna stood on guard outside the mouth of the cave, in case the attacker rushed out, while Adonair assisted Jairesse with the last rites for Thakian. Morgan looked away from the scene. Jairesse's whispery words, clearly not Onglan in nature, were completely foreign to him. Rayna, meanwhile, looked lost in contemplation.

"The chanting sounds nothing like the funerals I've been to," Morgan observed.

"Different people from different worlds may have different rites," Rayna reflected, "but Lon told me that the prayer for the metamorphosis of the departed, and their migration home, was once common to all of us."

Morgan didn't actually believe in the common prayer or the existence of what was known as "True Eurania," the mythical world of human origin. He thought that Rayna didn't either, but he had always tried to be respectful of people who did, as he assumed Rayna was doing now.

Adonair approached them. "He was the finest and bravest of our *Illito*." He stared up at the twin-peaked mountain. A passing hawk flew by. "We love peace; we have not had a murderer among our people in over five centuries. Whenever we've found someone killed, we've always traced the killing to a visitor from outside our valley."

Morgan found such a uniform peacefulness intriguing,

but unlikely for such a long period of time.

"Long ago," Adonair continued, "our leaders formed an elite corps to educate our people in peaceful ways. They learned and mastered the ancient *Illito* martial arts, but they also followed the *Illito* philosophy of understanding. Though they armed themselves, as all protectors must, they rarely had a confrontation that involved violence. Only intrusions of outsiders have broken the peace; only an outsider could explain the cruel massacre that occurred."

Uncomfortable with seeming insensitive, Morgan debated whether now was the time to question Adonair. But a killer still lurked somewhere inside the cave.

"What did Thakian mean when he said, 'The Xaturi'?" Morgan waited and tried to gauge Adonair's expression.

"The Xaturi..." After several slow breaths, Adonair's voice regained its strength. "This is our matter. You must understand, this is of no concern to you."

Morgan was growing tired of Adonair's evasion. They now had an unforeseen obstacle to finding the source of the particle beam, and Adonair was not helping. On the verge of losing his patience, Morgan struggled to keep his voice steady. "I do understand that this is your concern, not ours. But Thakian is dead. Jairesse is no warrior. Your priestess could be the next victim. I ask again: What is the Xaturi?"

Adonair's face contorted. He turned away and looked over the chasm, toward a distant mountain range. "It is a killer, a murderer, an evil creature that is supposed to inhabit these mountains but has not been seen in over a millennium."

"Myths and legends don't help," Morgan said. "Why didn't you bring a larger contingent for such a dangerous journey?"

Adonair shook his head. "Coming before the Timegazer is only for our priestess. It is a holy site. Thakian was the best of our warriors, and I am accompanying Jairesse because, as the administrator of the temple, I am already privileged to some of the sacred knowledge. But I will not set foot inside the sanctuary when we reach it." He eyed Morgan and Rayna, then opened a flap on his jacket and brought out several small pieces of paper. "I've been told my sketch is not very similar to the real article, but it was the best I could do, based on the description our ruler's great-uncle gave me." He unfolded one page to reveal a rough drawing of a black reptile with oversized scaly wings and a serpentine tail, accompanied by a line of unfamiliar symbols. Handing the drawing to Morgan and Rayna, he said, "The Xaturi."

After Jairesse concluded the Volonian last rites for Thakian, Morgan and Rayna helped Adonair carry Thakian's body into the rover. They then reentered the cave, Morgan and Rayna leading the way, Adonair and Jairesse following.

They paused before the statues of humans, semi-humans, and beasts lined up against the wall. Several were human in armor and helmets, with trident weapons in their hands and guns hanging from their belts. Others were tentacled creatures with human heads, large wings, and serpentine tails. Still others looked like amoebas covered with spiked fingers and eyes.

"Gods?" Morgan asked Adonair. "Monsters?"

"I'm not sure."

Morgan asked Rayna, "Ever seen anything like these before?"

Rayna examined the statues with her light, while Morgan kept an eye out for intruders. "There are excavated ruins in the Sestian Republic with old statues like these," Rayna said. "I think they're supposed to be from the ancient Etolian age."

"Not a collection of local artworks based on the old stories?" Morgan asked. "That would seem more likely to me."

"That wouldn't make sense," Rayna said. "Why would modern statues be hidden in underground tunnels?"

"Not necessarily modern," Morgan said, "but not over a thousand years old, either. It's dry and dark here, good for storage and preservation."

"But look at this," Rayna said, pointing at an inscription hanging over a statue's three heads. "That's not Onglan."

Morgan turned to Adonair. "Volonian writing?"

After an awkward silence, Jairesse stepped forward. "It's an older script. There are many stories among our people about nonhuman and superhuman beings that inhabited our world long ago. After the eruption of the Great Nebula, much was destroyed, and valuable Volonian knowledge was lost during the dark age. There are some among us who dedicate their lives to theorizing and reconstructing what was but no longer is."

Morgan eyed Adonair, suspicious that he hadn't offered an explanation like Jairesse had.

Jairesse swept her hand toward the wall of statues in a wide arc. "Rayna is correct. These are from the days of the Etolian Empire, when the people were far more enlightened in the ways of the *Pankoulda* than today. From before the cataclysm."

Thirteen hundred years earlier,
In the Year 6908 of the Old Memonan Calendar

Golden-robed High Priest Duo'ra silently approached the altar of the Great Temple of Almighty Euranos. Faint wisps of white smoke rose from a cobalt-blue bowl resting in the center of a wide raised slab of pure white stone. Twenty-foot-tall statues lined the walls of the cavernous sanctuary. On one side stood likenesses of green-skinned Lord Oscanos and six armored, weapon-wielding Dravies warriors. On the other side stood demure Mother Gheriah and six pixie-like winged messengers. Duo'ra inhaled the fumes with long, deep breaths as the people—over three thousand, seated in rows of gray stone pews—watched with anticipation.

Emperor Fur'thur, in the plush comfort of his private box high above the congregation and surrounded by dozens of aides, always enjoyed returning to his homeworld of Memona. Etolis was a recent construction, barely two centuries old, its sole purpose to be the administrative hub of the Imperial government. Memona, on the other hand, teemed with history and culture, a crossroads for people from throughout the empire. The temple itself was several thousand years old.

"In the days before the Great Migration," the high priest began, "a titanic conflict raged between the reptiloids of Sigorum and the humans of Amahl. And with them fought their lords and protectors, waging war throughout the cosmic multiverse."

While the high priest spoke, the emperor stared up at the shafts of sunshine beaming down from the crystal skylights lining the hundred-foot-high vaulted ceiling. His imagination drifted to a time long before the founding of the core worlds of the empire, when the human race still lived in the fabled cities of the lush forests of Amahl.

"By the invasion of Sigorum, the great Adelph and his army held the advantage against the Troggle and the reptiloids," High Priest Duo'ra continued, "and so the demonic creatures of Sigorum arose from the depths of the planet to aid the Troggles, slaughtering Adelph's forces in the bloodiest massacre in human history. Only the divine intervention of Lord Oscanos saved the human race."

The emperor lowered his head and pondered the meaning of what he had heard. The thought of how precarious life in the multiverse was chilled him to the bone. He wondered how many of the thousands in attendance grasped how close the human race had come to eternal enslavement—or extinction.

"I ask you." The high priest's voice boomed throughout the cavernous temple. "What does this mean?"

Indeed, the emperor mused. In the grand scheme of existence, what did it mean?

"In time, the human race relocated to new homeworlds," Duo'ra said, "our homeworlds. Over the millennia, we have flourished, expanding throughout the many star systems of Eurania, establishing our empire, the proud beacon of human existence."

He paused and lifted a finger. "But we are not to forget our predecessors, the divine beings of our creation, the fearsome entities of light and dark who fought for our survival. I ask you: Who among us keeps mindful of the prophesied return of the ancestral beings?"

The emperor understood. It could be tomorrow, or it could be a thousand years from now, but the deities of evil would try again. The human race—his subjects—had to remain vigilant. He would have to address the people about this.

The sound of a female voice interrupted his thoughts. "Your Majesty," his aide Andra whispered, her eyes wide with fear. She held up her comp-pad. "We have an emergency."

Emperor Fur'thur glanced at the message blinking in fiery red lettering: "Urgent: Massive Star Explosions Detected. Blast waves to reach the core worlds within weeks. No known defenses."

The emperor gasped. He squeezed the cushioned arms of his chair, his fingers digging in and ripping a piece of fabric.

"What should we do?" Andra's voice cracked with desperation. The other aides quickly gathered around, tense.

The emperor struggled to think. It couldn't be The End. There had to be a way to protect the people. "Contact Imperial Headquarters. I want a plan by tonight. Go!"

In the Imperial Headquarters orbital space city, high above the surface of Etolis, Pax Bn'dim, the watch commander, surveyed the scores of data monitors surrounding him. Human supervisors paced about the control center, studying the many data readouts. Dozens of android analysts walked alongside, their head and chest monitors displaying information.

Commander Bn'dim eyed the bank of displays above the long-range monitoring station. His patience was gone.

"What do you have?" he barked at the Central Region supervisor, a man half his height, twice his age, and nearing retirement.

The supervisor slowly shook his head. "We've picked up half a dozen more celestial explosions, all from the same catalyst."

Bn'dim sucked in his breath, waiting for the supervisor to finish his report. After a moment of silence, he seethed, "Well, Supervisor Jun?"

"Sir, the blast waves are destroying everything in their path."

Bn'dim pounded the console. "We need a viable defense."

"The sheer size alone is more than we can handle." Supervisor Jun sighed. "With each ensuing supernova, the path of destruction grows even more expansive. Nothing is going to stop it from reaching—and overwhelming—us." He stepped forward, reached up, and placed a warm hand on the younger man's shoulder. "I'm sorry."

Commander Bn'dim struggled to maintain his composure. "How could this have happened? Is this our end?" The watch commander's voice was barely a whisper.

"If this is our end, then I am truly saddened." Jun paused for a moment, then spoke in a soft tone. "I've lived a long and fruitful life, with few regrets. But I am sorry for your generation, those under your care, and for all the future children of Lord Oscanos and Mother Gheriah. Our people, our stories, deserve to live on. How, I don't know."

The military, led by the emperor's adviser, the general-superior, assumed command of the empire, and in a matter of days, commandeered every available spaceship. Almost immediately, crowds swarmed the spaceports. Orderliness was imposed at gunpoint by the soldiers controlling the ships. Outside the spaceports, chaos engulfed the masses. Bribes were offered, blood was shed, lives were lost.

Emperor Fur'thur watched his subjects descend into the depths of desperation from the safety and comfort of his royal yacht, *Star of Amahl*, in orbit above Etolis. His wife, Gemina, entered the mobile throne room and sat beside him, their infant son in her arms. Scenes of chaos and military-imposed order alternated on the four monitors lining the walls. Without warning, laser fire erupted on one of the monitors. The crowd scattered in all directions, leaving half a dozen fallen bodies on the blood-soaked pavement.

"They're animals," Gemina quietly said.

"They're dying," Emperor Fur'thur said with a heavy heart. "But we must keep faith that the Pan'kouldah will lead us to a new home, again."

"He is helpless," Gemina said as she stroked the baby's head. "He is at the mercy of others."

"He…" Fur'thur paused, unsure.

They were a doomed people. The chances of reaching the frontier planets—barely out of reach of the blast wave—were small. Nobody knew whether the probes that had launched over four hundred years ago to those distant worlds had survived. Without any known wormholes to traverse, the journey would take 250 years. They and their descendants would need to find food and fuel along the way.

Nobody could envision what the succeeding generations would be like, and whether the Imperial rule would be supported. Fur'thur looked into Gemina's eyes. She was right. Their son was at the mercy of the military, not just now as a baby, but even into adulthood.

"He should not be a target," Fur'thur said. "He must not wear the crown." He took a deep breath and spoke as firmly as he could. "Once we've departed, we will hide him within the general population, aboard one of the other ships. For his safety, he will have a different name, different parents, and a different upbringing. If it be the will of the Pan'kouldah, the crown will survive with our people."

He gave Gemina and the baby tender kisses and sent them out of the room as Andra entered with an unfamiliar young man at her side.

"Your Majesty," Andra said, as she and the man bowed, "may I introduce my new assistant, Pax Bn'dim."

"I bid you and your family welcome," Fur'thur said with a smile. "Your service record has been exemplary, the highest among many. I am delighted to have such a deserving person join my staff."

"Thank you so much for the opportunity," Bn'dim said. "I humbly serve at your pleasure."

"Notify the rest of the staff," Emperor Fur'thur said to Andra in a steady, stately tone that masked his sadness and uncertainty, "we will be departing in ten hours."

~ ~ ~

Leaving the ancient statues and proceeding deeper into the tunnels, Morgan followed Rayna around a turn in the cave, passing the spot where Thakian had been killed.

"What do you think about…him?" Rayna asked Morgan in Alscrasian, her voice low, her head tilting toward Adonair.

"I'm keeping my eye on him," Morgan said. "Do you want to lead, while I bring up the rear?"

Rayna nodded, then paused. "One more thing—just to be clear—*we* are searching for the source of the particle beam."

"Yes."

"And when we run into Thakian's killer?"

"We defend ourselves." Morgan raised his gun. "And your healer, too. I trust her. But keep your eye on our other friend." He felt a brief moment of anxiety over separating in the darkness, but it was the best way to maintain a defensive position in all directions.

"Got it."

Morgan drifted behind Adonair and Jairesse and pointed his light backward to confirm that they were alone.

They soon passed through an archway that opened into a circular cavern. Morgan stepped across a soft, carpet-like material that covered the floor in the deeper recesses of the cave. Although the ground cover exhibited the same blue-gray coloring as the surrounding rock, the texture differed. It was furry.

Rayna called from ahead, "Look at this."

She paused until Morgan and the others caught up. He shone his light on a dust-covered, rock-encrusted control console, thirty feet in height and width, built into the cavern's rock wall. Large gray tubes, emerging from the ground, entered the base of the console, rising through the top of the console along the wall. Morgan pointed his light upward, following the tubes up to the cavern ceiling, where they disappeared.

"Could be part of a massive construct," Morgan said. He knew that, during the golden age of Eurania, Onglus had been founded as a territorial outpost of the ancient Etolian Empire. If Jairesse's description of ancient lost knowledge was true, then it seemed possible that a powerful particle beam could have come from this location—given someone with the right knowledge to resurrect the machinery ruins. They could actually be pretty close to the source.

Rayna led the way forward, Adonair and Jairesse following, and Morgan bringing up the rear. Soon, they passed through a second archway that led out of the cavern and entered another passageway.

"Catacombs," Rayna said, pointing at more ruins lining the walls.

The passageway sloped upward. The right wall fell away, revealing a vast pit far below. Morgan picked up a fist-sized rock and tossed it over the edge. It bounced against the rock wall and plunged into the depths. Suddenly, a geyser of flame erupted from below. It vanished almost as quickly, leaving the echo of the blaze's roar vibrating through the cavern. A hint of sulfuric smoke drifted in the air.

Morgan began to piece together the image of a massive apparatus that drew unlimited power from the molten depths of Volon and channeled it up a tubular network, through an array of oversized transformer consoles similar to what they had passed.

The path continued to ascend, winding around the edge of the drop. Panning his light above, Morgan saw numerous overhanging boulders.

"Morgan!" Rayna called. She pointed up at a black shadow darting among the boulders.

Morgan tensed. Was it Thakian's killer?

Rayna panned her light along the rocky walls, unable to relocate the elusive figure. "I don't see how we can get up there without pulling down the boulders on top of ourselves."

"We need to be careful about this," Morgan said. "Maybe

we can climb up farther ahead. Let me go first."

As he took a step up the path, a loud creak sounded from above.

"Move!" Rayna yelled at Adonair and Jairesse, the first few small pebbles tumbling down past them.

They charged ahead as an avalanche of rocks and boulders rained down where they had stood and bounded over the edge. The crashes and rattles reverberated for several more seconds after the last of the rubble disappeared into the void.

Morgan and Rayna snapped their lights up at a gaping hole in a line of overhead boulders and caught a brief glimpse of the black shadow dashing off behind a crevice in the wall. Rayna fired, the bright energy charge sailing through the hole and exploding in the distance with a loud concussion.

Lowering her gun, she said, "It's gone."

Morgan put a firm hand on Jairesse's shoulder. She was hyperventilating, clearly terrified, her eyes wide as they looked about. "Are you okay with continuing?" he asked her.

Jairesse took a moment to steady herself, then slowly nodded.

Rayna led the way forward again. But before they ventured much farther, the path stopped. Several feet ahead, across a short chasm, was another small opening and the beginning of another narrow tunnel, this one lined with two strings of small, bead-like green lights.

"It's only a few feet," Rayna said to Morgan. "We can jump it."

Morgan paused. "Are you sure, Rayna?" With a flicker of his eyes, he indicated Jairesse and Adonair.

Rayna glanced around, pointing her light first to the left along the jagged crevice, then to her right, straight down into the darkness, and finally up above. "There," she said, pointing at a short, raised bridge, "I'll bring it down."

"Be careful," Morgan said.

"Morgan, don't fuss."

She stepped away from the drop, waved Adonair and Jairesse aside, then motioned to Morgan to keep his light steady on the chasm.

Morgan gave the go-ahead and held his breath.

Rayna took a short running start and gracefully leaped over the chasm, landing with a few inches to spare. She ventured into the mouth of the tunnel, where she looked over a series of power panels and switches and a maze of colored lights.

She scanned her side of the chasm in all directions and, stepping out and away from the tunnel, disappeared behind a formation of boulders. "Here it comes," she called out.

The short bridge lowered, the lift mechanism creaking softly, unpowered. Morgan watched it settle into place, approving of Rayna's decision not to activate any of the machinery and avoiding the possibility of automated detection.

After they all crossed to the other side, Morgan and Rayna surveyed the new tunnel—a dirty pathway lined with the green bead-like lights and covered with metal plates, some translucent, others warped or cracked. It reminded Morgan of some of the access tubes on *Ocelot*. They followed it a short distance before Morgan stopped and pointed his light at a perpendicular crawlway, partially obscured by stones, that he noticed to his left.

"What do you think?" Morgan asked, pushing the larger stones aside to peer up the sloping crawlway.

"I've got a feeling," Rayna replied.

"Female intuition again?" Morgan asked.

Rayna smiled. "Have I been wrong yet?"

After shaking his head and conceding her point, Morgan examined the crawlway and saw that it was rough but empty.

"Let me lead," Rayna said.

Morgan nodded and stepped aside.

After she climbed in, Morgan helped Adonair and Jairesse in. He made one last scan in all directions with his light, confirming that the shadowy figure was nowhere in the immediate vicinity, then entered the crawlway.

Rayna inched her way along the claustrophobic tunnel, crawling on all fours over alloy tiles caked with dirt, an occasional dust cloud feathering over her when she brushed a loose outcropping. Though she served as the commanding officer of the three squads that comprised *Pouton*'s onboard platoon, the Central Empire was at peace, and her assignments had amounted to little more than escorting Captain Jaron or Executive Officer Alteus when they disembarked at ports of call. In between, she organized the many hours of combat exercise.

Now, she found herself on a true expedition. Though she was off duty, and this was a self-initiated investigation, Rayna couldn't help but feel the adrenaline surging. She kept her eye out behind her, focusing on protecting everyone, and not on thoughts of being buried in a tunnel collapse.

After a long stretch of slithering over rounded and jagged rocks, and scraping through layers of dust and grit, Rayna came upon a small, closed access door at the end of the crawlway. She motioned for the others to stop. While they waited in silence, she put her ear against the door and listened for sounds from the other side. She thought she detected a distant melody. But hearing no voices, she gently pushed on the door and cracked it upward.

A sliver of light entered the crawlway.

Swinging the door farther, she saw the desolate ruins of a shadowy, musty room. The strains of an out-of-tune flutelike instrument floated through the thick air. Rayna swung her light about, examining the surroundings. To one side of the room, near a closed door, sat a disordered arrangement of old mismatched furniture: a table, two chairs, and a standing lamp. A sagging wooden case holding disheveled piles of discs and ancient decrepit books lined another wall. Next to the case sat a small desk with a vintage video reader and a chair with reader controls on its arms. Large self-illuminated landscape pictures hung on the walls. A small control board, one of its small lights alternately blinking blue and green, lay in the far corner, obscured behind an electronic globe, adjacent to a set of closed double doors. Next to it, a low, narrow pass-through gave a view of an unlit connecting room.

The setting looked similar to a simple Etolian-era parlor Rayna had once studied in history class at the academy. She wondered if the builders were settlers from the Etolian probes that had landed on Onglus.

She drew her gun and climbed out. After surveying the room a second time, Rayna helped Adonair, Jairesse, and Morgan out.

Turning to Jairesse, Adonair said, "The description in the Holy Book matches this room. I believe we have arrived."

Jairesse gave Morgan and Rayna a quick glance. "You will wait here." She removed her cape and handed it to Adonair. After a deep breath and a moment's hesitation, she opened the double doors and walked through, into a tunnel. A few seconds later, Rayna saw a flicker of light appear from an inner chamber deep within the tunnel. A wisp of reddish-brown vapors drifted in from the tunnel.

"The Timegazer?" Morgan asked Adonair.

Adonair nodded.

"What's inside?" Rayna asked. The scent seemed an odd blend of seductive sweetness and repulsive stench.

"It is not for us to know," Adonair said. "Certainly not for those who are not even our own people."

Stonewalled again. Rayna took several steps toward the doors, then stopped as she heard Jairesse begin a low, murmuring chant.

"You understand what she's saying, don't you, Adonair?" Morgan asked.

Adonair glared at Morgan, then walked away.

Rayna found Adonair useless, but she understood that Morgan was trying to keep Adonair engaged as a way to keep an eye on the man.

She walked over and asked Morgan, in Alscrasian, "What do you—?"

"Shh!" Morgan cut her off when the music stopped. "Move!"

They scrambled into hiding, Adonair back into the crawlway, Morgan and Rayna through the low pass-through into an adjoining compartment, a cluttered space filled with shelves of greasy machinery and tarnished tools. They shut off their lights, crouched, and listened.

Footsteps approached. A switch snapped, and a dim light illuminated the parlor. Morgan noticed a small, blurry but reflective metal box sitting on a low shelf within his reach. He quietly lifted it until he and Rayna could see through the pass-through on the metal's reflection.

A tall man appeared in the now-opened doorway, standing directly below a soft white light. The stranger seemed much taller than them, but otherwise looked human, with thin black hair and dark, beady eyes. He was dressed like an aristocratic gentleman from the Imperial worlds, in a white shirt, gray frock coat and trousers, and a small, golden disc in the middle of his shirt collar.

The gentleman gazed about the parlor. Morgan's fingers tightened around his gun. The man's eyes narrowed. Morgan tensed at the smile creeping into the stranger's face. The man quickly traversed the room and disappeared through the double doors.

Jairesse screamed.

Morgan and Rayna bounded out of the work room, passed through a short tunnel, and emerged into a large inner chamber, where they found Jairesse standing alone. Before her, the ruins of three earthen statues, all with their heads apparently broken off, were elevated on table-like pedestals along the back wall. Even without their heads, Morgan recognized the Three Guardians—the twin deities Cru and Thema, Guardians of the Past and Future, and Cqoeis, the Guardian of the Multiverse—from their birdlike wings and fishlike tails. A giant cauldron sat before the statues, odorous, red-brown smoke pouring out the top. Five-foot-tall flaming torches stood to either side of the statues, guarding two darkened exits. For an instant, Morgan thought he saw an image, something resembling a metropolis skyline with a hawklike shadow hovering over it, dissolving in the smoke. Jairesse had turned pale, and she shook uncontrollably. Rayna wrapped her arm around Jairesse's shoulder.

"Are you all right?" Morgan asked. He sneaked another quick glance at the cauldron, the smoke quickly fading away as

Adonair entered the chamber.

Jairesse whispered, "His aura…"

"Who?" Rayna asked. "What did you feel?"

Jairesse withdrew from Rayna and turned away. "Foulness. Putridness." She stared at the floor. "There is a decaying rot surrounding him, a centuries-old aura of corruption."

"How can you sense this?" Morgan asked. "Who was that?"

Jairesse faced them. "In the same way that I am connected to the *Pankoulda*, he also is connected to the *Pankoulda*. In the same way that I am connected to Lord Oscanos and Mother Gheriah, he is connected to Luzomi."

"Luzomi?" Morgan asked. The name conjured an uneasy feeling.

Jairesse looked grim. "Luzomi, he who is—"

"Everybody knows," Morgan interrupted. "He's in those old tales of the Euranian Ancestors. He supposedly fought Oscanos for control of the human race in the primordial days of the universe."

"There are reportedly underground cults of Luzomi scattered throughout Eurania," Rayna added. "Whether Luzomi is real or not, I've heard that his followers can be dangerous. Are you saying this man is one of them?"

"He is not just a follower." Jairesse looked at Rayna, then at Morgan. "He is receiving a channeling of Luzomi's presence. At one time he may have been human, but now he has become a vehicle for Luzomi."

Morgan considered her words. This description seemed too much like religious fanaticism for him to consider seriously. The man had looked like an ordinary gentleman. But Rayna's point about the cults was legitimate. The history of the Luzomi worshippers had been one of shadowy rumors and infrequent but shockingly violent appearances.

In the Year 6908 of the Old Memonan Calendar

Deep in an underground lair, hundreds of miles below the surface of Etolis, the thirty-seventh Masoule seethed with a blinding rage. With a high-collared black cloak fluttering like wings, the Master of Darkness hurled a comp-pad at the wall. It shattered into splinters, littering the floor of the office with shards of poly-fiber.

Three weeks, and then it would all be over.

Even the extreme reach of the Master's dark power paled in comparison to the mindless, soulless torrential wave that hurled through space toward them.

Black-gloved fingers grasped the air like claws seeking their prey. How could this have happened? Had the Three Guardians of time and space somehow affected the course of history? Had they circumvented the ancient prophecy of Lhuzo-mi's rising?

Whirling about, the Masoule stormed out of the office, brushed past a pair of soldiers standing in the hallway, and entered a dimly lit elevator.

The cold-hearted Soul of the Shadows didn't care for the fool emperor or the billions spread throughout the five Imperial core worlds and the many subsidiary dominions under their rule, only for the millions among the billions who faithfully worshipped the exiled Lord of the human race.

Within minutes, the elevator stopped, and the door opened, revealing a secret meditation chamber high above the city.

The Master of Darkness stepped in, stood before a large window, and stared into the pitch-black night sky. A tiny pinpoint of light—the deadly deluge of stellar debris and radiation that approached—was already flaring, destroying other stars in its path.

"We must survive!" the *Masoule* roared. "We will survive!"

A gloved hand, as black as a stone-cold heart, shook at the approaching light and pounded the window. The *Masoule* would give the order to infiltrate every available starcraft. As the human race had once migrated from a dead world to a new beginning, so they were now migrating from the doomed core worlds to the most distant settlements. Without a moment to lose, the *Masoule* sat and pondered a plan.

Probes to Upper and Lower Eurania had been launched nearly four hundred years ago. Surely, some of the targeted planets would have been found habitable. In particular, three worlds in Upper Eurania—Sestia, Bexel, and Onglus—should have had the best chance of success. They would be their new home.

Golden-robed High Priest Duo'ra approached the altar of the Great Temple. Faint wisps of white smoke rose from the cobalt-blue bowl resting in the center of the wide slab of pure white stone. He lowered his face into the smoke and inhaled the fumes with long, deep breaths. Over ten thousand people—a tiny fraction of the billions not chosen for the great exodus—stood shoulder to shoulder, between the towering statues and the many pews that were packed with children. Everyone prayed in silence.

The high priest raised his hands high. "Almighty Euranos, Lord Oscanos, Mother Gheriah, we come before you as helpless children! We appeal to your love." His voice echoed through the cavernous stone sanctuary. "We pray for those departing our home worlds. Let the chosen reach their destination. Let them find a new home. Let the human race survive!" He took a deep breath. "We beg for your mercy: may our end not be our end."

Whimpers sounded from the pews. Sobs filled the sanctuary. Wails started to cry out.

Tears rolled down High Priest Duo'ra's cheeks. "Let the memories of our existence live on after our demise," he pleaded.

A shadow approached from behind the altar. As it stepped forward, the sobs subsided, replaced by hushed whispers. Fingers pointed toward the mysterious person.

Duo'ra paused, unsure of the identity of the man or woman stepping toward him. Taking a deep breath to strengthen his voice, he asked, "Do you have a prayer to offer?"

"Yes." The voice was low, almost a growl. "May the Lord's will be done." A quiet scrape sounded like a long blade unsheathing. "Glory to Lord Lhuzomi!"

With lightning quickness, a silver blade flashed from the shadows, lopping off Duo'ra's head. A spray of bright red blood gushed over the altar as the high priest's body collapsed to the floor. A black-robed man ran out from behind the altar, scooped up Duo'ra's lifeless head, dropped it into the blue incense bowl, then dashed away as the horrified screams of panicked people reverberated throughout the temple sanctuary.

The followers of the Masoule secreted away on board the many evacuation ships throughout the empire, silently and swiftly eliminating innocent passengers and taking their places. Blood was shed, heads were decapitated, bodies and organs were sacrificed as offerings, supplications for survival.

When the main body of the exodus launched—only a few days before Etolis, Memona, and the other core worlds of the empire were destroyed by overwhelming waves of destructive solar matter and radiation in a spectacular eruption of light and energy visible throughout the entire galaxy—no one knew how many followers of Lhuzomi had embedded themselves within the population of survivors.

Two hundred and fifty-four years later,
In the Year 466 of the Sestian Calendar

The bulbous starcraft, Ark of Salvation, emerged through the morning clouds, its retro-thrusters firing powerful, colorful blasts to slow its descent.

Inside, twenty-thousand anxious men, women, and children peered through the portals at the surrounding landscape.

Outside, reddish, rocky mountains were surrounded by gleaming blue lakes. Waterfalls plunged from the high, jagged peaks into clouds of whitewater foam. Overhead, three moons— a large globe, a small faint disc, and an irregular rocky shape— floated in the clean, clear blue sky. A small settlement lay at the base of the mountain.

"We have arrived," the captain's voice announced over the speaker. The crowd cheered.

A loud clang echoed through the craft, signaling the release of the automatic locks. As the doors opened and the ramps lowered to the ground, the people received their first glimpse of the local settlers—men, women, children, and animals—who waited outside with a small caravan of vehicles.

Five men and women stepped forward from the welcoming party. A gray-bearded man raised an amp-horn to his mouth.

"We are overjoyed—and relieved—to have you join us," he greeted the new arrivals. "Welcome to your new home, the frontier planet of Sestia."

The human race had survived the destruction of the core worlds of the empire. After a journey of over 250 years, the descendants of the exodus had reached their destination in Upper Eurania. With grateful hearts, the people poured forth from the ship and out onto the floor of the caldera.

Among the many new arrivals, one person—a nondescript man carrying a gray bag—stepped out and quietly slipped away, heading for a nearby formation of large blue-gray boulders. He gave the people and the ship one last glance, then clambered into the center of the boulders.

Opening his bag, he brought out a small, jeweled medallion, a two-inch-tall clay figurine, and his handheld comp-pad. He switched the power on and waited for the device to come to life.

The image of a middle-aged woman with long black hair, wire-rimmed spectacles, and a gray work uniform appeared.

"By the time you see this, I will have been dead for over 250 years," the recording began.

"You are one of the few survivors amongst our people. Through you, our doctrine—the ancient teachings of our ancestors—will be preserved. Through you, the sacred worship of our Lord will be reestablished.

"Remember to keep your true identity a secret. Blend into your new society and wait patiently. Be alert for people of potential. In due time, an opportunity will present itself."

The speaker's eyes turned into a bright green glow. The *Masoule* donned a high-collared black cloak over the plain gray work clothes.

"When that day arrives, our Lord will return with vengeance to reclaim his crown."

The recording ended, and a puff of thick black smoke burst forth from the comp-pad.

After blowing the smoke away, the man raised his head at the sound of lighthearted play. Carefully concealing himself behind the largest boulder, he counted seven nearby children: four boys and three girls, one of whom had unfamiliar blue-and-yellow striped skin. A native Sestian, he mused, amongst six descendants of the original Memonan probe.

"One sacrifice to initiate six followers," he whispered. After hanging the star-shaped medallion around his neck, Polan

Bn'dim bowed to the winged figurine. "All power and glory to Lord Lhuzomi."

~ ~ ~

"Do not dismiss Jairesse's warning," Adonair said, raising his hands. "We are dealing with forces beyond our own." He put his hands on Morgan and Rayna's shoulders. "We do not know what will become of this, if we provoke Luzomi. What dark powers will enter into our lives?" He put his hands together. "I appeal to you: heed Jairesse's warning. Let us turn back."

Morgan didn't like the feel of this. More importantly, he wondered if this mysterious person could be connected to the particle beam. He made eye contact with Rayna, unsure of how she felt about venturing into what could turn into another mystical experience. But when she drew her gun, he knew she was ready to go. Turning to Adonair and Jairesse, he said, "We're going after him."

Adonair wrapped his arm around Jairesse's shoulder. "I will take Jairesse back to the rover. We will wait for you there."

The gentleman returned to his meditative pose, illuminated up to the waist by the circle of green candles. He took five long deep breaths, closed his eyes, and relaxed his muscles. The faint aroma, the hints of pomira tree bark and sulfur, seeped through his nostrils and entered his lungs. He took five more slow deep breaths; his limbs grew numb and faded away. His mind departed his body.

He found himself surrounded by the stars of deep space. Two tiny worlds orbited a giant red star. An atmosphere of dense, grayish-brown clouds cloaked the larger of the two planets, blocking out most of the sunlight and leaving the world in a perpetual twilight. Stray rays of light leaked through the cloud cover, the edges of the clouds glowing an eerie violet. The once-mighty cities of skyscraping buildings and towering structures lay in crumbled ruin. Countless bodies lay scattered on the ground, many burnt to fine ash.

The gentleman stood among the ruins and gazed up at the cloud-covered night sky, searching for his lord and master. Beyond a wrecked tower and the cracked sky arch, tiny stars twinkled in a solitary patch of clear midnight sky. He opened his mind to the stars of the night and relaxed, his vision migrating to other places and other times.

He saw Lord Luzomi and his followers disappear into a swirling vortex of pink-and-gray light rays. Deep within the timeless void, he felt their presence riding along the currents of time to another place and another era, their escape from the titanic devastation a success, but the outlet into the present closed. Ahead lay Luzomi's destination, a statue which eventually would become an object of worship to the little people of the new worlds.

The gentleman cleared his mind and the vision faded. *Yes, the sacrifice of a priestess of his master's arch-nemesis, Oscanos, would unlock the gateway of Lord Luzomi's reentry.*

Adonair and Jairesse paused during their journey back to the cave entrance. They reached the dirt-filled stretch of broken path where the boulders had crashed down earlier. Adonair shone his light in every direction, searching for the mysterious being. This time, all remained quiet and still.

"Perhaps we should have stayed with Morgan and Rayna," Adonair said, breaking the silence. "Here, we are alone, vulnerable—and you, not them, are his target."

"Please don't scare me." She wrapped her arms around

herself. "I know he is looking for me. With Thakian dead, I can only pray that they are able to destroy him."

Adonair put his arm around her, Thakian's firearm in his other hand. "I'll defend you, Jairesse."

Just then, a large boulder crashed down from high above. Jairesse screamed as it hit the path barely a few feet from them, breaking a section of the ledge off as it tumbled into the abyss. The echoes of the rumble trailed away.

"Run!" Adonair pushed Jairesse ahead.

Jairesse began to flee, but she stopped as more boulders cascaded down, surrounding them on both sides with falling dust and debris. She squeezed into a narrow crevice as a boulder ricocheted off the wall.

Adonair screamed.

Jairesse ran to where Adonair had stood. Her hands flew to her face as she looked over the edge. "Adonair!" she shrieked in horror. But she was too late to see his fate. As the crashes and rattles of the last of the rubble faded away, Jairesse collapsed to her knees in tears. "No, Adonair, no." Alone in the darkness, overcome by despair, and unable to move, she sat and cried, her face buried in her hands. She heard shuffling feet and raised her tear-stained face.

The being in black stood only a few feet away, towering over her, its wings outstretched, its foreclaws hooked, its fluorescent green eyes glaring.

Jairesse screamed.

Morgan and Rayna departed the inner chamber through one of the unlit doorways. Confronted with a long series of closed doors lining a darkened corridor, they explored slowly and carefully, opening several doors and peering inside.

"What do you think?" Rayna finally asked.

"This one." Morgan pointed at a doorway that led to an unlit ascending staircase. "Maybe this will take us to the top, where we can get a better view of this entire area."

They cautiously climbed a long circular staircase, eventually emerging into an observation room with a breathtaking view of the twin peaks through a translucent domed ceiling. One peak towered several hundred feet above them while the other rose high in the distance. In the far corner of the room, a small transparent door led outside onto the mountaintop.

A complex bank of tarnished instruments lined two walls of the room. At the intersection of the two long panels was a small seat, situated in front of a circular viewing screen and a set of controls. Directly above the viewing screen, two glowing yellow-and-orange energy tubes jutted out from the wall. The tubes ran parallel to the ceiling, one above each instrument panel, then turned down into the top of the machine at the two ends. A low hum droned from the machinery. In the opposite corner, partly hidden behind a scattering of portable equipment, was a partly open storage closet filled with coils, arrays, and a plethora of small transparent cases filled with jeweled crystals of different colors, shapes, and sizes.

Morgan said, excited, "Might this be the source of the particle beam?"

"But what *is* the particle beam?" Rayna asked.

Voices from outside interrupted them. Morgan and Rayna quickly stole away into the storage room and hid behind the equipment.

They spied from between two arrays of spare vintage power collectors and distributors as the transparent door swung open. The tall gentleman entered, now dressed in a long black cloak. Another man limped in, discarding a dented vest of armor and donning a hooded black robe. Morgan and Rayna exchanged looks when they recognized the limping man's bloodstained, dirt-covered face.

Adonair. Without Jairesse.

Why he was bloodied and disheveled, Morgan could only think the worst. Was Jairesse still alive? Was Adonair a prisoner?

"…your selfless dedication will be rewarded, my friend." The gentleman spoke Onglan with what sounded like an upper-crust Brozan accent.

Morgan froze. What was a Brozan doing on Volon? Broza currently held control of the Gearmlian Confederation, the largest and most militaristic constituent of the Central Empire. The Confederation was also nowhere near Volon. From the start, Morgan had felt uneasy about Adonair. Now he knew why the temple chief had acted so evasively. Had Adonair betrayed Jairesse?

"Do not worry about the intruders," the Brozan man continued.

"But, Mr. Saltos," Adonair said, "they are not like us. They are off-worlders."

"Off-worlders will not interfere with my plans." Saltos pointed at an arrangement of readouts on the panel. "I have repaired the traversal unit. The Timegazer will no longer rivet onto passing hyperspace ripples or currents." Saltos parted his lips, revealing short, yellow, sharpened incisors. "I will dispose of the two intruders already here, in my own time and means."

Adonair bowed his head. "I understand." He turned to the giant machine. "May I ask about this? I find it hard to comprehend that a scientific device, impressive as it may be, can reach into the realm of the spiritual."

"I have been slaving over this instrument for many, many decades," Saltos said. "Etolian script is not well understood. Without sufficient knowledge to repair the many worn and decayed components, the Timegazer sat in its own dust for centuries."

He swept his slender, bony hand toward the circular viewing screen, a grand gesture, and smiled.

"It is now in working condition and nearing final completion. I expect your assistance to prove most valuable. In its current state, there are many violent and uncontrolled effects." Saltos sat down in the control seat and activated the viewer. A pattern of spectrum waves appeared on the display, undulating like a school of sea snakes. "Watch the mountain peaks."

Morgan and Rayna peered toward the dome. A previously obscured disc, roughly ten feet in diameter and about one hundred feet above them on the peak, began emitting a whitish-yellow glow. A second disc, on the distant peak, also began glowing a soft yellow-and-orange light.

"When the underground accelerators power up," Saltos explained, "a chronon stream stretches between the two discs. I can focus a beam out into space, where it bursts open contact points between this universe and that of the ancient past." He switched off the viewer, and the glowing projectors faded. "Since my first successful test, I have been working on controlling the strength and duration of the contact points. They are weak and unstable, and the discharge is very violent."

"And the star medallion crystal?" Adonair asked.

"A powerful energy source," Saltos answered, "able to transcend the spatial-temporal boundaries of this universe, if channeled properly."

Morgan and Rayna exchanged glances. Third-hand stories about the mysterious ways of the Luzomi cults, ranging from ritualistic animal sacrifices to barbaric human mutations, were prevalent. But neither had ever crossed paths with Luzomi followers before. At least, none that they were aware of. Given the secretive nature of the followers, it was not inconceivable for ordinary-looking commoners—like Saltos and Adonair—to be Luzomi worshippers.

Saltos held out his hand. Adonair reached into the folds of his robe and drew out a dull, charcoal-gray box. He opened it, and a bright golden gleam illuminated both of their faces.

"Beautiful." Saltos smiled, his lips parting to reveal his pointed fangs. He brought out a tiny green crystal and held it up to examine it. A strange golden shine glistened around it like a small halo.

"It was difficult keeping its discovery secret," Adonair said. "During the expedition, many people roamed through the caves, looking for all kinds of precious stones and metals. I had to go into hiding with this crystal." He bowed his head. "I humbly apologize for not delivering this sooner."

"You have atoned for your delay," Saltos pronounced. He eyed the crystal. "This priceless gem is exquisite." Lowering the crystal, he turned his chair to face the controls. "As a reward, you will receive a place of prominence in the court of Lord Luzomi." Saltos brushed his fingers over a relay of levers, tripping them. "Watch as I engage the time projector and receiver."

The power lines pulsed at a rapid rate into the machine. The low hum rose. A faint, high-pitched whistle sounded from above. Images of static bolts shot across the viewer, and the speaker crackled to life. Saltos turned down the room lights as a blur of light took form on the viewer.

"Behold the beauty of the fountain of eternal passage."

A twisted, rainbowlike beam projected from the near disc and stretched across the chasm to the far disc. Short, jagged energy bolts of different colors shot out in random directions from the beam and scattered over the atmosphere. Soft explosions sounded above the dome. The spiraling strands of energy coalesced into a shimmering field of light that climbed through the atmosphere, narrowing into a tight beam projected into the stratosphere.

Morgan and Rayna watched as the static web on the screen solidified into a shadowy scene of heavy activity below a metropolis skyline. Garbled sounds of mechanical noises and human voices grew discernible through the crackles. The scene reminded Morgan of some of the metropolises of the empire, though he didn't recognize this one.

The picture settled into a nighttime scene. Flying beings filled the skies, and panicked people scattered in all directions. In the distance, beyond the buildings, a monstrous horned, winged silhouette towered. Energy beams shot into the sky and arced down to the surface, touching off explosions and fires. Bloodred screaming bodies and flailing body parts hurtled through the air.

Rayna winced. Morgan clenched his hands. The images were of a human massacre by animalistic beings.

"Now, let us test this," Saltos said to Adonair.

Saltos stood up and opened a small light-lined drawer at the base of the energy tubes. He removed a ring with five large red crystals from the vessel and put it aside. He then took the green star medallion crystal, gave it one last examination, and inserted it into the vessel. Once connected, the interior of the compartment illuminated. Saltos closed the drawer, pushed it back into its housing, and returned to his seat. The activity of the giant machine increased noticeably. The energy tubes intensified their glow.

Morgan felt Rayna's hand on his arm. He nodded toward her, recalling the memories of the giant tubular construct and the flaming geysers they had encountered in the tunnels.

The images on the viewer sharpened. The energy beams that flew skyward on the viewer appeared to shoot out from a sea of raised arms. On the speaker, a loud roar erupted, drowning out all other sounds. A moment later, a whalelike silhouette entered into the picture, high above the city. Tiny swarms of blue light descended from the underside of the bulbous shadow and zipped down to the city streets. Mile-high explosions burst wherever the blue lights impacted the ground. Arches cracked; towers fell. Blood splattered throughout the scene as bodies burst and collapsed in the street. Dark clouds rolled through the skies, obscuring the stars.

Morgan recognized what the images were depicting—the stories of the mythical war among the Euranian Ancestors—and wondered if that was what he had seen earlier in the smoke pouring out of the cauldron.

Saltos changed the display to show columns of numbers. "We have some contact points emerging." He changed the display again, and a second list of numbers began scrolling down. He frowned. "Most are unstable and closing already." He studied the numbers, then pointed to several. "Yes, we have a few perpetual points."

Adonair smiled, rubbing his hands together.

Morgan pointed out the rainbow to Rayna, its skyward beam achieving a tighter focus. A green tint shaded the edge of the rainbow. The beam developed a whirling, twisting movement, and the bolts that shot out from the beam turned to predominantly blinding pink and a light shade of gray.

"That's it," Morgan whispered to Rayna. They had found the particle beam that had shot them down. It had been fired from some sort of gargantuan space-time-transcending machine, under the control of a Luzomi worshipper.

"We have success," Saltos said. "It is nearly complete." He disengaged the power, and the rainbow dissipated. The picture froze. The echoes of the ancient destruction faded, and the ghostlike images on the viewer dissolved. Saltos turned to Adonair. "You should begin preparations for the sacrifice. The time is upon us to welcome Lord Luzomi into our midst."

Saltos rose from the chair and, with Adonair, departed down the stairs back to the parlor, leaving Morgan and Rayna to contemplate what they had witnessed, and what to do next.

From within the depths of the Great Nebula, whirling pink-and-gray radiances erupted, the fragile lattice of time ripped open by the pulsating burst of a zero-mass chronon beam firing through space. As the pulses hammered away at the areas of distortion, the explosion of light grew intense. The particle beam from the distant planet of Volon then ceased, and the pinwheel colors faded, leaving tiny, dark regions filled with no light, no mass, and no time.

Minutes passed, then hours.

A small, cylindrical vessel emerged through a black vortex. It sailed into a patch of plasma colors and slowed to float through, passing among the random drifts of radioactive rock and stellar debris. After exiting the Great Nebula and crossing a vast stretch of space, it banked away and entered a darkened cloud of ice, rock, and fine dust, where it came to a stop.

A section of the vessel opened, and a midnight-blue, multi-armed figure crawled out. It shut its many eyes and extended its sensory feelers for the flowing rhythms and dark energy of Eurania. It then closed the vessel and flew away, departing the comet cloud.

3. *Image of Luzomi*

Morgan stared at the monstrosity of machinery that dominated the observation room. He held his breath. His muscles tensed. The network of energy tubes extended upward like rising tentacles. The oversized circular viewer was like a glass eye. This was what had shot them down and almost killed Rayna.

It didn't matter that it hadn't been Saltos's intention to shoot them down. Apparently, the particle beam wasn't supposed to lock onto their passing spacecraft, nor even cross from normal space into hyperspace. It didn't matter that they were just in the wrong place at the wrong time.

Even though this was an ancient scientific marvel, it was also a deadly menace. Rayna had almost lost her life. The next shot into space could strike another passerby—one less fortunate than Rayna had been. It had to be disabled.

Rayna asked, "Do you understand what just happened?"

Morgan shook his head. "Not totally. We need to get Adonair. We know he's a traitor to his own people."

She nodded. "We can get some answers out of him."

They dove down the flights of stairs, reentered the deserted inner sanctuary, and slowed upon hearing the soft shuffling of footsteps. Morgan and Rayna quickly slipped back into the darkened passageway. Crouching out of sight, they waited.

The footsteps paused. A low scratching noise sounded for a few seconds. Then, more footsteps, followed by a grunt, a heavy thud, and hammering. After a short pause, the footsteps returned, and the sequence repeated. They continued waiting, Morgan listening for any change in the sequence of sounds as they repeated a third time. His muscles tensed, ready to spring. Rayna remained motionless. Was it Adonair or the mysterious Saltos?

The footsteps faded away. Except for the crackling flames of the torches, the chamber went quiet. Cautiously, Morgan and Rayna peered in. Three tall wooden poles had been erected, arranged in a semicircle on the side of the room opposite the statues of the Three Guardians.

Adonair backed into the room, dragging a fourth pole along the ground.

Perfect.

Adonair, standing only a few feet away, pushed the wooden post upright, completing the arrangement of poles. As Adonair began hammering wedges into its base, Morgan holstered his pistol and silently unsheathed one of his skiloblades. Rayna also brought out one of her skiloblades. Morgan pointed into the chamber, and she flung her blade across the room, the metallic weapon bouncing off the far wall with a soft clang. Adonair turned, startled, and Morgan exploded into the chamber. He gripped Adonair's mouth with his free hand and yanked Adonair backward until he was pressed tight against Morgan's chest.

"Don't make a sound," Morgan whispered, the two sharp points of the skiloblade pressing into Adonair's neck. "We don't want to hurt you. Do you understand?"

Adonair, his eyes bulging, nodded.

Morgan released one finger after another from Adonair's mouth and moved his grip along Adonair's collar until he held the back of the man's hood, leaving Adonair free to take a long, slow breath.

"What's that machine upstairs?" Rayna asked, stepping out to retrieve her blade. "And what did you do with Jairesse?"

"I don't know where she is," Adonair whimpered. "I left her in the tunnels."

"How?" Rayna asked.

"I took a fall to fake my death."

"That's why you're all bloody like *shat'oq*?" Morgan asked, incredulous. He wanted to know more about the fake death, but there were more pressing questions to ask. "Who's the other man?"

"Saltos, my master." Tears welled in Adonair's eyes. "Please, I only do as I am told."

"Why are you working for him?" Rayna asked. "How are you involved in all this?"

"Please, no." A tear rolled down Adonair's face.

"Don't stall!" Morgan snapped his head about, in case Saltos reappeared without warning. There were too many questions—the machine's purpose, the nature of the images they saw, who Saltos was. Who Adonair really was, for that matter. Morgan tightened his grip and gave the hood's collar a sharp twist, choking Adonair. "Answer her."

"I'll tell what I know," Adonair wheezed, as Morgan relaxed his grip. "But believe me, I honestly don't know much."

"Explain why a temple chief like you is a follower of Luzomi."

"Luzomi is our creator," Adonair said, "our true lord."

"You're a traitor to your people," Morgan said. "And to Jairesse."

Adonair flung a crazed gaze at the three headless statues. "If you knew the inner workings of the temple like I do, you would know that the institutional worship of the *Pankoulda* is corrupted." He swallowed, the light from the torches dancing across his face. "Mr. Saltos is a priest of Luzomi. He has a clear understanding of the ways of our creator, what is required, what is desired."

The guy talks like a crazy fanatic, Morgan thought, *like a cult follower*. Even though he didn't believe in the stories of the Euranian Ancestors, Morgan knew enough to understand that Adonair had reversed the traditional interpretation of those stories. Morgan switched tactics, hoping to get some useful information. "What is that machine upstairs?"

"I don't know."

Dox! This was taking too long. Morgan and Rayna probably knew as much about the Timegazer as Adonair did.

"What are you working on," Rayna asked, "now that you've delivered your crystal?"

"A perfect offering. With the means to welcome Luzomi into our universe, we can usher a new age to our present reality." Adonair smiled, another tear rolling down his cheek.

"You're *kroking* crazy!" Morgan snapped.

Rayna asked, "Who are you sacrificing, and what's the connection with that particle beam?"

Adonair stiffened and gave no answer.

They turned at the sound of approaching footsteps. Morgan muffled a curse and pulled Adonair back outside, through the connecting tunnel to the parlor. After giving Adonair a warning gesture with his skiloblade, Morgan motioned for Rayna to stand ready on one side of the double doors while he took the other side. Once in position, he replaced his skiloblade and readied his gun. Rayna stood ready with hers. Adonair, tears streaming down his face, backed step by step past the closed crawlway hatch, toward the opposite doorway.

The footsteps stopped. Morgan, with the tension of the moment getting on his nerves, felt certain that Saltos knew they were there. He resisted his instinct to jump out in front of the double doors and face his target. Instead, he glanced at Adonair, and for an instant, Morgan felt sorry for the clearly confused Volonian.

Without warning, a pair of bony hands appeared in the opposite doorway and, with a quick flip of the wrists, whipped a length of rope over Adonair's head, tightening it about his neck until Adonair winced from the strain. A black cloth immediately smothered Adonair's head and yanked him backward through the opening.

"Adonair!" Morgan charged after Adonair, Rayna hot on his heels. But a second before they reached the doorway, unseen trips snapped. Morgan and Rayna barely leaped back before metal bars slammed down over the doorway, the small access door, and the double doors, sealing them within the parlor.

Jairesse awoke, disoriented by the rotting stench of pomira and sulfur. A greenish-yellow flame flickered from a dark-green candle, alone in the middle of the gray, earthen floor. The ceiling and walls lay in the shadows, beyond the wavering flame's field of light.

She froze when she noticed that a shadowy figure stood only a few feet away, examining a collection of poles. Then, the strain of her arms, fastened behind her back, made her realize that she, herself, was bound to a pole. The figure made spine-tin-gling scratches as its feet dragged over the earthen floor, its long black robe sweeping up a thin wisp of dust. She recognized the being in black that had captured her in the tunnels. It approached one of the poles—and the blindfolded, sweat-drenched figure bound to it: Adonair.

Shocked, her heart pounding with fear, she did not dare make a sound.

A pair of long, thin, sharp talons extended toward Adon-air, and the pointy-nailed index fingers inched toward his face, the being's heavy breathing the only discernible sound in the room. One set of claws wrapped themselves around the side of Adonair's face.

Adonair whimpered helplessly. Tears streamed down from behind his blindfold. The other claw enclosed the other side of his face.

Jairesse almost cried out as a blinding flash of light erupted from the being's claws. Adonair's body suddenly jerked. He heaved against the ropes that held him taut against the pole, then jiggled with mild spasms that quickly grew violent. The be-ing gave a loud, ecstatic groan, and Adonair's body went limp. The two claws withdrew and disappeared beneath the being's black robes. It turned away and shuffled back toward the light.

With its back to Jairesse, it stood before the candle and lifted its arms. Its robes fanned out, assuming the appearance of giant black wings. The green flame dimmed, brightened, dimmed, then brightened. The light grew stronger as it pulsed, faster and faster, bathing the being in wave after wave of green light rays.

The being cried out in a hoarse voice, "Jakkum! Neide-mus! Luzomi!" and a blinding white light exploded around him.

When her vision returned, Jairesse nearly swooned from the sight of what now stood before the being.

It stood eight feet tall on two muscular legs, balanced itself on a long, thick tail, and seemed to be a gray, earthen statue. It had two tiny forearms and a pair of butterfly-shaped wings that slowly fanned in and out. Its elongated head ended in a gaping mouth that held two rows of tiny incisors and a long, red serpentine tongue. On each side of its head sat a large, round, pupil-less eyeball; on top protruded two large horns. Around its neck hung the only non-earthen element of the statue: a thick golden chain with a starlike medallion, which seemed to emit its own sparkling light.

The robed being in black knelt down before the reptilian statue and bowed its head. Its low, hoarse voice spoke in an unknown language with a passionate and reverent tone.

Jairesse did not know what to do, or even what she could do. She looked over at Adonair, who looked as lifeless as Thakian when he had died. She was alone, helpless, with a worshipper of the Entity of Evil. She could not tell if the object was, in fact, a statue. No real statue could move its wings or its tongue, as this one did. Otherwise, it stood perfectly still. It did not seem to be breathing, nor did it blink its eyes.

Without warning, the eyes changed to a stark yellow, and two green pupils appeared.

The being in black stopped talking, rose to its feet, pivoted around, its large wings flaring behind it, and stepped toward her, a growing, backlit silhouette of death. Its eyes were two tiny flickering green flames in the middle of a blackened face. Its breathing intensified as it approached. Its clawlike forearms rose out of the folds of the robe and inched their way toward her face.

Jairesse screamed.

The scream echoed throughout the halls, into the parlor.

"Jairesse," Rayna whispered.

"*Krok!*" Morgan cursed, slamming his fist against one of the bars. The loud clang echoed through the parlor. He took out one of his skiloblades, released the duo-blades, and tapped it against one of the bars, producing a tinny ping. He then placed the edge against the bar, made a hard, sharp slice, and examined the cut. Nothing.

"Let me try," Rayna said.

She twisted a small dial on the top of her charge-lock gun, pointed it at the bar, and squeezed the trigger. A tight, narrow shot exploded against the bar.

Morgan examined the bar. Still nothing. This alloy was stubborn.

Rayna fired again, this time holding the trigger down so that the gun rapid-fired at the bar. Explosions burst at the point of contact. White smoke poured out. The bar quickly changed from its gray metallic color to bright white.

"Let's take a look," Morgan said, holding up his hand.

Rayna let up, and after the bar faded back to gray, Morgan examined it. He ran his hand up and down the bar, feeling for any change or scarring. Again, nothing. *Dox!* As Rayna reholstered her gun, Morgan scanned the room.

"There's got to be a release somewhere." He tried the controls in the reader chair, but only managed to activate the old video reader. They checked the control console in the corner. Several of the switches lit the electronic globe with different lights; others dimmed or brightened the overhead lights. One controlled the lights that illuminated the artwork on the wall.

Rayna folded her arms in frustration. "He's sacrificing

Jairesse, isn't he?"

Somehow, they had stumbled into the midst of a religious conflict. Morgan took out his gun. "Double the power."

They fired simultaneously at the bar, drawing more blasts and smoke. The bar quickly returned to its white-hot appearance. Morgan could tell that, despite the searing energy cascading against it, the bar was still intact. His frustration mounting, he switched his gun to his off hand and, while maintaining a steady fire on the bar, brought his skiloblade back out with his free hand. He eyed the spot being pounded by the two sidearms, raised his blade, and swung as hard as he could. The skiloblade hit with a shower of sparks and a powerful blast that threw Morgan backward onto the ground.

"Morgan!" Rayna ran over to where Morgan lay.

Coughing, he tried to sit up, but collapsed back down. "Agh," he groaned. "That was brilliant."

"Don't try anything like that again," Rayna scolded. "Are you hurt?"

Morgan shook his head clear. "I'm all right."

Rayna picked up the seared skiloblade handle stub and showed it to Morgan. The duo-blades had vaporized, the end of the handle stub melted. He sucked his breath in. It could have been his hand or his arm. Or his whole body.

A laugh sounded.

Morgan and Rayna pivoted around to face Saltos, standing in the tunnel on the other side of the bars. His rage erupting at the sight of the mysterious man, Morgan charged and reached through the bars to grab Saltos.

Saltos gave Morgan's hand a sharp slap.

"Ah!" Morgan held his hand until the pain subsided. Three ragged scratches ran across his knuckles. "*Turkanaan!*"

Saltos merely smiled at Morgan's curse.

Rayna pointed her gun at Saltos. "Let us go!"

"Kill me, and you shall remain trapped in there for the rest of your mortal lives," Saltos declared. He chuckled again, baring his incisors and rubbing his hands together.

"*Krok*." Morgan struggled to contain his anger. Rayna had a clear shot at Saltos, but Morgan knew that Saltos was right —killing him wouldn't help them get out. Morgan took a deep breath to steady himself and try a different tactic. "Why are you sacrificing Jairesse to Luzomi?"

"She is the perfect offering for my master," Saltos said, "and she walked right into my parlor, of her own accord, thanks to your protective escort."

Morgan muffled a curse. Saltos—whoever he was—was sly, manipulative, and crazed. What was truth, and what was deception? "Where is Luzomi?" Morgan asked. While the activities of Saltos, Adonair, and the giant machine were very real, Luzomi was just a figure in a story.

"He will be arriving soon." With that, Saltos stepped away.

Rayna looked to Morgan for the order to fire.

Morgan shook his head. They still had to figure out how to get out before they could tackle Saltos and find out who, exactly, "Luzomi" was.

The statue towered before Jairesse, still and silent, its tongue slithering in and out with the same slow steady rhythm as its wings. Its yellow-green eyes oscillated from left to right.

Jairesse closed her eyes and tried to calm herself. She had never confronted Luzomi before. But with the statue before her, she knew she had to try to close the door of his passage. Now, before he appeared.

She slowed her breathing and focused on a different time and a different place. She inhaled long quiet breaths, the foul rot of pomira and sulfur filling her lungs, relaxing her and opening her mind to the windows of the universe. Away from the present world, she receded to an earlier epoch. The Great Nebula contracted into the giant red Euranian star with the two worlds of Amahl and Sigorum in orbit.

On Amahl, she felt the presence of Lord Oscanos, Mother Gheriah, the Three Guardians, and the others of the *Pankoulda.* On Sigorum, the shadows of Jakkum, Neidemus, Writher, and others floated about. Behind them towered their master, Luzomi, who turned, looked at her, and roared a beastly howl that shook the trees, rippled the waters, and echoed through the city ruins.

"What do you want with me?" she demanded.

Luzomi's wings expanded skyward, his claws opening, his tail whipping about behind him. He lowered his head, opened his mouth, and cackled a low-toned rumbling reply.

"You are pure," she heard his thoughts. *"You are pristine. You are perfect. I have been rendered repulsive by my enemies, a plague of boils and sores. Your beauty shall restore me to my rightful place. I am the creator of all higher life, and I have chosen you, Jairesse, as my favored consort."*

He stepped toward her, his arms open to embrace her. She could smell his stench, the repulsive mixture of a decaying Sigorum pomira tree and sulfur.

"I will not be yours," she said in defiance.

He groaned, his throat gurgling, his tongue slithering out. His wings began to close.

"Stay away from me!" she cried.

Jairesse screamed again from the other end of the tunnel, and a heavy metal door slammed shut, the concussion echoing through the tunnel.

"Jairesse!" Rayna called out.

Morgan, holding up his hand to silence Rayna, thrust his gun into her hand. He had an idea, but with Saltos in the vicinity, they had to work quietly. Morgan detached the empty skiloblade sheath from his vest, released the small oval cartridge from his gun barrel, and squeezed the charge-pak inside the empty sheath.

Morgan then pointed at Rayna's gun.

She gave him a questioning look. When she realized he was referring to her charge-pak, she mouthed, "Not mine, too?"

Morgan nodded. He knew he was blowing both of their firearms, but he had to make sure this was going to work. They had only one shot at this.

She drew in her breath, took Morgan's sheath, released her charge-pak, and added it to the bundle.

Morgan then detached his remaining sheath from his vest, sliced it open with his blade, and used it to tie the charge-pak bundle in place around the bar. After shaping the bundle with his fingers so that the two charge-paks bulged out together through the sheath, he whispered, "Not pretty."

Rayna cautioned, "I hope you know what you're doing."

"Me too." He gave her a quick, firm squeeze on her shoulder. He knew she was good at target practice; he hoped she would be just as good in a real-life situation.

They overturned the table and crouched behind it. Morgan nodded, and Rayna took out one of her skiloblades.

She released the duo-blade, took a deep breath to relax herself, peeked out from behind the table, and took aim. With blinding speed, she whipped the blade toward the bundle. A split second later, the two punctured charge-paks exploded, the two concussions rocking the room. The air filled with searing heat and suffocating smoke. Shrapnel rained down around them. After the cascade passed, Morgan and Rayna emerged from behind the debris-pelted table.

A large section of the bars gaped open.

As Morgan and Rayna squeezed through the hole in the bars, another scream sounded. They took out their remaining skiloblades and followed the scream down the short tunnel to the solitary, unmarked door, now closed.

Yet another scream.

Then, a low roar.

A swirling greenish light appeared in the Sigorum sky, high above Jairesse's and Luzomi's heads. It rotated, a pinwheel of pink and gray exploding in all directions. The sky darkened, and the light expanded as it revolved until it widened enough to extend over the heads of Jakkum, Neidemus, and the other malevolent followers.

Luzomi filled Jairesse's mind with thoughts of his mightiness. The swirling light descended, multicolored bolts engulfing her in a coruscation of energy. Jairesse summoned all her strength to fight the surge, but it was no use. His wings wrapped about her, smothering her in an oppressive foulness, lifting her up to him. The swirling colors grew intense, and the bolts multiplied into a tumultuous cascade of light.

Jairesse screamed, her face reflecting the terror of confronting the almighty Luzomi. "No! Please, no!" She screamed again.

Luzomi roared in delirious ecstasy as he entered her.

Morgan tried to kick the door open. Another scream sounded from inside. Frustrated, he pounded the door with his fist. Unable to budge it, he rested his head against it and tried to think of another way, his heart racing, his muscles tight with tension. He realized there must have been something holding the door in place. He raised his head and took a close look at the top edge of the door. Then he saw it: the track of the door. He inserted his skiloblade into the upper track and slid it until he tripped the lock.

The door swung open with a loud creak. Morgan switched on his light, revealing a squat green candle in the center of the room, still burning, a faint stench drifting in the stale air.

Swinging his light to one side of the room, he saw the statues of the Three Guardians with the extinguished torches on either side. Before the statues stood the cauldron, no longer smoldering, and an eight-foot-high earthen figure of a bipedal reptilian creature.

Morgan swung his light to the other side of the room and saw the four wooden poles. Adonair hung from one pole, limp and blindfolded. Jairesse hung from a second, her robe torn to tatters.

"*Krok!*" Morgan yelled as he and Rayna dashed to Jairesse.

Rayna placed her hand on Jairesse's shoulder and tried to rouse her. "She's still breathing," Rayna said to Morgan with a hint of hope.

Jairesse could not lift her head or open her eyes. But she could whisper. "…Prince…" She paused, her breathing difficult. "…of Evil…"

Morgan and Rayna listened, but Jairesse spoke no further.

"Stay with us," Rayna coaxed.

Morgan untied Jairesse and, as gently as he could, lowered her to the ground. They watched her to ascertain that she still breathed, though the breaths were slow and shallow. Morgan took off his jacket and covered her.

Rayna removed her jacket and placed it under Jairesse's head, cushioning it from the cold, hard ground. "She saved me," she whispered.

Morgan, trying to focus on their situation, stepped away and shone his light on Adonair. "Oh God." Adonair was not breathing. What Morgan could see of Adonair's face was as pale as a ghost. Morgan removed the black blindfold, studied Adonair's face, and felt his neck for a pulse. "Adonair's dead."

"Just like Thakian," Rayna whispered, grim.

Morgan had never liked Adonair, but he still felt sad for him. Morgan froze as he realized that the two empty poles might have been intended for himself and Rayna.

He turned to face the strange statue. It looked like a dinosaur with butterfly wings and oversized goat horns. He remembered frightening pictures from his childhood lessons of this beast, scenes of it and other giant creatures terrorizing crowds of people. In one particularly memorable image he once saw in a library, it was stomping across a hillside, trampling through people and animals, with a naked woman in its claw and a bloody, half-eaten man in its mouth. "This is Luzomi, isn't it?"

"I think you're right," Rayna said. "I never thought I would see this in real life."

Morgan stepped around it and looked it over. "It's just an earthen statue, like the others."

"He has the power to give life," said a low voice from the mouth of the tunnel, "or to take life."

Morgan whirled about and shone the light on Saltos.

Rayna demanded, "What did you do to her?" She raised her skiloblade and charged.

"Rayna—no!" Morgan yelled.

Saltos suddenly jumped high into the air, flying directly at Rayna, his cloak flaring like large black wings. Startled, Rayna took a quick step aside. Saltos landed with a bound and jump-kicked his legs into her stomach, knocking her to the wall with a blow so jarring that her skiloblade dislodged from her hand and fell to the ground. She gasped, out of breath and wincing from the pain of the blow, her arms wrapped about her abdomen.

Morgan froze for a second with the memory of Rayna lying unconscious in the forest before he turned his head to see Saltos charge. On reflex, he raised his blade and lunged at the approaching Saltos. But just as Morgan was about to strike, Saltos hurtled high over Morgan and descended upon Rayna. Off-balance, Morgan spun about, too late to defend her.

Rayna managed to roll aside, avoiding Saltos's downward strike. She swung a powerful blow into Saltos's head, knocking him back enough to give her an opening. She grabbed her blade and scrambled away on all fours into the corner.

Saltos spun around to face Morgan, his eyes now glowing an eerie green, his fangs protruding. "Behold," Saltos proclaimed, "the lord of the human race arrives!"

Morgan swung around to see the statue emit a glowing gray-green misty cloud into the air, directly above its head. Small puffs of pink-and-gray light appeared around the cloud. The wings swayed, folding and unfolding. Its tongue slithered in and out of its gaping mouth. Its tail swung back and forth like a giant serpent. The claws of its tiny forearms flexed, opening and closing. A red pinpoint sparkle radiated within the medallion that hung from its neck. Within seconds, a rainbow of tiny twinkles covered the jeweled surface of the medallion. The golden-green eyes of Luzomi blinked.

4. The Xaturi's Howl

Morgan didn't have time to think. Lightning bolts crackled from the shimmering multicolored cloud, covering the statue in a web of static electricity, transforming its surface from earthen clay to thick, scaly skin. He raised his twin-shaft skiloblade and charged the statue of Luzomi.

Saltos screamed.

Morgan swung as hard as he could, hacking into the statue's head. A blinding flash of light, an explosive burst of smoke, and a blast of energy destroyed Morgan's remaining blade and threw him, Rayna, and Saltos off their feet. The ceiling cracked, and the statue's medallion went flying into the corner. Morgan crashed into one of the poles. A jolt of excruciating pain shot from his ribs into his spine, radiating outward to his limbs. He struggled to regain his senses and clear his head.

The statue, headless and with thick black smoke pouring out of a gaping hole in its neck, toppled over and crashed to the floor, shattering into a thick blanket of dust and debris. As the multicolored cloud disappeared, a demonic cry echoed like the flapping of giant wings. The overpowering stench of pomira bark smothered the air.

Morgan felt a cold tentacle brush his body. Rayna, pushing herself off the ground, drew back and whirled about, as if startled by an invisible presence enveloping her. Then the rush of air from the blast died, and the howl blended into Saltos's cry.

Saltos raised his hands into the air, his shirt darkening to a charcoal-gray fur, his cloak unfolding and transforming into real wings of black, leathery skin. His arms bent at an awkward angle to become foreclaws. Saltos's clean-shaven face darkened into a rough, blackish visage, framed by uneven tufts of black hair and pointed sideburns. His eyebrows lengthened and thickened, sweeping over his slit-like green eyes. His nose hooked like a beak, and two long fangs extended from the row of upper incisors, descending out of his open mouth. A black, lizard-like tongue slithered in and out. Tiny brown horns rose from his scalp. The gold disc in the collar of his black cloak glowed.

The creature spread its wings and dove into Morgan. Morgan spun, sidestepping it. He swung his fist at the creature but missed. The black being landed on its feet and howled at Morgan, its incisors bared.

From her corner, Rayna charged at it. She swung her blade and swiped it in the arm, drawing a loud cry and a gush of green, oozing blood. She stumbled past the fallen statue, into the opposite corner of the room, and grabbed the still-lit medallion.

Morgan thought he could still recognize Saltos's distorted facial features within the black being's visage. "Are you Saltos or the Xaturi?"

The creature hissed and turned to face him. Holding its wounded arm, it said in a low, rumbling tone, "We are one."

A hybrid creature? Morgan took a quick glance at Jairesse, lying on the ground. She was unconscious but still alive, her chest rising and falling with shallow breaths. He made eye contact with Rayna, who was still holding the medallion out toward the Xaturi.

It suddenly whirled and extended its foreclaw toward Rayna. "Give!" It charged at her, its wings extended. She quickly tossed the medallion past the Xaturi's reach. The Xaturi howled and dove for the medallion, but the object sailed inches beyond its grasp into Morgan's hand.

The Xaturi raged with fury. There was something about this medallion, Morgan knew, something this creature wanted or needed. It had killed before to get it, and it would kill again.

Rayna dashed past the Xaturi, toward Jairesse. It ignored her and charged him. Morgan tensed, his breath drawn to steel himself against the pain, his fists cocked. But as it came upon him, Rayna whipped her remaining blade through the air, sinking it deep into its back.

The Xaturi cried out and crashed to the ground, the hilt protruding from the base of its neck. Relentless, it rebounded, its wings thrusting it upward from what should have been a fatal blow.

Rayna was now completely weaponless. Morgan had only one course of action that would protect her. He dangled the medallion before the Xaturi, then turned away and ran out of the inner chamber, the roaring Xaturi in hot pursuit.

Ignoring the shot of pain that erupted with each step, he mounted the staircase and burst into the observation room. He ran past the control seat, the banks of instruments, and the giant energy tubes, and out the side door.

On the mountaintop, a gust of cold wind blasted him, blowing him off his feet. Regaining his balance, Morgan wheeled around to survey his surroundings. Overhead, dark clouds swirled in the turbulent air. Deep-red rays from the rising sun gave the clouds an explosive, angry quality. Rumblings echoed throughout, and intermittent flashes illuminated the chasms. Large boulders, some jagged and black, others rounded and silver, dotted the blue ash that smoothed the surface of the mountain. A blue path, winding between some of the boulders, sloped up and away.

Perhaps it leads to the near projector disc. As he climbed the rocks, he kept glancing back to watch for the Xaturi. He paused when he reached a clearing formed by a circle of jagged boulders towering over him.

The path ahead narrowed to a short bridge that stretched over a crevasse between two sheer walls. Below, a layer of dark clouds swirled, concealing the depths of the crevasse. The wind raced through the corridor with a tremendous fury, buffeting both walls with blue ash. A bolt of lightning shot down from the overhead clouds into the heart of the chasm. The lower clouds blinked a soft orange glow. A muffled concussion echoed along the mountain walls.

Morgan took a deep breath and stepped onto the bridge. Halfway across, the bridge narrowed to less than five feet in width. A sudden gust of wind nearly blew him over. Pausing to regain his balance, he caught a glance of the precipitous drop through a break in the clouds below him. Not far above, lightning crackled through the dark clouds. Morgan could feel the static in his hair. Another lightning bolt flashed in front of him, striking the bridge with a glancing blow. The booming thunderclap pounded his ears. Determined, Morgan charged ahead.

Once on the other side, the steep slope wound around a giant rock formation. He found himself standing about fifty feet below the circular projector disc. He walked around it, studying the backside components that rose from the ground. There seemed to be a bundle of energy conduits that went into a transformer before connecting to the back of the disc.

Morgan jumped, startled by a lightning bolt flashing down into the drop. When he gathered himself, he saw a tall black figure descend in front of him. Morgan snapped into a defensive posture as the Xaturi stepped forward.

"Do not run!" Its voice echoed into the wind. It extended its foreclaw. "I am only my master's slave, serving his purposes. Do not fear me. I am condemned and am more a victim than those who have died at my hands."

Jairesse had said that Saltos had once been human but was now a vehicle for Luzomi. Was this creature speaking the truth about its nature?

"I am compelled to shed blood for my master's rule. Have mercy for a tortured soul."

Morgan tensed his jaw, his resolve stiffened. "You serve a liar, and you are a liar yourself. You ask for mercy, yet how many of *your* victims asked *you* for mercy?"

"If you must destroy me," it replied, "do so out of pity, not vengeance. Killing me would set me free."

Morgan gritted his teeth. He *would* kill it—but how? With rocks? Morgan held up the medallion. "Is this what you want?" He would bait it. "Would it have brought that statue to life?"

It took another step forward, its wings folding. "It is one of the ancient crystals that Lord Luzomi gave to us in former times, with the ability to tap its primordial power to further his aims."

"You used Adonair's crystal to power your machine. How many of these crystals are there?"

It held out its foreclaws. "Nobody knows, except Lord Luzomi himself."

"What did that machine do when you fired the particle beam?"

"Enough!" the Xaturi interrupted. "My master awaits the sacrifice that will unlock the door to his entrance."

Morgan kept his guard up, gauging the space between himself and the approaching Xaturi. He eyed the medallion. "Luzomi's entrance...with this?" It seemed the crystals—both Adonair's and the one embedded in this medallion—were key to this creature's aims. Morgan took a step back.

"It is mine," it roared. "It is of no use to you."

The Xaturi took another step toward Morgan, its arm outstretched. Keeping his eye on his opponent, Morgan knelt down and placed the medallion on the ground.

"No!" the Xaturi cried.

In one swift motion, Morgan grabbed a jagged black stone and brought it down on the medallion with all his might. The concussion rocked the area, the medallion disintegrating in a shower of light and sparks, shrapnel from the stone flying in all directions. The explosion blew Morgan toward the bridge, and he crashed to the ground onto his already bruised back.

Morgan fought against the pain and scrambled to his knees. Another lightning bolt lit up the sky. A faint groan and rot-like breath alerted him. He spun around just as it rushed him from behind. Roaring a monstrous cry, it butted its horns into his chest. Morgan's world turned upside down, and he crashed to the ground under the weight of the lunging creature, stunned by the pain in his back.

It thrust both foreclaws under Morgan and scooped him up, its wings extending to lift Morgan into the air. Realizing that the creature intended to throw him over the cliff, Morgan flailed his arms and legs about, helpless. He yanked his torso away, and the Xaturi lost its balance, crashing to the ground on top of Morgan, the blow punching into his abdomen.

Pinned at the edge of the bridge, Morgan struggled to roll away. The creature's leathery wings fell over his face, blinding him for a moment and smothering him in its stench. His legs free, Morgan kicked into its back with all his strength and, in one motion, rolled the creature under him. It roared and shot its scaly, forked tongue out at him, barely missing Morgan's eyes as he dodged to one side. With a split-second clear line of sight, Morgan shot his fist into its head, scoring a full-force strike between the eyes, stunning it.

Morgan scrambled to his feet, his hand throbbing from delivering the hit. As it regained its legs, Morgan booted a powerful kick into its head, sending it crashing to the ground with a cry of pain. With lightning quickness, he seized both claws and dragged the creature, like a heavy burden, back toward the edge of the cliff.

Regaining its senses, it planted a foothold and dove straight into him, slamming into his stomach, horns first, knocking Morgan's breath out. They both crashed to the ground, Morgan's head dangling over the cliff as a bolt of lightning shot into the crevasse. Morgan saw two balls of static electricity flash before his eyes. The Xaturi's glowing hands reached for Morgan's face.

This is how it killed Thakian and Adonair!

Morgan summoned all his remaining energy to deliver a bone-cracking kick to the side of its abdomen, drawing a spew of blood from its mouth as it fell over the edge, screaming. Morgan caught a brief glimpse of it disappearing into the clouds below.

Trembling, struggling to breathe, Morgan waited until the cold wind numbed the waves of pain. He rolled to his feet and staggered across the bridge to the dome of the observation room. Peering inside, he saw Rayna crouched by the control seat with her arm over her abdomen. She waved her free hand to him. He smiled, exhausted, and started back toward the control room's side door. But before he took his second step, he heard an ear-piercing howl from behind.

It was the Xaturi, reappearing out of the crevasse with its giant wings flapping. Its voice screaming at the top of its lungs, it soared high above the bridge.

Sheer terror engulfed Morgan as it banked and dove toward him, its bloody, incisor-lined mouth gaping open. He sprinted for the door, the shadow of the Xaturi looming large over him. Feeling the rush of air from its flapping wings, he doubled back, just as its talons swooped over his head. Now cut off from the door, he scrambled back across the bridge, looking madly for a rock or anything else that he could use against it. He saw a pulsating light and sprinted for it. He heard another roar as he rounded a boulder and ran past the glowing time-projector disc.

A sudden gust of wind blew, and the Xaturi's roar became a scream. Morgan looked back to see a twisted rainbow beam spiral out from the now-activated projector disc. Hurricane winds rushed through the chasm, slamming Morgan against the mountain wall. The ground shook with violent tremors. An ear-piercing howl drowned out the cascade of thunderclaps that accompanied the onslaught of lightning bolts rocketing between the cloud banks.

The particle beam enveloped the Xaturi in mid-flight, blanketing the creature in a bath of twisting colors. It cried out and burst into flames as it fought to free itself of the time distortion. Flailing its wings, it shredded itself into fine, burning cinder-like tatters of flesh and skin. On the other peak, the receiver disc blazed a blinding white, then exploded into an earth-shattering blast of energy, a dark-gray smoke cloud rising from it.

Morgan collapsed to the ground, battered by the blast. Everything came to a stop—the tremor, the high-pitched wind, the temporal beam, the dying scream of the Xaturi. Looking into the sky, Morgan saw a mist of thin, flaming remnants float down through the breeze. Above, the soft rumblings and occasional lightning flashes continued.

Rayna, staggering across the bridge, embraced Morgan. "Are you all right?"

Ignoring the pain in his back, he wrapped his sweat-drenched arms around her. "Are you?" Of all the things he admired about her, he was most grateful, at this moment, that they had been of one mind during their fight to the death. Their instinct to turn the particle beam against the Xaturi had destroyed the creature. He whispered, exhausted, "You're a lifesaver."

"I thought I'd lost you." Rayna buried her head in his shoulder. "I'm just glad it's dead."

Morgan gazed over at the other peak, where a flaming cloud of smoke and ash rose high into the stratosphere like an erupting volcano. "Good riddance, Luzomi."

A shock wave rippled through the stretches of space and time, the temblor radiating out from the tiny backwater planet of Volon.

The midnight-blue figure, floating through the depths of space, convulsed from the blow of the extinguishing of higher life. It flung its many arms out from the jolt of pain and spun out of control, reeling from the loss of a kindred being.

It didn't seem possible, but one of their own no longer

existed.

It stretched out its arms, its many podlike hands glowing like halos in the blackness of the void, reaching for anything that felt like any part of the Xaturi. It waited, its feelers extended, as it spiraled along on inertia. It felt the rhythmic pulse of the universe, the dark energy of its master, but no indication that the Xaturi still existed.

It was gone, destroyed.

The shock wave passed through, and the being eventually recovered its orientation. It would not be alone for very long. More would be arriving through the contact point.

It relocated its destination—a distant planetoid—and continued on.

Morgan and Rayna stared at the mammoth machinery—the now dead and silent Timegazer. The energy tubes sat dark. The view screen was blank. The controls that Rayna had worked, just minutes before, sat lifeless.

"Whatever it was," Morgan said, "it won't be shooting any more particle beams through space. At least we accomplished that much."

They supported each other down the long staircase, back into the dark inner sanctum. There, Jairesse lay at the feet of the Three Guardians, still unconscious, but breathing. Rayna knelt and took her hand, checking her pulse, while Morgan released Adonair's body from the pole and gently lowered it to the ground.

"How are we going to get her back to the rover?" Rayna asked.

Morgan sighed. He was drained, but they needed to get Jairesse back to her people. Hopefully, other Volonians could help revive her, as Jairesse had revived Rayna. He went back to Adonair's body, whispered, "Sorry," and removed Adonair's robe. "This will help us carry her out." After crossing Adonair's arms over his chest, similar to how Jairesse had crossed Thakian's arms, Morgan spread the robe out on the ground next to Jairesse, and together they lifted her and placed her on the robe. Morgan paused, flinching at the painful bruises in his ribs and back, and asked, "Do you think you're up to it?"

Rayna tilted her head at Morgan and sighed. "Do you really need to ask?"

At daybreak, Morgan and Rayna, driving the rover, returned to the crash site. Over a dozen Volonian men and women were gathered around four additional transport rovers, inspecting the Buggy.

"We'll have to tell them the truth," Rayna said. "What else can we do?"

"I hope they're friendly," Morgan said.

They brought the rover to a stop, and the crowd surrounded them. As they opened the door and limped out, two men stepped forward from the crowd. One, an older bearded man in a straw hat and dressed in a simple one-piece plaid outfit made of burlap, had his arm around the shoulders of a small blonde girl. Dressed in a flowing white robe, she looked to Morgan like a younger version of Jairesse, perhaps ten years old or so. Could she be the girl Jairesse and Adonair had spoken of?

The other man was a muscular *Illito* warrior, dressed and tattooed just as Thakian was, though a bit shorter and stockier. "Where are Thakian, Adonair, and Jairesse?" he asked.

Morgan grimaced. He decided his first words should be of good news, before breaking the bad.

"The Xaturi is destroyed," Morgan told the crowd, "and you are all safe." He saw no smiles or cheers among the people. He glanced over at Rayna. Maybe he should just give it to them straight, as she had suggested. "Adonair and Thakian were killed by the Xaturi."

That drew loud gasps from the crowd. The *Illito*'s mouth gaped open, his eyes wide.

Morgan quickly added, "Jairesse is alive." He pointed inside the rover. The young girl's large eyes looked up at him, as the people quieted. "But she is unconscious, and we don't know what her condition is."

"No," the girl whispered.

Morgan turned away to avoid the feelings of desperation he heard in her voice. He looked around at the people. "Thakian's body is also inside. Jairesse had already performed the last rites for your brave warrior. Unfortunately, we were unable to retrieve Adonair's body."

Hushed murmurs spread through the crowd.

"I am Panquo," the *Illito* warrior said.

"Ritoso," the older man introduced himself.

Morgan nodded. "Morgan Teggo and Rayna Choff."

"We saw the explosion on the peak," Panquo said. "We knew something terrible had happened."

Morgan said, "The explosion was the death of the Xaturi." He gazed at the people, hoping they would believe him. He turned to face Panquo and said, "I'm sorry for your loss, but it was a fight to the death."

Rayna bent down toward the girl and asked, "Are you learning to be a healer, like Jairesse?"

The girl looked up at the bearded man.

Rayna stood up and said to Panquo, "Jairesse saved my

life. She released the blockage around my *suromila* and reconnected me to the *Pankoulda*. Without her help, I would have died."

More murmurs sounded among the Volonians.

Returning her attention to the girl, Rayna said, "Jairesse was attacked, and I fear that her *suromila* may have been interrupted, as mine was. Are you able to help Jairesse, the way she helped me?" Rayna held her hands up, similar to how Jairesse held her hands when they glowed. "Jairesse showed this to me, after she healed me. Something like this?"

Morgan understood Rayna's thinking—that a young trainee might be Jairesse's only hope for survival. It was a heavy burden to place on someone so small and innocent-looking.

"Familla is very young," Panquo said to Rayna. "Yes, she is gifted, but inexperienced."

"I must try," Familla said to Panquo. She turned to Ritoso and said, "I understand what she is describing, father. If she is correct about the *suromila*, then Jairesse might die."

Her father thought for a moment, then nodded his head at Panquo. "Let her try."

"Are you certain that is best, Ritoso?" Panquo asked. "We all understand Jairesse's importance, and her importance to you. But what is the risk to Familla?"

Ritoso didn't answer.

Panquo turned to Familla and asked, "Do you know what to do?"

Familla hesitated.

Morgan, realizing he was the only witness to Rayna's revival, stepped forward. "Jairesse gathered seven different plant specimens and placed them on Rayna's body." The memory of those agonizing hours of anxiety and uncertainty returned.

"There was a small gold-colored flower on her head, a long purple vine across her collar, the stem of a red flower in her hands…"

"Yes," Familla said, brightening. She turned to Panquo. "Please have the men gather seven *quellates*."

Morgan smiled and nodded to the young girl. She knew enough to get started, at least.

"I must prepare myself," she said to her father and Panquo. Turning to Morgan and Rayna, she said, "Please take me to Jairesse."

While Panquo directed several of the men into the forest, Morgan and Rayna led Familla inside the rover, to the reclined seat where Jairesse lay next to the body of Thakian. Morgan and Rayna sat down while Familla stood at the priestess's side for a long time, apparently deep in thought.

"You are beautiful, even now," she whispered. "I am lost." She trembled, grasped her hands together, and brought them to Jairesse's face. "I don't know what to do. I don't know… how to help you."

Morgan bowed his head. The uncertainty weighed heavily on them all, and he felt for the girl.

Rayna rose from her seat and put her hands on Familla's shoulders. "Don't be afraid," Rayna said gently. "Panquo said you are gifted. Whatever you can do, whatever it might be, will be of help to her."

Familla nodded, a grim, determined look on her face. "Jairesse is our priestess; she is also my sister. I must not fail." She looked to Rayna and took a deep breath. "I will do my best for her."

Rayna stepped away as Familla sat on the floor next to Jairesse, closed her eyes, took three deep breaths, and placed her hands together in her lap.

Mixed feelings jumbled inside Morgan as Familla entered a meditative state. He was thankful that Rayna could reach and support Familla. Rayna was always patient. But despite this, he was also concerned that Familla's effectiveness could be compromised by her feelings of uncertainty.

As Rayna sat down, Morgan decided to step outside. Rayna could help her better than he could, at this point.

Back outside, he summarized for Panquo and Ritoso the events at the mountain: the mysterious Saltos, the giant machine, the Luzomi statue and the medallion, and the fight with the Xaturi. The people crowded around to listen. He judiciously omitted Adonair's role with Saltos to avoid raising too many questions. He didn't think the Volonians would believe that their temple chief could be a cult follower.

When Morgan finished, Panquo said, "Your presence is not a coincidence. The long reach of the *Pankoulda* brought you here, at the precise moment when your help was needed to stop Luzomi."

"An encouraging thought," Morgan said. "To be honest, I'm not a believer in the *Pankoulda*. The followers of Luzomi, though, are very real, just as the followers of the *Pankoulda* are real. And the Xaturi was definitely real, whatever it truly was."

Many heads nodded in agreement.

Panquo put his hands on Morgan's shoulders. "We believe that Luzomi is real and that he is still determined to subjugate us. We—and you—must remain alert. Be watchful of people and events around you. Just as Saltos was not as he seemed, others may also be not as they seem."

Morgan thought of Adonair's double identity. He wondered if there were others among the Volonian population lurking in plain sight.

The gatherers returned with the seven plant specimens, and Ritoso took them inside to Familla. Morgan followed and watched as Familla took the seven specimens and placed them on Jairesse's body. When she finished, Familla looked at Morgan and Rayna, a hint of hesitation in her eyes. She knelt at Jairesse's side again, took several deep breaths, and raised her arms to the ceiling, her sleeves falling aside to reveal thin, plain silver bracelets. She tilted her head back and began chanting.

"Ooooo, kha'tha, duolu, Oscanos, kha'tha, duolu, Gheri-ah, pan'dithy.

"Ooooo, kha'tha, duolu, kaandathi, maandathi, pan'dithy."

Familla brought her arms down, lowered her head so that her face disappeared beneath her wavy golden hair, and dropped her voice to a barely audible whisper.

"Hicith, cislema, jaka-jaka..."

She inhaled a long, deep breath, placed one hand on Jairesse's head, the other on her waist, and began singing a familiar soft, atonal melody.

Morgan glanced at Rayna, who watched with bated breath, finally able to see what had happened to her. He turned his attention back to Familla and waited. Her hands emitted no light.

Grim, Morgan stepped back outside again and watched as Panquo directed the crowd to gather into a semicircle facing the entrance to the rover. Panquo stood in complete silence, with his eyes closed and his arms raised. The people followed his lead, raising their arms.

Unsure what they were doing, Morgan sat under a tree and reflected on the struggle for life and death.

By midday, Ritoso came out from the rover and joined Morgan. They walked to the other side of the spacecraft, away from the crowd, into the shadows among the trees.

"Is Familla okay?" Morgan asked.

"I don't know," Ritoso said, shaking his head. "She has not left Jairesse's side in hours. She is very tired, but when I asked if she wanted to stop, she was adamant about continuing."

"Why don't her hands glow the way Jairesse's did?" Morgan asked. "Is she in any danger?"

"It only means that her abilities are very rudimentary. With time and proper training, she could achieve a level where she can command her powers." He paused. "But for now, she is following her instinctive feeling."

Morgan was amazed at how calmly Ritoso spoke, considering that both of his daughters were engaged in the struggle for life—and that the younger girl was fighting for the older one. He could only guess at the emotional turmoil raging within the man.

By late afternoon, half of the crowd decided to take one of the rovers back, while Panquo, Ritoso, and the others remained to wait for Familla.

The sun started to set, and the evening shadows of the forest began lengthening. Morgan went inside the rover to sit with Familla as Rayna stepped out to stretch. He found the young girl on her feet, standing by Jairesse's side with one hand over Jairesse's face, the other over Jairesse's chest. Familla tilted her head back, her eyes closed, breathing slowly but fully.

"Oscanos, ghethi bayillou Euranua,

"ghethi bayilou universalia."

Morgan paused. This part of the chant sounded unfamiliar. As he watched, the young girl's body began to rise up and sink down. Her feet levitated off the ground an inch, then returned back to the floor. He reached for a seat, uncertain of what he was watching. Again, he saw her rise into the air, this time two inches, before settling back down. He wondered why Jairesse hadn't shown this same ability during Rayna's revival. What did it mean? He wondered if she was nearing a successful revival.

Familla lowered her head to rest on Jairesse's chest, and her feet rose a third time off the ground, this time remaining an inch in the air. As she floated, a soft golden glow finally appeared—not projected from her hands, as Morgan would have expected, but over her hair, like a halo.

"Euranua, meno mino, meno."

Jairesse's body, with Familla's golden head resting on her chest, gently rose into the air, paused, then relaxed back down into the seat.

Without warning, Familla's head jerked up, eyes and mouth open, and she swayed and fell back, away from Jairesse. Morgan dashed over and caught her in his arms. The golden glow in her hair disappeared, and her eyes and mouth closed.

"Familla?" Morgan, alarmed by the abrupt end to the rite, gently shook the unconscious girl to try to rouse her. Hearing her whispering, he bent his ear down to try to make out her words. "Familla?"

"Jairesse...Jairesse..." Repeating Jairesse's name, Familla seemed delirious, her eyes closed, her voice but a mumble.

Morgan felt her forehead. It was warm and covered with a light sweat, as if she had a fever. He shouted, "Panquo! Ritoso!"

Panquo and Ritoso ran in, followed by Rayna and a couple of the remaining Volonians.

"What happened?" Rayna asked.

Morgan held Familla steady as Ritoso helped support her. Together, the two men eased the young girl into one of the seats. Panquo knelt before her and took her hands.

"Familla?" Morgan asked. "Can you hear me? Open your eyes!"

Rayna put her hand on Morgan's arm, calming his emotional rush. She knelt down beside Panquo and put her hand on Familla's shoulder. "Familla?"

"…Jairesse…"

Rayna bent down, close to the girl's ear. "Open your eyes, Familla."

Familla moaned and swayed her head from side to side.

"Come on," Rayna gently prompted. "Awaken, child."

Familla slowly opened her sleepy eyes, took a deep breath, gazed around at everyone, and after recognizing her surroundings, looked at her still-unconscious sister. "Jairesse," she sighed. She reached out and rubbed her fingers over Jairesse's hand. "She's no longer in danger of dying. But I'm not strong enough to revive her."

"Stasis?" Morgan asked.

Familla frowned. She turned to Ritoso and said, "I'm sorry."

Morgan looked at Rayna, touched by Familla's determination and depth of feeling but unsure of how to comfort—or at least encourage—the young girl.

Ritoso wrapped his arms around Familla. "No, you have done well, my child. You have saved her!"

"Jairesse lives," Panquo said, "and all the people will be grateful for what you have done."

Familla, still unsmiling, looked exhausted. She leaned forward, wrapped her arms around Ritoso, and buried her head in his shoulder.

Panquo turned to address Morgan and Rayna. "We will take Familla and Jairesse home and care for them. And we will lay Thakian to rest." He extended his arms. "Thank you for all you have done for us."

Morgan breathed a sigh of relief. Perhaps this incident on Volon—what should have been an enjoyable vacation to Toutle—was finally over. For the most part, the people of Volon seemed like nice agreeable folk, simple in their ways yet complex in their individuality. But he was more than ready to leave all this behind and return to familiar surroundings.

Morgan and Rayna, standing outside the Buggy, watched the four Volonian rovers depart the clearing, the vehicle lights disappearing into the overlapping shadows of the forest. Morgan thought of the unconscious Jairesse, departing inside one of the rovers, and felt bad for the Volonians. Given Familla's young age, it could be years—perhaps decades—before she mastered her abilities without Jairesse's guidance. Whether Jairesse could be kept alive until then, no one knew.

Jairesse's condition also meant that no one would know whether the appearance of the *Hruvrah* truly marked the beginning of a period of turmoil and conflict unseen since the mythical age.

Upon reentering the ruined Buggy, Morgan pointed at the message displayed on the console comm monitor. "Look, Rayna, a rescue craft has been dispatched."

"What a relief," Rayna said.

Morgan gazed out the window, waiting until the sounds

of the rovers had faded away into the distance. Part of him wanted to return, sometime in the future, to check on Jairesse and Familla. But part of him also wanted to leave this world of glowing hands, floating bodies, and Luzomi creatures behind—forever.

Rayna rubbed his shoulder, interrupting his musings. "We should get our belongings. The rescue craft will be arriving soon."

Morgan sighed. There was always something else to take care of. "Let me put out a response first." He sat in the pilot's seat and switched on the transmitter.

"Space Fortress C, this is *BG-832*, on the surface of Volon, Lieutenant Teggo speaking. Please advise the base commander that the source of the particle beam has been neutralized. We will be filing our reports with Captain Choff and Captain Jaron upon our return. Teggo out."

Mindful of his back and rib injuries, Morgan leaned back in his chair and placed his hands on the armrests. Rayna sat next to him, quiet. They had a couple hours alone now. The near loss of Rayna had made Morgan realize that nothing in life could be taken for granted.

He reached over and took her hand. "We won't make it to Toutle this time, but we still have our future to consider. I don't want to wait until we have another opportunity to go on leave together. I…"

It was hard to say the words. Rayna gave his hand a gentle squeeze.

"I almost lost you." Morgan's voice cracked, and he struggled to keep his composure.

Rayna's eyes were moist. "I almost lost you, too."

Morgan took a deep breath. "We both know that anything

can happen, at any time. But we've never actually gone through anything like this before, putting our lives on the line."

"It wasn't just another academy exercise, was it?"

Morgan hesitated. He knew he wasn't eloquent; he could only hope that she would understand what he intended to express. "I learned something important: you and I have something ethereal between us. When I thought I was going to die, I knew you would save me. We were of one mind. For an instant, we were of one soul. We are meant to be together."

Rayna smiled. "I felt it, too."

Morgan's body was beaten up, and he ached all over, but Rayna's words made everything feel better. He could see in her eyes that she understood what he meant. They had learned they didn't need a vacation. They needed the experience of life—to the brink of death—together.

When the moment came, it *felt* beautiful. A burst of heat stripped him clean, and a wave of pure emotion washed over him. Morgan couldn't treasure Rayna enough. He wanted their union to last an eternity, if that was possible. When it was over, he kissed her and said with a slight tremble in his voice, "I love you."

"I love you, too," she whispered. "I'll always love you."

Morgan smiled. "I wish we didn't have to go back. I wish we could just lie here and let the time pass." He gazed into her eyes and detected something amiss. "What is it?"

"I..." Rayna looked up at the ceiling. "I'm worried about all the strange things that happened to us here. Images we've never seen before and don't understand. Things we've never had to deal with." She let go of his hand and turned away—not a good sign. "I felt something when Saltos changed into the

Xaturi." She shivered.

Morgan bolted up, concerned. Had Saltos done something to her during their confrontation? Images of his jarring blow and her violent crash into the wall flashed in his mind. "Did he hurt you?"

"It's not that. I don't know how to describe it." She took a deep breath and looked into Morgan's eyes. "He didn't feel human. It was like a cold, damp wind flowing through the void, a presence coming into our midst—something demonic, like death itself."

Part 2

WAR CLOUDS

5. Mortal Enemies

The semi-human figure floated high above a dirt-gray planetoid, its many arms wrapped tight about its tubular torso. In the distance, a convoy of transports approached, slowly but surely. Turning its attention back to the barren surface, the being extended its four legs as it descended. The low gravity of the planetoid made for a slow, soft landing.

Once on the ground, the figure raised its midnight-blue, snakelike head and scanned the landscape, surveying the barren rock and sniffing at traces of methane, ammonia, and several other rare gases and metals. A dark-purplish volcanic mountain with white ash floating up from the crater stood in the distance. The being spied, at the base of the mountain, the lights of a wide, squat building blinking with a slow steady pulse. The figure lowered its head, turned, and scurried on its four lanky limbs toward the building.

At the entrance, it flattened itself against the ground and slid, inch by inch, past the automatic security camera, a silhouette as dark as the perpetual night and as slow as the drift of the planetoid.

It quickly found its target: a lengthy hairline crack in the outer wall, the result of natural, imperceptible ground movements. In utter silence, it slipped itself into the fissure.

Inside the wall, it worked its way against the slow seepage of artificial air until it reached the corresponding crack in the interior wall. It drained itself out and onto the floor, where it re-flattened itself and adjusted to the stronger artificial gravity. Now in the midst of a deserted corridor, it rose on its four limbs, lifted its head, surveyed both directions, and scurried away.

It stopped in front of a metallic-gray alloy door with a triple-paned viewing window in the middle. Next to the door was a sign with a human's name. The figure studied the name, looked inside the window at the occupant lying inside, sleeping on a bare platform bed, and lowered its head and moved on.

It passed one cell door after another—prisoners, both criminal and political, from distant dominions such as Asther, Belaan, Trak, and Othume, none of whom noticed that a silent being had taken a momentary glance at him.

Reaching the end of the long corridor, it turned the corner and came to a block of cells that held dead prisoners, still confined for the full term of their sentences. Most of the dead lay where they had fallen, in varying states of natural decomposition.

Certain individuals, though, rested in vacuum-sealed caskets with transparent lids, preserved. In those cells, scanners and recorders took continuous readings of the bodies. A stack of books contained printed study notes, hypothetical musings on the nature of evil, and other semi-scientific observations.

The figure stopped before the force-field-sealed door of cell 92456. A sign next to the door held an epitaph:

General e'Thuq Mapooly of Belaan, 1441-1490.

Terror of the Galactic Revolutions.

May Almighty Euranus have mercy on his soul.

Inside the cell sat a transparent casket. The body within

was clothed in a green-and-burgundy Belaanian dress uniform from fifty years earlier and adorned with a parade of colorful medals on both shoulders and across the chest. Though long dead, the man lay as if only asleep. His face, framed by a rodent-topped battle helmet, and with skin and lips whitened by the anemia of the passage of time, held a stoic, stonelike expression.

The figure inched its way across the floor, examining the wall, tile by tile, until it found a hairline crack that ran from floor to ceiling. It raised its head and looked about. A solitary guard had nodded off at a nearby desk, surrounded by a dozen monitors. The hallway remained deserted in both directions.

The shadowy creature rose on its hind legs, six forearms reaching for holds in the crack. It pulled itself through the crack, into the cell, and scurried to the casket, where it rose up again. Four additional forearms extended from its back, and it lifted all of its limbs into the air, straight, high above the lid.

It raised its head to the ceiling, opened its mouth, and began speaking a gruff, rhythmic chant that it had performed many millennia ago in a far distant region of the multiverse.

"Ooooo, kha'tha, duolu, Oscanos, kha'tha, duolu, Gheriah, pan'dithy."

The chant transitioned to a smooth, soaring melody.

"Ooooo, kha'tha, duolu, kaandathi, maandathi, pan'dithy."

The being brought its arms down, dropped its head, and lowered its voice.

"Hicith, cislema, jaka-jaka..."

It took a long, deep inhalation, placed one hand on the casket lid above Mapooly's head, the other next to the casket near his waist, and began singing a soft, atonal melody. A golden light emitted from the two pod-like hands; its head tilted back, its three insectile eyes closed, and it breathed slowly.

"Y'jili anhannou pakoso,

"Euranua, gomourouh."

As the rodent-like whispers continued, its body rose and sank. Its feet levitated off the ground an inch, then returned to the floor. Again, it rose into the air, this time two inches, before settling down. It lowered its flattened serpentine head to rest on the casket lid, and its feet rose a third time off the ground, this time remaining an inch in the air. As it floated, a soft golden glow developed into a halo around its midnight-blue head.

"Euranua, meno mino, meno."

Mapooly's body, with the figure's golden head still resting on the casket lid, gently rose, then relaxed. The figure's head jerked up into the air, eyes and mouth gaping open, and it fell away, its arms raised to the ceiling.

"Gartha, pixui, antizio, hellui!"

The being spread four hands across the casket lid and swung the heavy transparent slab up and open. It then placed one glowing hand on Mapooly's head, and the other on Mapooly's waist.

"Y'jili anhannou pakoso,

"ghethi bayilou unive'salia."

Mapooly levitated an inch off his bed. While the body remained floating in the air, the shadowy figure climbed into the casket, underneath Mapooly. It withdrew its many arms, its two legs, and disappeared from view, below the body of General Mapooly.

Metiar Walmsley excused his audience of ten clerical novices and sat in his high-backed, thick-cushioned chair on the portico, covering himself from his shoulders to his feet with a heavy, patch-patterned quilt. Removing his wire-rimmed spectacles, he closed his tired eyes and soaked in the warmth of the gentle breeze. After taking in a deep breath, he opened his eyes and looked at the pink sunset illuminating the sky. He then returned his lightweight glasses to his deep-wrinkled face. Below his overlook, the lights of the town of Frenius were blinking on. Walmsley turned his head at the sound of approaching footsteps.

A middle-aged man of short stature, in plain tan business dress, approached with two muscular men in sleeveless white tunics in tow. "Lord Walmsley," Dubian Trophet said, "Monseigneur Dhavail is asking for you." Walmsley's chief of staff knelt and lowered his voice. "He is weakening. I fear he may be near his time."

Walmsley sighed with a heavy heart. Even after four decades of living on this idyllic world of Wichloc, he hadn't tired of the view of the magnificent tropical forests that lay beyond the borders of the settlements. But the loneliness never ceased. Trophet motioned for the two muscle men to stand ready to assist, if necessary, while Walmsley grasped the hilt-shaped handle of his bronze-colored cane and rose to his feet.

As they made the slow walk through the stone corridors of the ancient fortress, Walmsley remembered the many joys he and High Priest Dhavail had shared since arriving on this planet. The many outings they led into the forests to view the wildlife. The many town gatherings they presided over to celebrate a wedding, a new home, or a birth. So much happiness over such an extended period of time.

Walmsley and his men reached the eastern residence wing and came before a large arched wooden door decorated with a mosaic depicting the forests of ancient Amahl. Trophet nudged the door open, and they entered. The men accompanied

Walmsley through the front parlor, where half a dozen men and women, members of the town council, sat in silence. Proceeding past the townsfolk, Walmsley entered a low-lit, spacious bedroom.

Six men and women in heavy white robes, members of the clergy, rose from their knees at the foot of the oversized bed to greet Walmsley.

"Monseigneur Navilla," Walmsley addressed the leader of the clergymen. Even now, Walmsley needed to remind himself that the "young man" had long ago reached his prime, his hairline already receding, and that he would soon be the next head priest of their people. "How is your father?"

The downcast look in Navilla's eyes saddened Walmsley.

"He seems delirious, and his breathing is difficult," Navilla said, "but he is at peace." He stepped forward and placed his hand on Walmsley's arm. "My father would be happy to see you."

"Thank you." Walmsley offered Navilla a gentle smile before stepping to the bedside.

Whinn Rexold, dressed in a royal-blue layered robe and shoulder-length headdress, both made of natural Wichlochian silk, sat beside the ailing high priest, praying with one hand resting on Dhavail's arm and the other grasping a string of wooden beads. Seeing Walmsley approach, Rexold released the high priest's arm and rose to her feet.

Walmsley motioned for Rexold to sit back down. The gray-haired consort of the high priest was not much younger than Dhavail and Walmsley. There was no need for her to vacate her seat. Navilla brought a chair for Walmsley.

As Rexold continued her quiet prayers, Walmsley gazed at his old friend, who was lying in silence under a soft, golden blanket, an occasional breath interrupting long moments of still-ness. Dhavail's eyes were closed. Walmsley took Dhavail's hand and slid his purple-and-gold wristband—which the monseigneur had blessed and given to him several decades ago—from his wrist to Dhavail's.

The old high priest smiled, and his eyes opened a slit. His mouth moved, but no words sounded.

"Just rest," Walmsley said, squeezing Dhavail's hand. "I will stay with you." He thought about their past.

How ironic that he had just recounted their first meeting to a new generation. The tale had brought the experience back with a powerful vividness—his views of the high priest, first as a figurehead, then as someone steeped in untold secrets and mys-teries, and finally as the one man with the courage to challenge the ancient Deity of Darkness.

That war had worn everyone out beyond exhaustion. With its conclusion, and the eventual formation of the new Eu-ranian order, Walmsley had withdrawn his militia, the Greyban Corps, to this remote world. Within a year of Walmsley's retire-ment from service, Monseigneur Dhavail also stepped down from the priesthood, citing the need for fresh leadership not tainted by decades of war. He quickly turned the Temple of Wiene, and the monumental task of reconstruction, over to a new high priest and journeyed to Wichloc, joining Walmsley for a respite and recovery that flowered into a lifelong friendship.

The entire experience still summoned feelings of sheer terror, even after the passing of half a lifetime. Walmsley kept the all-powerful *Gramm* locked away in a vault known only to him-self and Dhavail. But though it was out of sight, it was not out of mind—nor was the memory of Luzomi.

For Walmsley, the move to Wichloc had become his long-sought opportunity to reflect upon a new outlook on life and to take up a new and urgent purpose. He laid down his arms and, under Dhavail's tutelage, slowly and systematically studied what he had formerly dismissed as long-outdated mythical tales. *The Songs of the Euranians* contained the compendium of ancient stories of the Euranian Ancestors and the age-old annals of the early Euranian people. Perhaps the prophesied return of Luzomi would not occur in their lifetime, Dhavail had told him, but as the only other man able to invoke the power of the *Gramm*, Walmsley's mission now had to be the mastery of spiritual warfare. So they had spent the decades preparing for a larger battle.

Dhavail turned his head toward Walmsley. His mouth strained to form a word. Walmsley bent down to listen.

"...home..."

Walmsley felt a hint of a squeeze in his hand. He couldn't help but smile. For all the many years and decades they had lived here, the old priest never forgot where he truly belonged. Once a spiritual leader, always a spiritual leader, and the spiritual beacon of the Euranian people was the Temple of Wiene on Kelova.

"All right, my friend," Walmsley said. "I'll take you home."

Walmsley felt a second, stronger squeeze in his hand. The high priest's body tensed. Navilla rushed forward to join Walmsley and Rexold as Dhavail gasped, his body stiffening. Walmsley placed his free hand on Dhavail's soft cap and cradled his old friend's head.

Rexold took the high priest's free hand, held it tight, and closed her eyes. A tear rolled down her cheek.

"Mother Gheriah," Navilla prayed, "smile upon my father's face. Lord Oscanos, lift him up."

Dhavail released his breath and relaxed his body. His

eyes closed.

Walmsley also closed his eyes and lowered his head, a blanket of sadness engulfing him. He heard Rexold and Navilla weep.

Trophet said, "The high priest, our dear father, our friend and guide, has departed. Ring the bell, nine tolls, and let the people begin nine days of mourning."

Lifting his head, Walmsley saw the other members of the clergy kneel at the foot of Dhavail's bed, bow, and chant a short prayer. After they finished, they rose and covered High Priest Dhavail with his golden blanket.

"We will begin preparations for your ascension," one of the clergymen said to Navilla.

One of the clergywomen embraced Rexold. "We are all saddened."

They all bowed to her, then to Navilla, and finally to Walmsley before departing in silence.

"Lord Walmsley," Trophet said, "what are your wishes?"

"I don't know." Walmsley slowly shook his head. "I would like some time."

"Understood, sir." Trophet bowed and left with the two muscle men. They closed the bedroom chamber doors as they departed.

Walmsley, alone with the grieving Rexold and Navilla, took a deep breath to clear his mind. "Let us honor the memory of the high priest." He put his hand on Rexold's shoulder. She looked at him through her tears. "He was a great man and a powerful spiritual leader. Someday, he will be revered for the historic victory he achieved."

Rexold managed a smile. "Thank you, Lord Walmsley."

Navilla bowed and accompanied Rexold out.

With the help of his cane, Lord Walmsley walked alone to the chapel. He entered through the double doors and looked about, remembering the countless services High Priest Dhavail had led through the decades. Foremost among these memories were the myriad of holy festivals, both the traditional holidays from the Kelovan Temple and new observances created by the Corps population. He walked up to the chair in the front row where he always sat, now an empty chair among many empty chairs. He settled in and gazed at the altar. The chapel was vacant. The chapel *felt* vacant.

He stared at one of the paintings on the wall. It was a portrait of Lord Oscanos, whose taut upper-body muscles and slanted eyebrows expressed the intensity of a life-and-death war. His enemy was a gray-brown scaly serpent, horned and winged, with a tail coiled tight around Oscanos's legs. Behind them, throngs of bloodied, battered humans and reptiloids fought.

A rush of disquiet pressed down upon Walmsley, a cold vacuum of emptiness trailing off into the void of time and space. The feeling chilled Walmsley.

The last time he felt something like this was fifty years ago, when he and Monseigneur Dhavail were locked in a battle to the death against General Mapooly.

As a distant bell began tolling, Walmsley's thoughts returned to the old high priest. Of all the people who had settled on Wichloc after the war, Dhavail and Rexold were the last surviving members of Walmsley's generation, besides Walmsley himself. Together, they had survived the otherworldly terror of General Mapooly. Now, in this garden world, far from the new Central Empire and surrounded by the children and grandchildren of his late followers, Lord Walmsley felt alone, with only his memories, Dhavail's teachings, his new mission, a faint foul feeling that brushed by…and the most powerful weapon ever created at his disposal.

"Goodbye, my friend." Goodbye to the past.

Admiral Zerah stepped onto the boxy, low-lit bridge of the transport hauler, *Q'toz*. Converted from a fifty-year-old Gearmlian frigate, the dependable cargo carrier had served the towering but paunchy Zerah as the flagship of his forty-ship convoy with a distinction that filled him with pride.

"The admiral is on the bridge," Executive Officer Isaalt announced.

Zerah smiled to himself every time he heard the title. He wasn't a real, commissioned admiral. That was a title he gave himself three years ago, after leading a circumnavigation of the Central Empire, successfully delivering black market goods—hallucinogens, weapons, poached furs, and stolen gemstones—to twenty different planets.

With a fleet as large and well-armed as his, anything was possible. He relished the thought that throughout Euranian history, military leaders, even those who were self-made, often became conquerors and rulers of worlds.

Old space-dog Captain Bemone and his men, all clad in drab camouflage fatigues and obedient as docile pets, promptly saluted.

The haughty Zerah raised his hand to his hat and crisply returned the salutes. "What is it, Captain?"

Bemone and Isaalt stepped forward from the shadows. In his scratchy bass voice, Bemone said, "Admiral, we're picking up reflections from within the clouds."

Zerah glanced at the pastel-rainbow colors that filled the main monitor. Patches of plasma gas passed over and through one another, some sections wispy enough for the distant stars to shine through, other parts more dense. Sometimes colors combined, yellows and reds to make oranges, reds and blues into violets. Other times, the colors separated to reveal momentary glimpses of black, star-filled space.

The convoy of decommissioned warships and old creaky transports skimmed the boundary of the Great Nebula, the expansive remnant of the cataclysmic explosion of the Euranian home star that had torn the ancient Etolian Empire from its foundations. Within the last two decades, the construction of long-range ships capable of navigating the fluctuating perimeter of the nebula had finally bridged the centuries-long separation to Lower Eurania.

But few took that route—mostly smugglers and pirates. What little traffic existed journeyed at the risk of encountering the shadowy slave traders of Lower Eurania.

"The echoes don't match any of the natural pulsars," Captain Bemone said. "Nor do they resemble any of the known traffickers' beacons."

Mr. Isaalt spoke up. "Sir, I recommend we energize the weapons."

Captain Bemone shook his head. "No, the surge would give away our position, perhaps needlessly."

Admiral Zerah cleared his throat. It was time to inform his captain of what only he knew. "Captain, those reflections are camouflaged signals coming from Kaxuo, an unregistered prison facility—and our destination."

The security guard, a gruff, middle-aged grunt by the name of Grune, awoke to the annoying honk of the security monitor. The code for cell 92456 indicated that the casket lid was open. He pushed his oversized cap back out of his eyes and puzzled over the lack of any other alerts on his display. The triggers along the compound perimeter, in the hallways, and in the door to the cell were silent. The picture showed the cell quiet and darkened, the body resting in its casket, as always. But it did appear that the transparent lid was swung open.

"*Dox!*" he cursed. "*Thaaka'dox!*"

Both curious and annoyed, Grune took his firearm and left his station. At the cell door, he ran the diagnostic check on the lock. Nothing unusual. He released the lock, nudged the door open, and stepped into the darkness. With his free hand, he took out his handlight and shone it around the room. He then stepped over to the casket, confirmed that the lid was up, and studied the inanimate body of Mapooly. It was the same as always.

Grune held his stance. He thought he heard a soft atonal melody. Grune looked around, unsure where the strange sound came from. It sounded like a whisper.

"*Hicith, cislema, jaka-jaka…*"

Grune pivoted his light around, aimed his gun ahead, but saw nothing. He pivoted again, still saw nothing, and pivoted around a third time.

"*Tatiki!*" he cursed, disgusted. "*Thaaka'tatiki!*" He slammed the lid shut with a loud concussion that reverberated down the hall, drawing yelps and comments from the live prisoners in the far corridor. "*Thaaka'tatiki'dox…*"

Eyes.

Grune froze. The eyes of Mapooly, open and unblinking, stared at him through the transparent lid.

Without warning, the lid whipped open, slamming Grune in the face and knocking him into an awkward stumble. He tripped and fell backward onto the cell floor with a thud, his hand hitting the cold stone floor hard enough to jar his gun from his grip.

General Mapooly bolted upright and shot out of the casket into the air with his hands clenching, six more midnight-blue limbs fanning out from his back, his eyes still unblinking. His mouth gaped open, and he howled the cry of a drakothon, the elusive, near-extinct beast from the Outer Territories that the superstitious considered a descendant of Luzomi's mythical reptiloid, the Troggle.

His face bloodied by the hit from the lid, Grune never had a chance to scream before Mapooly's hands wrapped around his neck and crushed the life out of him.

General Mapooly sat on the floor of his unlit cell, deep in meditation, the body of the dead security guard dumped into the abandoned casket. The dark energy of the universe flowed in with each breath he took, the beat of his heart strengthening, his mind reforming into that of a man—the man he had been, one of the greatest, most mesmerizing, most powerful men in the history of the human race.

With his strength returned, he opened his eyes, raised his head, rose to his feet, drew his rypniblade from its scabbard, and flexed his muscles in a series of Vu'ng-discipline exercises. He began with simple poses, focusing on the feel of each part of his body. Once in command of his body, he stepped through the basic positions, slowly at first, then quickly, before expanding to blade-work exercises. He thrust into the darkness, spun around the casket, and with the quick flip of a switch, released the side fin-blades and swung the weapon down with both hands on the head of the casket, splitting it—and the body inside—into two bloody halves. Finished, he returned the long blade to the sheath on his belt, straightened his helmet and his uniform, and holstered the dead guard's gun on his belt. Four pitch-black limbs extended from his back, soft golden glows shining from the podlike hands. Mapooly stepped through the open door.

Lord Walmsley watched the gleaming golden casket of High Priest Dhavail descend through the opening in the sanctuary floor, into the underground vault below. The chapel choir sang the last refrain of "Hymn to Oscanos," the closing of the traditional requiem. Walmsley sang along by memory; the experience was far too familiar. He thought he would have grown callous to the hymn by now, but each new farewell brought its own sadness.

This farewell was the heaviest of all.

"To the Maker of the world, to the Giver of Life,

"We sing praises, we give thanks.

"We offer to Mother Gheriah our love,

"To the Three Guardians, our trust,

"And to you and Almighty Euranus, our lives.

"Home, we wait for home.

"Eurania, our home, Eurania.

"Bring us home to you, Lord Oscanos,

"Bring us home to you."

The final chorus concluded, the members of the clergy approached the altar, where Navilla stood alone. Walmsley remembered Navilla's christening in this same chapel by his father. Now, he watched as Navilla raised his arms above his head and whispered an invocation in old Etolian, the tongue of the ancient temple services. The clergymen then dressed Navilla in the adornments of the high priesthood—a white-and-red royal robe, a conical golden crown, and the gleaming green orb-handled scepter—while the choir chanted.

The people stood. With Trophet's help, Walmsley pushed himself to his feet. Together, they prayed for the new head priest: "The high priest has passed from our midst. May Lord Oscanos bless our new head priest."

After the conclusion of the service, Walmsley sat down to rest while the people filed out.

"Are you fatigued?" Trophet asked.

Walmsley nodded. "I just need a moment."

"It was a very long service," Trophet said. "Do you have tasks for me, sir?"

Walmsley sighed. "Yes. Monseigneur Dhavail wished to be returned to the Imperial capital. Please begin preparations for the journey. I will accompany him back to his home."

"You will?" Trophet asked, raising an eyebrow.

Walmsley leaned back in his seat. "It is different for the late high priest than for us. All of you were born here. You have lived your entire lives on Wichloc. And before settling here, I lived the life of a military man, always on the move, a vagabond. For us, this world is truly our home."

He had never felt any desire to return to the empire or to introduce the children of the Greyban Corps to where they came from. Dhavail, however, was different.

"For the monseigneur..." Walmsley paused, reflecting on his late friend, "he never forgot the place of his birth, his home for the first half of his life."

Trophet replied, "I understand."

Now was the time, Walmsley decided, to let the younger generation follow their own paths. "In honor of our late high priest, anyone who wishes to accompany him on the journey would be welcome to join us."

"Yes, sir." Trophet bowed and departed.

Walmsley gazed at Rexold and Navilla, who had remained to speak with him. Except for the tears in their eyes, both were stoic in dealing with their grief. "The high priest's last wish was to be taken home." He paused to assess whether they understood his meaning. "I would like the two of you to accompany me on the journey."

"To where?" Navilla asked.

Walmsley paused. Like the other members of his generation, Navilla had been born here on Wichloc and had never been off-planet. The core worlds of the Central Empire were only names of faraway locations.

"To the Great Temple on Kelova. There, the monseigneur will rest with the other great priests of Euranian history."

Rexold tensed for a moment. Walmsley knew that the old memories of the tombs of the great priests remained fresh in her mind.

"There, we will return the *Gramm* to its proper holding place, for the day when it will be called upon again."

With the passing of Monseigneur Dhavail, Walmsley now had to consider the possibility that Luzomi's prophesied return would not occur until a future generation. He didn't know who would be the next wielder of the *Gramm*. Rexold had vehemently refused on numerous occasions to take it. Navilla had expressed similar reservations, citing the need to strengthen his inner faith before considering such an undertaking. Perhaps some mild-mannered member of Navilla's generation would eventually emerge. Regardless, it was important for somebody other than just Walmsley to know where to retrieve the *Gramm*. By bringing both Rexold and Navilla to Kelova, he would be reasonably assured that the knowledge of the *Gramm* would be passed on.

Captain Bemone directed *Q'toz*'s approach toward the planetoid, his needlelike nose almost a pointer to follow. The helmsman—sandwiched between the weapons master and the comm operator—piloted the transport away from the convoy.

"No need for delicacies," Admiral Zerah said. "Our single ship commands more firepower than this entire complex."

"Yes, sir," Bemone answered. He ordered *Q'toz* into a headlong descent toward the surface. Directly ahead, the smoldering volcano, and the blinking lights of the prison building at its base, marked their destination.

"Set us right on top of them," Bemone ordered, watching the image of the building in the main monitor.

He knew that the ship's black color would hide it against the nighttime sky, allowing *Q'toz* to elude the prison's visual tracker for a few precious seconds.

Isaalt reached over and flipped open the craft's intercom. "All hands, prepare to disembark through the loading bay."

"Touchdown in ten seconds," the pilot reported.

Bemone watched the wide, flat roof of the building—a perfect landing pad—expand below them. Within seconds, security lights blazed on, triggered by detection of *Q'toz*'s thrust. Bemone, his adrenaline flowing and his instincts taking over, reached over the pilot's shoulder and pushed the steering yoke down, dumping the massive transport onto the building with a hard hit that jarred the ship and cracked the roof open.

"No delicacies," Bemone quipped.

"All right, *turkanaans*!" Zerah yelled into the intercom. "Go!"

Isaalt and others jumped down to the main hold, where

the rest of the assault team had assembled, wearing black fatigues and helmets, with military-grade firearms ready. Isaalt took a full breath, held it, and hit the airlock control. When the bay door opened, they jumped down the gangway tubes, through a ten-foot hole in the roof, and into the prison complex. Inside, the automatic life support systems were stabilizing the artificial air with an emergency force field against the leakage. Isaalt waited as everyone emerged through the opening.

Suddenly, two security guards rounded the corner. As they reached for their guns, Isaalt whipped about and opened fire, his blazing rifle cutting down the dumbfounded guards.

Soon, he led the two dozen men into the confiscation pool, where a cache of firearms had accumulated through the years in several storage rooms. Isaalt examined the first storage room's lock and frowned. He held his hand out for one of the crewmen's firearms.

Isaalt locked the weapon's release and squeezed the trigger to engage the charge-pak. A soft hum rose. He locked the trigger open, placed the gun at the base of the storage room door, and led everyone away to safety.

The explosion blew a gaping hole through the door, large enough for the men to squeeze through and bring out the collection of high-powered weaponry.

"Drop your weapons!"

A white-skinned, uniformed soldier, a string of vintage weapons hanging from his belt, emerged from the shadows between the storage units, his rifle aimed squarely at Isaalt's chest.

"Who are you?" Isaalt demanded, recognizing that the man before him resembled a notorious figure out of recent history.

"Look about you," the figure said in a low, rich voice.

"Your lives are meaningless, slaving away for your superiors on a lifeless planetoid populated by the shadows of the once-living." He held his free hand up. "Look at me. Who do you think I am?"

"You can't be." Isaalt blinked his eyes and shook his head in disbelief. "General Mapooly died fifty years ago."

"Yes," Mapooly said. "Died here, in cell 92456—which is now no longer occupied by General Mapooly." With his mesmerizing eyes held steady on Isaalt, he lowered his rifle. "Look upon me and realize my significance. We can rise again, the most powerful force to ever sweep across Eurania." Mapooly smiled, his piercing eyes narrowed. "The Grand Army of the People's Revolution."

Isaalt hesitated. The man looked like Mapooly, talked like Mapooly, and offered the same tantalizing visions of power as Mapooly had once offered to a prior generation.

"Join me." He extended his hand to Isaalt. "Follow me, and we will restore the past glory of Eurania." He nodded to Isaalt's men. "Resist, and you will join the dead who lie in their cells."

Without warning, one of the men swung his weapon at Mapooly and opened fire, pummeling the general in a blaze of explosive charges. Mapooly twisted and collapsed at an awkward angle to the floor. Isaalt held up his hand to stop the shooting, then stepped over Mapooly to examine him.

Mapooly lay still, his eyes closed, his chest rising and falling with a slow, labored rhythm. Smoking holes peppered what had been a pristine Belaanian period dress uniform.

But there was no blood.

Without warning, General Mapooly bolted upright and shot into the air, his eyes open, his mouth uttering the cry of the drakothon, six midnight-blue limbs fanning out from his back, his two hands crushing the neck of the shocked crewman who had fired.

Mapooly dropped the dead man to the floor, pressed his foot on the corpse, and said to Isaalt, "You're next."

Isaalt, hyperventilating, with his entire body trembling, could only stare. This wasn't the general Mapooly from history. It was something inhuman masquerading as him, something deadly and remorseless that could snuff anyone's life in an instant. Something, Isaalt reminded himself, that offered power and glory to its followers. He turned and nodded to his men. One by one, they threw their guns down and submitted to their new captor.

On the bridge, Admiral Zerah looked up from his fleet monitor as Captain Bemone approached at a brisk pace with a mini-comm unit in his ear.

"Mr. Isaalt requests you and I go below," Bemone reported. "He has a finding to report—in person. Sir, this doesn't feel right."

Zerah glanced at the prison complex again, cautious of their situation with the weapons cargo onboard. He took a deep breath and pointed to two armed men. "Myrane, Gorhoud, accompany Captain Bemone and myself. The rest of you, remain at your posts until our return."

They went to the narrow service ladder, wide enough for one person at a time, and climbed down to the dim, cramped lower decks, where unkempt mercenary personnel kept watch on the cache of weapons, ranging from hand weapons to ship-mount batteries and space cannons.

With Myrane and Gorhoud leading the way, they walked past crates of charge-paks, stacked from floor to ceiling, until they reached the entry nook holding two airlocks. Gorhoud opened the bay door, and Bemone and Zerah entered the gangway tube.

As they emerged on the outside, Zerah demanded, "All right, Mr. Isaalt, what is the meaning of this?" He stepped past Bemone to face Isaalt, who stood before a crowd of black-clad crewmen.

A voice from the rear of the assault team said, "I requested that he arrange for us to meet, Admiral."

The team members parted to allow a man passage to the front, a pale-skinned person in a green-and-burgundy dress uniform, a parade of colorful medals decorating his chest, a squat, rodent-topped helmet on his head, and a long blade and a gun hanging from his belt.

"Belaanian?" Admiral Zerah muttered. He recognized the figure: one of the most infamous, most notorious generals in history—under whom his own father had served—someone who had been dead for the last half century. Zerah paused, both bewildered and suspicious. "Who are you? Do you wish to join us?"

"No," the Belaanian said. "We wish *you* to join *us*."

General Mapooly drew his gun, and Isaalt's men followed suit, leveling weapons at Zerah and Bemone.

"Join us, Admiral." Mapooly flashed a vicious, downswept smile. "We will add your ships to those that await me, and your considerable armament to ours. Together, we will be invincible."

Zerah hesitated. His father had made a similar decision and lost his life.

"Look upon us and realize our significance." Mapooly's eyes mesmerized Zerah. "We rise again, the most powerful force to ever sweep across Eurania. Together, we will restore the lost glory of eons past." Mapooly pointed his gun at Zerah's head. "You will be rewarded beyond your wildest dreams."

Lord Walmsley gazed about the empty chapel, his mind on the upcoming voyage. The nightly dream of darkness persisted. He shook his head.

This was no dream. Something was happening in Eurania; something lay in wait. Now that they were within a few days of embarking, he couldn't help but feel something ominous approaching.

The door opened, and Head Priest Navilla walked in.

"My Lord?" Navilla rushed over. "Can I help you?"

Walmsley smiled at him. "I was just sitting for a moment, feeling at home."

Navilla nodded and sat down next to him.

Walmsley took a deep breath and turned his face away. "I don't think you should go on this trip."

"Why?" Navilla looked disappointed.

Walmsley paused to consider his next words carefully. "Something is in the air…" He could feel his heart race. "Something is upon us. From where, I don't know. From deep space." He turned to face Navilla. "You don't have a successor yet. It's imperative that you remain safe. In space, anything can happen."

"What do you think might happen?"

Walmsley gazed at the portrait of Lord Oscanos in his life-and-death battle against the gray-brown scaly serpent. "I'm hoping it's just anxiety," he said, "but the last time I felt this way was fifty years ago. In case something unforeseen does happen, you need to be here to guide the people."

Navilla's lips trembled. "Please give me a moment to

pray on this."

He rose abruptly, walked up to the altar, raised his arms above an oversized glittering-blue bowl built into the tabletop, and mumbled a silent chant.

A moment later, Walmsley saw thin wisps of smoke begin rising from the bowl, carrying the head priest's prayers up and away to Lord Oscanos.

6. Space Fortress

"Wake up, sleepyhead." Morgan tapped Rayna on the shoulder. "We're back."

She opened her eyes, sat up, and looked around the small passenger compartment of the rescue craft. Their belongings were piled on the two unoccupied seats facing them. Morgan pointed out a small, circular portal. Through it, they could see the first of the approaching buoys and the piercing, blinking lights of the signal beacons.

Ahead shone the welcoming lights of Space Fortress C. Arrays of spectrum transmitters and receivers, some combined with space cannons, surrounded the multiple watchtowers that stretched in all directions away from the central structure like the spokes of a giant wheel. Tiny taxis and transports darted about from pier to pier, ferrying personnel from one section to another. Large robotic arms and claws, some sporting humorous decorations and slogans—one proclaimed "Save a plant, eat recycled food"—reached in and out of the various capital and support ships tied up at the piers, loading or unloading equipment or payload. At the far side of the fortress complex, two escort destroyers, *Numa* (DE-58) and *Tagon* (DE-61), and the newly commissioned cruiser, *Castella* (CA-27), sat adjacent the gargantuan refueling depot. Beyond, another dozen ships of the Alscrasian fleet drifted at their assigned moorings.

The most prominent structure, the globular central Command Module, displayed the lighted insignia of the Central Empire, five stars radiating along purple-and-green stripes from the silhouetted crowned head of the hawk of Oscanos, the graftinop.

A short distance away, two dozen additional support craft, including the old frigate, *Epoch* (F-28), and three more cruisers—*Ancora* (CA-21), *Ocelot* (CA-23), and *Pouton* (CA-25)—sat at the repair facilities on the asteroid Canellis.

Rayna stretched. "It's good to be back."

The craft flew past a watchtower, over a line of munitions transports, toward an open pier, where several people stood inside the large window of the airlock.

"There they are," Morgan said, waving. "Such losers."

Burly, crewcut Otho Ennuk and smallish, narrow-faced Lon Prowzi, standing next to the airlock operator, waved back. Their tan service uniforms were embellished with the dual red star insignia of *Ocelot* over their left chest. Otho's copper buttons, pointed collar, and pair of silver shoulder stripes signified his lieutenant rank. Lon's pullover shirt and single silver shoulder stripe denoted his ensign rank.

The pilot brought the craft down on the landing pad, disengaged the engine, and deactivated the controllers. The airlock tube extended and clamped onto the craft's entry. Morgan and Rayna unstrapped themselves, reached for their bags, and headed for the door.

"Thanks," Morgan said to the pilot. "My compliments to the Patrol."

The door released, opened, and the ramp lowered to reveal Otho and Lon.

"What an awesome mess." Otho belly-laughed, pointing at the large bandage on Morgan's head.

"I *feel* like a mess, Oggy," Morgan deadpanned, gesturing at the layers of brown-and-blue dust and dirt caking him and Rayna from head to toe.

"A brief separation affords the gift of rest, but an extended disunion spirals into the agony of anticipation," Lon quipped, his Alscrasian laced with his Sestian accent.

Morgan shook his head at Lon. "Another wise Sestian proverb, Lon? So, you missed us, huh?"

"To those who hear, let them fathom." Lon gave him an innocent look.

"Or as my kid brother Edon used to say," Otho interjected, "'In due time, for some.'" He unsheathed the skiloblade hanging from his belt and raised it in salute. "*Maruga.*"

Lon drew likewise. "*Maruga.*"

"Sure," Morgan said, offering his arm. When Otho and Lon raised their eyebrows in question, Morgan added, "My blades got destroyed. I'm down to just hand-to-hand. *Maruga.*"

"Wow," Otho remarked, narrowing his eyes and cocking his head to reevaluate Morgan's and Rayna's worn and weary appearances.

He and Lon retracted their duo-blades, and the three servicemen "clinked" two hilts and an arm.

Rayna smiled. "Boys will be boys."

"Here," Lon offered his hand to take Rayna's bag. "Let me help."

"Not you too," Rayna said. "I'm fine." When Lon did not withdraw his hand, Rayna sighed and reluctantly handed her bag over. "Here. Sheesh." She quickly added, "You look a little run-down, Lon. Everything okay?"

Lon paused. "Nothing a drink couldn't help." He gave her a toothy grin. "You could use one, too, couldn't you?"

The four walked through the passageway and into the battle-gray terminal, where scores of military and civilian personnel crisscrossed about, some on foot, others on personal transports, some discussing logistical matters, others passing along the latest jokes and stories. They hopped into an available four-man motorzip, drove past a line of airlocks which connected to a series of piers, and entered an area hub, an expansive, high-ceilinged area filled with box-shaped supply stores and brightly lit eateries.

"You *both* need a drink, after your latest 'adventure,'" Otho said as he parked the motorzip and led them into the nearby Club 707 Wing.

"If you insist," Morgan said, following Otho in.

"I insist, Machoiss." Otho referred to Morgan's old street nickname. "You'll feel much better."

Inside, the strains of the latest popular songs competed with a wall full of monitors displaying a myriad of widecasts—some sharp, others fuzzy—of the latest news, markets, celebrity interviews, and sports. In the center of the floor were a dozen tables filled with base personnel and visitors. In one corner, two off-duty soldiers from the space fortress garrison sang along with the music, while a third soldier danced with a servicewoman from one of the visiting ships of the fleet.

"Cool song," Lon said.

Rayna nodded with a smile.

"Mr. Lendus said he'd join us," Otho said. Turning to the speaker on the host-kiosk, he ordered, "Table for six, please."

"Six?" Rayna asked.

"Your old man, checking up on you," Otho said, winking.

Morgan groaned, drawing a round of laughs.

A three-legged, three-armed robot led them to a window booth. From where he sat, Morgan could see dozens of pinpoint robot mechanics move about the larger ships in the shipyard at Canellis, illuminated under large clusters of work lights.

After the server departed with their orders, Otho asked, "So what's the story? Who the *krok* shot you down, and how'd you lose all your weapons?"

"And what are you going to put in your report?" Lon asked.

Morgan paused to consider his answer. It all seemed very far away, now that they were back among familiar surroundings. He glanced at Rayna. Her dirt-covered appearance reminded him of what they had experienced. "He's a Luzomi worshipper." He could not believe he'd actually said it, but it was true, and now others besides Rayna and himself knew. "He was using a gargantuan time-disrupting machine to try to bring Luzomi into our time—or so he said." Morgan spread his arms wide. "The machine was huge, apparently ancient, drawing power from deep within the planet core, and built into an abandoned complex inside a mountain."

Lon furrowed his brow. "I thought Luzomi cultists were secretive. I've heard that they only identify themselves to each other, and that you couldn't spot them in an open crowd."

Otho shook his head in disgust. "Too much idle time and nothing useful to do, so they make things up to feel busy. Bah! Where's my drink?"

"This guy was pretty weird," Morgan said, blowing out his breath at the memories. "He had an eight-foot statue of Luzomi, and he could transform himself into a big, black flying creature." He looked to Rayna, unsure if he wanted to relate all the other details of the trip. "It took everything we had to battle him and get out of there alive."

"Wow," Lon whispered.

"Well, I'm glad you guys are okay," Otho said. "Did you see the machine at work?"

Morgan and Rayna nodded their heads.

Lon leaned forward, his eyes wide. "What was it like?"

Morgan pondered the memories of the images they'd seen, the sight of the bombardment on the primeval founding worlds, and the feeling of uncertainty that remained over those images. He had tried his best to reassure Rayna. But the more he dwelled on the memories, the more he needed some reassurance of his own.

Captain Choff and Lendus entered with purposeful strides. Both were in white service uniforms—Commander Lendus's with copper buttons, three silver stripes on his shoulder boards, and a side cap; Captain Choff's with gold buttons, four silver stripes and a gold braid on his shoulder boards, and a combination cap.

"Well, look at the vacationers," Lendus said. "You both are a mess."

The four of them rose to their feet and crisply saluted the thickset, slightly diminutive captain.

Choff returned the salute, his fingers touching the brim of his captain's hat with a firm snap of the hand. "As you were." He pulled out a chair and removed his hat, revealing short-cropped, salt-and-pepper hair.

As they reseated, the robot waiter returned and delivered the set of drinks—Alscrasian whisky for Morgan and Otho, a "Crashing Blue Wave" for Rayna, and water for Lon. After taking Lendus's and Choff's orders, the waiter departed.

"Welcome back." A slight smile creased the edges of Captain Choff's mouth.

"It's good to be back, sir," Morgan replied. Seizing the topic of conversation, he asked Lendus, "How go the repairs?"

"Very well," Lendus said. Roughly ten years older than Morgan, the tall, dark-skinned, soft-voiced executive officer from the mining world of Enotha turned to face Choff. "We have another day of work on the upgrade to the topside engine, and then we'll be ready to begin refueling."

"The turret batteries?" Choff asked Otho.

"They should be fully charged by tonight," Otho replied.

Choff lowered his voice. "And the mods for the new torpedoes?"

"Slower, about a day behind," Otho reported, his voice also lowered, "but I'll have Mr. Fota shift people after tomorrow, and that should put us back on schedule." He paused while the waiter brought the remaining drinks—two brewed Kelovan teas. Once they were alone, Otho continued. "I'm targeting the diagnostic and control testing to begin three days from now. The holds are nearly ready, and tomorrow they'll be bringing the torpedo pack aboard."

"Do we know where we're going next, sir?" Morgan asked.

Choff took a drink, swirled it around in his mouth, and swallowed. "*I* know." He glanced at Lendus, Morgan, and Otho, each in turn, creases appearing in his forehead. "Now that we're all back, let's schedule a briefing for tomorrow morning, in the wardroom. The three of you."

"Understood," Lendus replied.

"Yes, sir," Morgan said.

"Yes, sir," Otho echoed.

Lon remained silent.

Choff turned to Rayna. "I'll let Captain Jaron fill you in, when she sees fit to do so."

"Yes, sir," Rayna echoed the others, straight-faced.

Choff paused, his face softening. He offered a hint of a smile. "How are you feeling, Rayna?"

Rayna chuckled. "I'm fine."

"You should have Dr. Creatoun look you over when you get back aboard."

"Yes, sir." Rayna sighed. "Look, I appreciate everybody's concern, but I'm fine. Really."

"You let the doctor decide that, Rayna."

Rayna gave up and folded her arms. "Yes, sir." She gave a half-hearted salute, which drew a mild look of disapproval from Choff and half-hidden smiles from Otho and Lon.

"And you?" Lendus asked Morgan.

"Just the bump on the head, sir."

"That's all, Mr. Teggo?"

Morgan knew that Lendus knew him better than that. "Well, maybe a bruised rib or two." Before Lendus could comment, Morgan added, "I'll check in with Dr. Hildermaan."

Choff emptied his cup. "I should get back to the ship. But before I go…" Choff turned to face Morgan. "I'd like a word with you, Mr. Teggo."

Morgan paused mid-drink, unsure of what this meant. Rayna, Otho, and Lon looked his way. Choff's terseness felt like a weight that had landed on Morgan's head. The first time he heard that tone of voice, the captain had reassigned him belowdecks for a week. Morgan put his drink down, rose to his feet, and followed Choff over to a quiet, unlit corner of the club, where a small window looked out into deep space.

"Yes, sir?"

Choff snapped around to face Morgan. "What the hell really happened out there, Teggo?"

Morgan's pulse raced. "Sir, I promise I'll have the report on your desk by—"

"To hell with the report." The captain kept his voice low, but the fire under containment was unmistakable. "First you get shot down, and Rayna's injured in the crash. Then she's miraculously fine and whatever the hell it was gets blown to all eternity. Is that a somewhat accurate summary of your messages?"

Morgan swallowed. "Yes, sir."

"I want an explanation, mister. Brief is fine, but I want some details of what the hell happened to the two of you."

Morgan dreaded having to relate what sounded like fanciful events. He doubted the captain would believe *any* of it. But it was the truth, and he would have to report it, sooner or later. Straightening his back and clearing his throat, he asked, "Sir, are you familiar with the cult of Luzomi?"

A small, unmarked transport downshifted to sub-light thrusters as it passed the buoys. It flew past Canellis, over a line of support ships moored at one of the perimeter piers, and headed for the maximum-security hangar in the Command Module. The transport slowed while exterior security scanners checked it over. Once cleared, it flew through four successive force fields, each checking for a different suite of threats, before entering the bay and landing on the pad. A final force field enclosed the shuttle in a protective bubble, and ten overhead scanners examined the craft. After a minute, the force field deactivated, the shuttle entry lock released, the door swung open, and the ramp lowered to the ground. A detachment of armored soldiers from the space fortress garrison stood at attention, their sidearms hanging from their belts.

Two Imperial guards in shiny black body armor with rich scarlet trim emerged from the transport, followed by four staffers in crisp white shirts and dark blue suits, and a small, balding man dressed in solid gray business clothing, thin spectacles, and carrying a small black binder.

The leader of the soldiers stepped forward and addressed the small man. "Welcome to Space Fortress Canellis, sir. I am Lieutenant Colonel Moton."

"Thank you," the man said in a soft tone. He bowed. "I am Kumatille."

Moton bowed. "The base commander is in his office. If you will follow me, we shall accompany you there."

They proceeded to the far wall of the hangar and entered a transparent elevator that lifted them to the top level. There, they received a bird's-eye view of the four craft that sat within the hangar. Leaving the bay, they followed a wide corridor into the Central Commons, the promenade where personnel went about their off-duty business. Overhead, large viewers displayed the current day's events, the arrival and departure schedules, and the *Galactic Times* widecast. The security guards formed a perimeter around Kumatille and his staff as they boarded a staff transport and drove through the Commons with the lighted Imperial graftinop insignia displayed. Even with all the passersby arriving at and departing from the space fortress each day, people still turned their heads at the sight of the Imperial party driving through their midst.

They disembarked at the wide, white gates of the administration tower, passed by the guards on duty, and entered through the double-door entrance. Walking past an information kiosk, they headed toward an unmarked elevator. Moton punched in the passcode, the doors opened, and they headed inside.

When the elevator doors reopened, they emerged at the entrance to the command center. Moton bypassed the double doors of the command center and walked, instead, to the unmarked door at the end of the corridor. He placed his hand on a scanner, and the door opened to reveal the base commander's assistants and two more security guards standing at attention outside the commander's office.

"Please inform the commander that the emperor's envoy is here," Moton said to one of the assistants.

The base commander, a tall, muscular man in black dress uniform and a chestful of medals, stepped out. Towering over Kumatille by a full foot, he removed his gray beret, revealing a smooth dome-like head that reflected the overhead lights. "Colonel Jetiah Chrystamme at your service." With a bow, the base commander invited the emperor's envoy in.

Once inside the office, Chrystamme activated the door locks, walked over to the bar, and offered Kumatille a drink. Kumatille declined. Chrystamme then offered a selection of teas, also declined, and finally water, also declined. "Don't mind if I drink alone, then." He reminded himself that office-bound bureaucrats such as Kumatille could be stiff. Chrystamme dispensed the dull-red tea into his cup and returned to his monitor-filled desk, while Kumatille took the guest chair and opened his binder.

"Have there been any changes in the situation?" Chrystamme asked, folding the four middle monitors into the desk, "We have not picked up any further ship movements along the Gearmlian or Heronian borders."

"No changes," Kumatille said, shaking his head. "Talks with the Grand *Primai* have broken off, while those with the Supreme Dictator never started. At this point, our 'friend,' Prince Fraither, has the full backing of both dominions." He took a reader out of his binder, glanced through it, and handed it to Chrystamme. "I'm afraid we must proceed as planned. You will have three days to make the necessary preparations and accommodations."

Chrystamme pursed his lips. The space fortresses were built to protect the Alscrasian region against threats from outside the empire, not inside. Politics always made a mess of everything. He had seen the trend developing for months. After nearly fifty years of relative stability, the Central Empire seemed past due for some ambitious troublemaking, and Prince Fraither of Bexel was a master of such maneuverings. With both the Heronian dominion and the Gearmlian Confederation backing the prince, Fraither now possessed enough muscle to challenge Emperor Otias of Alscras and his primary ally, Chancellor Wahren of Sestia, for the crown. With a deep breath, he flipped through the reader, skimming the contents, and wrinkled his brow. "The royal party?"

Kumatille sighed. "The emperor thinks it is a good opportunity to introduce the crown prince to the workings of a space fortress. Someday, the young prince may call upon such knowledge, as his father is doing now. Do you see any issues with any of the arrangements?"

Chrystamme shook his head dismissively. "It's an unusual movement, but one we're able to handle. I'll redirect some of the inbound vessels and relocate as many of the support ships as I can to Space Fortress B or D."

"Your judgment, Colonel." Kumatille rose. "The emperor

has complete confidence in you and your base to provide a... what shall we call it? 'Home away from home.'"

"Thank you, sir." Chrystamme rose and bowed as Kumatille turned to depart. *Thank you for dropping the heaviest weight I've ever received in my life.*

"I'll see you back aboard," Morgan told Otho and Lon as they climbed out of the motorzip and walked toward the Canellis-bound launch area.

"Back to celibacy," Otho said to Morgan with a wink and a grin. He and Lon then headed away.

Morgan accompanied Rayna to Passageway 3, where several maintenance workers waited for the next launch to return from *Pouton*.

"Here we are," he said, setting her bag down.

Rayna put her hand on his arm. "Was he very difficult?"

Morgan shrugged. "No more than that time I accidentally dumped you in the cooling tub." He tried to chuckle. "I'm sure he's just worried about your condition, like any good father would be. He just can't show it. He has a command presence to maintain." He rubbed her shoulders. "The sooner you get examined, the sooner his mind will ease."

"And the sooner he'll stop yelling at you." Rayna smiled. "As usual, you're saying all the right words, Morgan, but I know how you two feel about each other. Don't worry, I'll check in with the doctor as soon as I'm aboard." She poked him in the chest. "And the sooner *you* get examined, the sooner *my* mind will ease, too."

"I will, after I write up the report." Morgan sighed. The captain had not taken Morgan's hasty summary of their Volon incident too well. "You'll need to do better than *that* on your report, Lieutenant," he had pointedly said. Morgan offered Rayna a weak smile. "Wish me luck."

"Rayna?"

Morgan and Rayna turned. Approaching was a diminutive but muscular woman with a blonde ponytail, clad in a cobalt-blue drill uniform, sporting the blue comet insignia of *Pouton*'s platoon across her chest.

"Fiona!" Rayna smiled and embraced Fiona Cutxa, one of her three squad leaders.

"I was hoping to catch you," Fiona said. "Welcome back!"

"Thanks."

Fiona glanced at Morgan. "You too."

Morgan laughed. "Thanks."

The green lights on the gangway portal brightened, marking the arrival of the launch. A loud whoosh sounded as the portal door released and lowered, admitting half a dozen dock workers and their equipment into the passageway. The waiting crew members began heading into the empty launch.

Rayna gave Morgan a quick kiss, picked up her bag, and followed Fiona through the portal. "How's the platoon?" she asked Fiona as they entered the launch.

Morgan watched the door rise and lock after they boarded. The lights darkened, and he walked over to the window to follow the launch takeoff. From his vantage point, he watched the departing Rayna, sitting by a window, chatting with Fiona and waving to him.

Once the craft banked away, he picked up his own bag and headed for Passageway 1 to board his own launch. His mind was still mired in thoughts of his latest dressing down from "Captain Chump," the memories of the weekend, and the report he had to file. Soon enough, he was aboard the launch and approaching the shipyard at Canellis.

Ocelot and its gleaming hull designation of "CA-23" was a welcome sight. The ship had served as his home for the last two years, as they patrolled the Imperial boundary, occasionally calling on border worlds. Morgan watched a myriad of robot mechanics scuttle about the ship's turret batteries along the port and starboard sides of the main deck, assisting crew members with their work. Several test units scurried about the transmitter arrays, embedded in the bow and stern. Automated workabees scaled the three quantadrive pods, carrying personnel and equipment down to the two lower engines and up to the third.

Though it was the third of the seven *Ancora*-class cruisers, built immediately after *Haaxx*, it was the first retrofitted with an experimental third engine, the topside pod, which replaced the old traversal dorsal still sported on *Ancora* and *Haaxx*. About a year earlier, *Ocelot* had become the first cruiser to carry neutrino torpedoes. Now, they would be test-firing the new bosonic torpedoes, the most powerful ship-based weaponry to date.

The launch descended to the brightly lit surface of Canellis and landed alongside *Ocelot*. Once down, a short gangway tube extended out from the ship, and Morgan stepped through the airlock, onto the main deck of the ship, emerging near the command superstructure and the front of the line of turret batteries. Nearby, off-duty men and women milled about the deck, socializing in small groups, while maintenance workers and their many-limbed robot mechanics tested the oversized space cannons, one turret at a time. Morgan glanced over at *Pouton*, sitting a short distance away at a nearby pier, and gave himself a minute of quiet contemplation. With each passing moment, the memories of Volon were receding.

The transparent canopy of the deck afforded an expansive view of the shipyard and the assortment of military and merchant ships tied up among the robot cranes and lifts of the docks. A line of small, sleek escort destroyers sat alongside the boxy old frigate, *Epoch*. Next to them was a formation of auxiliary supply ships, lined up like neat rows of little boxes. Beyond, standing out from the midst of a crowd of support ships, *Ancora*'s lights were turning on. Soon, the work lights shining on it would be darkened and disassembled. Hovering in the sky above everything, the lights of the space fortress blinked like a beacon.

Morgan faced the approaching platoon officer.

"Permission to board?" Morgan saluted.

"Granted." Quino Schillary returned the salute.

Morgan quickly strolled past Ensign Schillary before a conversation could start. The man was competent enough, but he was also one of Captain Choff's favored officers. Morgan crossed the weapon-lined main deck to the rear entrance and descended into the hull.

Inside, he followed the narrow passageway that led to the officers' barracks. On the way, he passed through the enlisted men's barracks, exchanging salutes with CPO Semile, one of Schillary's squad leaders, who was listening to one of his many greatest hits collections, and PO1 Turons, chief quartermaster, who was reading a magazine on his porta-com. Passing a line of bunks with drawn shutters sheltering sleeping crewmen, he exited the barracks and continued through the corridor.

When he entered the crew's mess, a dozen men and women—some in drab brown service uniforms, others in off-duty attire—rose from their meals to salute.

"As you were," Morgan said, returning the salute before exiting the mess.

After a series of supply compartments, the main access tubes that led down to the lower decks and the ship's brightly lit central gyroscope, he crossed the double bulkhead into the forward half of the ship, walking past the officers' wardroom. Pausing briefly to glance at the star chart, he noted the ship's position. On the wall, a line of clocks denoted the current time aboard the ship, at the space fortress, and in the capital cities on Kelova, Alscras, and each of the other Imperial core worlds. Once he reached his own corner bunk in the officers' barracks, Morgan dumped his bag on the floor and headed into the sprayer for a thorough, soothing cleansing.

Nearly an hour later, after a therapeutic wash and rinse, and finally in a clean, crisp, tan uniform—a long-sleeved collared shirt with copper buttons and his rank insignia of two silver stripes on the shoulders, matching pants, and black boots—he sat back in his bunk and tossed his military cap onto his pillow. With his porta-com in his hands, he made one final review of his report for the captain. The only items judiciously omitted were the images from Saltos's machine. Everything else—the initial hit by the particle beam, Jairesse's healing of Rayna, Saltos and his Xaturi alter-ego, the discovery of the Luzomi statue, and the destruction of the machine—had to be included, as he had already mentioned them to Choff. Morgan did not want to mention the mythical images, not until he had consulted with Lendus. He pressed the speaker on the porta-com and buzzed the bridge.

"Bridge, Petty Officer Anibe here."

"Ms. Anibe, this is Lieutenant Teggo. What is Commander Lendus's current location?"

"Commander Lendus is meeting with the captain and the base commander at the space fortress, sir. He will return at approximately twenty-two-hundred, Canellis time."

Morgan thought it over. Lendus and the captain might be returning together from the meeting. Holding the report until he had a chance to consult with Lendus ran the risk of a late delivery to the captain. "Thank you, Ms. Anibe. Teggo out."

It was always possible that Lendus wouldn't have any important insights, so there was no need to risk inflaming the captain further. Morgan pushed the "send" button and filed the report to the captain's desktop, just as the porta-com buzzed.

It was Rayna. Morgan smiled. "Yes, Ensign Choff?"

"Very funny."

Morgan hunched forward and spoke in hushed tones into the porta-com. "So, what's the word from the doctor?"

A pause. "He wants to keep me for a day for observation. It seems my basic panel results are all over the map, and he can't put his finger on what it might be. He wants to run some tests."

Morgan sat up. He wasn't expecting this kind of indeterminate answer. "Rayna, how do you feel?"

"Still nothing unusual. I'm going to try to do some of my own research while I'm laid up, maybe see what I can find out about the *suromila*."

Morgan could feel his pulse quickening. He took a deep breath to calm his adrenaline. "Don't worry. Dr. Creatoun will get to the bottom of this."

"Right now, I'd be happy just to find out what's going on with my readings."

After Rayna switched off, Morgan stared at the wall, anxious breaths rushing in and out. He flexed his fists, itching to punch a hole through something to try to calm himself. The events on Volon were still with them—and now they had confirmation that Rayna was not okay.

After a night of restless tossing and turning, Morgan joined Otho and Lendus in the wardroom around the same table where they and the other officers had eaten breakfast earlier in the morning. While they waited for the captain, Morgan tried to focus his mind on the job. He glanced at Otho, then at Lendus. Neither spoke nor gave any indication that they had knowledge of what the captain would say.

As Choff entered, everyone rose and saluted.

"Be seated." Choff returned the salutes and took his customary chair facing the door. He tossed his hat on the table, then eyed the three officers before speaking. "Gentlemen, this base will be going on full alert tonight."

Morgan drew in a quiet breath. Now his mind was on the job.

"In five days, the emperor and his staff will be arriving for an extended stay."

Morgan, surprised, glanced at Lendus, who raised his eyebrows at the news. Morgan knew that the emperor often traveled to the regional capitals, sometimes for administrative needs or to be on the forefront of a high-profile initiative. Occasionally, he visited a military installation to give a morale-boosting address. But as far as Morgan knew, the emperor had never taken up residence at a military base, the way he did an administrative capital.

"For this visit," Choff continued, "the official purpose is a royal inspection of the fortress and the ships moored here. The crown prince of Alscras will be accompanying the emperor." Choff looked at each man in turn, his left eye squinting. "The real reason is not to leave this room."

Morgan hated secrets, but he loved the privilege of knowing them. Keeping things to himself was not one of his strong suits, though he had improved since coming aboard.

Choff cleared his throat. "Because of heightened tensions with the planet Bexel and military movements along the Gearmlian and Heronian borders—of which I have not been given any details—the emperor has decided to relocate his seat of power here until further notice."

"Whoa," Otho uttered, his rural accent slipping in.

Morgan stared at the captain, waiting for more. *What would* Ocelot's *assignment be?*

Deep-creased wrinkles appeared in the captain's forehead. "I've been told that the emperor feels a space fortress affords him a better command position, given the advanced communication and defense capabilities available. Over the next few days, some of the ships stationed here will be relocated, partly to reduce the population of this space fortress, and partly to reposition the home fleet."

Morgan could feel his palms start to perspire as Choff licked his lips. *Maybe the emperor's only taking a precaution.*

"We will not be departing," Choff said. "*Ocelot* has been selected for royal escort duty during the emperor's stay. His Majesty and his party will have free access to the ship at all times, and we will provide security detail to augment the royal guards. Should an incident break out—highly remote, at this point—*Ocelot* would be deployed for combat duty in defense of the emperor."

Morgan leaned back in his chair and took a deep breath. *So, if anything were to happen,* Ocelot *would be the first to start shooting.*

Choff turned to Otho. "Mr. Ennuk, prepare for firing drills. Start the exercises as soon as the last of the maintenance workers have departed. Run them continuously until further notice."

"Yes, sir," Otho said. "I'll prepare a schedule immediate-ly."

Choff addressed the table. "That's all I have, other than to say that it's imperative that this ship be combat-ready. Are there any questions?"

Morgan shook his head. Otho did likewise.

Choff took his hat and rose from the table. "We have a lot of work to do. Mr. Lendus, recall all personnel back to the ship. I'll need to address the crew." He saluted, and the others followed suit. "Dismissed."

After the captain departed, Morgan told Otho, "I'll catch up with you in a minute, Oggy. I need to talk with Mr. Lendus."

"Yes, Mr. Teggo?" Lendus asked as he and Morgan walked out together into the passageway. "You have a question?"

"I need your opinion, sir, about something we witnessed on Volon."

"Can I read about it in the report?"

Morgan paused, hesitant to spill the whole truth, but he had to level with Lendus. "I didn't put all the details in the report, sir."

Lendus stopped. "Why not? Morgan, you know it's a serious matter if you omit important information."

"Yes, sir, but I wanted to check with you first, and I couldn't reach you last night before I filed it."

Lendus crossed his arms. "All right, but we don't have a lot of time."

"Saltos's projector," Morgan said. "He described it as ripping open contact points between the present and sometime in the past. It had a large display viewer, and when he fired the beam, we were able to see some very strange images in it."

"How strange?"

Morgan paused to recall the details. "Do you remember the ancient stories about the war between Oscanos and Luzomi, and how the planets of Amahl and Sigorum were both destroyed? It looked like that: black toxic clouds, giant shadows, bizarre beings in combat, desolation everywhere." The memory felt surreal, like a bad dream. "Rayna thinks the projector might have tapped into a real, historical event." He stopped and waited, anxious for Lendus's response. "I didn't know who else to ask about this."

Lendus eyed him. "Morgan, you know I take your word on this. But honestly, I don't know what to make of what you're describing." He took a deep breath and put his hand to his chin, deep in thought. "We have more pressing matters, right now. I'll need you to help Schillary run combat drills with the platoon. That's our first priority, and we don't have much time for other concerns. We don't want to make the captain look bad in front of the emperor."

Morgan nodded. *First things first.* "I understand. But what about...?"

"Let me figure out how to approach the captain."

7. The Gathering

Two small, missile-like escort destroyers, their pulse cannons energized and armed, exited hyperspace and began their approach. A bulbous warning-and-control ship followed, the rainbow lights of its domed sensor cluster rotating. Finally, the largest vessel of the group, the sleek royal Starmaster, *Graftinop One*, appeared in a flash of light and banked toward the space fortress.

Colonel Chrystamme, in his formal dress uniform—a black collared shirt and pants, a long silver coat with gold buttons and a chestful of medals, and a black beret—waited near the entrance to a causeway, behind a large transparent airlock, accompanied by Kumatille, Captain Choff, and a detachment of armored guards. Though he tried to exude a calm command presence, Chrystamme definitely felt the excitement of the moment, and he took several long, slow breaths to ease himself.

The destroyers and the WAC ship came into view. While they held position a short distance from the space fortress, *Graftinop One* maneuvered toward the middle of the empty pier. After it made a smooth landing, a large underside bay opened and a short parade of three decorated military vehicles emerged. They rolled down the ship's ramp, leading a fourth vehicle—the emperor's armored sedan—onto the causeway for the short drive to the airlock. When they reached it, the walls of the large airlock closed over the four vehicles, sealing them from the pier. The oversized double doors to the Command Module opened, and the cavalcade drove the short distance into the space fortress, stopping before Chrystamme, Kumatille, and Choff.

Four horn players, in purple-and-orange dress uniforms, stepped onto the balcony of the Command Module and raised their cornicones. Four riflemen joined them and angled their weapons spaceward. A drummer stepped forward, called out, "Honors!" and began a drumroll. The horn players sounded the Imperial fanfare, three extended flourishes. The lead shooter called out, "Raise, aim, fire," and the four riflemen fired a series of three blanks over the heads of the people.

Emperor Otias II, in plain but stately dark blue travel wear, emerged from the sedan, followed by a diminutive middle-aged man in a business suit and the fleet admiral, who, apart from the four-star rank insignia across the front of his hat, was in a plain white uniform. The emperor stood eye to eye with the imposing Chrystamme, his aged, bearded face a sharp contrast to the square-jawed, clean-shaven head of the colonel.

"Welcome to Space Fortress Canellis, Your Majesty." Chrystamme offered a deep bow.

"Thank you, Colonel." The emperor nodded his head to the small, suited man by his side. "May I introduce my chief of staff, Mr. Franklen."

"Welcome, Mr. Franklen." Chrystamme saluted.

"Greetings," Franklin said with a bow. "The administrative staff follows in the next group of vehicles."

Chrystamme reported, "A three-floor complex within the administration tower has been converted to serve as the Imperial

Headquarters."

"Thank you, Colonel." Franklen stepped forward. "The royal guards will inspect the complex. Once they give approval, we will transfer the command structure from *Graftinop One*."

Chrystamme turned to salute the admiral, as Choff did likewise. "And welcome back, sir."

Admiral Kosolf promptly returned the salute. "Gentlemen."

The emperor then raised his arm, beckoning two more people from the sedan. "The crown prince of Alscras, Otias III, and the princess of Alscras, Thericia." Though the prince stood as tall as the emperor, he was much thinner, somewhat baby-faced, and stood with a slightly slouched posture. The princess, several years younger than her brother, stood barely taller than the chief of staff but looked more regal in her sash-accented outfit, ivory gloves, and tiara-accented golden-red hair than the prince did in his plain gray, nondescript suit.

Chrystamme raised an eyebrow, surprised at the presence of the princess. She had not been listed in Kumatille's manifest. Chrystamme knew that the young princess had been serving as the emperor's personal aide for over a year, but with Kumatille already here, he couldn't help but question the wisdom of bringing His Majesty's eighteen-year-old daughter to a military base. Nevertheless, Chrystamme broke off his momentary stare and refocused on the required protocol.

"Welcome." He smiled courteously and bowed. "Allow me to introduce Captain Antos Choff, commander of the cruiser *Ocelot*."

"We aim to serve," Choff said, bowing. "My ship is at your disposal."

"Your service is invaluable, Captain," the emperor said.

Looking to Kumatille, he added, "It's good to see you again, my friend."

Kumatille smiled, his eyes squinting. He bowed so deeply that his spectacles almost fell off.

As everyone returned to their vehicles to begin the parade through the Command Module, Franklen told Kumatille and Chrystamme, "You've done well. We should schedule a briefing with the admiral, once the emperor has settled in."

"Understood." Chrystamme bowed, beaming with pride.

As Dr. Creatoun paced at the foot of the exam bed, Rayna glanced over at Fiona and Petty Officers Tornique and Manion— the three squad leaders in her platoon—waiting by the door. Fiona quietly fiddled with one of the straps on the sleeve of her work fatigues. Tornique stood with arms crossed and a focused stare. Next to him, the six-and-a-half-foot-tall Manion stood still as a statue.

Flipping through the screens of his porta-com, Creatoun grumbled with disapproval. Rayna stifled a sigh, her patience gone. Creatoun lowered the reader and stared at her with his gray-browed but piercing eyes.

"Well, Ensign, the tests have resulted in a lot of data, some useful, some conflicting." He walked over to her bedside. "As far as I can tell, your brain activity has been altered. It's at a very low level, so you're probably not aware of it, but I believe some of your body functions have been adjusted in minute ways that are very difficult to detect."

Rayna shivered at the news. "Which functions?"

Creatoun checked his reader again. "Cellular repair, for one, specifically base excision repair, which appears to have become..." He glanced at the ceiling and inhaled a slow, deep breath. "...a bit...erratic. If I didn't know any better, I'd say it was being...selective...in what it excises." His gaze quickly lowered back to the reader. "Your immune system readings. Your electrochemical panel is changed as well, very minute changes, but the holistic balance of your organ functions are altered. You're in excellent health, but the data shows that your body is fighting *something*, and it's not autoimmune, either."

"Is Ensign Choff in danger?" Fiona asked.

Creatoun laid his porta-com on the bed and rubbed his dimpled chin. "I don't know yet. We need to research the ramifications of these changes to venture anything."

Rayna felt sick to her stomach. Her head reeled—what had happened to her, and why didn't she feel anything unusual?

"What can we do?" Fiona asked.

The porta-com chimed. "Dr. Creatoun, report to Power Junction 3."

Creatoun held Rayna's head in his hands and looked into her eyes and throat. "Bah, somebody probably stubbed his toe on a power wedge. You still don't feel anything unusual? Even a hint of dizziness?"

"Nothing but nerves," Rayna said.

He let go of her and jotted notes on the porta-com. "Let's schedule you for more in-depth labs, finer scanner readings, and some fitness tests to stress your body functions. I'll contact Zuhar medical base on Alscras and see what they can find out, too." He gave her a reassuring smile. "We'll get to the bottom of this. Don't worry." He turned to leave.

"Doctor!" Rayna hopped off the bed. "Do I have to stay here around the clock?"

Creatoun stopped at the door. "I think it's best for now. Don't you?"

"But I feel fine." She approached him. "The inactivity is killing me."

"You obviously can't go back on duty," Creatoun said.

"I know." Rayna lowered her head. "I'll need to speak to the captain about assigning Chief Petty Officer Cutxa as the acting platoon officer." After a pause, she quietly added, "I just want to be able to walk more than three steps."

Creatoun thought for a moment, then picked up his portacom and began entering orders. "Well, as long as you promise not to do anything foolish, I won't confine you."

Rayna smiled. "Thank you, Doctor."

After Creatoun, Tornique, and Manion left, Fiona said, "Don't worry about the platoon. I'll keep everyone sharp and alert until you get back."

"Thanks." Rayna gave Fiona a warm, grateful hug, then sent her back to duty.

As she changed into her purple jumpsuit, Rayna pondered her *suromila*, which she had not been able to find anything about. Jairesse had described it as a connection to the Euranian Ancestors. Did it seem reasonable that these impairments resulted from the temporary blockage? The more she thought about it, the more it made sense to her. Cellular repair and immunology both helped her to stay alive and healthy. If Jairesse had successfully restored the flow to her *suromila*, would these functions eventually return to normal? Or had the damage been done? The more she dwelled on it, the more fear she felt.

Morgan always made her feel better. She longed for the feel of his arms around her and the sound of his voice. He would find a way to reassure her that she would be all right. He always did.

Rayna broke out of her ruminations when Captain Boutah

Jaron, *Pouton*'s gray-haired "space madame," walked in.

"Well, Ms. Choff, how are you feeling?"

Rayna, fastening her belt and reaching for her shoes, smiled at the welcome. Captain Jaron sometimes felt like what Rayna would have wanted in another mother. "The good news is that I'm allowed to leave this bed."

"Excellent." Captain Jaron nodded. "The crew's starting to miss our star blade warrior."

"The bad news is that I get more tests before the doctor decides whether I can return to duty."

The captain reversed a chair and set her imposing frame down. "Now, don't worry. I have complete confidence that Dr. Creatoun will get to the bottom of this. He'll keep you safe."

"I'm not worried." Somehow, the captain's voice always put her at ease. "With your permission, I'd like Chief Petty Officer Cutxa to be the acting platoon officer in my absence."

"Approved," Jaron said. "Perhaps it's just as well. Repairs are complete, and nothing's happening. You're just missing all the talk about *Graftinop One*'s arrival." She chuckled. "Have you ever been this close to the emperor?"

Rayna smiled mischievously. "Princess Thericia and I go back a long way. She used to compete with me over a cute boy. Of course, the princess was far too young, and the boy would never have chosen her over me."

"Right." Jaron winked.

"You didn't know about my secret ties to royalty, did you, Captain?"

They both laughed.

"*Castella* has departed," Jaron continued, "and *Ancora* has taken her place. We're next in line for the depot. Once another ship leaves, we'll take up position to refuel. Then we're off."

Rayna smiled, but deep down she ached at the thought of leaving Morgan again. Who knew how long it would be before they could get together again—and in what condition would she be?

Morgan and Otho joined Schillary on the forward half of the main deck, near the central superstructure. Twelve infantrymen, one of the three squads that comprised the ship's platoon, stood along the starboard turret batteries, lined up in dark blue and white-trimmed drill outfits, with pairs of EE-stick-blades in their hands.

"Now that we've finished target practice, I've asked Mr. Teggo to join us," Schillary said. "You all know he's the best blade combatant in the crew. As security personnel assigned to the emperor and his heirs, you'll be expected to use whichever means are at your disposal to ensure the safety of the Crown and the royal family. That means, in addition to your sidearms, both blades and unarmed close-quarter combat. Understood?"

"Yes, sir!" the infantrymen barked.

Morgan looked to Otho, who nodded. Morgan then stepped before the soldiers, bowed, and said, "*Thu-senwu.*"

The fighters raised their two-foot-long EE-sticks and bowed at attention.

Morgan cleared his throat. "Protecting His Royal Majesty, the emperor, is not just a security assignment. It is a call to forfeit one's life for sovereign and homeland. Mr. Ennuk?" Time for the history lesson, Morgan mused as Otho began speaking.

"The Zahrin discipline was originally created for one purpose," Otho said. "It is not just one of the many styles of martial arts that flourished in the days of the Etolian kings. Master

Zahrin was the personal bodyguard of Vik'kung'auo, the legendary king of Memona and the first governor of the early Etolian Republic. Zahrin delved into the deepest centers of the human being to create the highest order of bodyguards for the king's protection.

"To attain this level of achievement, you must be constant in your focus, and your physical movements must be natural outflows of the internal fire within. Keep this in mind as you conduct your exercises. A single individual can be the most powerful weapon—and the most impenetrable protection—ever created."

Morgan stepped forward. "We'll start with basic warm-up drills. Pair up and assume the first combat position."

"Morgan," Otho said, checking his porta-com, "I'm needed on the bridge. Mr. Lendus must have started the emperor's tour."

"All right." Morgan continued addressing the infantrymen as Otho walked away. "This is a state of mind, a state of inner soul. Two deep breaths, everyone. Clear your *wacth.*"

The soldiers separated into six pairs and held their EE-sticks in a balanced position, ready to step forward or backward at the face-off, with one hand high for blocking and the other low for thrusting.

"*Maruga,*" signaled half of the combatants.

"*Maruga,*" replied their opponents.

Morgan held the moment, then blurted, "Attack!"

Lendus led the emperor, the crown prince, the princess, Franklen, and two royal guards onto the main deck of *Ocelot.* The prince looked about in all directions, taking in the two rows of giant turret batteries that lined the sides of the deck, and the view of Canellis and the brightly lit repair facilities through the transparent ceiling, while the princess took notes on her porta-com. The command superstructure rose high above them. The topside engine pod towered in the rear, dwarfing the wide-eyed prince and princess.

"A truly impressive engine room, Mr. Lendus," the prince said, taking a deep breath. "I've never seen a power plant of such size or scale."

"You've never been aboard a Gearmlian carrier," the emperor chided.

Lendus chuckled. "As I mentioned in the engine room, the main quantadrive pods are exterior of the hull, two pivotable units below, port and starboard, and a fixed unit right here." He laid his hand on the pylon that rose twenty feet from the deck. "*Ocelot* was the first ship to employ the Model-200 topside engine. It's now the standard configuration for all new heavy cruisers.

"Over there," Lendus pointed out to the guests, "you can see members of the ship's platoon, training under the watchful eye of our platoon officer, Ensign Schillary. They'll be assigned to you tomorrow."

"They look much more powerful and efficient than our own guards," the prince said.

"And more dangerous," the princess added. "I'm feeling safer already."

Lendus led them to a stout, gray-haired man standing by the batteries. "Chief Warrant Officer Fotablugen, Your Majesty."

"Fota" motioned toward the gunnery capsules. "On either side of you are twenty Costarking pulser turrets, grouped into ten-unit battery emplacements, each capable of recharging and firing within two seconds at a range of 2.2 light-seconds. The interconnected energizers are below the deck."

Lendus wasn't sure if the young royals or the emperor followed all the technical details, as Fota dispensed the information.

"The ship is armed with ten Externime neutrino torpedo launchers, two each at port, starboard, and aft, and four forward, with four magazines of twelve torpedoes each."

"So, can you battle a carrier?" the prince asked.

Lendus smiled at the question. "We've never tried, Your Highness. I don't know if we ever will. Even though the torpedoes are semi-adjustable in mid-flight and have demonstrated a range of up to 10.5 light-seconds, carriers pack twice our engine thrust and four times our firepower. Maybe two or three cruisers in a coordinated attack could stand a chance."

The prince quietly nodded.

"Thank you, Mr. Fota." Lendus held out his arm. "Now, if you'll follow me, I'll take you up to the command center."

They entered the command superstructure and stopped at a busy corridor, where personnel crisscrossed their way between the main hull and the superstructure. Lendus led everyone to the central circular staircase. "Please watch your head. It's a low ceiling."

They ascended to the Ops deck, where Lendus began a brief overview of the control room that coordinated the operations of the ship. He pointed out the many displays on either side of them and the two rows of control stations—one in front of the other. The forward row had four stations, one currently manned, two unmanned, and a third opened by technicians at work under Lon's supervision. "Here are the engine and environmental relays, long range lookouts, tactical monitors…" Lendus hoped that the "maintenance mess" would not be a turnoff to the emperor. "The Junior Officer of the Deck stands watch over the Ops deck, with a petty officer supporting from the second console," he continued. "Ensign Prowzi is currently on duty." He paused, noticing that the prince had fallen behind while peering curiously over the shoulders of a technician into the maze of circuitry inside an opened station.

"Young prince," the emperor called, directing the prince to rejoin the group.

While they waited, the princess stepped toward the front panorama-pane. Beyond *Pouton*, moored a short distance from *Ocelot* with running lights on, floated the space fortress.

"On both sides of the window are lines of display monitors," Lon said to her. "Some show views of the exterior cameras, some display power graphs, and others are off for maintenance. Along the walls are banks of circuitry and power relays, everything that ties the ship's operations to this command center."

"It's a lot to keep track of," the princess said. "The crew is very impressive."

After completing his overview, Lendus asked the emperor, "Your Majesty, would you like to mount the bridge?"

The emperor broke out into a wide smile. "You ask out of courtesy. Of course, who wouldn't like to stand on the bridge of a cruiser? Please lead the way."

They climbed the steep steps at the rear of the Ops deck to the platform overlooking the control floor. Otho stood on watch, near the ship's log. PO2 Anibe sat at the helm, running checks on the "big wheel." In front of her, overhanging the Ops deck, were the navigation displays of the short-, medium-, and long-range star charts summarizing the ship's position, and the unmanned combat station. To the left and right of the watch deck were the platoon officer's post and the signaling post, where

SCPO Elena was handling a call from the repair yard.

"Mr. Lendus," Otho said, "the yard is reporting that *Pouton* is ready to move to the depot. When *Tagon* departs tomorrow, we'll be next in line for refueling."

"Very good," Lendus said. Turning to the emperor, he said, "It's not spacious, Your Majesty, but do you like the view?"

The emperor chuckled. "The captain's chair is like a throne of its own. Someday, I should consider commissioning a redesign of my ship to something more regal, like this."

"Well done," Morgan told the infantrymen. "Dismissed."

As the squad departed to get cleaned up, Morgan collected the EE-sticks and turned to head back down. He stopped when he saw Schillary escort Rayna onto the deck.

"Thank you, Mr. Schillary," she said, as Schillary followed the infantrymen out.

Morgan threw down the stick-blades, ran to her, and wrapped his arms around her. "What did the doctor say?" Seeing her casual clothing, he asked, "You're still under medical watch?"

Rayna sighed. "I've been released from bed confinement, but I've not been cleared for duty." She looked into his eyes. "The doctor doesn't have any conclusions yet. He said the delicate balance of my body functions are altered. I don't know what that means. Whatever happened to me back on that planet, he can't figure it out."

Morgan tensed, then gave her the most heartfelt, most comforting hug he could. "The doctor will figure it out. What does he want to do?"

"More labs." Rayna sounded disgusted. "Exotic stuff, it sounds like, and fitness tests."

Morgan understood. "He wants to stress your body and see how it reacts. It makes sense. When?"

"Tomorrow." She looked down. "We're moving to the refueling station in twelve hours, and then we'll be departing for who-knows-where. I may not know how I am, even then."

Morgan couldn't help but worry about what Dr. Creatoun might uncover.

"Morgan, I've been thinking."

"What about?"

Rayna smiled and pointed to the stick-blades. "Let's do our own fitness test."

"What? Now?" *Was she crazy?*

"Why wait until tomorrow?" Rayna asked. "If I can fight Saltos, I can certainly do a little sparring against you." She took a deep breath. "If something's going to come out, then let it come out now—while you're still here to watch after me."

Morgan forced a smile. "Like a true warrior." He picked up two pairs of EE-stick-blades, tossed one pair to Rayna, and proceeded to fasten his pair together into one long FF-combo-stick. "All right, I'll try to be careful with you."

"I won't." Rayna energized the scoring sensor on her EE-sticks.

"You're on." With his competitive instinct snapping to life, he powered his FF-combo-stick and bowed. "*Maruga.*"

"*Maruga,*" Rayna replied, bowing.

The stick-blades whipped together and clashed. Rayna thrust with her right stick and blocked with her left, while Morgan alternately thrust and blocked with the two ends of his FF-combo. They separated for an instant, clearing the space between them with a series of defensive swipes, the slicing of the air echoing about the deck. They came back together with a burst of combative power; clangs and crashes sounded, Rayna's stick-blades higher-pitched, Morgan's combo lower.

A small crowd of off-duty onlookers gathered about to watch and cheer.

Morgan swung his FF-combo in a wide arc, forcing Rayna to leap back. Morgan swung again; again, Rayna leaped back. Morgan swung a third time. Rayna whirled her two EE-sticks together to block Morgan's stroke in a cross.

"Very good," Morgan said. "Ooph—"

Rayna kicked Morgan in the stomach, knocking him backward to the ground. He rolled away to avoid Rayna's quick left and right downward jabs. Without warning, he swung his legs inward in a tight arc, wrapped his feet around her legs, and heaved her as hard as he could.

"Oh!" she exclaimed, toppling to the ground.

"Ha!" Morgan thrust his arms up in the air in triumph. "I got the champ down!"

Rayna let her EE-sticks roll out of her hands and turned over on her back, out of breath. Morgan, also remaining on the ground, released his FF-combo and laughed at hearing the round of applause.

"I've never tried that before," Morgan said with a smile. "I didn't hurt you, did I?"

Rayna shook her head. "That's not in any of the moves," she said between breaths.

"Innovation is an important part of the Modern School," Morgan countered, "especially if it works in combat—and it worked on you."

"You're very proud of yourself, aren't you?"

"I've said it before—you're way too traditional."

"And I've said it before: the Zahrin School is fundamentally sounder. One surprise doesn't make one combatant superior to another." Rayna took a deep breath, picked up her EE-sticks and held them out to Morgan. "I still have the better record."

"All right, point conceded. For now." Morgan stood up and took her EE-sticks. He addressed the crowd. "That's all for today." As the onlookers dispersed, he asked Rayna, "Now, how are you feeling?"

Rayna sat up, took Morgan's hand, and pulled herself to her feet. "Winded."

Morgan stared at her. She usually didn't tire that easily.

Seeing his look, Rayna quickly added, "It's all the bed rest, nothing more. Otherwise, I feel fine."

"Are you sure?"

"For the hundredth time, yes."

The PA speaker crackled. "Lieutenant Teggo, report to the Command Module."

Morgan raised his head. "Oh, *turkanaan*! I forgot about the briefing. We've been assigned special detail to the emperor. I guess we're finding out what that's about."

"Well, aren't we the lucky one?" She squeezed him as they shared a quick kiss. "You'd better go. I'll check myself out with Schillary."

Morgan stood his ground. "Are you sure you're okay?"

"Go," she insisted, "before you get into any more trouble with my father!"

Morgan slipped into the Command Module conference room, closed the door behind him, and quietly headed for the remaining open seat, next to Otho and Lon. The captain stood at the front of the room, with Lendus, Admiral Kosolf, and Franklen seated around the table, and the other off-duty *Ocelot* officers crowded around the perimeter.

"Now that we're all here," Captain Choff began in a stern voice.

Morgan tensed at the pointed remark. He thought of apologizing but decided that keeping a quiet, low profile would be best.

"The emperor has sent his chief of staff and Admiral Kosolf to brief us on our upcoming responsibilities," Choff continued. "Mr. Franklen."

Choff took his seat, and Franklen rose to address the room.

"First of all, the emperor wishes to express his gratitude for the service you perform in the course of your normal duties." Franklen offered a smile for a couple seconds. "And for the special assignment you are about to undertake.

"As you know, Eurania has enjoyed a notable period of peace and stability, nearly half a century, and the Central Empire has settled into friendly relations with the Pharrian Republic, the Onglan League, and many neighboring planets. However, the large footprint of the empire affords the member dominions a large degree of regional autonomy, an autonomy which breeds ambitions toward the Imperial government."

Morgan, glancing at Otho and Lon, nodded his head. The Gearmlian Confederation, especially, was large enough—and powerful enough—to secede.

"Prince Fraither of Bexel," Franklen continued, "is one with such an eye toward opposing the emperor. Two other rulers also represent potential challenges. Supreme Dictator Quinn of Heron, as we know, commands a growing collection of territories and outlying colonies bordering Imperial space. And Grand *Primai* Ludzenia has cemented her rule over the Gearmlian Confederation in the last year."

Franklen gazed at the many attentive eyes around the room.

"Given recent developments within the Heronian and Gearmlian military, the emperor has decided to exercise precautionary moves. Admiral Kosolf will provide the details. Lights, please."

The room dimmed, and Admiral Kosolf rose to join Franklen as one of the aides projected a star map of the empire from a porta-com to the wall monitor.

"These positions are based on last year's intelligence sightings of the Heronian and Gearmlian task forces," Kosolf said, pointing at various groupings of ships.

Morgan saw three large task force markers in the upper half of the chart, along the Gearmlian border. To the right, two similar groups were positioned in Heronian space, with other ships situated in the more-distant Heronian colonies bordering the Trak States. Other task forces and ships were located in the lower half of the chart, along the Great Nebula, in the Sestian Republic and the Alscrasian Kingdom.

"You see nothing unusual," Kosolf said. "Each dominion's forces are within its own borders. Next, please."

The chart faded, and a similar but slightly different display appeared. Murmurs grew, spreading through the room.

"These positions are based on last month's sightings. A noticeable portion of the ships are missing from this graphic, indicating that they have either moved, or were on the move, to undetermined locations. Military intelligence is still analyzing the data and does not yet have a consensus theory on where the missing ships are headed."

Morgan counted two Gearmlian task forces and one of

the two Heronian task forces missing.

Franklen spoke again. "Given the backing of the high priest of Kelova, the chancellor of Sestia, and the council of the Onglan League, the emperor is secure in his rule. However, we are uncertain of the true intentions of Prince Fraither, Supreme Dictator Quinn, and Grand *Primai* Ludzenia."

"For this reason," Kosolf said, "we are moving *Pouton* to Alscras and *Castella* to Kelova, both within reasonable proximity to Bexel."

"The emperor," Franklen said, stepping forward as the lights returned, "has decided to remain at this base until the situation clarifies. We are monitoring communications from here, and the emperor's Starmaster has been placed on standby, should the need arise for the emperor to move to a spaceborne position." He paused to look at the *Ocelot* officers.

Morgan looked grimly at Captain Choff and Lendus. Now everybody knew the full picture. He wished his interpretation was wrong, that he was being too worked up, but as he saw it, they were staring at a military threat.

"*Ocelot* will serve as the backup to both the Command Module, while we are here, and *Graftinop One*, should we become spaceborne. You have the capabilities to both monitor the information needed and provide defense, if an incident were to break out." Franklen smiled. "You only lack a degree of basic comfort, which is why you will serve only as backup."

Everybody laughed, momentarily breaking the tension.

"In any event, you will be seeing a lot more of me. One of my staff will remain on board your ship at all times, keeping watch for the emperor." He looked to Choff. "I have given your captain my personal assurance that we will try our best to be unobtrusive."

More chuckles.

"In all seriousness, though, this is a key role in preserving the unity of the empire." Franklen looked around the table. "Since its launch, more than two decades ago, *Ocelot* has set many precedents, from new technology tests to special envoy passages to Pharry and Onglus. This special assignment will outweigh them all."

"Mr. Teggo," Captain Choff called from the head of the room as the meeting ended.

"Oh-oh," Morgan muttered. The rest of the personnel was already filing out, leaving him to face his commanding officer again.

Otho gave Morgan a firm pat on the shoulder, ostensibly for encouragement—or for condolences, Morgan pessimistically mused—before joining Lon and the rest of the exodus.

"Yes, Captain?" Morgan asked as innocently as he could.

Choff waited while Morgan walked up from the back of the room. "The reason for your tardiness, Mr. Teggo?"

Morgan paused and took a slow, deep breath. He hated implicating Rayna, but it seemed there was no way to avoid it. "Sir, I have no excuses. I was with Rayna, and I completely forgot the time."

Choff raised an eyebrow. "You were aboard *Pouton*?"

"No, sir," Morgan said, his tone even. "Rayna was aboard *Ocelot*. She had just been released from medical confinement."

Now Choff paused. "What's her condition?"

"Still undetermined, sir. She's scheduled for further labs and fitness tests."

A look of uncertainty appeared in Choff's eyes. "How did she look to you, Mr. Teggo?"

Morgan could tell that Choff was genuinely concerned. "I was a little surprised at how easily she tired, considering how athletic she normally is. Other than that, she seemed pretty normal to me." He tried to put Choff's mind at ease, but even as he spoke, he also worried about what was happening to Rayna.

"I'll excuse you," Choff said, "this time." He lowered his voice. "If you have any further insights on Rayna's condition, I trust you will...inform me?" Choff's eyes seemed to soften.

Morgan nodded. At least they could agree on how they felt about Rayna's current situation. "Yes, sir, I will do that."

Choff offered a very slight hint of a smile. "Then you're dismissed to return to your duties."

"Thank you, sir." Morgan saluted.

Kumatille weaved his way through the crisscrossing foot and transport traffic, exited the Command Module, and headed down a causeway toward a small complex of unmarked modules. He flipped through his porta-com until he found the screen he needed, looked at the first three structures that stood before him, and moved past them to the door of the fourth module. Hearing voices, he quickly ducked between two of the modules and waited.

"Morgan," one passerby said, "I really need some help with those piece-of-*shat'oq* bosonic torpedoes."

"I know, Oggy," Morgan said. "It's just that I've got my hands full preparing the platoon for royal escort duty. That *turkanaan* Schillary is so *kroking* useless."

Men returning to *Ocelot*, Kumatille recognized. He pressed tight against the wall of the module and listened to their boot steps as beads of sweat dripped down his underarm. He held his breath and listened to the thump of his racing heart. If either man saw him, the whole operation would be blown.

"Well, *any* time you can spare would be great," Oggy said.

"Sure, I'll stop by later," Morgan replied. "Maybe Lon can give you a hand until then..."

After their voices faded away, Kumatille stepped out from the shadows and returned to the fourth module. He looked over his shoulder, saw no one watching, took out two small electronic pieces from his pocket, and snapped them together. Using the tiny device, he unlocked the door, stepped inside, and secured the door behind him.

Inside, he scanned the shelves of machinery until he came to a small, handheld, octagonal device. He brought it down and slid three of the sides open, exposing an oval unit that hung suspended inside. He woke his porta-com and scrolled the text, skimming as he descended. The illustration matched the octagonal device with the sides up. He skimmed the remainder of the text, then closed the porta-com, reached inside the unit, and twisted an oval bulb until it emitted a pulsing purplish glow.

A low, quiet voice spoke through the light.

Kumatille removed his spectacles and watched the silent pulses, mesmerized by the whispers in his head. The voice abruptly stopped, the light dimmed, and Kumatille reflected on the words he had heard. He then returned his spectacles to his face, untwisted the bulb, closed the octagonal unit, and replaced it on the shelf.

Unlatching the door, Kumatille peeked outside, waited until the causeway was deserted, then headed back out.

Far from the alarming developments of the empire, Lord Walmsley smiled at the approaching Admiral Graft Kearn.

Always a meticulous dresser, the admiral wore the sharp blue-and-green-trimmed uniform of the Greyban Corps with the red stars of his rank lined up across his left breast pocket. He walked up to Walmsley and snapped his salute across the brim of his hat. Kearn had inherited command of the "fleet" from his father, Admiral Flan Kearn, in a rather smooth transition, some fifteen years ago, and he had proved as able an organizer as his father had been.

Walmsley returned the salute as best he could, given his age.

Together, they strolled through Hangar 1, where grease-covered mechanics, technicians in static-free coveralls, and muscular equipment movers worked on preparations for the upcoming trip, Kearn mindful to keep the pace slow as Walmsley walked with his cane.

"What's the count?" Walmsley asked.

"A little over three hundred men and women," Kearn said, "Five or six ships, a nice task force."

Walmsley paused to survey the formation parked before him. Hangar 1 housed five of the old cigar-shaped combat destroyers, seventeen of the smaller wedge-shaped corvettes, and Walmsley's own flagship, the heavy cruiser *Trion*. Next door, Hangar 2 held Commodore Sikka's frigates. During the Galactic Revolutions, the frigates, armed from bow to stern with every weapon the Corps possessed, had served as the workhorses of the fleet. Farther down the valley, Hangars 3 and 4 held three troop carriers, more of Commodore Rennious's destroyers, and an assortment of atmospheric craft.

Never needed for combat since leaving the empire, Admiral Kearn (first the father, then the son) nevertheless kept the ships in pristine condition with ongoing maintenance, continuing education, and regular training missions that sometimes ventured as far as the edge of the Outer Territories.

Walmsley was glad. Though Chairman Osterand, General Mapooly, and the other aggressors of the Galactic Revolutions were long gone, Wichloc was situated in the region between the Onglan League and the Fembournian star cluster, home of the Saolian Empire and other past expansionist powers who had ventured into Eurania on campaigns of conquest. Walmsley always felt it best to be ready for the next crisis, should one ever materialize.

"My lord," Kearn said, "I must admit that I'm as excited as a young farmer's spring hokhel about this voyage."

They laughed together.

"What do you remember about the empire, sir?"

Walmsley thought for only an instant. "Things have changed since those days." He reminisced for a moment longer. "The Central Empire hadn't formed yet when we left. None of the founding agreements had been signed." He paused to catch his breath, while Kearn grabbed a stool for Walmsley.

"Thank you." Walmsley sat, exhaled, and regained his stamina. "I remember attending many heated discussions among the representatives of the major planets. Bexel, Alscras, Pharry, and Sestia supported Monseigneur Dhavail's advocacy for a Grand Alliance. The Gearmlian planets—Breame, Kearo, Gassil, and the others—had felt self-sufficient and in no need for another layer of government, so they quickly re-formed their old confederation. Onglus, always an isolationist, attracted other like-minded planets, and the Trak systems had already agreed to remain separate and independent. I believe Heron had embarked on its own course of colonial expansion."

Kearn shook his head. "What a mess. It's amazing that

the empire formed at all."

"More so that it has stayed together, at peace, ever since," Walmsley said. "I understand that a key breakthrough in its initial formation was the agreement that the emperor would be elected by the Imperial Assembly, with the rulers of the core worlds being the eligible candidates. The assembly, equal in power to the emperor, is permanently on Kelova, while the emperor's court is relocatable, as people and situations change."

"So the Central Empire is not fashioned as closely to the ancient Etolian empire as I had thought?" Kearn asked.

"No, it is the result of diplomacy, not conquest." Walmsley paused to reflect. "A certain degree of tension persisted between the core worlds when I left. I suspect the real power still rests with the rulers of the core dominions. The continued relevance of the Imperial government all these decades has been a testament to the emperor's skills."

"Well, I am still looking forward to seeing it," Kearn said.

Walmsley nodded. Remembering the emotional volatility of the Euranian leaders of those days, he could only hope that attitudes and behaviors had changed for the better over the decades. As much as he tried to sound enthusiastic, he was not looking forward to seeing it.

Captain Pavon, the young commander of *Trion*, approached. He removed his hat, saluted, and reported, "Sir, the modifications are completed."

Walmsley smiled. The "modifications" were an assemblage of medical monitors being installed by Searus, his affectionate but overprotective nurse. "How soon, Captain?"

"We'll be ready for departure by tonight."

A dark-skinned, full-figured woman with short green hair, ear and nose studs, and light-blue work clothes ambled down the ramp from *Trion*, wiping her hands on a towel as she walked.

Walmsley chuckled with affection toward the woman. "I might have guessed you'd be inside."

Searus laughed, but with a touch of sarcasm. "My lord, you know how I feel about this trip."

"Yes, my dear Searus."

"Artificial life support systems are not the same as being on a real planet." Searus began her speech, waving her arms left and right. "Artificial gravity, artificial heat and light, recirculated air, recirculated water…"

"Yes, of course." Walmsley found her tirade charming.

"My lord," she said earnestly, "you must be mindful of your health. A voyage of this length will wear on you."

"Yes, I know."

"And it's been so long since you've been in deep space." She looked up into his eyes.

Walmsley nodded in understanding. She was excitable, but always dear to him like a surrogate daughter. "Searus, I owe the high priest a debt of gratitude. Our friendship was the outgrowth of fighting side by side during the most devastating war in human history." He saw in her eyes that she understood. "I made a promise to him, and I'll need your help to keep it."

Searus sighed and muttered, "I'm a sentimental fool."

"And I'll go get some rest before liftoff," Walmsley offered.

Q'toz plunged deeper and deeper into the dust and gasses of the Great Nebula, not far behind the rest of the convoy. Admiral Zerah stood on the bridge, silent, the tension of the situation weighing on him. General Mapooly wandered throughout the ship like an insect inhabiting its symbiotic host, ready to strike at anything that offered resistance.

The promise of riches dangled before the men, but Admiral Zerah hated the uneasiness. Everybody on board knew who General Mapooly was, but few believed that this was really the same figure from history, resurrected.

After several days of travel through the folds and layers of the nebula—days filled with hushed murmurs among the crew —the planet Yeros appeared, an extensive salvage complex sprawled on its burnt-orange, dust-covered surface. Captain Bemone ordered the magnification on the monitor to maximum, and a motley collection of spacecraft—two dozen ships of varying shapes and sizes—appeared among a near-random layout of uncovered enclosures and boxy, plume-spewing buildings. Two of the ships, much larger than *Q'toz*, resembled retired carriers. Some looked heavily armed, with rows of turrets protruding from their hulls. One had a distinctive tusk-lined wovren's head on its bow. Another had an array of yellow-and-red fins protruding from its topside, like spikes running along the back of an animal. A third sported turret arrays that extended left and right from the hull, like wings. Isaalt began running queries on the facility in the ship's computer records. Before he finished, General Mapooly stepped onto the bridge.

"Some of these ships are old Belaanian warcraft," Mapooly stated, "the remnants of my former Grand Fleet, the pride and power of Belaan. Once numbering over a hundred ships, we swept across Eurania, seizing control of every planet we landed on. When we lost the war, most of the ships were destroyed in battle, but this small group managed to flee to the safety of the nebula. In this remote location, the crews abandoned the ships and disappeared into the chaos that reigned over Eurania, with the hope that, one day, we could return here to reorganize and rise up. These ships remain, but over time, those men were all lost."

Zerah stared at Mapooly, still trying to determine who, or what, was speaking to him.

"But with the addition of your weapons-bearing armada," Mapooly said, "and with the multitude that is under your command, the day of my return has arrived. Begin landing operations at once, Admiral."

Once on the dust-whipped surface of Yeros, Admiral Zerah and his men headed straight into the cavernous warehouse, where representatives of each ship in the transport convoy gathered among the fifty-foot-tall storage towers that held scrap metal and pulled parts.

As he watched the people gather—some below the harsh white work lights, others in the shadows of the storage towers—he felt as if a prickly-legged giant insectoid crawled on his back, its pinchers poised to jab without warning. In reality, it was General Mapooly, whose rodent helmet rose prominently above the caps of black-clad *Q'toz* crewmen.

Admiral Zerah and Captain Bemone stood at the head of a crowd that included many unfamiliar faces—smugglers nursing black eyes, pirates with prosthetic limbs, outlaws sporting tattoos and scars, and assorted strangers from other vessels currently parked at Yeros. General Mapooly walked past Zerah and mounted a stack of crates to address the people of the convoy. He stood above the aim of the work lights, a silhouette towering over the crowd. Zerah spied a midnight-blue patch that rose from Mapooly's back. It seemed to move ever so slightly, every now and then.

"Come to me," Mapooly called out, "all who toil amongst

the stars. You have been abandoned on this godforsaken outpost of humanity, but I have come to relieve you of your misery."

The crowd hushed, all eyes wide, staring at the unlit figure speaking before them.

"How long have you waited in the midst of these blinding dust storms for your next destination? How far across the void of space are your superiors? How much longer can you hold out, waiting for faint whisperings from your so-called patrons?"

Zerah scanned the crowd, wondering if his late father had heard similar words from this man half a century ago. He thought of his own situation, commanding the convoy, and realized that he could have made similar recruitment efforts over the years.

"We stand at the forefront of a new revolution," Mapooly bellowed, his arms raised, "and you can stand with me, ready to reap the rewards of a return to glory. Come to me, all who seek a greater purpose in life. Your calling awaits you.

"I welcome all of you to the Grand Army of the People's Revolution. Together, we will restore the power and prestige of the Euranian people to what it once was. Together, we will mount the steps of the Imperial palace; together, we will toll the bells of the holy temples."

A low murmur rippled through the crowd as faces turned to peer at one another.

"All the people will gather, and we will relight the beacon of the Etolian empire. Then we—you—shall enjoy the fruits of our labor." Mapooly leaned into the light and flashed a snide, sneering smile, his fingers pointing at the people in a sweeping arc. "Your scavenger days are at an end," he shouted at the top of his lungs. "Years of scrounging for crumbs, a lifetime of waste and torment. Now is your moment to claim what is rightfully yours."

He spread his arms wide. "I claim more—the leadership of a new, revolutionary Euranian order. A new Etolian empire. Who will join me in our quest for legitimacy and restoration?"

Zerah and Bemone looked about. Little by little, voices began shouting all around them.

"I'll join," several shouted.

"I'm in," others yelled. "Me too!"

Zerah saw a contingent in the back waving their hands as they shouted, "We will follow you!"

Nearby, Zerah saw Shutha Zu, the pointy-nosed executive of the box carrier *Kiku*, with whom General Mapooly had briefly spoken in private earlier. What special role had Zu been given?

Mapooly looked down at Zerah. "Admiral?"

The chants of "We will follow you" had grown deafening, mixed in with shouts of "We will claim the Crown" and "We will prevail."

Captain Bemone whispered to Zerah, "Be careful, sir."

"Admiral," Mapooly repeated. "Join us, lead us to victory!"

Unsure, Zerah looked around at the multitudes who manned his armada. The outpouring of support for this specter was overwhelming. His men no longer followed him, Zerah realized. Only Mapooly—or whatever he truly was.

Had his father been in this same situation? What could one man do in the face of this mob?

Zerah took a long, deep breath and nodded. "Yes." He turned to address the crowd, his fist raised high. If he didn't claim his due, he would be left behind in this interstellar wasteland. "Yes! We will be victorious."

Mapooly, his eyes narrowing, smiled.

Zerah shrank back into the crowd, a feeling of uselessness gnawing at him. This "admiral" was a follower, not a leader.

Once the gathering concluded, Bemone dismissed his men to return to *Q'toz*, while Zerah waited and watched. Mapooly descended the crates, a crack of a smile showing on his darkened lips.

"Admiral," Mapooly said in a low tone, "I shall transfer to *Bakiraaqu*, my former flagship."

Zerah paused. Who would man the flagship? Recruits from the other ships not already with the convoy? Zerah obediently bowed. "Yes, sir."

Mapooly turned and walked away. "Captain Zu, I will now inspect your recruits."

Zerah stiffened. *Captain* Zu? Captain…of *Bakiraaqu*? He and Zu made eye contact. The young "captain" smiled. Zerah stared in silence as Captain Zu followed General Mapooly away.

Lord Walmsley awoke, his silk sleepwear drenched in a cold sweat, his heart pounding like a rapid-fire pulse cannon. He looked about, unsure for a moment where he was. Outside his cabin window, the textured folds of hyperspace whisked by, images of stars streaking into blurs.

Not much longer, Walmsley realized. After journeying for days from the far reaches of the Onglan League to the vast interior of Eurania, *Trion* and its small convoy had gained passage through Space Fortress E and was now traveling through Imperial space.

He took a deep breath to clear his mind.

A knock sounded at the door. "My lord?" It was Searus. "Is everything all right?"

Walmsley relaxed. Turning up the light, he said, "Come in, please."

Searus rushed in, wrapped in her robe and with a concerned look on her face. "My lord, your readings triggered an alert. Do you feel anything?"

Walmsley scanned the room. A favorite electro-painting of the forests of Wichloc hung on the wall. Two floor-standing indoor plants, one with star-like orange blossoms, the other with silky white leaves, were in the corners. His unfinished slice of cremeberry pie still sat on the table. Walmsley took a deep breath and shook his head. "It was just a bad dream, nothing more."

The chime sounded. "Lord Walmsley?" It was Admiral Kearn on the speaker.

"Yes, Admiral?" Walmsley asked.

"My lord, we are approaching Kelova. We'll be reentering normal space within the hour."

Walmsley paused a moment to gather his thoughts. "Inform me when we're ready to contact Space Control. We need to arrange an audience with the high priest."

"Yes, sir."

After switching the speaker off, Walmsley reached for his glass of water, his hand still shaking.

Searus quickly brought the glass over for him. After he took a sip, she sat down in the small bedside chair and asked, "Tell me about the dream."

Walmsley remembered a wave of coldness, a dank, rhythmic fluttering that radiated out from somewhere in the distant void of space. Kelova? No, it was extremely distant, from an area of pitch blackness, devoid of starlight or of life.

"My lord?"

Walmsley put the glass down and rubbed his cheeks with his fingertips.

Searus gazed at her digi-com. When Walmsley gave her a

look of curiosity, she showed him the readings of his vital signs, which were trending back toward normal.

"Maybe it was just nerves about our arrival," he began. "It's been so long since I left." He knew he had to tell somebody. If not Searus, then who? "It felt like something lying in wait for us," he whispered. "It was formless, shapeless, something dormant, but now awakening."

8. Secrets

A man in black, arriving at the Command Module, stepped off the one-man launch, weaved his way through the crisscrossing traffic, and headed down a causeway toward a small complex of unmarked modules. He flipped through his porta-com until he found the page he needed. He looked at the first three structures that stood before him, then moved past them until he stood before the door of the fourth module. He looked over his shoulder. No one watching. He took two small electronic pieces out of his pocket, snapped them together and, using the device to unlock the door, stepped inside, securing the door behind him.

The person in black went by the name Zukaaran, which meant "Phantom" in the ancient Etolian language.

Zukaaran walked along the shelves of machinery until he came to a small cylindrical device. He took the device off the shelf and unscrewed the top to reveal a small bulb. He then twisted the bulb until a dim green light illuminated. Setting the cylinder down on an open area of the floor, he backed away. The light began to blink, slowly at first, then faster, until it became a rapid pulse. He sank to his knees, lowered his head, closed his eyes, and allowed himself to be bathed in the waves of green light.

"Speak to me, my lord," he hissed, his jagged incisors inflicting a pronounced lisp.

As a low, quiet voice whispered through the light, Zukaaran extended his hand toward a shadowy being—a mysterious primeval entity known as Kinossah, the cosmic giant—that stepped out from the stars of the cosmos. The *Wilde'prim'ordia* reached into the folds of its robe, withdrew a small circular item, dropped it into Zukaaran's hand, and departed, disappearing into the luminous, impersonal energy of deep space.

When the voice ceased speaking and the light faded away, Zukaaran opened his eyes and gazed at the small golden disc resting in his hand. It felt warm, and he detected a faint pulse from it.

It was alive now, and events were in motion.

He stood, took a small star-shaped holder from his pocket, and snapped the disc into it. He then produced a chain from his other pocket and attached it to the star medallion.

"All power and glory to the Almighty Lord," he whispered. "Come and claim your crown."

Kumatille put down his copy of the *Galactic Times* to take a slurp of his noodle soup. The food tasted mediocre, but it helped with his hunger pangs. The featured contents of the periodical included an analysis of a hypothetical Imperial election, real-time widgets of the many financial exchanges throughout the empire, and the latest exotic fashions from the Outer Territories. Around him, other diners conversed, laughed, ate, and complained about the poor service. Over his head, cages housed the customers' pets. A few received occasional crumbs from their masters. He glanced at the clock on the wall. It was almost time.

A black-sleeved hand pulled out the chair across from

him. "May I join you, Mr. Kumatille?"

Kumatille downed his last bite, wiped his mouth with his napkin, and looked at Zukaaran, now seated with snakelike fangs protruding. Kumatille pushed a small bowl of nuts over. "For you."

Zukaaran stared at the nuts.

Kumatille sighed, tossed a single coin on the table, and took his jacket. They rose to their feet, and Kumatille followed Zukaaran to a small, unmarked door in the rear. Only special guests knew about this hidden room in the back, or that the owner of the diner was an underground sympathizer.

Once inside, Kumatille watched as Zukaaran, after locking the door, brought forth a small green light from his pocket.

"Kneel, Mr. Kumatille."

Kumatille obediently fell to his knees. Zukaaran brought the light directly under Kumatille's face. It radiated slow, steady waves of dim green light. Kumatille closed his eyes and let the warmth of the light soak into him. Minutes passed. Kumatille's body relaxed; he eased into a slight smile.

"For you, Mr. Kumatille: the gift of the Almighty."

Kumatille opened his eyes.

Zukaaran held the light steady with one hand, reached into his pocket with the other, and brought out the chain with the gold star medallion.

Kumatille gazed at the medallion, tears forming in his eyes. He reached out with his hands cupped. When the star touched his hands, they closed and held the medallion tight. A tear rolled down his cheek. "I am not worthy," he whispered.

"You have been made worthy."

Kumatille bowed his head. With one hand, Zukaaran draped the chain about Kumatille's neck, then he withdrew the light and stepped back. The golden light began to emit its own glow, bathing Kumatille's head and chest in a bright rainbow.

"Rise, Mr. Kumatille."

Kumatille raised his head and rose to his feet. The glow from the star settled down to a small light confined within the medallion itself. He put his jacket on and closed it over the medallion, the light disappearing beneath the dark covers, hidden from sight.

Morgan ran up the steps to the bridge. Otho, the Officer of the Deck, supervised a firing drill with Schillary from the combat station. Anibe manned the helm. On the Ops deck, Lon and several off-duty technicians helped the duty personnel test the upgraded control stations.

Lendus, conferring with Elena, caught Morgan's attention with a wave. Morgan hoped that this would finally be about his question regarding the Volon images.

"*Tagon* has completed refueling and is ready for departure," Elena reported. "We're next in line."

Lendus turned to Otho. "Prepare the ship for departure."

"Energize the environmental systems," Otho called down to Lon. "Signal all decks to prepare for the switchover."

Morgan stepped forward. "Lieutenant Teggo, reporting as ordered, sir."

Lendus turned to Morgan. "Let's talk in private." He led Morgan to the rear of the bridge, away from the others. "I had a brief discussion with the captain about your report. He has questions for you."

Morgan's anxiety surged.

"I think this would be a good opportunity for you to inform the captain of the images you saw."

Morgan's jaw sagged. "Just like that? Sir, he's going to think I'm crazy."

The lights blinked as the ship switched from the shipyard power grid to its onboard power plant.

"Switchover complete," Lon reported.

Lendus took a quick glance around the bridge before continuing. His tone was calm and steady. "We picked up a report from Alscras. Intelligence has finished the preliminary analysis of the telemetry your craft sent out. *Ancora* is being ordered to Volon to help a research team conduct an investigation."

The news encouraged Morgan. Something was being set in motion in response to what had happened to him and Rayna.

"The mission will need all the information that's available," Lendus said, "regardless of how crazy it might seem. Just answer his questions and tell the truth as you saw it. I'll support you."

Morgan nodded, taking a deep breath to prepare himself. *Here we go.*

As they descended the bridge, Lendus said to Otho, "Contact me when we're ready to push off."

They exited the command superstructure and stepped onto the empty main deck, where the captain was stretching his legs and loosening his arms with a brisk walk under the starlight. Lendus motioned to pick up the pace, and they jogged to catch up. The captain saw them but continued with his lap as they joined alongside.

"Keeping in shape, gentlemen?" the captain remarked. "Mr. Teggo, I've read your report. Nowhere in there do you offer an interpretation of what you witnessed."

Morgan pursed his lips. He had discreetly stuck to reporting just the facts, to avoid venturing into wild speculation about myths and legends. "Sir, I am…uncertain about what it meant."

"Any theories at all, Mr. Teggo?"

Morgan hesitated. The captain was giving him an opening with which to enter the whole mythical subject matter, but Morgan still wasn't sure if he wanted to sound that crazy.

"Mr. Teggo informs me that he has additional information on the particle beam projector," Lendus said. "Information to pass to *Ancora*, possibly worth pursuing on their upcoming mission."

Succinct and to the point, Morgan thought. He wished he could be as sure as Lendus sounded. "Possibly, sir."

Choff stopped. "What is it, Mr. Teggo?"

Morgan glanced to Lendus, who nodded. "As the machine shot the particle beam out into space, strange images appeared on a large viewing screen—scenes resembling the mythical war between the planets of Amahl and Sigorum." He paused to gauge Choff's reaction.

"Describe the images, Mr. Teggo."

Morgan recalled the surrealistic, nightmarish scenes. "Destructive beams and fire raining down from black rolling clouds, wreaking havoc on the metropolises on the surface. Blood everywhere. Death by the thousands. Bizarre beasts battling in the skies and on the ground, similar to Vinot's painting, *War of the Gods*." He stopped. Did the captain think he was off his rocker?

Choff squinted his left eye at Morgan, then turned to Lendus.

Lendus stood firm. "Mr. Teggo reported the same to me, that that was what he witnessed. I have no reason to doubt his word."

Choff snorted and turned back to Morgan. "How do you

know it wasn't a fake that Saltos had created and loaded into the viewer?"

Morgan considered sharing Rayna's viewpoint and feelings but, given the captain's apparent initial disbelief, decided against implicating her with him. "I agree, we don't know exactly what that machine was doing, but that was what I saw." He looked Choff in the eye.

Choff asked, "Opinion, Mr. Lendus?"

Lendus crossed his arms. "Clearly, that machine was doing something. I don't know if we'll understand much more until *Ancora* begins researching."

Choff looked down, lost in thought.

Unsure of where the conversation was headed, Morgan waited in silence.

Choff then looked up and eyed Morgan. "Mr. Teggo, I'm not sure what to make of what you're saying. I don't believe for a moment that you actually saw footage of gods and monsters from some mythical age."

Morgan tried to sort his thoughts, but he couldn't settle on the best way to answer him.

Choff blew out his breath. "All right, I'll pass this to *Ancora*'s captain and let him decide whether to pursue it further. There are more urgent matters for you, Mr. Teggo."

"Yes, sir?"

Choff scowled. "Mr. Ennuk has fallen behind on his work with the torpedoes. I need you to help him get back on schedule. We need progress, Mr. Teggo."

"And the platoon?"

"Mr. Schillary can handle the duty roster without your assistance."

Morgan tried his best to hide his dismay. The least he

could say was that Schillary was a lightweight, only good for routine tasks. For actual combat, though, he was nowhere near the fighter Morgan or Otho were. "Yes, sir."

"You're dismissed, gentlemen, and I'll continue with my exercise." Choff turned and walked away, leaving Morgan and Lendus behind.

"Maybe he didn't think I was all that crazy," Morgan said.

Lendus chuckled. "The captain is pragmatic. Your information will go to the *Ancora* team. That's what matters at this point. Now, I think you have some important work to attend to."

"Yes, sir. Thank you." Relieved, Morgan headed back inside. He first stopped by the officers' barracks to inform Schillary of his reassignment. Then he moved on to the lower decks.

As he entered the torpedo room, ducking his head to avoid a three-prong loader claw that was repositioning itself along the ceiling, he saw an agitated Otho issuing atypically terse orders over the monitor, one to crewman Kothol to retrieve a list of spare parts, another to Specialists Branke and Curob to recalibrate the launchers under Fota's supervision. Seeing Morgan, Otho muttered, "*Krok!* We almost had a backfire."

"What can I do to help?" Morgan hadn't seen his normally laconic friend unleash such a lengthy stream of expletive-laced orders before.

Otho heaved a sigh. "We have to *kroking* start all over. New torpedo, new launch codes. Can you help Fota ride on these idiots while I coordinate the other combat stations from up here?"

"Sure thing," Morgan said. "Don't worry, I'll get this going."

"And make sure those *turkanaans* don't arm the stupid thing again!"

After the monitor went dark, Morgan turned to Fota. "What seems to be the issue?"

Fota led Morgan away from the technicians and spoke in a low voice. "The men are doing everything they can, sir. It's just that we don't have any experience with this type of technology."

Morgan considered Fota's explanation. "Do the best you can. Double- and triple-check everything after each step. I'll talk with Mr. Ennuk when I get a chance."

Deep in the heart of the empire, Lord Walmsley pushed himself onto the command platform with his cane, joining Admiral Kearn high above *Trion*'s bridge. Goosebumps ran up and down his spine. Ignoring the scores of personnel, graphic displays, and activity all about him, he focused on the center of the oversized wraparound viewer that covered three walls of the bridge, and the enlarging image of the blue-green globe.

"It's been a long time." Walmsley reminisced back to the memories of half a century ago. All the bodies, all the body parts. All the blood, all the blackened skies blanketing the great metropolises of Eurania. War-torn devastation on every world, followed by endless summit meetings amidst reconstruction. Monsters, then men.

"I've never stepped foot in the Imperial capital," Kearn said.

"The settlement is only a few hundred years old, from what I remember," Walmsley said. "During the Saolian invasion, the high priest and the monks of the Wiene temple relocated to this quiet planet and went underground, building up a small fighting force. When the Saolies eventually withdrew, the army of the high priest became the sole unifying force in Eurania."

Walmsley paused, realizing for perhaps the first time the immense power of the old priesthood. He wondered what he would find when he arrived at the temple.

"From here sprang the reseeding of the ancient temples," he continued. "The high priest called the rulers of the five planets together to the Grand Assembly, the forerunner of today's empire."

Walmsley watched an extensive network of spacedocks emerge in orbit. He remembered that the planet was remarkably lush, and surprisingly sparse in population for an interstellar capital. From this altitude, the terrain looked green, but he was sure he would find a half century of development and modernization when he reached the surface.

Captain Pavon mounted the platform, saluted, and reported, "We've received clearance to dock."

"Proceed," Kearn ordered. "Please excuse me, my lord, while I monitor the docking."

As Kearn and Pavon dismounted the command platform, Walmsley's mind turned to the upcoming meeting with High Priest Merician XVI and the arrangements for the burial service.

Rayna stood on *Pouton*'s main deck, between two of the turret placements, deep in thought. She watched the dock workers direct the operator of the two massive fuel lines—one for liquified isolite, the other for tri-oxium gas. The operator brought the giant serpentine hoses from the depot station over to *Pouton*'s hull. Separate, either of the two fuels could power a small ship to near lightspeed. Combined, the disparate compounds formed an explosive mixture able to send *Pouton* into hyperspace. Or, should the reactor overheat, into oblivion. She wasn't an engineer, but what little she understood reminded her of her father and Morgan. Separately, they were two powerful personalities; combined, they could team for greatness—or for mutual destruction.

Rayna sighed. She admired her father and what he stood for. But his lack of regard for Morgan gave her heartache. The product of a rough, street-oriented upbringing, one without a proper family education, Morgan didn't fit the mold that the captain expected for a future son-in-law. Morgan conducted himself too often with an action-before-thinking tendency that her father disapproved of. The events that transpired on Volon, and her father's reaction, were no exception. Bottom line, the captain didn't feel Morgan deserved his only daughter.

Rayna only cared that Morgan's deeds always followed a good heart, with only honorable intentions toward her. She always remembered the time, early in their courtship, when he hustled her off to an available doctor to check into what turned out to be a harmless stomach virus. She knew he thought the world of her; if needed, she could do enough thinking for both of them. He had already progressed well in tempering his impulsiveness during his time on board *Ocelot,* something her father had noted in his recent review of Morgan's performance. If only her father could see more of what she saw in Morgan, she would be satisfied.

Now, she had the issue of her own well-being to deal with. She had never felt as unnerved as she felt now, with the strange readings that Dr. Creatoun still struggled to interpret. Rayna didn't think she was scared. It had been weeks, and she still felt fine. But she never did well with down time; now, all she had was down time, too much of it, and too much to think about.

Tagon idled nearby with the dock moorings withdrawn,

waiting for clearance to depart. Rayna looked over at Canellis, where *Ocelot* was the only remaining cruiser. Soon, it would be alongside again, taking *Tagon*'s place. Rayna thought of Morgan, smiled, and walked toward the gangway back to the space fortress.

After signing off, she headed for Soxos, a small trading shop she had discovered a few days earlier. Away from the Commons, Soxos offered an impressive collection of souvenir items from the Outer Territories. Though its wares were chaotically piled high on overcrowded shelves and poorly presented, it was a great place to find a unique spur-of-the-moment gift for Morgan when he arrived.

She stopped when she approached the shop's entrance. Two armored royal guards, in black-and-scarlet uniforms and small but menacing sidearms, blocked the oversized tiki mouth that formed the doorway.

Rayna walked up to the guards, smiled to them, and asked, "Is there a problem?"

"No problem," one of the guards said. "The princess is shopping inside."

"Oh," Rayna said with a nod. "I'll wait."

Standing before the two guards, Rayna could peer between them to get a glimpse of Princess Thericia, dressed in a simple, light-blue suit and long ivory gloves, browsing through some of the less cluttered shelves.

Despite her joking with Captain Jaron, Rayna had never been this close to royalty before. She wondered if the princess signed autographs. That would make a wonderful souvenir that she and Morgan could share. But what could she ask the princess to sign? Rayna's pockets were empty. The only thing she had was her skiloblade and its sheath. One side of the sheath was soft and flexible, the other side seemed solid enough to write on.

When she noticed the guards looking at her handling the blade, she asked them, "Do you think the princess would sign my sheath?" She offered them the skiloblade.

At that moment, the guards snapped to attention as the princess appeared at the door, a small package in her hand.

"Hello," she said to Rayna, who stood with her sheath in one hand and the skiloblade in the other.

"Hold!" the two guards said in unison, their guns drawn. "Step away and hand over the dagger."

Rayna, taken aback at being put at gunpoint by the guards, handed them the skiloblade. "Sir, I'm the platoon officer on *Pouton*, and I offered you my skiloblade."

"You are out of uniform." The security guard motioned to a spot along the wall of a neighboring store, about fifteen feet away. "Step over there, please. Now."

Rayna slowly backed away, embarrassed and confused by the guards' treatment.

"Your Highness." A short balding man appeared on the scene. He squeezed between the two guards and walked straight up to the princess, undeterred. "A moment, if you please."

"Yes, Mr. Kumatille?" the princess asked.

Rayna paused at a portent that rose up from within her. She did not know who Mr. Kumatille was, but she immediately sensed something wrong with him. She stared at him, studying the man. There was nothing in his walk or his appearance that seemed sinister or threatening. But the feeling was unmistakable—he reminded her of Saltos.

"Your Highness," he continued, "the emperor requests you to join him and the prince at the Imperial Headquarters. Please come with me."

"Of course," the princess said.

An alarming urgency erupted from within Rayna. Unsure of what else to do, she stepped forward, her empty sheath in her hand, and interrupted the princess. "Your Highness, I am Ensign Rayna Choff, platoon officer of *Pouton*. May I speak with you? Before you depart?" When the princess hesitated, Rayna added, "I am unarmed, as you can see." She motioned to the guards, who still held her skiloblade.

"Your Highness," Kumatille urged, "the matter with your father is urgent."

"Is he all right?" the princess asked.

"He's fine, but he needs to speak with both of you. In person."

"Just a very brief moment," Rayna pressed. "It's about your personal safety."

Princess Thericia froze and looked at Rayna. "What about my safety?"

Finally! With nothing more than a hunch to go on and the weight of significant consequences looming over her head if she turned out to be wrong, Rayna pointed toward Kumatille and asked, "Sir, what are you wearing under your jacket?"

Kumatille raised his eyebrows. "I beg your pardon, Ensign?" He sounded insulted.

Rayna took a deep breath but kept her voice authoritative. "Sir, please remove your jacket."

Kumatille crossed his arms. "I will not." He looked at the guards. "What is the meaning of this?"

"Ensign, what are you suspecting?" the princess asked.

"Your Highness, this is ridiculous," Kumatille ranted as he threw his hands up. "Your father—*the emperor*—needs to confer with you. Immediately."

The princess kept her eyes on Rayna, but she addressed Kumatille. "Mr. Kumatille, perhaps you should go ahead and open your jacket. And then we can be off."

"Your Highness, this is an invasion of privacy." He jabbed his finger at Rayna. "What reasonable suspicion can she point to? We are a people of laws, not personal power."

"Mr. Kumatille," the princess said quietly. "Please, let's settle this and be done with it."

"We are very late." Kumatille turned his nose and walked away. "I'll report to the emperor before any more time is lost. I suggest you do the same." He charged away, down the walkway, and rounded the corner toward the Command Module.

This was not how Rayna had wanted the situation to play out. Now, she didn't know how to address the young but potentially powerful princess. "I'm very sorry, Your Highness."

The princess seemed deeply troubled, her eyes narrowing. She stepped around Rayna, maintaining a discreet distance, and looked her over. When she returned to the two guards, she held out her hand for the skiloblade.

The guard handed it over with a bow.

The princess carefully released the duo-blades. "Very sharp, very pointed," she remarked. "Very dangerous, in the wrong hands." She retracted the blades and handed the weapon back to the guard. "Explain yourself, Ensign. Why did you ask poor Kumatille to open his jacket? What did you suspect?"

Rayna took a deep breath. "Honestly, it was a feeling, Your Highness. A very strong, disturbing feeling, but only a feeling, which is why I only asked him to open his jacket, and nothing more."

"Female intuition, Ensign?" The question carried a hint of sarcasm.

"If I may ask, how well do you know him?" Rayna, having stepped this far, had little more to lose by pursuing her suspicion. "How long has he worked for the emperor?"

"I know very little about him, Ensign."

"Doesn't it seem strange that he would refuse such a harmless request?" It was her best argument. She held her breath in anticipation.

The princess looked to each of her guards in turn before deciding on a course of action. She turned to Rayna, stern. "I don't like how this is going, Ensign. You will follow us back, and we will discuss this with my father and Mr. Kumatille. Then we will arrive at the truth of your suspicion."

Rayna stiffened. "I should inform my commander."

"My guards will contact your captain and brief him or her on the situation." The princess was all business. "I hope this will not take long. Let's go."

As they walked away from the shop, Rayna's porta-com buzzed. She looked to the two guards, who walked on either side of her. The guard on her right held his hand out.

She handed the porta-com over. "It's probably my barrack mate, looking for me."

The guard checked the screen and said, "Teggo."

"Oh." Rayna turned to the princess. "That's not my barrack mate. He's a friend aboard *Ocelot*."

The princess eyed her. "A friend?"

Rayna offered a half smile. "A special friend."

The princess softened her gaze and nodded to the guard to return the porta-com.

Rayna hoped they would afford her a small measure of privacy, but they didn't. She took the porta-com and answered it. "Hi, Morgan."

"Rayna, you're not aboard *Pouton*," he said. "Where are you?"

Rayna looked at the three, standing around her. "I'm at the space fortress."

"We'll be heading over shortly. I thought I'd come visit."

"I can't talk right now." She looked back at the princess and the guards, who seemed to be growing impatient. "How about if I contact you when I get back aboard the ship?"

"Is everything okay? Did the doctor come back with any more information?"

"Nothing's happened. I'm just...busy." Rayna tried to think of a way to let Morgan in on what was happening. But with the princess and her guards waiting on—and watching—her, she could only offer a vague response. "I'm headed for an important meeting at the Command Module. I'll contact you when I'm done. Okay?"

Morgan paused. "Okay."

Rayna held the speaker close and whispered, "Love you. Later." She quickly shut the porta-com off and replaced it on her belt. "I'm sorry for the delay. We can continue."

Morgan puzzled over Rayna's behavior. She was off duty. What important meeting could she be involved in? Neither Schillary nor his squad leaders had been scheduled for any meetings at the Command Module, as far as he knew. As Morgan headed for the bridge, he made a mental note to ask Schillary, the next time he saw him, about any security developments on the space fortress.

When he arrived, he took over for Otho as the Officer of the Deck. Lendus had decided to stick around for a return call from Colonel Chrystamme while the captain was away. PO1

Turons took over the helm and began running final checks. Through the panorama-pane, the main row of the Canellis shipyard sat empty, as both *Ancora* and *Pouton* had moved to the refueling depot.

"Canellis reports that moorings are ready to withdraw," CPO Grisconne said from the signaling post.

"Launch stations," Morgan ordered.

"Bridge to all hands: launch stations," Grisconne's husky voice announced.

A buzzer sounded. On the Ops deck, the lights of the main status panel began switching on as the different sections of the ship signaled their readiness. The Ops crew technicians readied control systems and activated readouts.

"Feeder relays energizing," Turons said. "Thrusters will be online in one minute, main engines in an additional four minutes."

Morgan reviewed the activity on the Ops deck, noting the status displays on the many monitors. "Operations?" he called down to the Junior Officer of the Deck.

"All decks signal ready," Ensign Violette said.

"Helm?" Morgan asked.

Turons flipped a display and brought up a screen showing ten green lights. "Thrusters are online and standing by."

Morgan turned to Grisconne. "Signal Canellis: retract moorings."

"Yes, sir," Grisconne said. "Mr. Lendus, the space fortress reports that Colonel Chrystamme is on his way to a meeting with the emperor. He'll contact us when he is finished."

"It seems like everybody's going to meetings over there," Morgan muttered.

In the Command Module's conference room, Chrystamme reclined in his chair while Prince Otias stepped past two
broad-leafed potted plants and a small cascading water fountain
to a series of ornately framed pictures on the wall. Chrystamme
pointed out Admiral Kosolf's portrait to the prince, along with
those of some of Kosolf's predecessors: Admiral B'toon, the first
Imperial fleet commander; General Petis, the joint war commander during the Galactic Revolutions; and Lord Walmsley, the
man who had defeated General Mapooly to end that war.

"Lord Walmsley is the only one not portrayed in an official uniform of one of the Imperial dominions," the prince observed.

"Lord Walmsley never joined any star fleet," Chrystamme said. "He was a great hero of the war, the man who
brought an end to the fighting, but he fought his own battles, using his own militia. He departed for the outer regions during the
early reconstruction summit meetings—before the core planets
had united to form the empire—and never returned."

"Why?"

Chrystamme sighed. "Nobody knows why. He simply
left."

The prince took a seat, opposite Chrystamme. "That's too
bad. I'm sure the empire could have used his leadership."

Chrystamme looked up at the wall clock. "I've heard that
the emperor is rarely late. Is everything okay with His Majesty?"

"He's waiting for word from his aides on where Princess
Thericia and Mr. Franklen are," the prince said.

The door opened and the emperor walked in, saying,
"Well, it seems Mr. Franklen is still at Canellis, on board *Ocelot*,
and the princess is shopping somewhere." He stopped, looked
around, and asked, "Where is Mr. Kumatille?"

"Wasn't he with you?" the prince asked.

"No." The emperor took his seat at the front of the table. "Do either of you know what this meeting is about?"

The question surprised Chrystamme. "Your Majesty, we were told that *you* called for us to meet."

"You were told...what?" The emperor turned to the prince.

"I was told the same thing," the prince said.

The emperor threw his hands up. "Who told you I called for this meeting?"

"Kumatille," the prince said.

"Yes, sir," Chrystamme said. "Mr. Kumatille."

The emperor glared at both of them, then at the door, then at the clock. Chrystamme puzzled at the confusion. Had Kumatille delivered the wrong message?

Eventually, the door opened and Kumatille hurried in, out of breath, a stack of porta-coms under his arm. "I'm terribly sorry, Your Majesty." He handed a porta-com to Chrystamme.

"What is the meaning of this?" Chrystamme demanded. "Why did you tell the two of us that His Majesty called for this meeting?"

"So sorry, Colonel," Kumatille stammered, "but I had no choice." Finished with passing out the porta-coms, including two to empty seats for Franklen and the princess, he walked back to the head of the table.

"Explain yourself, Mr. Kumatille." The emperor rose and stepped over to Kumatille, towering over the diminutive staffer. "You've been a diligent and loyal worker. Why the dishonesty?"

"It's all very simple, Your Majesty, nothing to get excited about. If you'll be patient, everything will become clear." He eyed the two empty chairs. "We should wait until Mr. Franklen and the princess arrive."

"We will *not* wait for Mr. Franklen or the princess," the emperor said, his voice rising a touch. "Franklin is at Canellis, and the princess is not critical."

"But, Your Majesty—"

"I demand to know. Now!"

Kumatille paused.

Chrystamme looked at the enraged emperor, then back at Kumatille, who looked oddly defiant for a brief moment before taking a deep breath and relaxing his stiffened pose.

Kumatille finally said, "Very well." He took a step back and began unbuttoning his jacket. "I had hoped the princess would be here, as the matter involves the Imperial Crown."

The prince glanced at the contents of the porta-com reader. Seeing this, Chrystamme switched his on and read aloud, "The Plan for a Return to the True Monarchy of the Empire."

The emperor snapped his head toward Chrystamme upon hearing this.

Chrystamme shot a quizzical look at Kumatille. "What is this supposed to mean?"

After an awkward silence, the emperor demanded, "Well?"

Kumatille cleared his throat. "Prince Fraither of Bexel plans to lay claim to the crown."

"That is not news to us," Chrystamme said.

"But his claim is not through a call for election. I've run across sources that appear to support a lineage claim, tying the Fraither name back to the last ruler of the original Etolian Empire."

"That's what this is all about?" the emperor roared, his eyes bulging. "Whatever sources exist, even if verified, are not relevant."

Chrystamme quickly added, "It's unlikely that they can be verified, given the state of records from the old empire."

"We are a different empire," the emperor stated, "with a different system of government. The Imperial election, not dynastic succession, is the basic foundation of our empire. You know that as well as we do." He took a deep breath to calm himself. "What is the real issue, Mr. Kumatille? Be honest with me."

Kumatille paused. He glanced at the prince, then returned his attention to the emperor.

"Sir, I highly respect you as my current ruler." Kumatille bowed his head. "But we must all recognize that the Central Empire is, in fact, an attempt by the five core worlds to reconstitute the Etolian Empire, to bring back the golden age that existed during that era.

"Recall the legendary kings of the founding worlds, the many centuries of rulers from Memona, Jahop-thune, Paebih, Oscanos, and Hoscanis, who forged the greatest achievement in human history."

Kumatille clenched his fist and raised his voice.

"Think of how much was irreparably lost when that empire was destroyed: the glory of existence, the pride of the children of the Euranian Ancestors. Eurania suffered tremendously in the centuries since the fall of the empire. Chaos, invasion, war, conquest and occupation. So much suffering, so much humiliation, unworthy of our people. We must not squander the last half century of peace and self-determination. We must not be weak or vulnerable."

He stepped closer to the emperor.

"We must reestablish ourselves as the beacon of life. We must bring back the true greatness of the Etolian Empire, which includes reinstituting the dynastic crown—a strong central ruler who gave, and held, a unified vision to the empire, not a poor substitute empire with a powerless figurehead who is subject to the electoral whims of the Assembly."

Chrystamme frowned and folded his arms as he listened to Kumatille's long-winded rambling.

"Prince Fraither would be such a ruler. He is strong, a long-entrenched leader, and his vision for the empire is the unifying vision that we need. He is the descendant of the ancient kings, the heir to the crown of Emperor Fur'thur, the last Etolian Emperor. However, in order for Prince Fraither to be elevated"—Kumatille opened his jacket and revealed his gold-lighted disc—"the elected emperor must be removed."

"No!" Prince Otias cried out, leaping from his chair.

With Kumatille's intent suddenly dawning upon him, Chrystamme dove across the table, his arms outstretched to try to shove the emperor out of the path of destruction.

Kumatille cried out an ear-piercing, maniacal howl that echoed off the walls. A blinding flash of pure whiteness flared out as a deafening concussion shattered the room.

9. The Diadochi

"Sir! An explosion!"

Morgan and Lendus turned at the sound of Turons's voice and saw, through the panorama-pane, a massive fireball flare outward from the center of the Command Module. They shielded their eyes from the brightness of the blinding flash until the automatic tint adjusted to compensate. Then they saw a large section of the superstructure break away and a shower of debris blow into space.

"Oh my God!" Grisconne said.

Morgan froze, breathless, his curse muffled, his fists locked white. He had just spoken to Rayna. She was somewhere on the space fortress.

Lendus stepped over and took command of the bridge. "Try to raise the Command Module."

"Yes, sir," Grisconne said.

"What happened?" Otho asked, bounding back up the steps.

Motioning for Otho to man the combat station, Lendus said, "Scan for hostile craft." He then said to Morgan, "Mr. Teggo, try to locate the explosion."

Morgan relayed a string of coordinates down to Violette

for the Ops deck crew to investigate. Activity and reports whirled about him, but even as he worked, he couldn't help thinking of Rayna.

Turning to Grisconne, Lendus asked, "Anything?"

"Still trying." Grisconne paused. One of her lights came on. "I'm receiving a signal from Captain Jaron."

Lendus nodded for Grisconne to activate the speaker. "Captain Jaron, Lendus here."

"My God, Lendus, what happened?"

"We're trying to determine the location of the blast," Lendus said. "Did you see anything?"

"There was no warning whatsoever."

"General Quarters," Lendus ordered. "Signal the dockmaster for emergency launch."

The alarm sounded, and all the standby stations on the Ops deck automatically quick-started, while the lights over them dimmed to maximize the readability of the colorful screens. Additional personnel raced in to assist the Ops crew. A platoon soldier flipped open a wall panel marked "Emergency" and released overhead compartments over each station, while Schillary ran onto the bridge to do the same. Life support jumpsuits rolled down to everyone.

Morgan quickly slipped into his suit and placed his helmet on the console hook. As he did, he kept his eye on the scanner readings relaying from the Ops deck to the navigation monitor.

Otho, also in his e-suit, activated the firing controls and called down, "Energize all turret batteries. Load torpedoes."

While Otho ran startup tests, Morgan monitored activities throughout the ship. Weapons personnel engaged the arming mechanisms of the lightspeed-capable neutrino torpedoes, while others initiated the startup sequences of the firing computers. Robotic arms loaded the first set of torpedoes into the launchers and set the automatic relays for firing. On the main deck, gunnery crews climbed into the Costarking capsules below each cannon and powered up the turrets.

"Canellis Yards signals the moorings are released," Grisconne said.

"Push off, Mr. Turons," Lendus ordered. "Thrusters ahead, as soon as we clear the pier."

Turons fired a short burst from reactive jets along *Ocelot*'s hull, propelling the heavy cruiser away from the dock. The underside port and starboard engines powered up, and the ship departed Canellis under full power.

"The captain is on the bridge," Schillary called out as Choff stepped onto the bridge and assumed command. Franklen, out of breath, followed at the captain's heels, his head swinging from side to side, wild eyes darting from monitor to monitor.

"Any word from the Command Module?" Choff asked.

"Still trying," Grisconne said. "Nothing yet."

"We'll be at the space fortress in two minutes," Morgan reported.

Without warning, a blinding flash erupted from the vicinity of the depot. A massive fireball engulfed *Ancora*. An ominous silence descended onto the *Ocelot* bridge and Ops deck.

"*Tatik*—!" Morgan said under his breath, his surroundings seeming to shatter before him. One hundred seventy officers and crew served aboard *Ancora*, the same as *Ocelot*. What happened, and what was their condition now?

The fireball quickly dissipated, revealing an expanding cloud of debris and *Ancora*'s blasted carcass. The refueling station, though badly seared from the heat, miraculously survived.

Pouton, nudged down the pier by the blast until the fuel lines held it in place, also escaped without significant damage.

Morgan glanced at the assortment of monitors throughout the Ops center. He gazed at the wreckage wrought on both *Ancora* and the Command Module, uncontrolled thoughts of undetermined dead and dying crossing his mind. A timer light blinked on his console. "One minute to the space fortress."

"No sign of enemy vessels," Otho reported.

"Bring us alongside *Graftinop One*," Choff said. "Ahead slow."

"Another call from *Pouton*, sir," Grisconne said. "Captain Jaron."

"Put her on the speaker," Choff said. "Captain Jaron, what's your condition?"

"A little shaken, Captain Choff, but on the whole, we escaped in decent shape. We've got some work to do here, but we can give you assistance, if you wish. We're trying to raise *Ancora*, but there's no response yet."

"We've been trying to contact the Command Module," Choff said. "Our priority right now is the emperor and his family and staff. Can we leave *Ancora* to you, while we proceed to the explosion site?"

"Of course."

"There's *Graftinop One*." Turons pointed to the left half of the monitor, where the large, sleek Starmaster sat alone. "It looks unharmed."

"It was far enough away from the explosion site," Lendus said.

Morgan took a deep breath as a new reading appeared on his display. "Sir, the blast looks to have been centered on the Imperial Headquarters."

Choff spun around, his jaw dropping.

They looked at the gaping hole in the space fortress's central structure, a black maw-like abyss filled with twisted metals.

Morgan quietly signaled on his porta-com, hoping that Rayna would answer.

"Anything?" Choff asked Grisconne. Receiving a shake of her head, he said, "Mr. Lendus, take Mr. Schillary, one of his squads, and Dr. Hildermaan over to search for the emperor while we make a pass to survey the site. Include a demolition man with your team."

Lendus turned to Grisconne and said, "Call Dr. Hildermaan and Mr. Prowzi to the hangar."

As he and Lendus turned to leave, Schillary switched on his mini-com. "Mr. Semile, report to the hangar with your squad."

"I should go," Franklen said. "His Highness may need—"

"It's too dangerous." Choff shook his head. "Especially given your position. Let's wait until they've ascertained the situation over there."

"Captain Choff." Morgan, seeing Lendus and Schillary head down, sprang to his feet and broke in through all the activity. He stepped up to the captain. "Can we speak in private?"

Choff glared. "What? Now?"

Morgan lowered his voice into a fierce whisper. "It's about Rayna, sir."

Choff froze, facial muscles taut. He motioned for Morgan to follow him to the back of the bridge, next to the captain's private handset. "What is it?" Choff asked in a low voice.

"She's at the space fortress, sir; I was talking to her earlier. I just tried contacting her, but she didn't answer."

Choff stiffened. Clearing his throat, he asked, "What was she doing over there?"

Morgan's pulse was racing. "I only know that she hadn't been cleared for duty yet."

As Choff paused, deep in thought, Morgan stole a glance at Otho, who was directing the Ops crew in conducting the survey of the damage to the Command Module, compiling picture after picture, scanner reading after scanner reading, and pushing the crew to work with increased urgency.

"Mr. Lendus." Choff stepped forward and called down. "Take Mr. Teggo with you."

When the explosion hit, it blasted apart the walls of the administration tower, and the vacuum of space created a storm like a wind tunnel, blowing the contents of the Commons—tables, chairs, signage, decoration, personal effects, and screaming people—through the many large and small holes that punctured the admin tower, until the emergency bulkheads inside the building shut and repressurized the interior.

Rayna immediately pulled the princess behind one of the giant pillars that supported the structure of the Commons and sheltered her in a protective crouch while their world whirled about them. Despite the cover of the pillar, small flying projectiles pelted them.

One of the royal guards jerked high into the air, to the horrified screams of the princess, and flattened against one of the holes at the fifth level of the tower, helpless. A few seconds later, he was sucked in while a massive block toppled onto the other guard, crushing him under a heap of crumbling building ruins.

Within moments, loud slams reverberated through the storm, as the automatic bulkheads inside the admin tower released and sealed. As each barrier shut, the chaos dampened until it finally died away, leaving the cries of the injured to wail throughout the Commons.

Rayna held Thericia steady in her arms, letting the princess's hysteria run its course. She fought against the temptation to look around, driven by thoughts of the deadly falling debris all about them. Remarkably, the life support systems, including gravitation and climate control, held steady, likely due to the strategic layout of redundant units throughout the space fortress. When the princess's sobs lessened, Rayna released her, saying, "I think it's over. Are you all right?"

The princess, still hyperventilating, whispered, "I think so. Oh God, what happened?" She buried her face in her hands.

Rayna put her arm around the princess's shoulder and stared at the wrecked administration tower, her thoughts turning to the fate of the occupants. "Can you stand?" she asked. "Can you walk?" When the princess raised her head and nodded, Rayna said, "Let's try to find the emperor."

Working their way through the chaos of fallen wreckage and debris—overturned tables and chairs, merchandise, signage, and the bruised and bloodied crowds of injured on the promenade floor—they reached the base of the administration tower. The main entrance sat ajar. Rayna tried to kick the door back onto its tracks, to no avail.

"There's another entrance," the princess said.

Rayna followed her to a much smaller side entrance, hidden in the unlit alley between the admin tower and the adjacent services annex. Though protected from the whirlwind by the narrowness of the alley, the door had been knocked off its tracks. The opening, however, was wide enough to squeeze through. Rayna peered into the darkness inside. An unmarked service staircase led up through an empty stairwell, where a cold draft blew down.

"The Imperial complex is on the sixth through eighth floors," the princess said.

"Do you want to wait here while I take a look?" Rayna asked.

The princess shook her head. "I need to find my father and brother." She paused. "I'd also feel safer if we stayed together."

Rayna nodded, and they mounted the stairs. They paused to note the same chaotic mess of rubble surrounding shaken and injured staffers on each level before bypassing the entrance and moving on. On the fourth floor, they encountered their first signs of structural damage: large wall cracks and a bent, exposed girder. Rayna looked around the corner and spotted, down a darkened corridor, a collapsed ceiling, buckled interior walls, and people gathered around unconscious victims, many with head injuries. The princess gasped at the sight.

On the fifth floor, a locked overhead bulkhead prevented further climbing. Rayna touched the emergency door and immediately jerked her hand back. Something that icy cold could only be deep space on the other side of the door.

The regular entrance still worked, and they stepped onto the floor. They found themselves surrounded on both sides and overhead by the dull shine of the emergency walls and ceiling and bathed by sweeping amber lights. With no other direction possible, they moved forward in search of a second staircase, until they came to a door sitting slightly ajar.

Rayna pushed it open, and the princess screamed, turning away from the sight of a dead body partially crushed under a fallen wall. Rayna threw her arms around the princess, shielding her face, and led her through another doorway, damaged but still standing.

"Oh my God," Rayna gasped, entering a room littered with bodies and topped by an emergency bulkhead ceiling. In the far wall, the large blast doors were closed tight, automatically released to reinforce compromises in the wall. Through one of the adjacent windows, she could see another room with the shattered remains of furniture, monstrous blast holes in the ceiling, giant cracks in the walls, and two bodies floating inside. In front of the doors, one bloodied person, lying crumpled on the floor, moved an arm and groaned.

"Otias!" The princess broke away from Rayna and ran to the fallen prince, lying battered and beaten. "Oh my God, Otias," the princess cried, collapsing at his side. "Don't move. Be still. Please, be still." Tears rolled down her face.

"Thericia…"

Rayna knelt and took his arm, trying to focus on the crisis. "Don't talk. I'll see what I can do." His hand felt as icy cold as the bulkhead she had touched.

The prince shivered, his eyes only slits. "Thericia…"

"I'm here," the princess whispered.

"Protect…" He squeezed Rayna's hand. "…the Crown…"

The prince drew his final breath, stiffened, and withdrew to the cosmos.

The princess sobbed, vigorously shaking her head in denial. "Otias…" She dropped her head and let her tears flow.

As the prince's hand fell from her grasp, Rayna turned away to look through the window. She stifled a gasp at what she saw. Rayna squeezed her fists to steady her tremble. She touched the young princess's arm. "Your Highness…" Rayna couldn't bring herself to say what she saw. She wanted to shelter the young princess—who had just lost her only brother—from the horror that was on the other side of the window. But Rayna knew that the princess had to find out, and the sooner, the better. She gently touched the princess's chin and coaxed her to raise her head and look through the window. The two mangled, but recognizable, dead bodies floating inside the remains of the sealed room were those of Colonel Chrystamme and the emperor.

The princess screamed and bolted to the window, clawing at the transparency. "No! Father, no!" She collapsed to the floor, her cry of distress echoing off the walls.

"Your Highness, I'm so sorry." Rayna wrapped her arms around the princess's shoulders. This was no accident, Rayna knew. This was a palace overthrow. She couldn't even hazard a guess at who could be behind this unthinkable act. The ramification of what they were facing felt like a crushing weight. With the emperor and the crown prince both dead, the empire was now wide open. Only the young princess stood in the way of the usurper, whoever that was. "I have to get you to safety."

The princess whirled on Rayna. "I don't want the *kroking* crown! I don't want it! I want my father!" She buried her head on Rayna's shoulder and cried hysterically. "I want to go home. I don't want this…"

Rayna's heart broke at the princess's torment. She held the young ruler tight and wept with her.

Nearby, the doors to the decompressed room, unreinforced without emergency bulkheads, strained against the pressure.

Morgan and Lon exited the launch and charged through the ruined Commons to the administration tower, Schillary,

Semile and his twelve-man squad hot on their heels, while Lendus and Hildermaan brought up the rear. After two unsuccessful attempts to open the main entrance, the team used portable wedges to force the doors apart.

With the lifts dead, they mounted the main staircase. Hildermaan hesitated on both the first and second floors to look over the injured, but Lendus urged him on to their main objective, the safety of the emperor and the Imperial personnel. They soon reached the fifth floor, where the sealed emergency bulkhead blocked further advancement.

Lendus put his hand on the door and jerked it back. "It's like ice," he said. "The Imperial floors are gone."

A sinking feeling descended upon Morgan. A half century of peace and order in Imperial society could collapse under the threat of regional rivalries. The consequences for the Central Empire could be devastating.

"Come in, *Ocelot*," Lendus called into his collar-com. "Ms. Grisconne, inform the captain that Imperial Headquarters is gone. Destroyed."

A pause. "Yes, sir."

"We'll continue searching for survivors of I-HQ and for clues to what happened. Lendus out."

Morgan and Schillary watched as Lon analyzed samples of the blast damage with his porta-com.

"Anything, Lon?" Morgan asked.

"Doesn't look like a standard explosive, Imperial or Pharrian," Lon said. "I'm checking the residues against some of the known explosives from the bordering dominions, but our information on those is pretty sparse." He finished processing, took out a carrier, and deposited the samples inside. "Maybe the ship will have access to better information for analysis." He looked around. "I would normally use the fortress databank, but I don't know what shape that's in."

The walls creaked, drawing stares from the team.

"We'd better hustle," Morgan said, worried that they could get caught in a collapse of their own.

"Helmets on," Lendus ordered. "Fan out. Check the entire floor—whatever parts are accessible."

Lon told Semile, "Stay here and continue collecting samples. I'll go ahead and assist Mr. Teggo."

Morgan and Lon slapped on their helmets and plunged forward, keeping watchful eyes on the integrity of the walls, ceilings, and especially the doors. They quickly reached a closed door at the end of a long hallway. Morgan felt the door with his hand, nodded to Lon, and pushed the button.

Nothing happened.

Recalling a similar situation on Volon, Morgan whipped out his skiloblade. Lon followed suit, and they ran their blades along the track of the door until they triggered the lock mechanism. The door slid open, revealing a room full of dead bodies and two women, standing before a large window, sobbing.

"Rayna!" Morgan said in astonishment. She looked all right, to his relief. The princess seemed uninjured, too.

"Rayna?" Lon echoed.

Both men ran toward Rayna and the princess, both ripping their helmets off. Rayna and Morgan quickly embraced.

"What are you doing here?" Morgan asked Rayna. "Are you all right?" Relieved after receiving a quick nod, he turned to the princess and asked, "Your Highness?"

The princess, who looked overwhelmed with emotion, only stared at them through her tears.

"She was with me." Rayna's face turned grim. "Morgan,

the emperor is dead." She indicated the bodies in the window. "The crown prince, too."

The princess erupted in a loud wail and sobbed against Rayna's shoulder.

"Oh no," Morgan said. The foundation of the empire was gone. They had failed their emperor. Now, a nightmare scenario—a pack of vicious successors and an upcoming feeding frenzy—stared all of them in the face. "Your Highness, I'm sorry."

"Mr. Lendus," Lon called on his collar-com, "we've found the princess. She appears unhurt. Follow my signal to our location." He paused. "The emperor and the crown prince are both dead."

"We're on our way," Lendus replied.

Morgan said to the princess, "We've got to get you to safety immediately."

The princess turned away to face the window.

Morgan put a protective arm around the young princess's shoulder. "We'll defend you, Your Highness."

Lon felt the doors, inspected the bulge in the center, and said, "They're holding, but I don't know for how much longer." He looked through the window and said, "They were blown down from above." He pointed at a jagged blast hole in the ceiling. "There's got to be a way to retrieve them."

"From outside," Morgan said. "*Ocelot* can send someone to take care of it." He turned at the sound of running footsteps.

As Lendus and his team entered the room, they paused to survey the scene before removing their helmets.

"Your Highness," Lendus addressed the princess, who had her back to everyone.

After the princess's sobs calmed, Rayna gently turned the

young heir to face the *Ocelot* team. Morgan raised his skiloblade, descended to one knee, and lowered his head before the Ruling Princess of Alscras. Lendus and the others followed suit. Rayna then joined the others in kneeling, the final person to raise her blade.

Princess Thericia, her eyes still glistening with tears, took a deep breath and said, in almost a whisper, "Please rise. We should go."

A loud creak sounded. Morgan, seeing the doors increase their bulge, called out, "Hurry, it's not going to hold!" He pushed Rayna and the princess out ahead of the team.

Lendus, the last man out, manually closed and locked the emergency bulkhead, sealing off the floor.

A moment later, a tremendous concussion from the other side rocked the walls and the ceiling as the fifth floor blew out into space.

"Thank Oscanos and Gheriah," Franklen said, as Rayna, Princess Thericia, Captain Choff, and Captain Jaron entered the conference room aboard *Graftinop One*, joining Admiral Kosolf and an assortment of somber, red-eyed Imperial staffers at the table. The blanket of collective grief in the air was overwhelming, and the lineup of powerful men and women around Rayna felt imposing. She hoped she would not have to give a report, though she was the only witness to the calamity that befell the princess.

Princess Thericia, covered in dust, stepped forward, accepted a hug from the chief of staff, and dissolved into tears again. Others—both women and men—broke down within seconds.

The emperor was dead. Despair threatened to break Rayna down as well. She placed her hand on the princess's shoulder. "We *will* protect you, Your Highness," Rayna said.

"Yes," Kosolf said. "We will defend you to the last man and woman."

The people gathered around the princess and Franklen, many repeating, "We will defend you, Your Highness," until the words grew into a collective chant.

Without warning, the princess lifted her head, turned to face everyone, and said in a trembling voice, "We should thank Captain Choff and Captain Jaron for our safety." Turning to the two captains, she bowed, and everyone in the room followed suit. "I especially wish to thank Ensign Rayna Choff, who personally watched after me from the moment she suspected trouble until our rescue." She held her hand out to Rayna, who initially hesitated, but then accepted a warm, heartfelt embrace from the princess as the people applauded.

At that moment, Rayna caught a glance from Captain Jaron and remembered their brief joking aside about personal friendships with royalty. *How ironic.*

"Mr. Franklen," the princess said, her voice steadying, "I would like Ensign Choff to be my personal attendant for the time being."

Rayna, dumbstruck by what she had heard, looked around at some of the more-familiar faces in the room: Captain Jaron; Commander Alteus, *Pouton*'s executive; Admiral Kosolf; Lt. Colonel Moton, now the acting base commander; Commander Lendus; and Captain Choff, her father.

"Captain?" Franklen asked.

Jaron gazed at Rayna with her penetrating gray eyes before voicing her concern. "Ensign Choff is still under medical observation, Mr. Franklen, recovering from recent injuries."

"Dr. Doxuit, my personal physician, can attend to her," the princess said. "As she would be with me at all times, and I am now under constant guard, it is unlikely that she would be put in harm's way."

Jaron put her hand to her chin for a moment, then said, "Well, if it's only light duty." Jaron smiled at Rayna. "It is a great honor for Ensign Choff. I would request that Dr. Creatoun be kept abreast of her medical status."

"Agreed, Captain," the princess said.

"Then it's done." Franklen extended his hand to Rayna. "Welcome to the royal staff, Ensign."

Captain Jaron's words echoed in Rayna's mind. *It is a great honor for Ensign Choff.* Her hands started to tremble, but she took deep breaths until they steadied. The princess took her seat at the head of the table, Franklen directed Rayna to the chair next to his, and everyone else took their seats around the table.

Rayna looked to her father, who sat quietly, his dark eyes reflecting a pensive mood. When he looked up, she managed a slight smile toward him, which he returned, equally slight.

"Admiral," Moton said, "what do we know about the *Ancora* explosion?"

Kosolf shook his head. "Only that it originated from within the ship. A small explosive, if planted within the feeder lines that energize the torpedo magazines, could have resulted in the extremely large blast that destroyed the ship. All aboard were killed, and the ship is a total loss." He paused, while murmurs passed through the room. "Captain Doring and 170 young men and women were among the finest in the space service."

Rayna lowered her head. *All those servicemen, all lost. All those families, all the grieving to come.*

"We have reviewed the logs of people boarding and deboarding the ship," Kosolf said. "It looks to be an inside attack."

"Just like Mr. Kumatille," Franklen said.

Rayna stiffened. There was that name again.

"We are reviewing everything we have on him," Franklen said. "With your cooperation, Admiral, we will try to find a connection between Kumatille and someone aboard *Ancora*."

"We have a lot to deal with," Kosolf said. "With all due respect to the colonel, this space fortress has been compromised to the point of ineffectiveness. We have a gaping hole in our border with the outer dominions now."

"We'll do what we can with what we have," Moton said, "but I agree with the admiral. Central controls over the watchtower cannons were destroyed in the blast. We need reinforcements from the fleet to restore firepower and capability. Can we recall the other cruisers that were here?"

"No," Kosolf said, "their strategic repositioning is now more vital than ever. The closest available task force, *Freemon*, is already en route. But even at maximum velocity, it will take nearly two weeks to return from the Outer Territories. For now, we have the two cruisers and the remaining support ships. They still pack some firepower, Colonel."

Moton, hearing the situation, looked about, grim. The room went quiet.

Franklen broke the silence. "I have something important to share." He reached into his pocket, took out a micro-cartridge, and inserted it into the computer. "This was just passed to me by the fortress security team. It's the automatic recording from the emperor's final minutes." He looked to the princess. "Prepare yourself, Your Highness. It's disturbing."

The monitor came to life with the video recording of the emperor standing over Kumatille, at the head of the conference room. The prince and Chrystamme were seated on either side of the table, poring over their porta-coms.

Rayna leaned forward in her seat, her pulse picking up. There was Kumatille, exactly as he had looked at the tiki shop.

"What is the real issue, Mr. Kumatille? Be honest with me."

"Sir, I highly respect you as my current ruler. But we must all recognize that the Central Empire is, in fact, an attempt by the five core worlds to reconstitute the Etolian Empire..."

Rayna found Kumatille long-winded. As he rambled on, she wondered how the emperor put up with him for a year.

"...and that includes reinstituting the dynastic Crown..."

Rayna's ears perked up.

"...he is the heir to the crown of Emperor Fur'thur, the last Etolian Emperor. However, in order for Prince Fraither to be elevated, the elected emperor must be removed."

"No!"

Rayna saw the princess suddenly grasp the armrests of her chair.

On the recording, the prince leaped to his feet. Chrystamme dove across the table and pushed the emperor away as Kumatille tore open his jacket to reveal a blinding light emitting from a tiny disc hanging from his neck.

That was it! The memory of Saltos and the disc *he* wore flashed into Rayna's mind.

The screen suddenly flashed into a blinding white, then faded to black, as several of the viewers gasped.

Rayna heard a labored whimper and glanced over at the teary princess. The memory of their final meeting with Kumatille at the trading shop was still fresh. Rayna still couldn't identify the ominous feeling that had come over her or why she suspected that Kumatille harbored something dangerous. But that feeling had turned out to be what had saved the princess from the fate that befell her father and brother.

"I'm very sorry, Your Highness," Franklen said, as others around the room bowed their heads, "but now we know the truth. The assassination of the emperor, coupled with the bombing of *Ancora*, is an act of treason. We must identify who Kumatille was working for—whether Prince Fraither was involved—and whether we are facing the possibility of a military response."

The princess buried her face in her hands.

"I will carry that burden." Kosolf quickly stood up. "My staff will review recent fleet movements, and I will prepare a comprehensive assessment and my recommendations to Her Highness."

After a long pause, the princess lifted her head, her composure regained. She quietly said, "Thank you, Admiral." She wiped her eyes. "Mr. Franklen, how should we proceed?"

"The most important thing is stability during this crisis," Franklen answered. "You are now the interim ruler, the Ruling Princess of the Kingdom of Alscras, and as you have been training for this contingency for the past two years, I anticipate no opposition to your confirmation by the Alscrasian Council. Count Haagewyn?"

The gray-haired elder statesman who advised the emperor as the liaison to the Alscrasian Council cleared his throat. "Yes, I agree. However, the council will need strong leadership during this crisis."

"I understand," the princess said.

"As for the empire," Franklen continued as he turned to face a short, balding man, "what are your recommendations, Dr. Docherae?"

"As you know, the emperor is elected," the adviser on Imperial relations said to the princess. "There is no heir to the Imperial Crown, nor is there an acting emperor. Therefore, you must contact Mr. Duc Ilwatu, the chief of the Imperial Assembly, and have him call a special session of the Inner Chamber of the Assembly to begin the work of organizing an election. You should also meet with the high priest of Kelova as soon as possible; his voice is crucial to the unity of the empire. You must then go on a widecast and reassure the people that the empire, its institutions, and its workings continue without interruption. Finally, as the Ruling Princess of Alscras, you must declare that you will seek election in your father's stead."

Franklen turned to address the entire conference room. "If what Kumatille said is true, we cannot allow Prince Fraither to usurp sovereignty undeterred."

Kosolf said, "I agree. With the death of the emperor, I see a struggle coming that will engulf the Imperial Assembly, one that could turn ugly, potentially paralyzing the empire. Chancellor Wahren of Sestia has proved consistently passive in Imperial affairs, so the contenders for succession are Prince Fraither, Supreme Dictator Quinn, your old 'friend' Grand *Primai* Ludzenia, and yourself."

The princess looked unsure to Rayna. Franklen and the admiral had laid things out as clearly and succinctly as possible. It seemed the sudden weight of responsibility might crush the poor princess.

"Admiral," the princess said, "you know that my father came to this fortress precisely because he suspected the Grand *Primai* or the Supreme Dictator of making a move against him." She glanced at Franklin before continuing. "I am not comfortable with the idea of journeying to Kelova and walking into the presence of potential enemies in such a simple-minded manner."

"You must at least assume authority and establish a strong presence, for the good of Alscras and the empire at large," Kosolf said. "The alternative is an uncertainty that could lead to weakness in Alscras and civil war between the core worlds." Seeing the princess's hesitation, he paused for a second. "We will transfer your seat of power to this ship. You will be well-protected. For now, you can speak from the safety of the throne room on board."

The princess lowered her head and took a deep breath. "I understand." She turned to the Imperial spokesman. "Mr. Myhmik, please help me prepare my speech."

Franklen nodded toward the princess. "I think the admiral can now turn his attention to the military aspects of this crisis."

Rayna glanced at the assortment of *Pouton* and *Ocelot* personnel with mixed feelings. While she was being transferred away from her regular duties, they—her father, Morgan, and the others—would be left with carrying out the admiral's order to defend the princess.

When Morgan heard the news coming out of the meeting aboard *Graftinop One*, he rushed off *Ocelot*, conflicted between excitement and concern. He ran up to the hull of the Starmaster and caught a glimpse of Rayna, standing at the head of the airlock.

She waved to him and headed down.

"Rayna," he called out, "Lendus told me the news about you." He embraced her. "Are you going to do it?"

"It's already done," she said. "The princess asked for me at the beginning of the meeting."

Morgan paused. "It's done? So you're going?"

Rayna hesitated. She released him and took a step back. "Captain Jaron signed off on it. Is something wrong?"

"No." Morgan took a deep breath. The conversation now felt precarious. "But…you're on medical watch."

"They know," Rayna said. "The princess's personal physician will watch after me."

"Rayna, how are you going to be a bodyguard when you're not cleared for active duty?"

Rayna looked dumbfounded at Morgan's question. "You're not going to be like my father, are you? He didn't like the idea."

"I'm not sure I like it, either."

Rayna took a deep breath. "Try to understand, Morgan. The princess is scared. She's surrounded by powerful men and women, both friendly and not, and all eyes are looking to her for action. She didn't know this was going to happen, that her family would be murdered, and she would suddenly be the ruler of Alscras. She's trying her best, but she's only eighteen, still a kid. She *is* our princess, and she *did* ask for my help."

Morgan considered his words. "It's a great honor and all. You're just in no condition to be the bodyguard of an assassination target. You know they're going to try again, don't you?"

Rayna shook her head. "The princess is going to be under so much coverage that I won't be called upon to do anything. I'll probably be more of a glorified handmaiden than anything else."

Morgan scoffed. "Don't be naive. Kumatille was an inside job. *Ancora* probably was too, and how many did they kill there? The next attack *will* be from the inside."

"Morgan, don't—"

"Rayna…!" Morgan knew he was getting too worked up, but he also knew when he was right. Though he tried to be as calm and steady as possible, he had to speak his mind. "Look, you know I didn't think it was such a great idea for you to go into the mountains with me, when we were on Volon. I'm glad you went, believe me. But this time, you're pushing the risk factor too far." He took a deep breath. "The captain is right. This is too dangerous for you."

Rayna stared at him. "You're always so overprotective—just like Dad! Aren't you happy for me?" She folded her arms, her eyes reflecting the hurt. "I had hoped you'd be proud of me."

"I am," Morgan said.

"Then why are you so negative about this?"

Morgan, frustrated by her stubbornness, blurted out, "You're too carried away by all this. Think! Would you assign someone this duty if you knew that that person wasn't up to the highest calling?"

Rayna went quiet. A long silence imposed itself between them.

Morgan always knew that Rayna was too stubborn for her own good. At least this time, it sounded like the captain also thought this was too dangerous for Rayna—one of the few times he could remember them being of the same mind.

In a soft but angry voice, Rayna said, "You're right about one thing. The personal protection of a ruler is the highest calling of a Zahrin warrior." She took a step back. "My duty is not to myself but to my princess." With a fierce look in her eyes, she turned and headed away for *Pouton*.

Morgan cursed under his breath, realizing he had pushed too hard. "Rayna." He tried to reach out after her.

"Go away, Morgan."

Hearing footsteps approaching from behind, Morgan pivoted and faced Captain Choff. The captain must have come down a different airlock—and undoubtedly caught the end of his exchange with Rayna. *Always the overprotective parent. Dox!* Morgan braced for the inevitable tongue-lashing.

"Mr. Teggo," Choff began in a measured tone, "that was cold, especially toward someone for whom you claim to care so much. I would never have thought you capable of it."

Morgan's eyes turned down toward the captain's boots. He waited in silence, obedient.

To his surprise, Choff turned and walked away, saying, "Sometimes it's needed."

With each article of clothing that she tossed onto her bunk, Rayna muttered a longer string of curses. "Such a *kroking turkanaan*, Morgan! *Dox kroking shat'oq*-face, Morgan!" She paused and took in a deep breath to calm herself.

"Are you all right?" Fiona asked, entering the barracks.

"Yes." Rayna blew out her breath. "In the long run."

"I'm so excited for you," Fiona said. "But I'll miss you."

Rayna smiled. "I'll be back."

"When?"

Rayna thought about it. "Whenever the princess sends me back." She grabbed her bag and began stuffing her belongings into it.

Tornique knocked before entering the women's barracks. "Anybody home?"

Rayna gave a stern face and cleared her throat.

Fiona and Tornique immediately snapped crisp salutes to their commander, then laughed after she returned the salute.

"I'm going to miss the fun," Rayna said, fastening her bag shut.

"But I can't think of a more deserving officer," Tornique

said. He extended his hand to take Rayna's bag.

"I can get it," Rayna said.

"Please, I'd like the honor," Tornique said.

"This feels so strange," Rayna said. Handing the bag over, she quickly tied up her hair and put her hat on. "Leaving home for the big time."

"Keep a log," Fiona said as they exited the barracks. "Let us read all about it after you get back."

When they mounted the main deck, Fiona called out, "Attention on deck!"

Rayna stopped, stunned. She was not prepared for the lineup that greeted her. The entire ship's company had come to see her off. With a lump in her throat, she tried to smile and look each of her shipmates in the eye as she passed them. Not one word was spoken, but none were needed. The memories of the last two years—the training, the drilling, the landings—and the feelings of camaraderie they evoked were overwhelming.

At the end of the lineup stood Manion and the three squads that comprised the ship's platoon. Tornique took his place at the head of one of the squads, alongside Manion.

Fiona, doubling as the acting platoon officer in Rayna's absence, stood at the head of the platoon, unsheathed her skiloblade and held it high. "Raise thy blades!" she called out.

In unison, the soldiers of the platoon unsheathed their skiloblades and saluted, "*Maruga!*"

In response, Rayna unsheathed her skiloblade and returned the salute. "*Maruga!*" After returning the weapon to its sheath, she turned her attention forward.

Captain Jaron, flanked by Commander Alteus, stood before the airlock.

Rayna put her bag down and saluted her captain. "Permission to depart the ship?"

Captain Jaron returned the salute. "Permission granted. I wish you all the best on your assignment, Ensign."

"Thank you, Captain."

After a final, heartfelt hug with Fiona, Rayna took her bag and disembarked *Pouton*.

On Kelova, Lord Walmsley sat in the foyer of the Holy Office with Searus, Admiral Kearn, and Kearn's yeoman, all dressed in the crisp, clean blue-and-green dress uniforms of the Greyban Corps, patiently awaiting this meeting. The high priest was almost an hour late. Walmsley turned his attention to the line of portraits on the wall, studying three of the most prominent depictions with special interest.

The first was of Zeltius, from the pre-Etolian era. Portrayed in an arid, desolate location dominated by barren hillsides and caverns, and under layers of charcoal-gray robes suggesting an ascetic lifestyle, he had prophesied the destruction of the original Euranian homeworlds—those that would form the Etolian Empire—and the eventual return of Luzomi in a later age. The first prophecy had already been fulfilled. The second deeply concerned Walmsley.

The portrait of Merician II, known as "the Great," illustrated the founding of the Order of Oscanos and Gheriah—black-clad warrior monks who had eluded capture during the early years of the Saolian invasion to settle on Kelova and construct the Great Temple.

Finally, the picture of Merician VI, who had led the order during the post-Saolian feudal era, portrayed him like a royal sovereign in a grand palace setting and in a tall, jeweled crown and a purple and ivory robe that stretched to the floor, intervening in the conflict between the old Gearmlian Confederation and the Alscras-led Milanian League by imposing the Treaty of Kelova on representatives from both factions.

Walmsley felt bad for asking Navilla to remain on Wichloc. At the time, it had seemed the sensible thing to do. But now, he felt lonely, despite not being alone. Neither Searus nor Kearn were especially religious, though both were respectful to the beliefs. Whinn Rexold had declined the invitation to the meeting with Dhavail's successor. Instead, she had opted to visit the Gherian nunnery that adjoined the Great Temple. Visiting the Great Temple and meeting with the current high priest would have been as meaningful an experience for Navilla as for Walmsley.

The door opened and a middle-aged priestess, simply dressed in a cream-colored robe and cap, stepped forward with outstretched hands to receive Walmsley. "I am Jarrumina, first assistant to His Holiness."

Walmsley bowed. "Madame Jarrumina."

"I am terribly sorry for the delay," Jarrumina said, "but His Holiness is ready to receive you now. Please follow me."

Walmsley's spirits picked up. The High Priest of the Great Temple. For someone who had devoted his retirement to a spiritual quest, this was a watershed moment. With Searus's help, Walmsley grasped his cane and rose to his feet. "Now *I* feel like a young spring hokhel," he said to Kearn with a wink.

After stepping through the doorway, Jarrumina closed the door, leaving Walmsley and the others to gaze in all directions. The room was as bare as a business office, as plain as the unadorned hallways they had walked through. The gleaming white and golden crystal exterior of the Great Temple, extensively rebuilt since its devastation fifty years earlier during the Galactic

Revolutions, had been as grand as he had imagined. Magnificent rainbow-colored jewels decorated the ornate front facade, and massive stone statues of the Etolian high priests adorned the steps leading up from the tree-lined plaza. But inside the foot-thick stone doors, the interior presented a completely different look.

This was the high priest's sitting room? Where were the statues of the Three Guardians? The soothing wisps of incense and fresh flowers? The beautifully colored glass depictions of Mother Gheriah?

Directly ahead, backed by an electro-painting of geometric patterns, was an old wooden desk with holographic monitors on either side. To Walmsley's left sat four chairs and an end table with a tea service. To his right stood two men and two women, all but one sharply dressed in gray business suits and holding light-topped corder-coms. The second man, middle-aged and noticeably paunchy in a layered ivory robe and a tasseled cap, stepped forward with a wide smile.

"Well, it is true!" He clasped his hands together and bowed as the other three recorded the moment. "Lord Walmsley, welcome home."

Walmsley also bowed. "Your Holiness, I am honored to come before thee."

"Let us sit."

With the aides in tow, High Priest Merician XVI—a name of obvious significance—led Walmsley and his party over to the four chairs. Walmsley sat facing the high priest, while Kearn and Searus sat to either side. Kearn's yeoman stood behind Kearn, out of the way. The receiving priest poured cups of tea for the high priest, Walmsley, Kearn, and Searus.

"To your health." Merician lifted his cup.

"And to yours," Walmsley said, surprised that the high priest had not asked for a moment of prayer.

After the ceremonial sip of aromatic tea and a myriad of lights flashing from the corder-coms, Merician handed his cup back to the receiving priest and folded his hands together. "Lord Walmsley," he began, "I am more than delighted to see you. To be honest, we had no idea that you were…how shall I put it?" He chuckled. "Alive and well. This is indeed amazing!"

Walmsley smiled. It had never occurred to him that his sudden, unannounced appearance might be shocking.

"May I inquire as to your whereabouts these past decades?" Merician asked. "If I may be candid, I have always wondered why you abandoned the summit talks at the very time when the people were in need of strong leadership such as yours. Suffice it to say that many were disappointed, even discouraged."

Walmsley lowered his head. He had been afraid that this might come up.

"It's been a long time without any contact," Merician continued. "You'll forgive me if I say that many—myself included—assumed that you had died in obscurity. Of course, I am glad that assumption was incorrect." He cleared his throat. "I hope that you have returned to stay."

Walmsley wondered about the course of this conversation. This was not how he had pictured the high priest. Merician had not brought up any spiritual topics. He had not even mentioned any of the Euranian Ancestors by name. He could not imagine Dhavail or Navilla avoiding their religion during conversation.

"High Priest Dhavail and I had journeyed to the far reaches of the Onglan League," Walmsley said, "for a long-term spiritual retreat."

Merician's eyes bulged at the mention of Dhavail's name. "Is His Holiness...with you?"

Walmsley sadly shook his head. "That is the purpose of my visit. As you can see, I am stricken with age and require much assistance." He motioned toward Kearn and Searus. "So was the high priest. He departed us for his final journey several weeks ago. His last wish was to be returned to his home, to Kelova." Walmsley took a deep breath. "It is my hope that he be laid to rest with the great high priests." He could feel his heartbeat race with anticipation at the request.

"Of course," Merician said, easing Walmsley's mind. "I will soon be addressing all the dominions. We can send notice regarding the high priest to the far reaches of the empire at the same time. He will be given a fittingly majestic memorial."

"Thank you." Walmsley bowed. "May the Euranian Ancestors bestow their blessings upon..." He paused as Madame Jarrumina entered and stepped over to whisper to Merician.

The high priest's face turned serious as Jarrumina pointed out something on one of the aides' corder-coms. "Put it on one of the monitors," he said, terse.

The aide pointed her corder-com at the closest holographic desk monitor, and it came to life with the image of a middle-aged man in a midnight-blue business suit speaking from a podium.

"...the princess of Alscras will now address us."

Walmsley leaned forward in his chair to get a better look at the young princess as she stepped to the podium. She wore a dark suit without adornment of any kind, her golden-red hair tucked under a black headpiece. Walmsley wondered why she, rather than the emperor, was addressing the empire.

The princess stared at the camera for a moment before she began speaking.

"People of the Kingdom of Alscras, and citizens of the empire, I speak to you tonight from Space Fortress Canellis. As you may be aware, the emperor had been on an official visit of this base. Unfortunately, I must share some terrible news with all of you."

Walmsley noticed the high priest struggling to steady his trembling hands as he listened. Was Merician already aware of this terrible news? "What is the time delay here?" Walmsley asked.

"At this distance, almost two and a half days," the aide said.

"So this address is over two days old," Kearn said.

"Yesterday morning, this base was attacked by two individuals—two suicide bombers. One explosion devastated the cruiser Ancora. *Captain Noel Doring and all hands—170 servicemen and women, including the bomber—were killed, and the ship was destroyed."*

The princess looked down for a moment, then continued speaking in a slow, monotone voice, and with an unblinking stare.

"The other explosion occurred in the Command Module of this space fortress. Three hundred eighty-six men and women were killed, including the base commander, Colonel Jetiah Chrystamme, Crown Prince Otias, and the emperor."

Walmsley tensed, his fists clenched. A cold, terrifying dampness rushed through him. He felt a strong grip choke his throat.

"My lord," Searus said, her hand grasping Walmsley's arm.

"I'm okay," Walmsley whispered, though he knew he wasn't. The shock of the devastating news felt overwhelming. This was not how he had pictured his return visit to the empire.

"In accordance with the Order of Succession, I am assuming the duties of the interim monarch of the kingdom. I have issued a call to bring the Alscrasian Council into emergency session and have dispatched communiques to both the Speaker of the Imperial Assembly and the high priest of Kelova."

Merician leaned over to Walmsley. "That is why our meeting was delayed. I was composing a reply to Her Highness."

"It is only right and proper to pause and honor His Majesty's life and work. Therefore, it is my wish that all citizens of the empire enter a period of Royal Mourning for the next five days. Dominion governments may extend their mourning periods as appropriate for local needs and customs. Together, may we cherish our individual and collective memories of a great man, and only together may we ensure that this terrible attack does not jeopardize the empire or the lives of its citizens..."

Walmsley stopped listening. He closed his eyes and began praying. An ominous, oppressive weight pressed down upon him. It was the memory of a nightmare he had lived through—a black, demonic entity that Eurania had not seen in half a century.

"Lord Walmsley," Merician said, interrupting his thoughts. "Now you understand what I meant earlier. I do hope you are back to stay. Now, as before, the empire is in need of strong, experienced leaders—like you."

A pair of eyes, hidden in darkness, studied the image of the princess of Alscras on the widecast monitor as she delivered her speech. Behind the eyes, a sinister mind schemed in silence.

The princess looked weak, hesitant, lacking in confidence, and hastily prepared by her staff. She was not suitable to be the ruler of the most powerful empire in Eurania. She was perfect.

"Though the emperor is no longer with us, he remains in our hearts and our minds. I shall miss my father terribly. I shall miss my dear brother as well. However, the institutions which they worked so hard to establish remain vital and active. They bind all of us, the inhabitants of the empire, together in a common identity and common ways. Though the emperor is no longer with us, we will continue his work, as he would wish us to."

The princess was young, inexperienced. Ripe. Soon enough, the Inner Chamber of the Imperial Assembly would be electing the new emperor or empress, but what really mattered was who could gain command of the Imperial fleet.

The buzzer sounded.

A gloved fingertip activated the speaker. "Yes?"

"Master, are you watching the princess's speech?"

"Of course."

"The admiral is with her. She appears to have the backing of the military."

"Some of the military, not all."

"What are your orders, Master?"

"She is insignificant, a gnat to be swatted. We will advance our timeline."

"But what about—?"

The glove released the switch, and the speaker cut off mid-sentence. With the flip of another switch, the princess's irrelevant speech silenced in similar fashion.

Smoke from a pile of smoldering pomira bark drifted in the air, seeping into the Master's lungs, relaxing them. On the shelf, next to the widecast monitor, stood a miniature figurine of a bipedal reptilian creature with an elongated head, two tiny forearms, butterfly-shaped wings, horns, and a starlike medallion stud around its neck.

The Master—the third *Masoule* of the modern era—rose and bowed before the statuette of Luzomi.

Part 3

BORDER CROSSING

10. Beat to Quarters

In the eons before the formation of the Great Nebula, multi-limbed, multicolored Azixi glanced up at the tinted glow of the giant red Euranian star. As it floated silently through the darkened skies of Amahl with its many tentacles writhing about, it caught brief glimpses of powerful cloudlike manifestations of Oscanos, Gheriah, and the Three Guardians, Cru, Thema, and Cqoeis. Azixi spun about and fled high into the stratosphere, out into space.

It descended to neighboring Sigorum, where it flew under the swooping bi-wings of fiery Jakkum. Below, the many multi-segmented, podlike legs of Neidemus trampled through the rubble. Lightning from the nine spiked heads of legless Writher crackled throughout the air. Ahead, towering over the distant craggy black mountains and surrounded by ghostly gray apparitions of surviving followers of all sizes and shapes, stood their master.

Luzomi's beastly howl shook the trees, rippled the water, and echoed through the city ruins. A swirling cloud rotated high in the sky above the head of Luzomi, emitting a greenish light, with puffs of pink and gray exploding in all directions.

"You summoned me?" Azixi asked.

Luzomi's wings expanded skyward, his claws opening, his tail whipping about behind him. He lowered his head, opened his mouth, and cackled in a low tone.

"You are pure," Azixi read Luzomi's thoughts. *"You are powerful. You are perfect. I have been rendered impotent by my enemies, but your ruthlessness shall restore me to my rightful place. I am the creator of all higher life, and I have chosen you to replace Oscanos. You shall be my favored warrior, Mapooly."*

A pair of eyes, hidden in darkness, focused on the figurine of Luzomi, the starlike medallion stud around the statue's neck glistening while smoke from burning pomira bark drifted in the air.

The buzzer sounded, and a gloved fingertip activated the speaker.

"Yes?"

"A signal, Master. The Grand Army has secured additional vessels and personnel and is departing from the rendezvous point."

"Prepare my ship. I will transmit the coordinates myself."

"Yes, Master. Shall I—?"

With the flip of a switch, the speaker cut off mid-sentence. The eyes closed and the *Masoule*'s mind focused on a different time and place. With slow, quiet breaths, smoke filled the lungs, and the bright medallion stud radiated warm light rays. The mind relaxed, opening to the windows of the universe. Soon, the *Masoule* drifted off.

The rhythmic dark energy of the universe, fanned by the flutter of Luzomi's wings and flavored by the decay of the pomira bark, pulsed into the *Masoule*'s mind, strengthening the body.

Time passed.

The *Masoule*'s eyes reopened to the sight of the Great Nebula. Now repositioned to the spaceborne replica office, the delays of the long-range comm-network would be avoided, with communications directly tapping the short-range relays.

The speaker activated, and General Mapooly appeared on the monitor.

"Welcome, mighty drakothon," the *Masoule* said.

The image of Mapooly bowed. "The Grand Army is assembled and awaits your orders."

Now was the time. The *Masoule*'s forces stood ready for the campaign.

"You shall be our vanguard, the forefront of our charge to restore Eurania to its former glory. The Grand Army of the People's Revolution shall be your scythe, sharpened to slice the multitudes. The little people will be the offering to our sovereign, to burn in the fire of subjugation. General, proceed to your first target. Once you have secured a landing, capture the temple of Oscanos and erect, in its stead, an altar to Almighty Lord Luzomi. Destroy any resistance you encounter."

"Understood," Mapooly said, bowing.

Admiral Zerah squeezed his fist in anticipation, his stare glued to the main monitor. *Q'toz* neared the last vestiges of the Great Nebula, the dust and particles having thinned enough to allow the stars of Upper Eurania to reappear.

"Sir"—the comm operator pointed at his display—"we're receiving a signal from *Bakiraaqu*."

Zerah dashed to the comm station, Bemone hot on his heels. "Let's hear it," he snapped.

"Men and women of the Grand Army..." Mapooly's voice boomed over the speaker. "We now embark upon our great crusade. To this magnificent endeavor, we dedicate our lives and our blood. May we be rewarded with glorious victory and a new golden age for all Euranians."

Cheers rose from all about Zerah.

This was it, he realized, trepidation descending upon him. Whatever General Mapooly's scheme was, they were now committed.

Aboard *Graftinop One*, Rayna waited patiently as the gray-bearded physician dictated into his porta-com.

After he finished, Dr. Doxuit said, "Your ship's doctor left very thorough notes. Everything is consistent with your last series of exams."

"So I'm okay?" Rayna asked.

Doxuit looked up from his porta-com. "You are as you've been, no further changes."

Whatever had happened to her on Volon, it hadn't killed her yet. "Am I finished?"

He gave her a reassuring smile. "For today. Contact me if you feel anything different."

Rayna hopped off the examination table and departed the doctor's office. Passing through the main corridor of the ship, she slowed and gazed at the men and women who had gathered about the wall monitors to watch an incoming widecast from the interstellar comm-network. Trying to peer between the staffers, she caught glimpses of a long procession of people dressed in many subdued but colorful religious dresses of the empire, all singing a familiar hymn.

It was the funeral of High Priest Dhavail.

News of the arrival of the high priest's party at Kelova had set off a wave of excitement throughout the space fortress over the past several days. The stories shared among the many descendants of the fighters of the Galactic Revolutions were a welcome respite from the arduous recovery work after Kumatille's attack. As she listened to the hymn on the monitor, Rayna recalled some of the old war stories from her childhood, especially those of the victory of Monseigneur Dhavail and Lord Walmsley over General Mapooly.

Unable to gain a good view, Rayna gave up and headed up the steps for the princess's chamber. No doubt, Her Highness would also be watching on her private viewer. When she reached the end of the upper-level corridor, the guards flanking the entry saluted and admitted Rayna into the receiving room. Inside, Princess Thericia sat alone with the lights dimmed, clad from head to foot in black and charcoal-gray mourning attire, the ceremony showing on her viewer.

Rayna paused. "Your Highness?"

The princess slowly turned her face. After a moment, she offered a hint of a smile. "Did the doctor find anything new?"

Rayna shook her head. "May I join you?"

Thericia nodded and motioned for her to take one of the nearby seats.

"I hope I'm not intruding," Rayna continued. "The wall monitors are so crowded. I couldn't see anything." She waited for the princess to reply but received none. Sighing, Rayna remembered the sadness she had felt when her own mother had died. She wished she could say something to comfort the princess, but she knew that nothing would really help this soon.

Rayna turned her attention to the footage of the ceremony. The camera slowly panned over the many dignitaries in attendance. Sitting in the front pew with a group of men and women in period military dress uniforms of the Galactic Revolutionary era and an elderly woman in an ivory robe was a man who looked like a frail, aged version of Lord Walmsley from the history videos.

Rayna's jaw dropped. "I don't believe it..." She carefully scrutinized the image on the monitor. "Lord Walmsley...*alive?*"

The princess raised her eyebrows. "He is?"

Rayna pointed at the monitor. "He's right there."

The princess blinked, then took a slow, deep inhale, seeming to rouse herself out of her state of grief. "A living legend, right before our very eyes," she whispered. She turned to Rayna, her eyes now alive, and switched on her comm. "Mr. Franklen, are you seeing what I'm seeing?"

"Your Highness, we're *all* looking at Lord Walmsley!"

"Perhaps we can extend him an invitation?" She glanced over at Rayna, seemingly for her approval, to which Rayna gave a quick nod.

"Yes, Your Highness, I will see what I can do."

"After we ensure the stability the empire, of course."

"And complete the period of mourning for the emperor, Your Highness."

The princess paused and, after a quiet sigh, said, "Yes, Mr. Franklen."

As she switched the speaker off, the bell chimed, and Admiral Kosolf entered. "Your Highness, Colonel Moton has received a signal from the *Freemon* task force. Their estimated arrival is in three days."

Rayna smiled at the news. The space fortress had been vulnerable ever since Kumatille's bomb disabled many of the space cannons. The carrier would restore firepower until repairs could be completed.

"How many ships in the task force?" the princess asked.

"Twenty," Kosolf said. "Eight escort destroyers, three long range scout ships, a troop carrier, three fuelers, and four supply ships."

"I'll feel much better when they've arrived." She motioned for Kosolf to sit. "Any news from the council?"

"Count Haagewyn reports that the council is divided," Kosolf said, as the princess raised the lighting level. "A small faction is advocating a criminal investigation through Imperial channels. The majority of the body, however, is split between a swift military response against Prince Fraither and a diplomatic solution." He handed her a black binder. "Here is my report. Dr. Docherae and his intelligence staff have reviewed it and confirmed the assessment on the major dominions. Each of our options is summarized for you."

The princess opened the binder and glanced at the porta-com inside. After taking a slow breath, she began reading aloud. "...*If the attack was sponsored by the prince of Bexel, a swift military strike should be considered. Bexel's military is not large enough to mount an effective defense against Alscras. However, such military action would risk a response from Heron or the Gearmlian Confederation...*" She lowered the porta-com. "Admiral, I know that Prince Fraither had been a vocal opponent of my father for a long time, but do *you* believe that he was behind the bombing?"

"We are researching whether a link exists between Prince Fraither and Emperor Fur'thur," Kosolf said. "But there's no guarantee that anything definitive will be discovered. With his new alliances, it's possible the prince could be emboldened now."

The princess frowned, then continued skimming the report. "...*Even if the attack was not state-sponsored, mobilization may still be required."* She paused, then read more slowly. *"In the absence of an Imperial succession, and in the interest of maintaining a balance of power between the core worlds, opportunistic Gearmlian and Heronian aspirations for expansion must be deterred..."*

"There have been subtle movements by the Gearmlian and Heronian fleets," Kosolf said. "They appear to be taking defensive positions around their home worlds and along the dominion borders. These could be precautionary moves, anticipating retaliation on our part, or they could be preparatory for more aggressive actions."

Rayna listened to the discussion while watching the widecast of the funeral service. As a succession of eulogists spoke, quick views of the attending dignitaries were shown. She recognized the mustached, silver-haired man in the midnight-blue dress uniform of the Bexelian army. Prince Fraither of Bexel, who looked old enough to be the princess's grandfather, had been one of the founding fathers of the Central Empire, and the primary catalyst in ushering the Gearmlian Confederation into the empire. In the decades since the formation, he had remained strangely quiet as the other core worlds vied for control. However, as she remembered Kumatille's words about elevating Prince Fraither to the Imperial Crown, Rayna could not help but feel suspicious.

In succession, the camera showed Duc Ilwatu, the aged chairman of the Imperial Assembly in a charcoal-gray robe and tasseled hat; Chancellor Moh Wahren of Sestia, a handsome man in a dark business suit; Premier Jhangoria of the Pharrian Republic, draped from head to foot in a flowing black funerary dress; bronze-haired Chairman Astoph Estini of the Onglan Congress; Supreme Dictator Quinn, in the traditional black cape of Heron;

and Lady Ludzenia of Broza, the olive-skinned, shock-white-haired Grand *Primai* of the Gearmlian Confederation in flowing, bright red Brozan robes.

"Your Highness," Kosolf said, "I recommend that we also reposition our capital ships closer to Alscras. *Castella* and her task force would be the quickest to pull back."

"Wouldn't that leave Kelova undefended?" the princess asked.

"I don't think it will be an issue, while all the heads of state—and all their protective details—are on Kelova for the funeral and the upcoming emergency session," Kosolf said. "Protecting our home world is the prudent first move."

The princess slowly, almost reluctantly, nodded in silence. "I won't lie to you, Admiral. My worst fear is that we may be heading toward a conflict in which there will be no victors."

"I understand your concern," Kosolf said, "but I should remind Her Highness that we are not the aggressors, but the defenders of the empire."

The princess paused, then quietly said, "Thank you, Admiral. I will study your report and send you my thoughts."

Kosolf rose and saluted.

After he departed, the princess put the porta-com down and said to Rayna, "I was wrong." Pointing at the monitor, she said, "Even though I should be in mourning on Alscras, I feel that I should be there, on Kelova. Alscras is the only major dominion with its head of state not in attendance."

A wave of sadness swept over Rayna. There wasn't even a little time for the princess to grieve her loss. "Your safety is paramount for now," she said. "Kumatille's last words were of support for Prince Fraither."

"It's not Prince Fraither that I'm worried about." The

princess's eyes narrowed. "It's Lady Ludzenia. People have forgotten that her ascension coincided with the disappearance of the rightful ruler of the Confederation."

"I don't think the people have forgotten," Rayna said. "It's just that her administration has achieved many notable reforms that have benefitted the Gearmlians."

The princess shook her head. "The woman is crafty and secretive. I know. We crossed paths two years ago."

Rayna saw a disturbing darkness appear in the princess's eyes.

"I was young," she said. "I was curious, naive, and headstrong. She accused me of spying on her, and to preserve the peace between Alscras and the Confederation, I was ordered to perform restitution. But what I witnessed convinced me of her true nature. She is a vile sorceress, able to summon the presence of the Keeper of Souls."

"Wa'ohl'thu?" Rayna asked. She was familiar with the name. During childhood, one of the neighbors—an old, solitary woman who dressed exclusively in black—often told her tales of the mysterious Wa'ohl'thu appearing in people's dreams, claiming their lives, and transporting their souls to the underverse.

"Despite what Kumatille said on the recording, I don't believe Prince Fraither to be the real threat," the princess said. "Lady Ludzenia already has control of the Confederation. I suspect that she intends to take the empire."

Lord Walmsley, dressed in funerary white as pure as light, listened stoically to the five hundred voices of the children's choir. They sang "The Song of Jhoraine," the tale of the death of the great Adelph, the legendary warrior and first high priest of Lord Oscanos. In the song, the spirit of Adelph was transformed into that of a monarch butterfly by Almighty Euranus, so that Adelph could fly home to True Eurania and spend eternity in utter bliss with Lord Oscanos, Mother Gheriah, and the other Euranian Ancestors.

Walmsley saw tears stream down the face of His Most Holiness, Merician XVI. The high priest of the Temple of Wiene stood at the massive stone altar, dressed in layers of bronze, silver, and ivory fabric, with a shiny gold vest over his robe and a hawk's head for a cowl. He held a large glittering jewel butterfly in his hands.

The fakir, Walmsley stewed. The tale was one of the most moving in all the ancient stories. Set to the beauty of music, the raw emotions of loss and redemption tugged at the depths of Walmsley's heart. But the bitter taste of his meeting with the high priest still lingered.

Merician was nothing like his predecessor. He was the head of a massive bureaucratic establishment, not a spiritual crusader as Monseigneur Dhavail had been. The meeting started off a disappointment, and after it was mercifully interrupted by the princess's address, ended up utterly forgettable.

"I have always wondered why you abandoned the summit talks at the very time when the people were in need of strong leadership." Merician's pointed words echoed in Walmsley's mind. *"Many were disappointed, even discouraged."* The high priest could have simply stated what he really meant—that, despite all his victories in battle, Walmsley had ultimately failed the people of Eurania.

The statement stung like an accusation of cowardice. He had decided, then and there, not to reveal that the *Gramm* was in his possession. Something in the back of his mind told him that this high priest would covet such a legendary artifact, not empower it.

As the song ended, Merician placed the jewel butterfly on the altar and began the final reading from *The Songs of the Euranians*, a poem known as "Hoscanis's Prayer to Mother Gheriah."

Next to Walmsley, Whinn Rexold wept quietly. Her hands shook and her body trembled, but as befit a consort of a late high priest, she maintained her dignity through the reading.

Surrounding them, dignitary delegations of all sizes and manner of traditional colors sat in attendance. Above, uncounted hundreds, perhaps thousands, from throughout the empire and the neighboring dominions filled the uppermost galleries, sending reports and images back to their respective home planets.

Below the starlike twinkling lights of the hundred-foot-high vaulted stone ceiling of the Great Temple, Walmsley wished again that he had not told Navilla to stay on Wichloc. He had not been prepared for the immense scale of the service or the superficiality of Merician's presence. Walmsley sadly lowered his head. Navilla would have been a more suitable spiritual leader of the temple.

The final reading concluded, High Priest Merician closed the massive book. He raised his arms to bestow the final blessings to the body of High Priest Dhavail. Walmsley marveled at the solid gold casket Dhavail lay in. Navilla would have been pleased that it sat next to the smoking Eternal Cauldron of Creation. The service concluded with "Hymn to Oscanos," sung by the angelic voices of a thousand-woman choir.

Walmsley clutched his pouch as the unsettled feeling surfaced again. Inside, the all-powerful *Gramm* lay dormant. After the service finished, High Priest Dhavail would be taken below, to the subterranean levels below the Great Temple, where he would be laid to final rest with the many great temple leaders of the past.

Similarly, Walmsley would take the *Gramm* below, to the same subterranean levels, to return it to where it had been retrieved fifty years ago.

Walmsley couldn't shake the vividness of his foreboding. He knew in his bones that it wasn't simple apprehension he felt. The cold, clammy presence was unique, a feeling—and a memory—that remained as stark as when it first occurred. He would never forget the images of sheer terror.

Large slabs opened, and High Priest Dhavail's casket slowly lowered into the floor. Walmsley held his breath to maintain his composure and his dignity. This was truly goodbye. The slab doors closed, sealing the tomb of High Priest Dhavail. Walmsley's friend was home.

As the audience filed out in silence, Walmsley remained where he sat. He could hear Dhavail's voice reciting the teachings that he had conveyed to Walmsley over the decades.

"Thank you, my friend," Walmsley whispered.

He had to remain on guard. He had to heed his feelings. Until another was found who could power the *Gramm*, Lord Walmsley remained the only hope for the human race.

"My lord." It was Admiral Kearn, approaching through the departing crowd.

"Yes, Admiral?"

Kearn sat in the seat vacated by Rexold, next to Walmsley. "I ran across some very strange news at Space Control. Apparently, deep space relays have picked up a set of unusual readings from within the Great Nebula. Zero readings."

"Zero readings?" Walmsley asked, not sure if he heard correctly. "As in, no readings at all?"

Kearn nodded his head. "Complete voids. No particles,

no energy, no light. Nothing."

Walmsley tensed. Pitch blackness, devoid of light or life. He fingered his pouch. The feeling—*his* feeling—was it real? "Did they say how many?"

"Not many," Kearn said. "No more than half a dozen, and they seemed randomly scattered across the perimeter of the Great Nebula, stretching from the Onglan League all the way to the Sestian republic."

Even without Searus's monitors, Walmsley could feel his readings elevate. The appearance of the voids could not be a coincidence. Something was approaching—an entity crouching in the shadows of space, preparing to pounce upon them. *Was this the moment that Dhavail had warned of?* Walmsley knew his old teacher was still with him in spirit, but now he needed him in person, too.

Kearn added, "Some were suggesting a connection between the zero patches and a report of an ancient projectile gun recently discovered on the planet Volon."

Walmsley raised his eyebrows. "The name sounds familiar. Is it an Onglan planet?"

Kearn nodded. "On our way home, in fact."

Walmsley looked down at his pouch. He pressed down on the fabric until he could make out the shape of the *Gramm* inside. Walmsley knew he had to act. A leader, even one as aged as he, could not stay put while a threat emerged.

He would not retire the *Gramm*. Not while this oppressive darkness—this suffocating stench of Luzomi—still weighed on him so heavily. What was happening, and what was yet to come? He had to find out.

"I hope that you have returned to stay." The sooner he left the religious bureaucracy behind, the better. *"Now, as before,*

the empire is in need of strong, experienced leaders, like you."

Now, as before, the empire was disappointing. Walmsley had hoped for a shining beacon of the Euranian people. Instead, he had arrived at the exact moment of a palace assassination. Decades had passed, but the turmoil remained the same.

"We have brought High Priest Dhavail home; our job here is finished." With a strong grip on his cane, Walmsley pushed himself to his feet. "Admiral Kearn, prepare for departure."

Admiral Zerah did not like following orders from a mystery man. He couldn't stand the fact that his convoy was following a young nobody—one who had been elevated to flagship captain by the mysterious Mapooly—on an unknown course. Captain Bemone and Isaalt stood nearby, silent. The tension of the situation weighed on Zerah.

By order of General Mapooly, the weapons caches had been opened and distributed, and Bemone's crew had begun training in their usage. Some practiced sidearms, filled with blanks. Others were adapting the ship-mounted weapons for use on *Q'toz*. Similar activities were taking place aboard the other ships, including *Bakiraaqu* and the other old Belaanian warcraft manned by the former crews of the other vessels parked at Yeros.

The promise of riches dangled before everyone. They were being transformed into a mammoth strike force, capable of seizing control of any target they chose.

Bemone walked over from the comm station, handwritten notes in hand, and spoke to Zerah in a low voice. "Sir, we have new orders from Captain Zu." Bemone handed Zerah the paper. "Our new heading."

Paper? What is this? Zerah couldn't believe he was being

handed a piece of paper. Nevertheless, he studied the directional coordinates. "This takes us away from the protective cover of the nebula. What's our destination?"

"No word, sir, except that the convoy will rendezvous later for further instructions."

Zerah stopped studying the coordinates and only stared at them. He hated his situation but didn't know how to get out of it. He glanced at Captain Bemone. Where General Mapooly was taking them, nobody knew. He offered power and prestige, and the crews of the convoy fell in line behind their new leader.

Zerah had no choice other than to plunge ahead with full force into whatever Mapooly's plans were. He reminded himself that, if they were successful, he would have an excellent chance at a high-ranking fleet command in Mapooly's new Imperial military.

He was now in the same situation that his father had been in and had been offered the same tantalizing reward. Perhaps he could succeed where his father had failed.

Walmsley sadly embraced Rexold. Her decision to remain on Kelova meant that he would make the return voyage without the companionship of someone of his own generation. On Wichloc, he would truly be the last survivor of the Galactic Revolutions.

He understood her reasoning. She wished to stay close to Dhavail, even in death. Walmsley always suspected that their relationship was based more on her devotion to everything the former high priest stood for than anything resembling conventional love. She would remain devoted to Dhavail and to the worship of the Euranian Ancestors for the rest of her life. Perhaps longer than that.

"How will you support yourself among Kelovan society?" he asked as members of *Trion*'s crew passed them and ascended the ramp to the ship.

Rexold smiled. "I may not need to. The keepers of Mother Gheriah's gardens have offered me a place among them." She brought out a small medallion from the folds of her ivory funerary robe. "The senior keeper gave this to me." She held it up to show Walmsley. On it was a porcelain depiction of Mother Gheriah, draped in a beautifully elaborate arrangement of leafy vines and long-stemmed flowers. "I will learn to be one of them and help take care of the many gardens that surround the temple grounds. In my remaining years, I hope to devote myself to the service of the Gherian priestesses."

Walmsley smiled. It was a decision befitting the consort of a high priest. "You will be missed on Wichloc."

Captain Pavon walked up to them, saluting. "My lord, the ship is ready for departure."

Walmsley saluted. "Thank you, Captain."

Rexold grasped Walmsley's arm. "Please tell Navilla that I will pray each morning and evening for him and all the people under his care."

"I will." Walmsley reached into his pocket and brought out a digi-com chip. "I wish to leave this with you."

"What is it?"

"The location where the *Gramm* is to be laid to rest. Someone other than myself needs to know where it ultimately belongs." Walmsley paused. He still had the opportunity to change his mind. He could still return the *Gramm*. But no, not when something approached. At some point in the future, it would be returned to its proper resting place. When, he didn't know. "I have been feeling something, ever since the high priest left us." Of all the people, Rexold would understand. "Something dark and foreboding. Something that I can only associate with the terror of Mapooly."

Rexold's eyes widened with surprise, then with fear. "Are you sure, my lord?"

"I have tried to reflect on this feeling, but I am not certain." Walmsley had to decide. "The high priest had devoted himself to teaching me and preparing me for the possibility that the *Gramm* may need to be called upon again." Walmsley straightened his back. "I am keeping the *Gramm* at my side. When I am certain that it is safe to put the *Gramm* away, I will arrange for its return here. Be ready to receive it, should I send you word."

Rexold nodded. "I will be here, my lord."

Walmsley had committed to his decision. He felt the weight of the universe on his shoulders. He also remembered the horror of the past.

Lord Walmsley sat in his room, alone. He felt empty inside. He felt lonely.

He still couldn't believe that Monseigneur Dhavail was gone. Though she was away, he could contact Whinn Rexold on Kelova at any time. But Dhavail—as Walmsley watched the pink clouds of Kelova's sunset whisk by outside his cabin window aboard *Trion*—the realization sank in that the high priest would never return.

Walmsley walked over to the bureau and opened the top drawer. With a heavy heart, he unstrapped his pouch and placed it inside the empty compartment.

"I wish you were still here, my friend," Walmsley whispered. "I need your wisdom. Your courage." He sighed and lowered his head. "Your faith. I wish I was imagining things, imagining monsters and demons. I don't want to face what might be coming."

There was no answer. There would *not* be an answer.

Downcast, Walmsley closed the drawer and locked the *Gramm* away.

The buzzer sounded, breaking the silence.

Walmsley hit the wall switch, opening the door. "Come in." He watched as two muscle men entered his cabin with his luggage cart in tow. Searus also entered. After unloading his possessions and departing with deep, reverent bows, the door closed behind them.

Searus reached for her digi-com and checked Walmsley's readings.

"Am I good?" Walmsley asked, taking hold of his cane.

"Elevated pulse and adrenaline levels." She paused the digi-com. "Are you sure this side trip is wise?" She reached forward and put her hand on Walmsley's arm. "You should seek rest, not stress."

Walmsley gazed out his window at the shrinking globe of Kelova. He closed his eyes and let his mind drift back to the nightmares. Now that they were leaving the empire, the ominous feelings threatened to engulf him. Deep within the darkness, he could sense a cold, calculating personality.

"My lord?"

Walmsley opened his eyes. He wished that Navilla was aboard. Turning to Searus, he asked, "Would you pray with me?"

Searus nodded. "By all means, my lord."

Walmsley smiled. Though not particularly religious, Searus—always so devoted—was a comforting presence.

Together, the two of them stepped to the back of the par-

lor, where they came before a small table with three white candles. Searus pulled a set of cushions from beneath the table and
helped Lord Walmsley kneel. Once he was situated, Searus took
his cane, rested it against the wall, and then knelt down next to
him.

They closed their eyes as Lord Walmsley recited in a soft,
soothing voice, "Let your innermost thoughts lift up through the
smoke rising from the candle flame. Lord Oscanos, Mother Gheriah, and the Three Guardians will hear our prayers." He tried to
think rationally, but he could feel his anxiety growing. He
opened his eyes and gazed at the three white candles that sat on
the small table before him. "Please light the candles."

Searus ignited the striker and held the tiny flame before
Walmsley's eyes.

*A tiny spark of life, a beacon of hope in the void of dark-
ness.*

She lit the center candle, the initial burn flaring in a
bright flash before settling down.

Walmsley took a deep breath, clutched his hands together,
lowered his head and prayed for goodness and light, for themselves and for all the people. He prayed for strength and wisdom.
An entity of evil was approaching. He prayed for mercy.

Hi, Mom -

*I'm sorry I haven't had a chance to write until now. I un-
derstand that you have inquired about us, so you must know by
now that we are all fine and unharmed. Our current assignment
is classified, so all I can tell you is that there is a lot of work to
do here, and that it's in service to the princess. She is very capable, so even though she is young, I think she will make a good*

queen, if the council will give her a chance.

How are you holding up? I know the death of the emperor must be a major shock to you and—

At the sound of his porta-com's chime, Morgan sat up in his bunk. It was time to go. With a sigh, he stopped writing. He wondered how his mother was doing. Her new husband (he wasn't *that* new, Morgan reminded himself) was a good man. But he wasn't the same as Morgan's father, wherever he was. After so many years, Morgan still wrestled with mixed feelings and theories of what-if.

He placed his porta-com back on its holder and hopped to his feet. He'd have to finish after dinner.

Morgan walked through the *Ocelot* corridors, observing the many men and women at work, his mind racing down a list of detailed goings-on. Except for a momentary pause to watch High Priest Dhavail's funeral, life at the space fortress had overturned into a blend of triage and the routine. A very brief, very somber service had been hastily performed for the officers and crew of *Ancora* before the bodies were ferried back to fleet headquarters on Alscras.

Aboard *Ocelot*, Otho's testing on the bosonic torpedoes finally began showing some progress as the firing computers were successfully calibrated. Meanwhile, Franklen appeared less often, and Imperial staffers converted a utility room below the Ops deck into their work area.

Rounding a corner, Morgan headed for the large door at the end of the hallway. He wasn't sure how he should feel. It was an honor to be invited, with Otho and Lon, to the captain's quarters for the evening, while Lendus covered the watch. Perhaps it was a sign that the captain was starting to warm to Morgan, finally.

But right now, the invitation reminded him of how badly his last conversation with Rayna had ended and how terribly he felt about it. Besides, he reminded himself, the evening could take a sudden turn for the worse with the mercurial captain. Perhaps he was being evaluated by an uptight, overprotective father. Morgan thought of Rayna's travails on Volon and her current medical status, and he stifled a sigh as Otho and Lon joined him in front of the captain's door.

"Ready?" Lon asked.

"Sure," Morgan said.

"Go for it," Otho said. "My stomach's growling already."

Lon hit the buzzer. As soon as the door opened, they saluted in unison.

"At ease, gentlemen," Captain Choff said, admitting them.

Morgan, Otho, and Lon stepped into a suite consisting of the front parlor, where Yeoman Smyra was setting up for dinner, and the interior private quarters. Morgan gazed around, never having been invited inside before. A miniature torpedo boat sat on a shelf, next to the captain's desk. Above it hung a medal of commendation and the accompanying certificate from the admiral. In the opposite corner, Morgan saw a ten-stringed instrument, an *eth-wu-pia*, sitting on a small chair. Next to it, on a modest table, was a sepia-toned picture of a pretty young woman with a wide-brimmed hat over her dark wavy hair, holding a bald baby.

"Sir," Otho abruptly said, "we've finally reached phase four on the torpedo tests."

Choff held up his hand, silencing Otho. "That's all right, Mr. Ennuk. You're off duty tonight."

As Otho nodded, Morgan's attention returned to the baby picture.

"Yes, Mr. Teggo," Choff said, "that's Rayna with her late mother." The captain paused. "I still miss her to this day."

Morgan smiled at his apparent transparency. Rayna's soft eyes and mischievous smile still looked the same, even as an infant.

"How is your mother, Mr. Teggo?" Choff asked.

"I'm very lucky," Morgan said. "She's remarried and moved to a new and better home." He paused to think of all the hardships during his childhood—for both himself and his mother—growing up alone after his father had abandoned them for a life of wild pursuits. He lowered his head and stared at the floor, though he wasn't sure if it was from relief or the old feelings of shame. "Her husband's a good man, and she's happy, finally." He took a deep breath and relaxed.

"Glad to hear that. Do you play, Mr. Teggo?" Choff asked, changing the subject and gesturing with his hand toward the *eth-wu-pia*.

Morgan shook his head. "No, sir. But I think Lon does. Don't you?"

Lon managed a weak smile. "Not very well. I haven't played since I was a boy. You, sir?"

Choff shook his head. "It's been a long time for me as well, Mr. Prowzi." Choff inhaled, slow and deep. "I taught Rayna, when she was very small. She was very good for her age, able to sing and accompany herself. But I doubt if I'm much better than you now." He turned to Morgan. "Does she sing for you, Mr. Teggo?"

"She used to, when we were together." Morgan smiled. "She has a beautiful singing voice."

"That she does." Choff nodded.

Otho read the commendation: "'For bravery above and beyond the call of duty.'"

"Near the planet Cidon, many years ago," Choff explained. "You won't read any accounts about it, though. It happened far out, beyond the Outer Territories." He cleared his throat. "Our task force was ambushed by a swarm of Tenotan pirates. The ships scattered, and when my torpedo craft's engine was hit, we were left behind."

Morgan saw the captain's eyes darken, his voice slowing and turning grim.

"We eventually reached Cidon. But being an isolationist world, they refused our request for help, and when a straggler Tenotan ship appeared and attacked"—he paused for an instant— "I had no choice but to evacuate the crew to the planet before the pirates destroyed the ship.

"Of course, we were not welcome, and once the Tenotan ship landed, our situation quickly deteriorated into a fight for survival. We managed to escape in a Cidonian craft and journeyed through deep space for a month." He sighed. "We soon ran out of ammunition and food. In all, we lost twenty-one men and women on that accursed planet. Not one received a proper burial."

Morgan noticed that Choff seemed to be staring off into the distance. The captain's eyes barely blinked.

"The cuxioblade is the greatest weapon ever created. I must have killed at least a dozen Tenotans and another dozen Cidonians by myself. I was soaked from head to foot in two different colors of blood. It was the worst thing I ever did in my entire life. And when we finally reached the Outer Territories, and civilization, they gave me this medal."

A somber silence filled the air.

Choff took another deep breath and relaxed. "Like I said, it was a long time ago." He forced a chuckle. "I did manage to steal a set of Cidonian dinnerware from the vicar's residence." He indicated Smyra's setting. "Well, gentlemen, with that tall tale, shall we dine?"

Morgan awoke from the haunting story. Somehow, shifting to dinner conversation felt a little awkward. But he followed the others to the table.

The food itself was nothing particularly special, being the same gravy-laden chonquet loin and roasted rhisomn roots that were served to the rest of the officers.

"Someday," Choff said, slicing his meat, "each of you will be up for discharge. Have you given thought to what you'll be doing afterward?"

"I'm thinking of staying with the service," Otho said.

"Not going back to the ranch?" Morgan asked.

"It's a nice place to retire," Otho said. "Kick back and watch the cows eat grass. But the service is an honorable career. My kid brother Alenn is planetside with the Royal Army. I figure the star fleet is a good chance to see the different corners of the empire. Maybe I'd like to stay aboard *Ocelot* for a little longer, then see if I can move up to one of the carriers. I've started training Mr. Turons as my assistant, and it's going very well, so I may expand to the other quartermasters as well. I understand that's how they do things on the carriers."

"You're a fine officer, Mr. Ennuk," Choff said with a smile. "The service will be for the better with you staying." He then turned to Lon. "Mr. Prowzi?"

Lon cleared his throat. "I'm considering entering the clergy."

"There's certainly nothing wrong with that," Choff said, taking a bite. "If I knew, I would have asked you to say a few words before we started eating. Mr. Lendus has mused, from time to time, on possibly pursuing that path as well."

"He's not ordained?" Otho asked.

Morgan sighed. "How many times have I tried to tell you, Oggy, that's just a rumor."

Choff smiled. "Mr. Lendus is not ordained. Yet." He turned to Morgan. "Mr. Teggo?"

Morgan swallowed. *Here it comes.* He cleared his throat. "Sir, we haven't talked at length about it, but Rayna and I, uh…"

With his plate emptied, Choff put his utensils down. "Speak freely, Mr. Teggo. This is a social occasion."

Morgan took a breath and glanced at Otho and Lon, whose irksome smiles hinted their enjoyment of the moment. "We haven't actually talked about it, sir, but I would like, uh, Rayna's hand in marriage." There, he'd said it, and Choff seemed calm. Morgan took another deep breath, this one for relaxation. "Eventually, of course. We have a lot of practical details to figure out first."

"Such as, how are you going to support yourselves?" Choff leaned back in his chair and folded his arms. "You must understand, I have a vested interest in this."

"Of course, sir." Morgan quickly gathered his thoughts. "One idea, which we haven't talked about in detail, is that, well, given that we're both very good bladesmen, we could return to Alscras and open a martial arts school. We could train teams to participate in tournaments for prize money. Nothing grand, but it would be a comfortable life, and we would both be doing something we enjoy and are good at."

"Hmm. Interesting." Choff's left eye squinted.

"Like I said, it's just an idea, sir."

Choff mused for a moment. "So it is, Mr. Teggo. There are good ideas, and there are, well…other ideas…"

Morgan went silent. Other ideas, as in "*not*-good ideas."

Smyra cleared the table, set out four glasses and a bottle of liquor, and placed a small case in front of Choff.

"Archari Red," Choff introduced, opening the bottle and pouring the sunset-red liquid into the four glasses. "Archarion is an independent world in the region between the empire and Pharry. Hospitable enough, and with a long history—you may be more familiar with its ancient name of Zagon—but now they mostly keep to themselves." He passed out the four glasses. "A word of caution: this has a strong kick."

Morgan accepted his glass and, as he waited for Otho and Lon to receive theirs, tried to push aside his feelings about the captain's "ideas" remark.

"Gentlemen"—the captain held out his glass—"you are part of the command structure of this ship, and as such, extensions of me and the orders that I operate under. After the despicable attack on *Ancora* and the assassination of both the emperor and the crown prince, no one can predict what the coming days and weeks will bring. But you will be counted upon to help lead the crew of this ship, regardless of how things unfold, whether it be in peace or otherwise." He glanced at Lon. "May the Euranian Ancestors light our way?"

Lon nodded. "Amen to that, sir."

"To you," Choff toasted, "and your futures."

Morgan smiled, relieved, and sipped the stinging drink.

Several columns of starcraft crossed the starless void that separated the Central Empire from its neighbors. A hybrid of small needle-nosed destroyers, an armada of converted box transports, aging battlecruisers sporting rows of fiery red spikes along their main decks, and two winged Belaanian dreadnoughts, the combined force maintained communications blackout for the duration of the journey, employing shuttles to ferry personnel and orders between ships.

On board the flagship dreadnought, *Bakiraaqu,* General Mapooly sat, slumped over in his chair, his eyes closed, while the multiarmed midnight-blue figure scurried up and down his back.

A buzzer sounded.

The figure withdrew its many arms and buried itself within Mapooly. Slowly, Mapooly opened his eyes, raised his head, sat up, and activated the monitor on his desk. "Yes?"

Captain Zu appeared on the monitor. "General, Admiral Zerah's liaison reports that the first of the advanced scouts have reached the Imperial borders. One of the space fortresses exhibits extensive wreckage and is lightly guarded by a flotilla of two cruisers, a dozen escort destroyers, and other smaller craft."

Mapooly's lips curled. "We have our point of attack, Captain. Break silence. Relay to all ships: prepare for battle."

"Yes, sir."

Mapooly switched the monitor off. He closed his eyes, lowered his head, and slumped over. One by one, four silhouette-like limbs extended out from his back, reaching out, grasping, clutching, clawing.

"The game is 'Seven Red Revolution.'" Choff opened the game set. "Mr. Prowzi, would you care to deal?"

Lon shuffled the square maroon-and-gold cards, dealt them out, and placed the five candy-colored translucent dice and the stack of remaining cards in the middle of the board. Each person selected a token, and play commenced. After three rounds, Lon became the first victim, losing the last of his cards into the center pit on a double-dice-roll gambit.

"A valiant effort," Morgan exhorted with a hint of sarcastic delight. Exposing his weakest card, he rolled the dice. The total came up to fifteen. Morgan advanced his token and drew three cards, including a powerful Green Queen.

Otho, down to just four cards, exposed three of them and rolled the dice. Four, two, two, one, and zero. Otho grimaced and threw his remaining card into the pit in the middle of the board.

"Welcome, Oggy," Lon said, smiling to Otho.

"Mr. Ennuk, you actually had the right idea," Choff said, "if only you had the right hand to put down. So, Mr. Teggo..." Choff leaned forward in his chair. "It's down to us." He put all but one of his ten cards down and rolled the dice. Four, four, one, one, one. "Ha!" He drew ten new cards, advanced his token two steps ahead of Morgan's, and leaned back in his chair to survey the state of the game. "I'll have you defeated in the next round."

Morgan knew his situation. The honorable move would be to concede. The smart strategic play would be to let his captain, the father of his intended, win. But as he studied the subtle smirk on Choff's face, ire rose up from within. The occasional scowl, the passive-aggressive zingers, a scut-work assignment in the cargo hold a year ago, and the temperamental outbursts, as upon their return from Volon. Even in a friendly game against Otho or Lon, it wasn't in Morgan's nature to lie down without a fight. But in a match against this captain—and on his own turf, no less—it became total bravura.

Morgan exposed all but one of his ten cards and reached for the dice.

The speaker buzzed just as the dice landed. Five, five, four, two, one—enough to move past the captain for the win.

"Bridge to all decks." It was Turons's voice. "General Quarters. This is *not* a drill."

"*Krok*—" Morgan stifled his curse as the klaxon sounded.

Choff switched on the monitor. "Report, Mr. Lendus."

"Captain, a large formation of unidentified vessels is entering the perimeter. The space fortress has just gone on alert."

Morgan tensed, then jumped to his feet as the captain said, "Let's go, men."

Morgan's eyes swept over the array of display panels as he, Otho, and Captain Choff mounted the bridge. Lendus had the long-range scanner on the bridge monitor. The approaching vessels already numbered twenty; as they advanced, more ships entered the picture.

"Captain Jaron and Lt. Colonel Moton are both standing by on the speaker," Grisconne reported as Choff, Morgan, and Otho donned their e-suits.

"Captain Jaron, do you have an ID?" Choff asked.

"We're not picking anything up yet," Jaron said.

"Neither are we," Moton added. "The flotilla appears to be primarily destroyer-sized craft of all differing makes. It's difficult to make out. A private merchant fleet, perhaps?"

"Box transports confirmed," Turons said. "They are all painted black, which makes visual contact difficult, but they look like cargo carriers from several decades ago. Wait. There's something different now."

A larger vessel, about five times the size of the preceding ships, appeared on the monitor, followed by a second identical vessel. Both had two sets of bright green wings flaring out from the main deck and a pair of long spikes pointed forward from the bow.

"Distance: one hundred light-seconds," Morgan reported. "Closing fast."

"What is that?" Grisconne asked, pointing to the next group of ships to appear.

Everyone stared at the ferocious, animal-headed man-of-war in the center of the group. The lower half of the bow was covered with bloodred incisors that extended forward and curved into pointed tips, while the upper half of the bow was pitch black. The long main deck was painted in a fiery orange-and-black striped pattern.

"Never saw a ship that looked hungry before," Otho said.

Morgan pulled up the databank and began searching through it. Nothing from the Imperial fleet resembled the animal-striped, tusk-lined, pupil-less visage staring at them. Just as he was about to give up and begin searching through known vessels from the nearby Fembournian star cluster, he ran across some-thing very similar. "This doesn't make sense," he said, puzzled.

"What is it, Mr. Teggo?" Choff asked.

"A Belaanian dreadnought," Morgan said. "I thought Be-laan was destroyed at the end of the Galactic Revolutions."

Choff said, "Before he was killed by Lord Walmsley's forces, General Mapooly set off a neutrino shower that devastat-ed his planet and wiped out all the historical records. His people were all destroyed."

"Then how do we explain the dreadnought?" Otho asked.

"That's the head of a Belaanian wovren on the bow," Morgan reported. "The stripes and upturned tusks are supposed to be unique to that species of wovren."

"There's more coming," Otho interrupted.

Morgan ran the same query on the next group of ships. Strange as they looked, with curved rows of pointed spikes running the length of the main decks, they resembled old vintage cruisers.

"I recognize those," Lendus said. "They're Belaanian also."

Morgan checked his readout. "Distance now seventy-five LS."

"A show parade, sir?" Turons asked.

"No," Lendus said. He turned to Choff. "It's a strike force, sir."

"*Krok*," Morgan muttered under his breath. He hoped Lendus was wrong, but deep down, Morgan knew that was unlikely. The space fortress had been severely crippled. The sudden appearance of this unidentified fleet couldn't have been a coincidence. Why the ships looked fifty years old was a mystery. Whether they exhibited the limitations of fifty-year-old ships remained to be seen, but their large numbers were daunting. Morgan flexed his fists and double-checked the monitors on his panel. *Freemon* was still more than a day away.

"Mr. Franklen is on the speaker," Grisconne reported.

"We're picking up the approaching force, Captain," Franklen broke in. "What should we do?"

"Recommend you prepare for immediate departure," Choff said. "We'll hold them off as best we can, but they outnumber us badly. Mr. Teggo?"

Morgan, after considering the need for natural camouflage away from the space fortress—but not too far away—gave his recommendation. "There's a comet cloud within two days travel. The space debris will provide ample cover for hiding."

"We can rendezvous with you there," Choff said. "Mr.

Teggo will send you the course heading."

"Thank you, Captain. Join us as soon as you are able."

"We'll be going dark," Admiral Kosolf said. "Captain Jaron, you have seniority. Set up a two-line defense."

"Yes, sir," Jaron replied. "Good luck. Captain Choff, you have *Epoch*, *Lexay*, and *Silmarro* with you," she said, naming the three slower ships.

Choff took a deep breath. "Understood, Captain. Colonel Moton, it looks like it's up to us."

"Are you kidding, Captain?" Moton said. "We'll be fighting without a central command structure, each watchtower firing at its own discretion."

"It's still a viable defense, Colonel," Jaron interjected. "We'll lead the destroyers out to meet the strike force while you prepare."

"We'll set up the second line behind you, Captain Jaron," Choff said. Turning to Lendus, he ordered, "Prepare for departure. Relay to Commander Streat of *Epoch* and the two cutters."

Morgan stared at the screen, watching *Pouton* lead a task force of twenty ships away. The approaching strike force numbered over fifty ships and was still growing.

The captain looked at Morgan. "Mr. Teggo, if I believed in spirits, I'd say that the ghost of General Mapooly has returned with his old fleet. But I don't."

Morgan didn't believe in spirits, either. It felt assuring that he and the captain were on the same page. But who was this?

"Commander Streat signals they're ready," Grisconne said.

"Operations?" Lendus called down.

"Ready for combat," Lon reported, with Violette by his side.

Lendus turned to Otho. "Weapons, Mr. Ennuk?"

"Standing by, sir."

"Let's go, Mr. Lendus," Choff ordered. "Take us away from the space fortress, interception course."

In the circular Ops deck of *Graftinop One*, Rayna stood beside Princess Thericia and watched the personnel secure the ship. The expansive array of displays lining the walls—some for operation of the Starmaster, others for monitoring the comm traffic of the empire—seemed to surround everyone, including Admiral Kosolf, standing with Captain Udahl up on the bridge.

"Located, sir," the navigator reported. "It's the Qirrous comet cloud. At maximum velocity, about two days travel, as Mr. Teggo reported."

Rayna gazed at the main monitor. The WAC ship and the two escort destroyers sat on the pier, next to *Graftinop One*. Giant robot arms were pulling the moorings back from the four ships.

Admiral Kosolf said, "We don't dare signal the other ships with the heading. They'll just have to follow our lead."

"Understood, sir." Captain Udahl turned to the executive officer. "You may depart when all hands are ready."

The young empire that had emerged from the Galactic Revolutions was now in danger, Rayna realized. She remembered her history lessons from school: how, in the last days of the ancient Etolian Empire, the devastated dying central government struggled to maintain authority as breakaway regions declared independence in an anarchic grab for power. Once civil war engulfed the settlements in Upper Eurania, Saolian invaders from nearby Fembournia swept in and conquered the region, plunging all humanity into a centuries-long dark age from which finally emerged the Central Empire and the current half century of peace and stability.

She reached out and took the princess's hand. Would the core worlds rally behind the princess, or would they splinter?

"I don't know how to prevent the fight," the princess confessed. "How to keep the empire at peace." She turned to Rayna. "The core worlds are sure to mobilize now. Where do I begin?"

"First, you must survive," Rayna urged. "Stay strong and in command. As long as you're viable, you'll have defenders of the Crown and of the empire."

"I wish I could be as sure as you," the princess whispered.

"You have the authority," Rayna said. "You must have the will to wield your power."

"Captain," Grisconne said, "Commander Streat reports that *Epoch* and the cutters have taken up their positions."

Choff ordered, "Weapons on combat command."

Morgan posted the tactical layout on the navigation monitor, then shot a quick glance at Otho, who was immersed in the many surrounding displays, as the captain had turned the ship's combat command over to his combat officer. While *Ocelot* held position with the frigate *Epoch* and the cutters *Lexay* and *Silmarro*, *Pouton* headed for the center of the mammoth strike force, its twenty-ship task force dwarfed by the opposition. "Distance is now twenty-five LS," Morgan reported.

"This is Captain Jaron of the cruiser *Pouton*," Jaron's voice sounded over the *Ocelot* bridge speaker. "Identify yourselves and your intentions."

Static filled the speaker for a moment. Then it cleared with an automatic translation of the reply.

"This is General Mapooly of Belaan, commanding the Grand Army of the People's Revolution."

Morgan gasped at the declaration. A ghost from the past? He looked over at Otho, then at Captain Choff and Lendus.

"General Mapooly," Jaron said, "state your heading."

Mapooly cackled. "I am not a fool, Captain. We are entering Imperial space; that is all I will state."

"Hold your position for boarding, General."

"Captain Jaron," Mapooly countered, "withdraw your task force, and we will relent from opening fire."

Morgan switched a side monitor to display another view of the tactical positions. The lead Belaanian destroyers broke formation, swung wide, and surrounded *Pouton* on three sides. The two Belaanian carriers and the Belaanian dreadnoughts were far behind, deep in the formation and well protected.

"Withdraw *immediately*," Mapooly continued, "or we will destroy you without mercy."

Pouton's escort destroyers broke formation and swung in wide arcs toward the front of Mapooly's strike force.

"Distance: ten LS. Torpedo range." As Morgan watched the two swarms of destroyers approach each other at attack speed, first on a tactical display, then on a visual monitor, the realization sank in that, for the first time in half a century, hostilities were breaking out.

General Mapooly descended the steps from the *Baki-raaqu* pilothouse, entering the command center. Captain Zu and the rest of the bridge crew stood before Mapooly. On the command monitor, the faces of Admiral Zerah, Captain Bemone, and Isaalt waited in silence. With the internal speaker on and the relays to the other ships open, Mapooly addressed his followers.

"To do all that one is able to do, that is the potential of the human race; but to do all that one *wishes* to do, that is to approach the realm of the gods. Fifty years ago, a magnificent dream was cut short and left unfulfilled. Power is my mistress, glory my courtesan, and I have toiled too hard in my conquests to allow either to be taken away from me. Today, we return to that path—the path to power and glory.

"You must do as I do, dream as I dream. Be gods. As I am a god, you can be gods. Do not fear death; gods cannot die. Defy death, drive him into the enemy's ranks, and you can defeat him, as we will defeat all our enemies. Above all else, victory belongs to those who persevere. Follow me, and we will persevere to victory. Victory!"

He paused, staring at the men standing around him. Four slender black limbs reached out from behind him. On the monitor, he saw the reflection of his own eyes blaze fiery red.

"This moment will be remembered forever," he said. "The return of General Mapooly." The small Imperial flotilla came into firing range. His lips curled. His teeth bared. "Open fire!"

Cannon shots blazed out from three Belaanian destroyers.

Captain Jaron's deep, husky voice bellowed over the speaker. "All ships, fire at will."

A storm of laser blasts erupted, blanketing the formation of battling warships, the bright explosions lighting up the black box craft like silhouettes. One of the Belaanian destroyers reeled from a succession of rapid-fire hits. An explosion erupted from its engine, sending it spiraling between two other ships and away.

"They got one!" a voice from *Pouton* called out over the speaker.

"Lord Oscanos, have mercy on us all," Lendus muttered.

"Signal Alscras, maximum gain," Captain Choff told Grisconne. "Inform the council that we have engaged the Belaanian strike force."

Admiral Zerah watched as Captain Bemone ordered *Q'toz* to open fire on the formation of Imperial destroyers. He doubted if any of the warships packed as much firepower as his own ship, which bulged from bow to stern with military-grade weaponry.

"Target approaching," Isaalt reported, indicating the ships on the monitors. "They're maintaining formation."

"Hard over," Bemone ordered. "Bring our starboard broadside to bear."

Zerah glanced at one of the side monitors, noting that *Pouton* had plunged deep into the main body of convoy transports, while *Ocelot* pivoted toward the Belaanian warships. On the one hand, it felt surrealistic that he was now commanding a battle force. On the other, fleeting thoughts of conquest crisscrossed his mind. He knew how he could end the battle in short order. "Signal all ships," Zerah ordered the communications man. "Concentrate fire on the two cruisers."

"All weapons open fire," Bemone ordered.

Q'toz roared to life, its high-powered pulsers peppering the enemy with a deadly barrage of explosive blasts. Two Imperial destroyers suffered a cascade of hits amidship and lost power. Other ships scattered in all directions.

"Captain," Zerah broke in, "let's back *Q'toz* off. Let the other ships spearhead the attack." *No need to get personally entangled*, he thought, *when we have an overwhelming numerical advantage*.

"Yes, sir," Bemone said. "Helm, reverse course."

While the ship backed away from the point of engagement under Zerah's watchful gaze, one of the large transports fired half a dozen torpedoes at *Pouton*, scoring three hits across the cruiser's hull.

"Sir," Morgan reported, his pulse quickening, "the Belaanian ships have broken through *Pouton*'s line."

Pulser fire littered the formation of ships as rapid-fire coordinates raced across Otho's monitors.

The battle was not going well, and having seen footage of old Lord Walmsley at High Priest Dhavail's funeral, Morgan wished he had a chance to retrieve and study Walmsley's successful tactics against Mapooly. "Enemy approaching," he said. "Distance: five LS. Bearing: 2.25 by 15 degrees."

"Trackers locked," Lon reported.

"Forward launchers," Otho called down, "fire."

Power surged through the control systems and a rumble vibrated the ship as four energy torpedoes shot out.

A Belaanian battlecruiser, firing a web of defensive countermeasures, tried to weave around the pattern of *Ocelot* torpedoes. A moment later, it took a brilliant blast on its bow. *Epoch* flew into view and opened fire, its forward batteries blanketing the battlecruiser in a barrage of detonations.

"There's our target, Mr. Ennuk," Choff said, indicating one of the Belaanian carriers sitting behind the struggling Belaanian battlecruiser.

Otho reset the automatic trackers. On his monitor, the launchers reloaded while crews readied the next set of torpedoes. On the panorama-pane, an explosion hit *Epoch*'s stern. Its maneuverability compromised, the frigate tilted and began drifting. The two Belaanian destroyers circled around and fired, bombarding *Epoch* on two sides. Without warning, *Epoch*'s batteries roared to life, showering the destroyers with pulser fire.

"Full ahead," Choff ordered. "Bring us to course 136-16."

As Turons banked the ship in a wide arc, *Ocelot* maneuvered between two enemy destroyers on a path to intercept the carrier.

"Broadside batteries," Otho called down, "target destroyers and open fire."

The Costarking turrets roared to life, pounding the destroyers with pulser fire. The ship on *Ocelot*'s port side erupted in a rapid-fire succession of magazine explosions along the length of its hull, blowing the ship apart and showering debris in all directions.

"Oh yeah," Morgan shouted. Ahead, the carrier grew larger. "Clear path to target. Distance: 3.2 LS. Bearing: 23.3 by 348 degrees."

Just then, a salvo of mega-pulser fire from the Belaanian dreadnought hit *Ocelot*, rocking the cruiser with explosions across the bow. On the Ops deck, one of the control stations erupted in a shower of sparks and smoke, throwing the crewman to the floor. In response, Lon dashed over and took the controls.

"Sir, the helm's not answering!" Turons yelled.

"Auxiliary controls," Lendus ordered.

Turons threw the switch, and the helm went dead. He flipped it back and tried again. "The backup's not responding."

Another salvo hit rocked the bridge.

"*Dox!*" Morgan followed the line of diagnostic numbers on his board until he found a blank reading. "The relay's been hit." The ship was a sitting target. He called down to Lon. "Can you bypass the relays?"

"We're dead here, too." Lon rose from the Ops deck control station. "I'll have to go take care of it."

As another salvo hit the hull and rocked the ship, Lon turned the Ops deck over to Violette and bound out.

Graftinop One pushed off from the pier and, once clear of the space fortress, led the two escorts and the WAC ship into space.

Rayna watched *Pouton* and *Ocelot* put up valiant fights against overwhelming forces. *Ocelot* appeared to be in trouble, drifting off course as the carrier pounded it relentlessly.

The princess had managed to keep her composure while they watched the battle, but Rayna wrestled with her uncertainty about *Ocelot*'s situation. Images of her father and Morgan, struggling to regain control of the ship, worried her. She put her hands together in a tight grip and hoped that the two of them would be able to put their differences aside and work together.

Her final, dismissive words to Morgan echoed within her. Deep down, she knew he must have meant differently than what he had said. She didn't really want to brush him away. Not if she knew that those would be her last words to him.

She had told him to go away. Now, she was the one going away, leaving him to the fight. She watched the space fortress, and the battle, shrink into the distance, and her conflicted feelings about Morgan welled up from the depths of her heart.

Belowdecks on *Ocelot*, crewmen in e-suits raced about, effecting repairs, both structural and electronic, as coolant leaked into the air all about them.

"Hand me that servo-socket," a crewman called out.

"Gravitation holding?" another asked.

"There…it's back," Fota said. "Good job."

"Bridge to all decks." It was Turons's voice over the speaker. "Brace for impact."

Another salvo hit, the jolt throwing the crewmen off their feet.

Through all the activity on *Ocelot*, the Phantom slipped by, unnoticed, as he made his way to the banks of engineering relays. Once hidden from view by the deep columns of equipment, he searched each unit, one by one, until he found the Fire Controller. He put his hand on it. Very warm.

The front panel included four service doors. The top held the relays to the port batteries, the second the starboard batteries. The third controlled all the torpedo launchers. The final door held the master relays that connected the power source in the engine room to the firing controls on the bridge.

Zukaaran opened the fourth door, deposited a tiny circular device inside, and closed the door. He then emerged from the depths of the relay banks and blended back into the surrounding activity.

11. Metamorphosis

As General Mapooly watched the battle from the relative safety of the *Bakiraaqu* pilothouse, he felt disgusted—soiled—by Admiral Zerah's incompetence. After *Q'toz*'s withdrawal from the battle, the small Imperial forces stiffened their resistance. Two of the slower transports took hits amidship, and as they drifted apart with their engines disabled, *Q'toz* suddenly became exposed to the main crossfire.

Directly below, Captain Zu, who commanded a dozen men in the ship's command center, called up to the pilot, sitting next to Mapooly with an unfettered view in all directions. "Hard to port. Bring all torpedoes to bear on the lead Imperial destroyers."

The pilot swung the flagship about in a wide arc on an interception course with *Q'toz*'s opponents.

At that moment, *Q'toz* launched a barrage of cannonade fire, catching the lead Imperial destroyer in an onslaught across its bow. A brilliant arc display erupted from the underside of the destroyer's forecastle, ran up through the bow, engulfed the superstructure, and raced through the ship, until the forward magazines exploded in a fireball that shattered the hull. *Q'toz* then turned its weapons on the second destroyer, bombarding its bow and forcing it to retreat.

"Retarget," Mapooly ordered, seeing *Q'toz* no longer threatened. *Maybe Zerah wasn't all that inept.* "Where are the Imperial cruisers?"

"One appears in trouble, sir," Zu reported.

Mapooly looked at two of the nearby monitors. On one, *Pouton* was in pursuit of one of the Belaanian dreadnoughts. The other display showed *Ocelot*, adrift and helpless.

"Target the cripple," Mapooly ordered Zu. "Take it out."

"Lon," Morgan called down belowdecks. "What's happening down there?"

"I'm on it, Morgan. I'll have it back in a minute."

Morgan pounded his fist on the console in frustration. The ship drifted farther off course as shot after shot exploded against the portside plating.

"Sir!" Turons called out. "Incoming!"

On the monitor, a telltale flash of red light from the wovren-headed Belaanian flagship marked the launching of a torpedo in their direction.

Lendus hit the speaker. "All decks, brace for impact."

The torpedo streaked into the port side of the main deck, the blast setting off a chain explosion and sending the ship spiraling, three turrets torn away. Alarms blared throughout the Ops deck as emergency bulkheads released to seal the gaping holes in the hull.

"Another one!" Turons pointed at the fleeting red light on the panorama-pane.

"Bridge," Lon called over the PA. "You've got manual."

"Evasive!" Choff ordered.

Turons regained control of the thrusters and righted the

ship, banking it across the trajectory of the approaching torpedo, just as electronic countermeasures fired into its flight path. Its guidance signals scrambled, the torpedo veered enough to barely miss the ship and detonate harmlessly.

"Starboard broadside," Otho ordered. "Fire."

The ship swung laterally, and the starboard batteries bombarded the Belaanian dreadnought, scoring several hits.

"Hard to starboard," Choff ordered. "Arm the bosonic torpedoes."

Otho pivoted in his chair with his mouth gaping. "Sir? The *bosonic* torpedoes?"

"You heard the order, Lieutenant."

Otho swallowed. "But, sir, we haven't had a successful test fire yet."

"Captain," Lendus stepped over to intervene.

"I want that *krok*-head dreadnought taken out!" Choff barked, silencing everyone.

Morgan targeted the tusk-lined enemy flagship as Turons maneuvered the ship, the three quantadrive pods powering *Ocelot* back around. On the window, the Belaanian dreadnought pivoted away from the suddenly resurgent cruiser. Morgan kept an eye on the tactical display as *Ocelot* closed rapidly on Mapooly.

"Bosonic torpedoes armed," Otho reported.

"Distance: 2.9 LS. Bearing: 38.9 by 21.7 degrees," Morgan said.

"Trackers locked," Violette reported.

"Fire torpedoes," Otho called down. A second passed with no indication on his monitors. "Forward launchers," he repeated. "Fire!"

"We're getting no response," came the reply on the

speaker.

"We have a blowout in the firing control's main panel!" a second voice yelled.

"*Krok!*" Otho cursed. "Switch to backup."

"Switching."

Another explosion rocked the ship from belowdecks. Otho's panel suddenly became a brilliant display of flashing red lights. "Captain, I've lost firing control."

Lendus raced over to Otho's station, switching two of the adjacent monitors to diagnostic displays. "Explosion in the firing relays," he called out.

"*Dox!*" Morgan's eyes darted through the many diagnostic displays on his panel. "We've lost all our weaponry."

"Another torpedo coming!" Turons called out.

"Evasive," Choff ordered. Turning to Otho, he asked, "Countermeasures?"

Otho shook his head. "Launchers are offline." Punching the speaker, he called down, "All stations, switch to manual." He eyed the bridge monitor. "*Krok*, it won't be in time—!"

"All decks, brace for impact," Morgan called down as the torpedo hit.

Explosions erupted throughout the Ops deck, noxious fumes spewing out. The bridge lights blacked out, and confusion broke out amongst the Ops deck crew as power surges arced across the control panels. Without warning, the helm exploded in a blinding flash of light.

"Pito!" Morgan jumped to his feet and caught Turons as the young helmsman fell away from the cloud of thick black smoke with a loud cry.

Lendus and Schillary ran over and helped Morgan ease Turons to the floor. A single bank of emergency lights activated in the ceiling, bathing the bridge in dim, subdued lighting as Grisconne called for Dr. Hildermaan.

Morgan quickly looked Turons over. Massive burns scarred the chest of Turons's suit and part of his face. "Hang on, Pito."

Turons shivered. "Morgan, it hurts…ahh…"

"The doctor's on his way," Lendus, who was at the helm, tried to reassure Turons.

"…ah…ah…"

Morgan winced at the sight of Turons, writhing in pain. He grasped Turons's hand, the roar of the power vents and the noisy chaos below them only a faint echo.

"Take the helm," Lendus told Morgan.

Morgan nodded and stepped aside as Hildermaan arrived and began placing medi-monitors on Turons.

"Hard about!" Choff ordered.

Morgan scrambled to assess how to regain control of the ship. The majority of the helm's control panel was either dead or damaged from the blowout, and the seared and blackened "big wheel" had lost power. Fortunately, enough of the board still worked that he could reprogram the functions and connect the helm to the manual relays. "Lon," he called down, "what's your status?"

"We have fires raging," Lon said through the static. "We're trying to get them under control."

Morgan completed the reprogramming and swung the ship about, taking it away from the dreadnought. He heard another cry from Turons.

"It's all right, Pito," Hildermaan said, working feverishly. "The painkiller should take effect in just a moment."

"I…I'm…c-c-col-d-d…" Turons went into a coughing

spasm, flicks of blood splattering on Hildermaan. "Ah...I...s-s-see...stars-s..."

Morgan saw Hildermaan shake his head at Choff, saying, "He's going too fast." The pulse on the medi-monitor was slow and erratic. "There's nothing I can do."

Morgan increased speed just as a volley of pulser shots hit the stern of the ship. The powerful blasts jolted everyone on the bridge.

"Combat status, Mr. Ennuk," Choff called out as he and Lendus regained their feet.

"Crews are battling the fire," Otho said. "The firing relays are still inaccessible."

Morgan saw Choff glare at the battle scenes on the array of monitors. The flagship dreadnought was now out of range, but an enemy carrier still loomed in the center of the stern monitor. *Epoch* looked adrift.

Morgan glanced back again as Hildermaan administered a second injection. Though breathing with difficulty, Turons seemed calm and pain-free, his eyes nearly closed. Without warning, the young helmsman gasped. He stiffened, time froze for an instant, and he released his breath. Hildermaan bowed his head, then switched off the medi-monitor.

"Sir," Lendus quietly said to Choff, "recommend we withdraw."

Choff clenched his jaw. "Mr. Ennuk, how long until you can reroute the firing controls?"

"Sir," Lendus repeated, louder, "I recommend we withdraw."

Morgan saw Choff glare at Lendus.

"Mr. Lendus," Choff said, "without us, Space Fortress C is doomed. They break through, and the empire is wide open.

Now is not the time to turn coward and run."

"Captain," Lendus pressed, "*Pouton* is hit, *Epoch* has lost engine power, and we've lost firing control and can barely maintain helm control. *Graftinop One* is away, and we must withdraw to rendezvous with the princess."

Morgan's blood boiled. *Dox! This is no time for the commanders to be arguing!* On the tactical display, he saw a formation of Belaanian destroyers and battlecruisers close on *Ocelot* from two sides. "Enemy approaching: three LS, closing fast."

"Sir!" Lendus said. "I respectfully remind you of our orders."

Choff froze, an ugly, twisted grimace of disgust on his face. Morgan held his breath as the captain scowled at Lendus. With his facial blood vessels seemingly ready to burst, Choff growled, "Withdraw!" He whipped about and stormed down the steps, abandoning a stunned Lendus to command the bridge.

Morgan stared after the captain. Battery blasts from the pursuing attackers rocked the ship. He tensed, expecting a shattering explosion at any moment, but kept his focus on directing the ship toward the space fortress.

"Inform Captain Jaron," Lendus quickly told Grisconne.

"Incoming!" Otho called out.

All eyes turned to the aft monitor, and the red-light launch of another torpedo from the lead Belaanian battlecruiser in pursuit.

"Aft torpedoes," Lendus ordered as he ran to Otho's station. "Visual targeting."

"Widen proximity 0.2," Otho quickly added.

Lendus turned to Morgan. "Maintain a straight line, Mr. Teggo."

"I hope this works," Morgan said.

"So do I," Lendus said under his breath.

From the corner of his eye, Morgan saw Choff pause at the base of the steps to watch Lendus. "Target: point-blank range."

Lendus called into the speaker, "Manual launch—now!"

The lights blinked and the ship shuddered from the power surge. Two *Ocelot* torpedoes shot out and flew toward the incoming menace. A split second later, a spectacular explosion punctuated the collision of the warheads. Cheers erupted on the bridge and the Ops deck.

At that moment, the three nearest watchtowers of the space fortress began firing their cannons at the enemy strike force. The ships broke formation and turned their assault to the watchtowers with a barrage of pulser fire. *Ocelot* flew under the crossfire, past the space fortress, and out into open space, leaving the fortress to defend itself.

Mapooly slammed his hand down on the console, cracking one of the displays and drawing a startled look from the pilot. Catching his breath, Mapooly turned from the sight of the departing *Ocelot* to address the crew on his speaker. Though *Bakiraaqu* had overwhelming firepower, it didn't have the agility to catch its prey.

"Reverse course," he ordered. "There's still one cruiser within range. Maintain the advantage and persevere to victory!"

The craft pivoted around, and Mapooly's eyes turned to the aft monitor. He stared at *Ocelot*, disappearing into the distance, and silently vowed to capture the prize that had eluded him.

"Status of navigation beacons?" Morgan called down to the Ops deck.

"Minor battle damage," Violette reported, "but backups are fully operational."

With Lendus at the helm, Morgan hopped back to the navigation board to plot the course for the comet cloud. "Signal all decks: prepare to jump."

Violette immediately relayed the order to the operations personnel.

"Send Captain Jaron our regrets," Lendus said to Grisconne. He called down to the lower decks, "Mr. Prowzi, what's your situation?"

"Fires under control, sir. Do you want me to stay and help, or return?"

"I need you to repair the primary beacons," Lendus said.

"On my way."

Morgan glanced at Lendus in admiration. For the first time, he began to question Captain Choff's character under real pressure. Morgan took a deep breath, not sure what to think, and conflicted about abandoning the space fortress while it was still under attack. He felt worse about leaving *Pouton*, *Epoch*, and the other ships still defending it. But he also knew that their orders to protect the Ruling Princess were now paramount. He shot a look toward the steps.

The captain was gone.

"The captain is off the bridge," Schillary belatedly stuttered.

"Mr. Lendus," Grisconne reported, "Captain Jaron wishes us all the best."

His calculations finished, Morgan punched them into the controls. "Course plotted, sir." He stole a glance at the aft monitor and saw the Belaanian flagship in the midst of the attacking ships. General Mapooly—or whoever it was—plunging the empire into war.

"Backup beacons active," Violette reported. "All decks report ready."

"Engaging quantadrive," Lendus said, activating the controls to send *Ocelot* out of the region. Turning to Schillary, he quietly said, "Help the doctor with Mr. Turons."

Morgan watched as Schillary called the platoon officer up from the Ops deck. Turons was young, an efficient and effective crewman who everybody liked. It was a gross injustice to take his life away before he had a chance to grow into the man he could become. An eerie silence surrounded Morgan as he succumbed to the grief of losing a friend. Would there be more? Morgan could only think the worst as Schillary and the soldier lifted the fallen serviceman and followed Hildermaan off the bridge.

Admiral Zerah struggled to maintain his command presence. It wasn't so much the loss of five transports, painful as that had been, as it was the chokehold of General Mapooly, or whoever he really was. Zerah cursed his own ego and his own dreams of commanding a fleet on a military campaign. His father had served under General Mapooly; he came away from the liberation of Sestia with no riches, only enough battle scars to cut short his life. Zerah understood now that he, like his father, was but a puppet, an underling obeying the whims of his superior.

"Captain Bemone," he said in a slow monotone, "send to all ships: submit damage reports within the hour."

Zerah surveyed the faces of the bridge crew, the words of Mapooly's speech on Yeros still fresh in his mind. For himself and for his convoy, there was nothing to be gained from the invasion. Only more losses. With each destroyed weapon, he lost more of the profit on this shipment. And with each destroyed ship, he lost more of his ability to make subsequent gains on future jobs.

"Belaanian ships signaling new course," the comm officer reported.

Zerah gave another glance at the monitor, where *Bakiraaqu* and other Belaanian ships were starting to shrink into the distance. He grimaced, then said with a scowl, "Let's take a look, Captain." He motioned Bemone over to review the new heading.

"Yes, sir," Bemone said, before relaying the order to Isaalt.

"Signal all ships: prepare for new course." Zerah sensed the bitter disgust in his own voice. "And hasten repairs. We won't have much time before we go into battle again."

A pair of eyes, hidden in darkness, opened from a deep slumber. A long, slow breath inhaled sweet, intoxicating fumes, relaxing the nerves, drifting down into the depths of the lungs. A miniature figurine, bathed in a soft, streaming purplish light of a starlike medallion stud around its neck, stood on the shelf. A day had passed since the battle at the space fortress with no news. Yet.

The buzzer sounded.

"Yes?"

The speaker crackled to life. "General Mapooly reporting, Master."

"Yes, mighty drakothon?"

"We have penetrated Imperial space. The space fortress has been neutralized, with manageable impact to the fleet, and we are proceeding as planned. As the swift conquest of Eurania remains our objective, both of the Imperial cruisers were allowed to escape." The general's voice, already distorted by the high-intensity electronic relay signal, echoed in the *Masoule*'s ears as if snarled by the thickness of the pomira smoke in a dreamlike morass.

"And the princess's ship?"

A momentary pause. "Also escaped, under the cover of the battle."

The *Masoule* fumed. The eyes narrowed into a pair of slits. "Estimated time to arrival, General?"

"Five days, at top speed. Landing operations to commence immediately upon—"

The speaker cut off mid-sentence. The *Masoule* preferred the complete, utter silence of the void to the drivel and noise of minutiae. Penetrating the empire was but the beginning. The real target—the first conquest of the master plan—was still to come.

Far from the devastating battle at the space fortress, Admiral Kearn saluted and reported, "My lord, we are approaching Volon. We will scan the surface for the Timegazer before selecting a landing site."

Lord Walmsley, arriving on the bridge with Searus at his side, gazed at the small blue-green globe rotating slowly on the wraparound viewer. From this altitude, the planet looked lush and untamed, not unlike Wichloc. He puzzled over this out-of-the-way world, of which he knew almost nothing. The survey report from the databank gave no indication of the inhabitants being capable of constructing a deep-space projector gun—the "Timegazer," a name mentioned in the report retrieved from Space Control on Kelova. It all felt very mysterious.

"Admiral?" Captain Pavon stepped over from the survey-or station and saluted. "We've found what appears to be a pair of large mountaintop dishes, possibly centuries-old Onglan projectors. One is burned out and in ruins."

Walmsley raised an eyebrow. Could they be so lucky this quickly? He weighed possible courses of action.

"Can we see it?" Kearn asked.

"Not yet," Pavon said. "We should be in visual range within the hour."

Walmsley made his mind up quickly. "Admiral, select an elite team to survey the site."

"Yes, my lord." Kearn relayed the order to Pavon.

Walmsley considered the possible ramifications of a connection between the projector dishes and the zero-readings within the Great Nebula. It would be almost as if the projector gun had punched holes into the fabric of the nebula. But what did the name "Timegazer" mean?

"My lord," Searus interrupted, "what do you think they'll find at the site?"

Answers? Lord Walmsley wished he could say. "Whatever they find, Searus, we must be open to whatever possibilities might come out of it."

He paused and drew in a slow breath. It could even be something connected to the foreboding feeling that had been haunting him since Monseigneur Dhavail's passing. Deeply disturbed by the possibility, Walmsley departed the bridge and returned to his cabin, lost in thought, Searus walking alongside every step of the way.

Walmsley went straight to his bedside and took his well-worn copy of *The Songs of the Euranians*. His hands shook as he turned the old paper pages. Why he persisted in eschewing a digi-com, he didn't know. But as long as he could work his fingers, he clung stubbornly to the book he had received half a century ago from Dhavail.

"A projector dish," he muttered to himself as he searched. "There is something. A passage, an eternal passage. A passage... to eternity?" His eyes scanned the words, looking, seeking.

"What is it, my lord?" Searus asked.

"A term," Walmsley said. "A passage...of the gods. Yes." He let out a deep breath and pointed to the text. "Here." He nodded his head. "An alternate account of the war between the humans of Amahl and the reptiloids of Sigorum, written in the ancient proto-Memonan language. I hope I can still read all of it." He cleared his throat.

"Death and desolation, everywhere. The survivors, uncounted millions on both worlds, were but shadows. No life, no future, no hope.

"It seemed the Lords of Almighty Euranus had disappeared, leaving the people to care and fend for themselves.

"'Where is Lord Oscanos? Where is Mother Gheriah?' The people cried out, but they received no answer. 'It is a terrible, hollow victory,' they said, 'merely a brief respite before we perish as well.'

"Time passed: months, years, decades. Finally, Xukas, the old decrepit prophet, emerged from the ruins of Amahl, announcing the traversal of the gods to unknown regions of the multiverse.

"'They will continue to watch over all of us,' Xukas proclaimed, 'but they will no longer mingle amongst us.'

"The people listened, waited, and prayed for hope. And so, the Pan'kouldah departed through the eternal passage, never to be seen again by human eyes."

Walmsley studied the following paragraph, then closed the book. He glanced at Searus, who looked mesmerized by the reading. "In here," he told her, "is something called the *Hru-vrah*—the rainbow of the gods—through which the Euranian Ancestors departed the physical realm. It is described as a focusing of high-energy particles, powerful enough to pierce the fabric of space and time and allow passage into unknown regions of the multiverse."

"Do you believe they used the same means to reenter our universe?" Searus asked.

"Not them. Not Lord Oscanos or Mother Gheriah." Walmsley tensed. "The other one."

Morgan accompanied Lendus to the smoke- and gas-permeated areas below the main deck, where wreckage, splatters of fluids, and debris littered the narrow, dimly lit corridors. Bruised and bloodied crewmen covered in ash and oils struggled to coax components of the ship back to life.

"Mr. Teggo," Lendus said, as they headed down another level, "how well did you know Mr. Turons?"

"We weren't close," Morgan answered. "He'd been mostly working with Otho, but we had many conversations about different things."

"Did he ever mention his family?"

Morgan thought for a moment. "I think his father owned a small scrap metal business, and his mother may have been a librarian or a teacher. I think he also had a brother who's still in school." The thought of Turons's family mourning their loss saddened Morgan. It could have easily been his own mother grieving a dead son. He tried to think of something positive to say. "Considering the size of the attack force and the direct hit we took, we were lucky we didn't lose more men, especially the gunnery crews manning those three batteries."

"That's true, but it's still a shame," Lendus said. "I don't know how long it will be before we can send him home to his family." He stopped to face Morgan. "The captain would like you to prepare a brief memorial for Mr. Turons."

"Yes, sir." Morgan stopped to consider something that had been eating at him since the battle. "Sir, I have a concern."

"About?"

Morgan took a deep breath. "Several people have asked me about the captain's conduct during the battle." He paused, not wanting to name any of the crewmen who had spoken to him in private. How could he convince Lendus it was a genuine concern, not an insubordinate attitude? "I…have the same question as well."

Lendus knitted his brows. "Your concern is noted." Turning away, he continued through the corridor, effectively closing the subject.

They reached the relay banks and the blackened remains of the firing control relays. The units were open, and parts sat on the floor in an orderly layout, while the technicians made replacements. Chief engineer Petre supervised the hookup of the power.

"Good news, sir," the gray-haired, well-seasoned Petre said as she lifted her visor and rose from the power compartment. "The converter's holding. We'll have weapons on manual shortly."

"What about the automatic relays?" Lendus asked.

Petre shook her head. "We've tried powering up a replacement unit, but it didn't work. There appears to be extensive internal damage."

"Estimate?"

"We can have it scoped out by the end of the day, sir. Then we'll know what it'll take to make the repairs."

Lendus nodded and moved on. "I've seen enough," he said to Morgan. "I'll head back to the bridge. Continue with the survey, Mr. Teggo."

"Yes, sir."

After Lendus departed, Morgan stayed and watched the technicians work. He glanced at some of the porta-com displays that the techs were working with and noticed an unusual indicator. "Ms. Petre," he said. "What's that?"

"That's something we've been working on analyzing," Petre said. "Traces of an unidentified element in the corrosion. I've never seen anything like it in all my years. Do you recognize it?"

Morgan looked at the damaged relay unit, his mind racing. "An unidentified element? So something was introduced from the outside? *Dox!*" He tensed at the memory of the *Ancora* explosion, then dashed away to call after Lendus. This wasn't damage from a hit—it was an explosive!

That evening, Lendus reviewed the details of Morgan's damage report. As he walked through the ship, now on lockdown, he couldn't help but eye each crewman, wondering who might have planted an explosive. Was the culprit setting up another attempt, even as everyone worked on repairing the ship?

One hundred seventy officers and crewmen served aboard *Ocelot*. He knew everyone by name. But for many, especially the enlisted men assigned below the main deck, he didn't know much beyond the contents of their paperwork. Schillary was running everyone's records and reviewing the extensive automatic recordings, but how long before Schillary presented his list of suspects, Lendus didn't know.

"Mr. Lendus!" It was Fota, his short gray hair unkempt, his face looking a bit haggard with deeper-than-usual creases across his forehead. Lowering his voice, he said, "We've worked together for a long time."

Lendus smiled. "Over five years, since the day I came aboard as the captain's exec."

Fota did not smile. "I've been with this ship for nearly two decades and served under three captains."

Lendus turned serious. "Your service record has been impeccable, and you probably know more about this ship and its crew than anyone aboard. What is it?"

"Please believe me when I tell you that…well, sir, I have no ulterior motives…" He sighed. "I fear that the crew may be losing confidence in the captain."

This caught Lendus's attention. "Okay, tell me."

"Many have been asking me in private, and I have told each one to keep faith, to not lose focus on our work." He sighed again. "But, sir, in all my time on this ship, I have not seen this level of sudden uncertainty."

Lendus knew that he had to tackle this one head-on. "Is this because of what happened during the battle?"

Fota's eyes and voice saddened. "The captain abandoned his command during battle." He sighed a third time, now looking aged and worn. "I haven't spoken a word of this to anyone."

Lendus knew that this was serious, not just for the captain but for the entire ship. "I will speak to the captain about your concern."

"Thank you, sir." Fota turned to depart.

"Keep me apprised of any further developments," Lendus

quickly interjected.

"I will, sir."

Lendus walked away, contemplating the state of the ship. He hadn't seen the captain in person since the battle, and he wondered whether he would be welcome. They had never had a public disagreement before. In fact, they hadn't had a major difference, public or private, in the three years since Lendus's promotion to commander. But, if this wasn't addressed, it could quickly balloon into a full-blown crisis. First, Morgan had asked him about the captain's conduct, and now Fota. Lendus could only steel his nerves with a slow, deep breath as he buzzed the captain's cabin.

The door opened.

"Come in, sir," Yeoman Smyra said, admitting Lendus.

The captain sat at his desk, staring at his monitor.

Lendus walked straight up to the captain and handed over his porta-com. "The damage survey, sir. The three port batteries are gone. The port engine also took a hit. Though it's still operational, we've taken it offline and shifted some personnel to do preventive work on it. The men are still working on restoring the automatic relays to the steering array and the firing controls. The hits were pretty bad, sir; they'll have a better idea by the end of the day if they'll succeed or not. Other areas of damage along the hull are under control."

Choff asked, "Sections that are vulnerable to torpedoes?"

"The areas surrounding those three batteries," Lendus said. "A hit might breech the main hull."

"And the lockdown?"

"All off-duty personnel are confined to their barracks. Mr. Schillary is conducting a thorough investigation of ship's personnel. He will notify me when his report is ready."

Still staring at the porta-com, Choff said, "Have a seat." He switched off the monitor, his eyes looking sleep-deprived, hollow and darkened. "What's your assessment of Otho Ennuk's conduct during the battle?"

"Exemplary." Lendus paused. He knew what the captain was referring to, and it bothered him as well. "Except for the order to arm the bosonic torpedoes."

"I don't need to state the obvious. Every second is crucial," Choff said. "How much time did he spend questioning the order? Would anything have changed if there hadn't been a delay? Could they have fired before the explosion knocked out the relays?"

"I will remind Mr. Ennuk of his duty," Lendus said, hoping to placate the captain. "A strong, stern reminder, sir."

"You do that. Who knows what we're up against or where we're headed next."

Lendus knew the captain had a good point. Now was not the time for a lapse in discipline, Lendus reminded himself. *Especially for the commanding officer.* "Captain, I must speak to you about something."

Choff held up his hand, slumped back in his chair, and glanced up at the ceiling. "I know, Kaleb. I'm sure that..." He stumbled. "The crew has been talking...about *my* performance during the battle."

So, the captain is giving me an opening. "Sir, the crew is confused. Both Lieutenant Teggo and Chief Fota have received...more than one question on that."

Choff nodded. "Kaleb, I admit—to you—that my judgment in those moments might have been...in error. But I can't have the crew lose confidence."

Lendus shook his head; he hadn't expected a quick concession. "I don't think the men have lost confidence in you."

"We need to make *sure* that that doesn't happen," Choff emphasized. Pausing, his eyes softened a bit. "We could all use a little shaping up, including the captain. But I'll need your help to make sure the officers are with me. Teggo, Ennuk, the rest of them."

Lendus felt better, now that the captain had admitted his own failing. "I'll speak with all the officers and make sure everyone is aware of the importance of maintaining focus and discipline."

Work on the major systems was completed. Though still damaged, the nav and comm arrays and the port engine had been restored to operational status. As the ship continued its journey to rendezvous with *Graftinop One*, Morgan and Schillary paced along the main deck, deep in discussion, both in crisp midnight-blue dress uniforms, with white gloves, shiny black boots, low-brimmed hats, skiloblades on their belts, and silver stripes over their left breast denoting their ranks. While they talked, members of the crew trickled out from below, some alone, others in pairs or trios. Lendus stood at the base of the topside engine pylon, studying a recitation. One by one, the injured from the ward appeared, some with assistance, on crutches, in slings, wearing bandages or other badges of bravery, but all in dress uniform.

Morgan and Schillary were interrupted by the frantic appearance of Lon. "Have you seen Otho? I can't find him."

Morgan asked, "He's not at the barracks?"

Lon shook his head. "He's not on the bridge or in any of the torpedo rooms, and he's not answering."

Morgan glanced at the clock on the forecastle wall. Otho, known for his efficiency and dependability, was usually very punctual. It wasn't like him to be late for something important.

"I'll go look for him," Morgan said, leaving Schillary to oversee the arrival of the crew. "Call me if he shows up."

Morgan plunged down the steps into the aftcastle. He passed several groups of crewmen heading for the deck as he made his way to the ship's quarter galleries, figuring that he would start at the stern of the ship and work his way forward until he found Otho. He took a quick peek into the port quarter gallery, saw that it was deserted, and moved to the starboard quarter gallery.

Just as he was starting to feel anxious, he found the missing Otho, standing alone before the window, watching the stars and the perimeter of the comet cloud. "Otho?"

No answer. Otho was crying.

Unsure of what had happened, Morgan joined Otho at the window and watched the mass of approaching ice rocks and space dust. "Want to talk about it?"

A violent shake of Otho's head.

Morgan put his hand on Otho's shoulder. "All right if I stay with you for a few minutes?"

"I dunno why I'm crying. It just came…" Otho heaved a sob. "…outta nowhere."

Morgan was shocked to find the dependable Otho, his buddy since the academy, in this state, all semblance of formality and propriety gone. He took a deep breath and exhaled. The release felt good, one moment for his muscles to relax. "Must be the pressure, Oggy. I feel it. We all do. We've never gone through anything like this before. None of us."

"Who am I kiddin'?" Otho pleaded. "A career officer, I told the captain. What a joke."

"Hey," Morgan interrupted, "how you're feeling inside

has no bearing on your standing as an officer."

"An officer shouldn't need to be reminded of his duty by the exec. I buckled under pressure!"

"You've been exemplary," Morgan said. "Handling the ship's weapons, the firing crews, the fighting. How many enemy ships were attacking? Fifty? Sixty? Manual firing, repair crews, all that *kroking* testing. You've been a star."

Otho paused, seeming to consider Morgan's words. "It's just...I dunno what I'm feeling. Witherall just regained consciousness, an hour ago. Eckles lost an arm. Vevo, an arm *and* a leg."

Morgan recognized the names of the three gunners whose turrets had been blown apart.

"Pito, he was like a kid brother. He was smart and eager, and now he's...gone." He looked to Morgan. "Is he really gone? What's going to happen to the rest of us?"

Morgan looked down at his shoes. He didn't know. Was Turons really gone, or could he still exist—in some other place, in some other form? "I wish I knew." He had witnessed—even participated in—and subsequently considered things that seemed to suggest a bigger existence than what his eye could see. But who really knew? What had really happened to Rayna? He couldn't help but worry about where she was and how she was doing. Had anything changed in her medical status? "I don't know if *anyone* really knows."

They stood together and gazed at the distant stars. Space was so wonderfully—and so terribly—expansive. The minutes passed in silence. As Otho inhaled a long and deep breath, Morgan sensed his friend's composure returning.

"Mr. Teggo?"

Morgan turned to face CPO Baer, standing at the doorway. "Is it time?"

"Just about, sir."

"Thank you, Ms. Baer."

After she departed, Otho said, "She's an excellent torpedo crew supervisor. She did the manual launch during the battle."

Morgan nodded. "We have an excellent crew."

"Thanks, Morgan." Otho put his hand on Morgan's shoulder and gave him a solid squeeze. "We should go pay our respects."

Morgan smiled. In the midst of chaos, friendship had to endure.

One hundred sixty-three men and women—all but the three recovering gunners, an attending medic, the assistant chief engineer, and Ensign Violette manning the bridge—lined both sides of the main deck, the silent turret batteries arrayed behind them, the transparent ceiling admitting the star-filled canopy of the universe. Captain Antos Choff stood before the crew, in front of the forecastle. Commander Kaleb Lendus, Lieutenant Morgan Teggo, and Lieutenant Otho Ennuk stood at his side. The flag-draped casket of Petty Officer Pito Turons lay between them and the rest of the crew. The purple silhouette of the hawk of Oscanos, the graftinop, was displayed on top.

Morgan brought the crew to attention with three long blasts of his whistle.

Lendus stepped forward to recite "Metamorphosis," the most traditional of all funeral poems, and one of the few texts surviving the fall of the Etolian Empire to be completely translated into modern language.

"A monarch emerges from his cocoon with pure white
wings that dazzle the eyes.

"His majesty rises and smiles as we rejoice in his rebirth.

"Lift up to the heavens. You will be welcomed by the gods.

"Farewell, Pito Turons. Begin your journey to a new and better world.

"Leave the empty cocoon, let it sleep in silence.

"Soon, it will be gone."

Lendus stepped aside, and Captain Choff stepped forward to address the crew.

"We are gathered here to pay our final respects to Petty Officer First Class Pito Turons, who gave his life yesterday while in the performance of his duty. His bravery is noted, his fortitude is commended, and his loyalty is praised. He was a son and a brother, and he was like a son to me, and like a brother to you.

"His service was cut short by a despicable act of aggression which we will not forget. Though he was aboard *Ocelot* for less than a year, he made a lasting impression on those of us who worked with him. He began in the engine room, then quickly advanced to the forward torpedo room, and finally to the operations deck and the bridge of the ship. He was a bright young man, a tireless worker, a loyal subject to the Crown, and a patriot to his homeland. He will be missed."

Morgan gazed down the two rows of crewmen. They were not just the shipmates that he served with. It was more than that, he realized. Everyone on *Ocelot* would be bound together, forever.

"None of us know what the future holds. Even now, none of us knows where this journey will lead us. But we can be certain in our hope for Mr. Turons. He has begun his journey to a new and better world."

Morgan knew the traditional closing used by nearly every

funeral eulogy by heart.

"To those who follow Euranus, they will find their home in True Eurania. There, we are told, they will smile."

Choff stepped aside, and Morgan stepped forward. He gazed down at Turons's casket before calling out his command.

"Raise thy blades!"

In unison, the crew of *Ocelot* unsheathed their skilo-blades, held them aloft, pointed them outward to the stars, and shouted, "*Maruga!*"

Otho, stepping forward to join Morgan, commanded, "All batteries!"

The port and starboard turrets rotated in unison with a low, steady hum. With a series of mechanical clangs, they pointed up and away.

Otho completed his command. "Salute!"

As one, each of the thirty-seven operational cannons fired a blank shot into the depths of space, the concussion sending shivers through the deck, the shots symbolically sending Turons's spirit to the cosmos, home to the long-lost mythological world of origin, True Eurania.

Their swords still held high, the crew then sang "Hymn to Oscanos."

> *To the Maker of the world, to the Giver of Life,*
> *We sing praises, we give thanks.*
> *We offer to Mother Gheriah our love,*
> *To the Three Guardians, our trust,*
> *And to you and Almighty Euranus, our lives.*
>
> *Home, we long for home.*
> *Eurania, our home, Eurania.*
> *Bring us home to you, Lord Oscanos,*

Bring us home to you.

Morgan had never given the Euranian mythology much thought, and though he sang more out of respect for Pito than any sort of genuine belief in his final resting place, the consideration crossed his mind for the first time.

When the hymn concluded, Morgan called out, "Lower thy blades!" He began to dismiss the crew but stopped as Schillary stepped forward and interrupted him. Unsure of the new development, Morgan stepped aside and gave the deck to Schillary.

"The following persons, remain after dismissal," Schillary announced. "Technicians Blaise, Sequeme, and Kothol; Specialists Ophil, Toroh, Branke, and Cikul; Petty Officer Leory; and Ensign Prowzi."

Schillary then gave the deck back to Morgan, who stepped forward, unsure of what Lon had gotten himself mixed up in. Not receiving any looks or signals from Schillary, Lendus, or Captain Choff, Morgan dismissed the crew. Lendus, Morgan, Otho, and Schillary remained as Choff stepped before the nine crewmen.

"Yesterday," Choff began, "during the battle, an explosion occurred within the firing control relay banks, effectively destroying the ship's ability to fire automatically. We have determined from traces of an unidentified element that something was planted inside one of the relay banks. As such, we have no choice but to treat this as an act of sabotage, an attack upon this ship."

The captain looked at each of the nine, one at a time, before proceeding.

"Each of you was in the vicinity of the firing control relays, within one day prior to the explosion. As such, you are sub-

ject to questioning on this incident. Until we make a determination, you are all relieved of duty and confined to your barracks."

Choff paced back and forth before the nine as he spoke.

"One of you—and you know who you are—is a traitor. A
traitor to your shipmates, a traitor to your monarch, and a traitor
to me." His face twisted as he spoke. "One of you—and you
know who you are—is among the lowest of lifeforms in this universe. You are like the monoworms or plasma-sponges of the
deep, parasites that feed off the living."

Morgan, after seeing the frightened look on Lon's face,
exchanged worried glances with Otho.

"Treason is a capital offense. One of you—and you know
who you are—will be captured and caged like an animal. Petty
Officer Turons lost his life because of this abhorrent act, and I
shall see to it that you lose yours. I promise you that."

Choff stopped pacing. He then took one step toward the
nine suspects.

"One of you—and you know who you are—is already as
good as dead. Dismissed."

Except for the quiet hum of machinery, the main deck
was as silent as a morgue.

Choff turned to Lendus. "Maintain shipwide lockdown
until further notice. Ensign Schillary will report directly to me on
this matter."

Morgan paused, surprised at the change of reporting
structure. It was the captain's prerogative, but he wondered how
Lendus would take to being removed from oversight of the investigation. As the captain stalked off, Morgan pondered the
mercurial man. He thought he had finally reached an understanding about Rayna's father, but now Morgan was more perplexed
than ever.

Slowly, the suspects left for their barracks—all but Lon.

"Sir," Lon said to Lendus, "there must be some mistake. You know why I was down among the relays. I was restoring helm control. I can't possibly be a suspect, can I?"

"We can't treat you differently than anyone else recorded in the vicinity," Lendus said. "As long as you know you're innocent, you don't have to worry."

"But, sir!"

"I'm sorry, Mr. Prowzi." Lendus shook his head. "Just so we're clear about this: you are one of nine suspects in the bombing of the firing control relays. You will conduct yourself accordingly."

Morgan stepped in and put his hand on Lon's shoulder. "Come on, Lon. Otho and I will accompany you back to the barracks. Don't worry."

Lon stared at Morgan and Otho. "I don't believe this...!"

Sitting next to the pilot of *Trion*'s lander, Lord Walmsley watched mile after mile of dense foliage pass underneath. Ahead, a mountain range rose in the distance, a formation of pointed peaks.

"My lord, we've found something interesting." Admiral Kearn stepped forward with one of his men and handed Walmsley a digi-com. "Apparently, an Onglan expedition, about a thousand years ago, reported evidence of an underground Apelian settlement."

Walmsley raised an eyebrow. He had heard of the Apelians—a race of beings who had inhabited Upper Eurania before the arrival of the Etolian settlers. But except for three brief prophecies quoted in *The Songs of the Euranians*, he had never seen evidence of their existence.

A tingle ran up his spine. He hadn't expected to feel excited, but investigating an unexpected mystery on an unfamiliar planet seemed thrilling.

"There it is," the pilot said, pointing at a black projector dish at the top of a mountain peak. "We'll touch down in one minute."

Walmsley saw a second projector dish appear on the top of a second peak, and he wondered about Volon. He understood the inhabitants to be fairly rudimentary in their technology. Based on Kearn's survey report, it didn't seem likely the Volonians could have constructed these dishes.

Could the ancient Apelians have built them?

"There's a spot we can land." The pilot pointed at a small section of flat ground near the first dish.

"Proceed," Kearn said.

As the lander descended, Walmsley got a quick glance of a dozen Volonians emerging from beneath the dish. Except for the machinery they were working with, they looked like primitive but powerfully built natives. Then the lander flew past the towering projector dish and descended to a smooth landing.

"Well done," Walmsley said to the pilot.

As he opened the door, Kearn said to Walmsley, "Please watch your step."

Accompanied by half a dozen crewmen clad in dull-blue and moss-green camouflage fatigues, Walmsley walked down the lander's ramp onto the surface of Volon.

A crowd of tall, muscular men, many sporting tattoos of various designs—skulls, spiders, tridents, and lightning bolts—stood before them. Most were tanned and drenched in sweat from the heat of the midday sun. Many were caked in a fine blue ash, the same dusting that covered the jagged boulders surrounding the site. Their work among the ruins interrupted by Walmsley's landing, the people gathered about with their tools, spiral-coiled wires, and other equipment still in their hands. The gargantuan blackened projector dish, mounted high on a massive rock formation with what looked like an array of power relay units, cast a shadow over the people.

"Hello." Walmsley greeted the native Volonians in Onglan. "Who is the leader here?"

One of the Volonians stepped forward and replied with a thick accent, "I am Panquo, leader of the *Illito*."

Walmsley bowed. "Metiar Walmsley."

"Are you friends of Morgan Teggo and Rayna Choff?" Panquo asked.

Walmsley remembered reading those names in the report, but he had focused mainly on the account of the Timegazer, not the people involved. "No, I have never met them."

"But you are here for this, are you not?" Panquo swept his hand upward toward the dish.

"We are." Walmsley sized up Panquo. The Volonian was clearly more of a warrior than a researcher. "Are you conducting analysis of this dish or repairing it?"

Panquo shook his head. "We are only our people's warriors. We are disassembling a part of this to take back to our people, for our council of elders to examine. Some of them possess scientific knowledge, while others are steeped in our beliefs. Together, they will try to determine if this is merely a highly advanced machine left by an ancient civilization or something of prophetic significance."

"Have you considered contacting the Onglan Congress?" Walmsley asked. "They could provide experts and resources to aid this endeavor."

Some of the Volonians grumbled. Others shook their heads.

"We are a simple people," Panquo said. "We have our own traditions and way of life. We would prefer not to have more out-worlders descend upon us."

Walmsley frowned. The Volonians may have been self-sufficient in their livelihood, but this felt as if they were too proud to ask for help with something that seemed beyond their capabilities. Walmsley blew out his breath and turned his attention back to the purpose of his visit. "What can you tell us about it? Before it was destroyed, did it shoot some sort of high-energy particle beam into space?"

Panquo nodded his head. "The *Hruvrah*."

Walmsley raised an eyebrow. The rainbow of the gods—the same ancient word he had read in *The Songs of the Euranians*. "Tell me."

"The Timegazer did shoot into the sky, several times," Panquo said. "Then it was destroyed by Morgan Teggo and Rayna Choff." He spread his arms wide. "None of us saw how this happened. The only surviving witness among our people, our priestess, has been lying unconscious in the temple for weeks."

"I am sorry to hear that," Walmsley said. "Whom did they confront?"

Panquo's eyes narrowed. With a venomous tone, he hissed, "A Luzomi worshipper."

Walmsley froze, his fist clenched. He felt a trickle of sweat roll down his neck. *Luzomi.* He held his breath and thought of the darkness that had been haunting him—the oppressive, nefarious spirit of evil.

"According to prophecy," Panquo continued, "the appearance of the *Hruvrah* marks the beginning of a period of turmoil and conflict unseen since the ancient days." He lowered his head, his voice softening. "But without our priestess, we cannot know any more than that. What kind of turmoil, how long-lasting, how far-reaching the conflict will spread..." He slowly shook his head.

Walmsley concentrated on understanding the true meaning of what he had felt. A priestess of the Euranian Ancestors lay in danger, the victim of the heinous Luzomi. The Prince of Evil lurked in the shadowy folds of existence, waiting for the shattering power of the *Hruvrah*, waiting for the doorway to open, waiting to effect his return into the physical universe.

What had happened to the priestess? Nobody knew. Her life was on the line—for now and possibly for all eternity.

Walmsley clutched his pouch. His fingers caressed the outline of the *Gramm* inside. He had spent so many years—so many decades—preparing for a moment like this. Was there anything he could do for her?

"Perhaps I can try to help your priestess," Walmsley said to Panquo. "Please take me to her."

The Volonian temple was modest, a single-storied earthen building with a pointed roof in the middle and a towering stone smokestack in the rear spewing burnt-red billows, surrounded by a ring of torches taller than the Volonian warriors. An arrangement of statues even taller than the torches lined the steps leading up to the entrance. On either side of the main doors stood clay likenesses of ancient Dravies warriors in helmets, battle garments, shields, and with fanged attack wovrens at their sides.

It all seemed very rustic to Lord Walmsley compared to the equally small but significantly more modern chapel on Wichloc. The Volonian temple seemed primitive to the point of suggesting an ancient worship site, more reminiscent of the mythical setting of Amahl than anything he'd seen before.

"Shall we go?" Panquo asked as his men opened the heavy double doors.

Walmsley turned to face Kearn and the other crewmen. "Please wait here." With a strong grip on his cane, he joined Panquo at the entrance.

They entered and walked through a short torch-lit corridor lined with earthen statues of humans, semi-humans, and beasts. Walmsley wondered if any of these might have been of Apelian origin. He heard a flute and the soft musical strains of a woman's voice chanting. A hint of incense wafted through the air, a sweet aroma of wild tropical fruits that pleased the Euranian Ancestors.

Walmsley recognized some of the minor deities of the Euranian pantheon, such as Jhoraine, the young fairylike messenger of Mother Gheriah, and Aegoia and Xan, the aides to Almighty Euranus that were depicted as brilliant balls of radiant energy. Renderings of the lush forests of Amahl were positioned around the entrance to the inner sanctum, with tree trunks to the left and right and a dense, leafy canopy above the heavy wooden door. Lurking within the leaves and blended into the tree roots were disembodied limbs of all shapes and sizes, suggesting the presence of the mysterious *Wilde'prim'ordia*—enigmatic deities of chaos, such as Helaz, the Flesh Being; Emul'kiq, the Black Star; Wa'ohl'thu, the Keeper of Souls; and Serpea'tiq, the Edge of Existence.

Just inside the entryway, Panquo and Walmsley knelt before a small basin of still water.

"I cleanse myself to come before thee," Panquo recited, dipping his hand into the water and rinsing his face.

Walmsley followed suit. "I cleanse myself to come before thee." It was an ancient rite he had read about but never performed, having been abandoned at the modern temples during the centuries of Saolian occupation.

Panquo led Walmsley past a dozen rows of floor-standing torches to the candlelit altar, which was covered with fruits and leaves of all shapes and colors. Behind the altar stood statues of men, women, and animals, all in purple-and-green diagonally-striped gowns—attendants to the Euranian Ancestors—and behind them, enormous wooden statues of Lord Oscanos, Mother Gheriah, and the Three Guardians that reached to the apex of the sanctuary's vaulted ceiling. Thin wisps of white smoke rose from a small blue bowl on the altar.

In front of the altar knelt two women in light-blue robes and conical hats, with their dark hair flowing down to their waists. One played a long wooden flute; the other chanted in ancient Etolian. Situated between them, a young blonde girl sat before a golden casket with her head bowed. Panquo knelt behind the blonde girl and lowered his head. Walmsley also knelt. Though it was an unfamiliar setting, he felt comforted in the presence of the Euranian Ancestors. The dark oppression that had weighed on him lessened.

He silently stared at the casket, noting the circle-and-halo emblem of Mother Gheriah positioned above the head. Realizing that this must be Jairesse, the fallen priestess of the Volonians, Walmsley lowered his head and prayed to Lord Oscanos for restoration for these simple people.

On the ride down from the mountaintop, Panquo had told Walmsley about the Xaturi, what Morgan had told them about its destruction, and how the young novice—the girl praying before them—had attempted to revive Jairesse.

She looked about ten years old, merely a child. Walmsley could not imagine her having the power to perform a death-defying ritual. Even Monseigneur Dhavail had never dared venturing into the subject.

The music stopped. Hearing the sounds of Panquo and the girl rising to their feet, Walmsley opened his eyes.

"Welcome," the girl said in lightly accented Onglan. Her voice was soft and serene.

Walmsley gripped his cane, rose to his feet, and bowed. "Walmsley of Wichloc, at your service."

"I am Familla." She bowed to Walmsley. The girl was small, her head level with only the middle of Walmsley's chest. "I am learning to be a priestess."

"Lord Walmsley has come to help Jairesse," Panquo said.

"Can you revive her?" Familla asked.

Walmsley drew in his breath. He had to be honest with her from the start. "I don't know. I have been a student of the Euranian Ancestors for a long time, but I have never ventured into anything like this."

Familla reached for his hand. "Please come." After motioning for the two women to step outside, she looked into his eyes. "We must try."

As Walmsley took Familla's hand, her sleeve fell away, revealing a silver bracelet etched with Etolian script. One specific symbol caught his eye: a vertical line crossed by short horizontal bars near the top and bottom.

The emblem of Lord Oscanos, the *Gramm.*

Familla drew upon the same power, spiritual and physical, as he did. Could they work together to attempt a revival?

"Please place the *quellates*," Familla said to Panquo.

As they stood before the casket, Walmsley gazed at

Jairesse. She was a beautiful young woman, seemingly at peace in her bed of gold. However, he knew her outward appearance merely hid the truth of her condition. She had been a victim of Luzomi. Whether her spirit was still in torment or not—whether she had been in torment ever since the attack—nobody knew. Walmsley's heart broke at the thought of her pain.

Panquo placed an assortment of colorful plant samples— red and yellow blossoms, green and blue vines, golden leaves— on Jairesse's head and body, then stepped away.

Familla asked Walmsley, "Do you require time to prepare?"

Walmsley shook his head. "Do you?"

"I made my preparations many weeks ago."

Walmsley understood. The young girl had not stopped praying, all this time. "Then I am ready."

Familla lowered her head, closed her eyes, and took several long, deep breaths. As she did, her hair fell forward, obscuring her face.

Walmsley also lowered his head and closed his eyes. Not having any idea what was about to transpire, he waited in silence. From outside the chamber, a gong clanged. Deep, heavy drumming reverberated through the walls of the temple. Within seconds, he started to feel a warmth radiating from Familla's small hand, still in his grasp. With each breath she took, and as the drumming quickened, the warmth grew stronger and seeped farther up his arm. He realized that she was reaching deep within him.

"Ooooo, kha'tha, duolu, Oscanos, kha'tha, duolu, Gheriah, pan'dithy."

Walmsley recognized the ancient words. Familla chanted not in Etolian but in early Memonan, a much older, music-based language. In the era before the Etolian empire, stories were told of the primeval world of Amahl, where the early humans mingled with the Euranian Ancestors. Most of these stories had disappeared during the Saolian occupation, but Walmsley recognized the tale of the resurrection of Kaliak.

His eyes still closed, he felt a feathery tingling along his arm. It was a power he had never experienced before. The incense vapors began turning foul. The gong sounded again, startling him for a second. With deep breaths, he fought to dampen the rising doubts—and fears.

"Ooooo, kha'tha, duolu, kaandathi, maandathi, pan'dithy."

The tingling entered his chest and settled around his heart. Now he understood. The chant sought to connect the subject's inner spirit with the powers of the Euranian Ancestors, especially those of Mother Gheriah, the creator of the human race, and Lord Oscanos, the eternal defender of humanity. Similar to how her warmth was extending farther into his inner being, Familla was reaching into the deepest areas of Jairesse's existence.

The drumming ceased, replaced by irregular but rhythmic scratches. The dense smoke reeked of decay.

"Hicith, cislema, jaka-jaka..."

The musical chant gone, the bestial whisperings unsettled Walmsley. He knew that what Familla was attempting was extremely dangerous. In the mythical story, Kaliak, the explorer who discovered Sigorum, had been killed by the reptiloids inhabiting that world. Somehow resurrected by Luzomi, Kaliak eventually became the enemy—and assassin—of the great Adelph.

Familla's ritual was adapted from that resurrection, altered from the power of evil to the power of good. Walmsley understood that it was up to him, the bearer of the *Gramm*, to keep her pure.

The rotten air was suffocating. The damp, dark feeling deep within fluttered and fought against the feathery tingling that wound its way throughout his body. He could not allow this glimmer of Luzomi to interfere or influence Familla in any way. He *would* not allow it. He concentrated, focusing on Lord Oscanos and the power of the *Gramm* that he had once wielded.

He recited with Familla what he could recall of the old chant.

"Oscanos, ghethi bayillou Euranua,
"ghethi bayilou universalia."

He felt a new power radiating from within. It spread down his arm, weaving through his hands and fingers and over to Familla.

The gong boomed a third time. The scratching ceased, and the pounding drums resumed. Familla's voice grew louder, stronger. Walmsley could feel her inner power growing. Something was happening. Some sort of spiritual energy seemed to drain from his body. With deep breaths, he fought to stay strong, even as the energy flowed from him to Familla.

"Euranua, meno mino, meno," they chanted together. *Euranus, my creator, my protector, my God.*

Familla uttered a cry…

…and Walmsley found himself whisked away down a long black spiraling void, into a nightmarish morass within the hidden reaches of the multiverse. He saw Jairesse in the distance, her pure white robe tattered and torn, her skin glistening with sweat, screaming at the monstrous winged shadow of Luzomi as he squeezed her writhing flesh to himself and his mightiness. A warm stickiness filled the void. Blood gushed forth from their union, a violation of all things clean and good by all things corrupt and evil.

Outraged by the defilement, Walmsley raised his arms high, drew upon a spiritual power of the Euranian Ancestors that defied the weakness of his aged body, and shouted into the darkness, "By the power of Oscanos, I cast you out!"

A whirling, cascading rainbow of brilliant colors channeled through the void and bombarded the shadow in a blinding blaze of pure light. Luzomi emitted a howling demonic scream, shattering the void…

…and Walmsley heard a gasp, then a new voice.

Overcome by a sudden wave of weakness, his knees buckled. He let go of Familla's hand and gripped the edge of the casket to steady himself. The drums had stopped; the air had cleared. He opened his eyes and saw, beneath the golden glowing figure of Familla, the sweat-drenched face of Jairesse, her eyes wide open, her mouth sucking in rapid breaths.

Familla cried, "Jairesse!" As the golden glow faded away, Familla wrapped both her arms about Jairesse's neck and buried her head in Jairesse's shoulder. "Are you really back?"

Jairesse heaved deep breaths, her eyes bulging with shock.

"Jairesse?" Walmsley whispered. Clearing his throat, he repeated in a stronger voice, "Jairesse?"

Jairesse stared at him, still silent.

Familla lifted her head, her eyes filled with tears. "Can you speak?"

Walmsley reached out and touched Jairesse's hand. It was icy cold. He rubbed her hand until he felt it beginning to warm.

"Jairesse? You are safe," he reassured her. "You're back among your people."

Jairesse shook her head. She mouthed a word.

"What is it?" Familla asked.

Jairesse's answer, a hushed, ghostlike whisper, chilled Walmsley to his bones. "Luzomi. He is here. For you, for me, for us. All of us." She suddenly broke into a maniacal hysteria. With tears pouring out, and her body trembling, she let loose a cry that echoed throughout the sanctuary.

Epilogue: The Ancient Prophecy

Morgan, back in his daily fatigues, looked up from his porta-com as Otho approached.

"Lon's not speaking," Otho said, pointing to the other end of the line of bunks.

"I'll try to talk to him," Morgan said, rising from his bunk. He handed Otho the porta-com. "See what you make of this."

"What is it?" Otho asked as he opened the locker to change out of his dress uniform.

"A *kroking* long shot," Morgan said. "We were routed at the space fortress. Who knows where General Mapooly's next target is."

"*If* that's really him," Otho said, setting the porta-com down to grab a shirt. "I still can't believe we're fighting a ghost."

"I've been studying his tactics at the space fortress," Morgan said. "If it's not him, it's a good copycat." He pointed at the porta-com. "Those are some of the accounts of Lord Walmsley's victory over Mapooly. I can't figure out how he won. In fact, I can't find a single head-to-head battle, not at Pharry, not at Sestia, not even at Belaan." He shook his head. "Somehow, Mapooly's home planet was just destroyed."

"Okay, I'll take a look." Finished changing, Otho picked up the porta-com and closed the locker. "You know, Lord Walmsley's still alive—maybe we can find a way to contact him." He paused. "But I'm worried about Lon."

"We all know he's innocent," Morgan said. "He'll be okay."

"I know," Otho said. "But we don't know who the real bomber is. Security can be broken, computer records changed. Innocent people can be framed, and the guilty can hide. I don't want Lon to get caught in all that."

Morgan sank into deep thought. Otho had been shaken by Turons's death. Now Lon was in trouble. Though Morgan was sure their buddy would be exonerated, he shared Otho's concern. And then there was Rayna, keeping watch over Princess Thericia. They were all going into hiding within the comet cloud now, so with ship-to-ship communications restricted, there would be no way to contact her. "Oggy, we were charged with protecting the emperor...and we failed. Then Mapooly suddenly appears with an attack force. It can't be a coincidence. The princess has got to keep the empire together. If she can't, who knows what will happen. She *is* our princess. It's now our job to help her, any way we can."

Otho nodded. "I know."

"One other thing—like you said, we don't know who the real bomber is." Morgan turned and headed down the aisle. "*Our* ship can't end up like *Ancora*."

On board *Trion*, Walmsley turned away from his monitor to look out the window at the passing stars. They were back on course for Wichloc, and home never felt so good. He rested his eyes. During his waking hours, he could keep himself busy following the news of the empire. But when he lay down, he couldn't sleep.

The vision of Luzomi's shadow in the void terrified him. *Luzomi.* Jairesse's words haunted him to his bones.

Walmsley looked up as Admiral Kearn and Searus entered his cabin. With a sigh, he pointed at his monitor and said to them, "This is disturbing."

"What is it?" Searus asked as she and Kearn joined Walmsley in front of the monitor.

"A news report off the comm-network," Walmsley said with a grim tone. "An attack upon the empire."

On the monitor, an angry red headline in bold lettering flashed: "Attack on Space Fortress Canellis." A reporter spoke as footage showed emergency crews repairing battle damage while rescue workers attended to injured personnel. *"According to reports, Ruling Princess Thericia escaped before the enemy assault began. However, the Alscrasian Council reports that there have been no communications with* Graftinop One, *and so Her Highness's current whereabouts remain unknown."*

"First the emperor, now this," Searus said.

"We've picked up a report," Kearn said. "The Onglan Congress has been called into special session."

"Somebody is trying to overthrow the empire." Walmsley lowered his head. "We don't need a new war. The last one was horrible enough."

"As for the attackers, the only information we have is the claimed identity of General Mapooly, the long-dead Belaanian warlord from the Galactic Revolutions."

Walmsley froze, his mouth gaping. Searus's monitor beeped a rapid beat.

"This footage, obtained from the space fortress's deep

space recorders, shows some of the attacking ships."

Walmsley held his breath as he watched the footage of the battle. He recognized some of the Imperial ships, none larger than cruiser class. Strangely, most of the attacking ships looked to be merchant vessels—slow but well-armed cargo carriers.

"What are *those*?" Searus asked, pointing at the footage.

"It can't be," Walmsley whispered in disbelief.

The merchant ships were accompanied by a number of vintage warships, flamboyantly decorated with wings, horns, and spiked hulls. The largest vessel sported a tusked wovren head on its bow.

Jairesse's words of warning repeated in Walmsley's head. He now understood the truth about the cold presence he had been feeling.

The attackers were not a conventional fighting force. They were ghosts from the past. He didn't want to relive the nightmare of fifty years ago. He desperately wished for the feeling to fade, for it to be a bad dream. But despite his best efforts to block out the memories, the images of towering black shadows, scaly reptilian limbs, and giant wings flapping above his head persisted. As if it was yesterday, he could hear the screeching demonic howls and feel the warm splash of blood against his skin.

Luzomi was back, and despite the decades of learning and preparation, Walmsley couldn't help but tremble.

"My lord," Kearn said, "I understand your desire to let the empire handle its own problems."

"One war is enough for a lifetime," Walmsley said.

"For you, I agree." Kearn turned down the volume on the monitor. "But our generation has not served the empire that our parents fought to create."

Walmsley eyed Kearn. "Admiral, do you know what this will entail?"

Kearn stood tall. "I know that the Onglan League has been a centuries-old ally of the kingdom of Alscras, that they once fought side by side." He took a step toward Walmsley; their eyes met. "My lord, the empire is in jeopardy. You know how to defeat Mapooly. We can do the fighting in your stead. At least, we can go before the Onglan Congress and propose action to end this incursion before it goes any further."

Walmsley dropped his head and stared at the floor. He felt a surge of pride in Kearn's loyalty to Onglus's history, but he also feared what his admiral was ignorant of. And yet...as foreboding as it had been, as fearful as he had felt, he couldn't deny that saving Jairesse from the evil presence of Luzomi had been a moment of triumph he hadn't experienced in half a century. The power of the Euranian Ancestors pouring through his feeble body and bombarding the Prince of Darkness into a pained retreat had, somehow, renewed and refocused his life's mission. Walmsley lifted his head. "You are correct, Admiral. We can—and we will —take action to help. If need be, the Greyban Corps can mobilize to defend our ally, the Central Empire."

Kearn bowed, saying, "Thank you, my lord," and turned to depart the cabin.

"Please wait," Walmsley said, holding up his hand. He glanced at Searus, who stood nearby adjusting the medical monitors. "This is a serious matter, with serious implications. I must pray about this." With a surprising tremble in his voice, he asked, "Will you pray with me?"

Searus's eyes reflected her concern. "Of course, my lord."

"Of course, my lord," Kearn echoed.

With her gentle help, Walmsley made his way to the back of the parlor, where three unlit candles sat on a small table. The experience with Familla and Jairesse had physically drained him. Though he walked with determination, each step seemed as if he would collapse to the floor. He had never felt as old as he did now.

Kearn set out the cushions. Searus held Walmsley steady as he kneeled. Once he was situated, she took his cane, rested it against the wall, and knelt down to his left, while Kearn knelt to his right.

They closed their eyes, and with great effort, Lord Walmsley began reciting in halting, hushed whispers: "Let our innermost thoughts...lift up through the smoke...rising from the candle flame. Lord Oscanos, Mother Gheriah, and the Three Guardians..."—he took a deep breath in his struggle to stay focused on the rite—"...hear our prayers."

He paused, dwelling on the ominous words of Jairesse. The oppressive, malevolent feeling was real. The prophecy of the *Hruvrah* was upon them. Somewhere, Luzomi waited at a portal, ready to enter the universe, ready to rule the human race.

Monsters. Demons. These were not ghost stories told to naughty children. These were the realities of existence, unseen by human eyes, but felt from the depths of the human heart.

He cowered from the thoughts of doom and despair, but he also remembered the power of Lord Oscanos and the love of Mother Gheriah. The human race had triumphed once before. That was a fact, a real victory. The initiative to confront Mapooly again would be another victory.

Walmsley opened his eyes and gazed at the trio of white candles on the small table before him. It seemed a futile gesture, but he knew that the candles were a symbol of his faith, and his faith was stronger than the power of the Prince of Darkness. It had to be stronger. He said to Searus, "Please light the candles."

Searus ignited the striker and held the tiny flame before Walmsley's eyes.

A tiny spark of life, like a beacon of hope in the void of darkness. It felt so small and insignificant, compared to the threat that awaited him. Walmsley tried to calm himself, but he could feel his anxiety growing with each breath he took.

"My lord?" Kearn asked.

Walmsley clutched his hands together, lowered his head, and silently prayed for goodness and light, for strength and wisdom. The Entity of Evil was approaching. He prayed for mercy, for themselves and for all the people.

Searus extended the striker and lit the center candle, the initial burn flaring in a bright flash before settling down. The dazzling spark caught Walmsley's eye just as a cold, dank numbness swept over and seized him, binding him still. A cold, oppressive weight, as tight as a metal vise, clamped on the innards of his very being and twisted him until the psychological pain was unbearable.

A vicious, bestial roar rumbled from within. He felt beads of cold sweat break out across his forehead.

A deep, seething voice whispered to him: *"You assail me and my existence. You are the bane of my rule. You have pilfered my people—my possessions—for the last time. I shall avenge myself upon you. You shall be consumed by my fury and forever enslaved in eternal chains of everlasting torment."*

Walmsley tensed the feeble muscles of his body. He struggled to focus on his adversary. He opened his mouth—but no words came out.

Without warning, his body went numb, and he lost his

balance. As utter desperation overtook him, Walmsley realized that the decades of preparation had been in vain. The all-powerful *Gramm* remained locked away in his bureau. It was not in his grasp, as it should have been. *Now* was the moment, and he had failed to see it.

Luzomi had him in his clutches.

A jeweled maw, lined with incisors of blinding light, opened before Walmsley, revealing a ring of searing red flame. Beyond was the endless, pitch-black void of nonexistence—the same tunnel of eternity that had entrapped Jairesse. In the distance, dozens of bead-like fiery eyes flared. With blinding speed, brilliant rainbow colors surrounded him. Within the chaos of colors and shapes, an uncountable number of shadowy, flame-tipped claws emerged, reaching out toward Walmsley like writhing tentacles.

As his vision blurred and spun out of control, Walmsley heard Searus cry, "My lord!" He fell forward and plunged headlong through the flames into the void and the awaiting clutches of Luzomi. An excruciating pain seized him, and with a sudden spasm of violent convulsions, he lost consciousness.

As told in *The Songs of the Euranians*, the Prince of Darkness, Luzomi, and his nefarious followers escaped the destruction of Sigorum by traversing the rainbow of the gods to the nether regions of the multiverse. With the passing of the eons, while the human race flourished in Eurania, the evil lord of terror plotted his return—and his revenge upon the descendants of Amahl.

And the legendary prophet Zeltius wrote these words about the reappearance of the rainbow of the gods and the opening of the door for Luzomi and his followers to reenter the universe:

"I will conquer those who had defeated me. I will chain my enemies and enslave them. The multitudes will worship me as their true master, or they will be doomed to suffer excruciating torment for all eternity."

Characters

Alscrasian cruiser, *Ocelot*:

    Antos Choff (AHN-toss CHOFF) - Captain

    Kaleb Lendus (KAY-leb LEN-dus) - executive officer (Commander)

    Morgan Teggo (MOR-gun TEE-go) - navigator and 2nd officer (Lieutenant)

    Otho Ennuk (OH-tho EE-nik) - combat officer and 3rd officer (Lieutenant)

    Quino Schillary (QUEEN-o schi-LAR-ee) - platoon officer (Ensign)

    Lon Prowzi (LON PROW-zee) - operations officer, chief (Ensign)

    Violette (VEE-o-LET) - operations officer, swing (Ensign)

    Elena (ay-LEE-nah) - signaler, chief (SCPO)

    Grisconne (gris-CONE) - signaler, swing (CPO)

    Pito Turons (PEE-to TUR-rens) - quartermaster, chief (PO1)

    Anibe (ah-NEE-bay) - quartermaster, swing (PO2)

    Meek (MEEK) - quartermaster, graveyard (PO2)

    Semile (seh-MEE-lee) - squad 'A' leader (SCPO)

    Dr. Arrit Hildermaan (AIR-reet HIL-da-mon) - medical officer (Lieutenant)

    Fotablugen (FO-tuh-BLU-gen) - operations & maintenance supervisor(MCWO)

Bena Petre Bearn (BE-nah PET-tree Burn) - chief engineer (SCPO)

Baer (BAY-er) - torpedo supervisor (CPO)

Branke (BRANG-kee) - torpedo specialist (Spec)

Curob (KOOR-rob) - torpedo specialist (Spec)

Witherall (WITH-er-ohl) - gunner (spec, referenced only)

Eckles (EK-lees) - gunner (spec, referenced only)

Vevo (VEE-voh) - gunner (spec, referenced only)

Kothol (KO-thahl) - engine technician (Tech)

Smyra (SMEAR-rah) - captain's yeoman (Sr Spec)

Villains:

General e'Thuq Mapooly (ee-THOOK ma-PU-lee) - ruler of Belaan (ba-LON)

Prince Fraither (FRAY-thur) - ruler of Bexel (BEK-sul)

Grand *Primai* Ludzenia (Grand PREE-may lud-ZEN-ee-ah) - ruler of Broza (BRO-zah) and the Gearmlian Confederation (GEAR-mil; gear-MIL-ee-an)

Supreme Dictator Quinn (QUINN) - ruler of Heron (her-RONE)

Zukaaran (zu-KAR-run) - follower of Luzomi

Saltos (SAL-toes) - follower of Luzomi on Volon (vo-LON)

Imperial Headquarters:

Emperor Otias II (OH-tee-us) - king of Alscras (al-SCRAHZ) and ruler of the Central Empire

Prince Otias III - crown prince of Alscras

Princess Thericia (ter-REE-cee-ah) - princess of Alscras

Franklen (FRANK-lin) - chief of staff

Admiral Kosolf (KO-zolf) - fleet commander

Captain Udahl (U-doll) - captain of *Graftinop One* (GRAF-tin-nop)

Kumatille (KU-ma-teel) - Imperial aide

Dr. Doxuit (du-QUIT) - Imperial physician

Myhmik (MIM-mik) - Imperial speaker
Dr. Docherae (DOK-ur-Ay-ah) - adviser, Imperial affairs
Count Haagewyn (HOG-ah-win) - Alscrasian council liaison

Alscrasian cruiser, *Pouton*:
  Boutah Jaron (BU-tah JAIR-ron) - Captain
  Alteus (ALL-tee-us) - executive officer (Commander)
  Rayna Choff (RAY-nah CHOFF) - platoon officer (Ensign)
  Fiona Cutxa (fee-OH-nah KUT-zah) - squad 'A' leader (SCPO)
  Tornique (tor-NEEK) - squad 'B' leader (CPO)
  Manion (MAN-yun) - squad 'C' leader (CPO)
  Dr. Korr Creatoun (KOR CRE-a-toon) - medical officer (Lieutenant)

Wichloc:
  Metiar Walmsley (MEET-ee-ahr WALMS-lee) - leader of the
    Greyban Corps (GRAY-bon)
  Dubian Trophet (DU-bee-an tro-FET) - chief of staff
  Monseigneur Navilla (na-VIL-lah) - head priest of Wichloc
  Monseigneur Dhavail (da-VAIL) - former High Priest of Wiene
    Temple
  Whinn Rexold (WIN REX-ald) - consort of Dhavail
  Admiral Graft Kearn (KERN) - fleet commander
  Captain Pavon (PAY-von) - captain of *Trion* (TRI-on)
  Searus (SEAR-rus) - Walmsley's nurse

Volon:
  Jairesse (jair-REESE) - temple priestess
  Adonair (add-o-NAIR) - temple chief and expedition leader
  Thakian (THAK-ee-an) - master of *Illito* warriors (il-LEE-to)
  Panquo (PONG-quo) - Volonian leader
  Ritoso (ri-TO-so) - Familla's father
  Familla (fa-MIL-ah) - novice

Kaxuo:

Grune (GROON) - security guard

Space Fortress Canellis:

Colonel Jetiah Chrystamme (KRIS-stam) - base commander
Lt. Colonel Moton (MO-ton) - deputy base commander
Commander Streat (STREET) - commander of *Epoch*

Mapooly's forces:

Admiral Uchiusus Zerah (u-KI-uh-sus ZEAR-ah) - commander
of mercenary arms convoy
Dithri Bemone (DITH-ree be-MOAN) - captain of *Q'toz* (Q-
toz)
Isaalt (EE-salt) - executive officer of *Q'toz*
Shutha Zu (ZU) - captain of *Bakiraaqu* (ba-KEER-a-ku)
Myrane (mur-RANE) - security man
Gorhoud (gor-HUDE) - security man

Kelova (keh-LO-vah):

Duc Ilwatu (DUKE ill-WOT-tu) - chief of the Imperial Assem-
bly
Monseigneur Merician XVI (mer-EE-see-an) - High Priest of
Wiene Temple
Jarrumina (JAH-ru-MEE-na) - chief aide to the high priest
Jhangoria (Jang-GOR-ee-ah) - premier of Pharry (FAR-ee)
Moh Wahren (MO WAH-ren) - chancellor of Sestia (SES-tee-
ah)

Etolian Empire Flashback:

Emperor Fur'thur (FUR-thur) - ruler of the Etolian Empire
Empress Gemina (jeh-MEEN-uh) - empress consort of the Eto-
lian Empire
High Priest Duo'ra (DOO-oh-rah) - High Priest of the Great
Temple

Pax Bn'dim (PAX BIN-dim) - watch commander, Imperial Headquarters

Jun (JOON) - Central Region supervisor, Imperial Headquarters

Andra (ON-dra) - Imperial aide

Polan Bn'dim (PO-lon BIN-dim) - follower of Luzomi on ancient Sestia

The conclusion of
The Ruler of the Galaxy

Preview: Red Spike

"How's your Kelovan, Oggy?" Morgan asked as he and Otho approached the wardroom.

"Out of practice, Machoiss," Otho replied. He reached for the door switch. "I haven't watched official proceedings since our academy days."

Up to their ears in work, the two buddies hadn't found any time to just hang out, even for a few minutes. Though it had been a mere couple of years since graduation, their days of goofing around at the academy with Rayna and Lon seemed a distant memory now.

"It'll come back." Morgan tried to sound confident, knowing that his Kelovan wasn't much better than Otho's.

The door opened, and Morgan and Otho joined Captain Choff and Lendus in the wardroom. Two monitors had been set up on adjacent walls. The left monitor was blank; the right displayed footage from *Graftinop One*, where an arrangement of chairs flanked the oversized graftinop-like throne, facing a block of contiguous monitors on the back wall. Franklen was directing

Rayna to stand at the seat immediately to the throne's left, next to Mr. Myhmik, the briefcase-toting spokesman.

The princess then walked into the throne room carrying the large royal scepter tipped by a silver graftinop with a golden orb in its beak, a diamond-studded tiara accenting her hair. Her eyes never wavered in any direction; she stared straight at the throne, and her heavy royal-blue robe flowed behind her. As she took her seat, Franklen signaled the others to follow suit.

Kosolf's voice sounded over the speaker. "Signal coming in from Kelova."

"Thank you, Admiral," the princess replied.

In the wardroom, the blank monitor, and the monitors in the throne room, sprang to life with a transmission of the Inner Chamber of the Imperial Assembly, the signal having traveled for two days from Kelova to their current position within the comet cloud. Morgan, returning to his seat, noted the myriad of Kelovan staffers who wandered about, straightening chairs, providing drinks and porta-coms. Assembly Speaker Duc Ilwatu, wearing his gold-and-red official robe, entered through the large ceremonial double doors, accompanied by his guards, and took his place at the podium. Behind him, four large men carried the white-robed High Priest Merician XIV to his ornately ornamented high-backed chair.

A mustached elderly man wearing the midnight-blue dress uniform of the Bexelian army and displaying a Palm Leaf with Binary Star medal on his chest, entered the Inner Chamber. Prince Fraither, old enough to be the princess's grandfather, was one of the founding fathers of the Central Empire and the main catalyst in ushering the powerful Gearmlian Confederation into the empire after its formation. Strangely, Morgan reflected, the prince had remained politically quiet over the decades since.

Within minutes, Supreme Dictator Quinn, wearing the traditional black cape of Heron, and the olive-skinned, shock-white-haired Grand *Primai* Ludzenia of Broza, the new capital of the Gearmlian Confederation, followed, her bright red Brozan robes flowing behind her. Speaker Ilwatu greeted each ruler as they walked in and took their seats along the conference table. Shortly after, Chancellor Moh Wahren of Sestia arrived in a plain dark business suit and went to his seat next to the vacant chair for the monarch of Alscras.

Around the perimeter of the chamber, tables marked in Kelovan, the language of official Imperial proceedings, with placards, such as "Taorus Cluster," "Qimori Cluster," "Trak States," and "Ghike Cluster," filled up with Imperial representatives in all manner of dress and physical variation of height, weight, color, and body shape.

The secretary of the Assembly stepped up to the podium. "The Inner Chamber of the Imperial Assembly is now in session, Speaker Duc Ilwatu presiding. All rise at attention."

Following the playing of the Imperial anthem, the high priest stood and said, with a powerful voice, "We will now have a moment of silence for the memory of our late ruler, His Royal Majesty, Emperor Otias, and Crown Prince Otias."

After a long pause, he raised his right arm high into the air and proclaimed,

"Lord Oscanos, Mother Gheriah, and the Three
  Guardians,
"while we mourn the passing of our emperor,
"we know that he is with all the immortals in Eurania.
"Guide our proceedings, give us wisdom,
"Bring us peace to our worlds.
As you will, so will we all."

Everybody echoed, "So will we all."

The high priest sat back down. A murmur began throughout the Inner Chamber.

"Order, please," the secretary implored, sounding a loud
horn.

"This an emergency session of the Inner Chamber. The
first order of business will address the invading force of General
Mapooly," Speaker Ilwatu announced. "The princess of Alscras
has relayed a statement, to be read during these proceedings."

"Regardless of who the interim monarch is, a swift response is needed," Chancellor Wahren said in a slow, measured
tone.

"Really," Prince Fraither said, a hint of sarcasm in his
voice. "What course of action does the young princess of Alscras
suggest this body take?"

As Speaker Ilwatu nodded, the secretary played the
princess's recording over the speakers. "Speaker Ilwatu and
members of the Imperial Assembly, we face a dangerous situation. The armada that attacked the space fortress numbered over
fifty vessels, a combination of arms transports and aged warships. Combined, General Mapooly's fleet carries more firepower than a typical modern attack force. A single dominion may not
be able to organize an effective counterattack force without re-
ducing the defense of its home worlds. I propose forming a joint
Imperial fleet to seek out the invaders. Together, we would have
enough capital ships and troops to initiate a counterstrike against
the attackers. I urge the Assembly to take action and enact this
proposal with the utmost haste, lest the invading armada strike
again at a more strategic location and with greater loss of life.
Thank you."

Prince Fraither turned to address Speaker Ilwatu. "By our

constitution, only the emperor can call upon military forces across the empire. Absent that, each dominion is autonomous and under the command of its own ruler. If we follow the young princess's suggestion, then we have no choice but to address the issue of the interim emperor first."

Speaker Ilwatu shook his head. "An election will take time to organize."

"I agree." Prince Fraither nodded. "We need to look at another, quicker means." He looked at each person in the Inner Chamber. "In this time of crisis, the empire needs experience. I have been ruler of my dominion for over forty years, far longer than any other head of state." He motioned to the rulers from Heron and Broza. "And I have the support of the majority of the core planets." He turned to the Speaker. "I mean no disrespect, but the princess is clearly not qualified to rule the empire. I, on the other hand, have alternate grounds—as lineage successor to Emperor Fur'thur, the last Etolian emperor."

Various delegates jumped to their feet. "Inadmissible, Mr. Speaker!"

"Please wait to be recognized!" Speaker Ilwatu called out.

"Mr. Speaker," Chancellor Wahren interrupted. "Lineage succession is not recognized by our constitution. The prince is well aware of this. Also..." He paused as he turned to address Prince Fraither. "Your ally, Grand *Primai* Ludzenia of Broza, is not the legitimate ruler of the Confederation."

Morgan saw the grand *primai* smile. Other than that subtle gesture, the mysterious woman remained calm and unchanged.

"With all due respect to Your Excellency," Prince Fraither mocked, "Prince Jomin capitulated and went into exile. Grand

Primai Ludzenia assigned executive authority over the Gearm-lian Confederation to General Faut over a year ago."

"With all due respect," Chancellor Wahren pressed, "Prince Jomin did not capitulate. He was usurped by an assassination attempt."

Prince Fraither pointed at the chancellor, his voice rising. "The fact remains that Grand *Primai* Ludzenia is in power and no one challenges that. This is the reality, Your Excellency."

Chancellor Wahren rose. "The fact remains that we are dealing with an invasion, and you rely upon the capabilities of your allies, Supreme Dictator Quinn and Grand *Primai* Ludzenia, and their military strongmen, Field Marshall Tonkar and General Faut. Bexel is but a shell of its former glory, and you, sir, are merely a mouthpiece, a figurehead."

The prince slapped the table, affronted. "You, sir, are not worthy to rule the Sestian republic." He turned to Speaker Il-watu. "My delegation will introduce a resolution to remove Princess Thericia as the interim monarch of Alscras. She is not qualified to serve. She should devote her energies to comforting her mother during this time of mourning."

The secretary called out, "Order! Please, be seated."

"The Republic of Sestia objects to the tactics of the prince of Bexel," Chancellor Wahren said. "The resolution is no more than political maneuverings to seize control of the empire."

"Order!"

"Once the House of Bexel takes over the crown," the chancellor pushed, "the prince will never relinquish control back to this body."

"Please," Speaker Ilwatu said, rising, "the crown of Alscras is an internal matter; there is no need for hostilities." He looked to Prince Fraither, who fumed in silence.

"I have stated my position, and I have humbly offered my services, as the ruler with the most experience," the prince finally hissed, motioning for his representative to follow him out.

Morgan glanced at Otho, then at Lendus, who shook his head and let out a quiet sigh. Had the chancellor been too aggressive? Had he not been diplomatic enough? Morgan looked at the captain and saw lines of tension pull across his face as he took long, slow breaths. Morgan took another deep breath. Even just watching the proceedings, he felt the stress of the situation.

Speaker Ilwatu said, "The chair recognizes the delegation from the planet Xundan."

The blue-skinned, four-armed representative from Xundan, one of the many planets from the Outer Territories, stood and spoke. "Mr. Speaker, Your Highness, fellow delegates, I speak for a majority of the planets from the Taorus Cluster. We are extremely concerned about the recent developments, including the attack on Space Fortress C. If the core worlds cannot agree on a course of action, where does that leave those of us along the outskirts of the empire? We are wide open to attack."

Cheers erupted among the majority of the delegations as the Xundan representative sat down.

"Mr. Speaker, Mr. Speaker!" several other delegations called out.

"Order, order…"

A large, egg-shaped delegate stood up and began speaking into his microphone. "Mr. Speaker, the planets of the Qimori cluster—"

"Would the delegation from Oblinough please wait until called upon?" Speaker Ilwatu called out.

"Mr. Speaker!" an exoskeletal representative began speaking. "The planets of the Ghike cluster demand unified action on the current crisis. What about the renegade armada?"

A staffer ran up to Speaker Ilwatu and pulled him aside to confer.

While they spoke, Morgan glanced at the others, who remained stoic through the growing chaos. He then looked to the monitor, at the grand *primai*, who appeared to be stifling a smile. A loud horn blast momentarily interrupted the proceedings.

Speaker Ilwatu rushed to his microphone. "Members of the Inner Chamber, please proceed to the emergency exits. We have an urgent signal from space command—the planet is coming under attack!"

About the author:

Moses Solomon's first publication, *The Santamobile*, a tale of Santa Claus in the 21st century, has received the following words of praise:

"...even readers not into fantasy will enjoy this nice short Christmas story."

"What can I say? This is a really well put-together book that everyone preteen and up should read..."

He is also the author of the YA novella, *Star Princess: Encounter in the Dark*, which takes place two years before *The Ruler of the Galaxy* and tells the tale of Princess Thericia's first foray into the Central Empire's precarious dealings and dangers.

Morgan Teggo, Rayna Choff, and the cruiser *Ocelot* will return in the conclusion of *The Ruler of the Galaxy*, coming soon.

Follow Moses Solomon's tales of the Euranians at eurania-moso.com and on Facebook.